In ALien FLeSH

GREGORY BENFORD

TOR

A TOM DOHERTY ASSOCIATES BOOK

Acknowledgments

To two who tolerated the time it took
Alyson and Mark

Contents

Blood on Glass _____

Nature knows nothing of death.
Not in the cat's lazy smug *meeeeooow*
not in the antelope's mad kick
as the lion makes its meal.
Neither in the tidal lifting of a sluggish sea
by a star's blunt gradients,
nor a flower's nod, an insect's frantic dance.
Live is all the world ever says.
Of alternatives it lies mute.

But ponder aliens lounging in lattices,
of ancient ice-cased memories
from the first beings, born beneath
Suns now gone to shot and scatteration.
They have forgotten birth and,
sheltered in cool cubits, face no end.
If we meet them they will see
bags of ropy guts
skin shiny with grease
food stuck between our teeth
in our rush from interrupted breakfast.
Moving garbage, yellow fat jammed between
brittle calcium rods, stringy muscles
clenching, stretching to make the puppet cage
of bones yearn forward.

In our bookstores there are texts
on dying's art, a new kind of skill
we must learn: identify the six stages

(rejection of news; depression; calm plateau;
world-gobbling; slide; will to go on).
We are works in progress,
suspended between the mouse's unsuspecting struggle
and promises of crystalline infinities.
These aliens, then, are as animals.
Only in us and our unending forward tilt
can death live.
Each sharp moment is free.
And all that could happen
might yet be.

In Alien Flesh

I.

—green surf lapping, chilling—

Reginri's hand jerked convulsively on the sheets. His eyes were closed.

—silver coins gliding and turning in the speckled sky, eclipsing the sun—

The sheets were a clinging swamp. He twisted in their grip.

—a chiming song, tinkling cool rivulets washing his skin—

He opened his eyes.

A yellow blade of afternoon sunlight hung in the room, dust motes swimming through it. He panted in shallow gasps. Belej was standing beside the bed.

"They came again, didn't they?" she said, almost whispering.

"Ye . . . yes." His throat was tight and dry.

"This can't go *on*, darling. We thought you could sleep better in the daytime, with everyone out in the fields, but—"

"Got to get out of here," he mumbled. He rolled out of bed and pulled on his black work suit. Belej stood silent, blinking rapidly, chewing at her lower lip. Reginri fastened his boots and slammed out of the room. His steps thumped hollowly on the planking. She listened to them hurrying down the hallway. They paused; the airless silence returned. Then the outer door creaked, banged shut.

She hurried after him.

She caught up near the rim of the canyon, a hundred

3

meters from the log buildings. He looked at her. He scratched at his matted hair and hunched his shoulders forward.

"That one was pretty bad," he said woodenly.

"If they keep on getting worse . . ."

"They won't."

"We hope. But we don't know that. If I understood what they're about . . ."

"I can't quite describe it. They're different each time. The *feeling* seems the same, even though . . ." Some warmth had returned to his voice. "It's hard."

Belej sat down near the canyon edge. She looked up at him. Her eyebrows knitted together above large dark eyes. "All right," she said, her mood shifting suddenly, an edge coming into her voice. "One, I don't know what these nightmares are about. Two, I don't know where they come from. That horrible expedition you went on, I suppose, but you're not even clear about that. Three, I don't know why you insisted on joining their dirty expedition in the—"

"I told you, dammit. I had to go."

"You wanted the extra money," Belej said flatly. She cupped her chin in a tiny hand.

"It wasn't *extra* money, it was *any* money." He glowered at the jagged canyon below them. Her calm, accusing manner irritated him.

"You're a pod cutter. You could have found work."

"The season was bad. This was last year, remember. Rates weren't good."

"But you had heard about this Sasuke and Leo, what people said about them—"

"Vanleo, that's the name. Not Leo."

"Well, whatever. You didn't have to work for them."

"No, of course not," he said savagely. "I could've busted my ass on a field-hopper in planting season, twelve hours a day for thirty units pay, max. And when I got tired of that, or broke a leg, maybe I could've signed on to mold circuitry like a drone." He picked up a stone and flung it far over the canyon edge. "A great life."

Belej paused a long moment. At the far angular end of the canyon a pink mist seeped between the highest peaks and began spilling downward, gathering speed. Zeta Reticuli still rode high in the mottled blue sky, but a chill was sweeping up from the canyon. The wind carried an acrid tang.

He wrinkled his nose. Within an hour they would have to move inside. The faint reddish haze would thicken. It was good for the plant life of northern Persenuae, but to human lungs the fog was an itching irritant.

Belej sighed. "Still," she said softly, "you weren't forced to go. If you had known it would be so—"

"Yes," he said, and something turned in his stomach. "If anybody had known."

II

At first it was not the Drongheda that he found disquieting. It was the beach itself and, most of all, the waves.

They lapped at his feet with a slow, sucking energy, undermining the coarse sand beneath his boots. They began as little ripples that marched in from the gray horizon and slowly hissed up the black beach. Reginri watched one curl into greenish foam farther out; the tide was falling.

"Why are they so slow?" he said.

Sasuke looked up from the carry-pouches. "What?"

"Why do the waves take so long?"

Sasuke stopped for a moment and studied the ponderous swell, flecked with yellow waterweed. An occasional large wave broke and splashed on the sharp lava rocks farther out. "I never thought about it," Sasuke said. "Guess it's the lower gravity."

"Uh-hum." Reginri shrugged.

A skimmer fish broke water and snapped at something in the air. Somehow, the small matter of the waves unnerved him. He stretched restlessly in his skinsuit.

"I guess the low-gee sim doesn't prepare you for everything," he said. Sasuke didn't hear; he was folding out the tappers, coils and other gear.

Reginri could put it off no longer. He fished out his binocs and looked at the Drongheda.

At first it seemed like a smooth brown rock, water-worn and timeless. And the reports were correct: it moved landward. It rose like an immense blister on the rippled sea. He squinted, trying to see the dark circle of the pithole. There, yes, a shadowed blur ringed with dappled red. At the center, darker, lay his entranceway. It looked impossibly small.

He lowered the binocs, blinking. Zeta Reticuli burned low on the flat horizon, a fierce orange point that sliced through this planet's thin air.

"God, I could do with a burn," Reginri said.

"None of that, you'll need your wits in there," Sasuke said stiffly. "Anyway, there's no smoking blowby in these suits."

"Right." Reginri wondered if the goddamned money was worth all this. Back on Persenuae—he glanced up into the purpling sky and found it, a pearly glimmer nestling in closer to Zeta—it had seemed a good bet, a fast and easy bit of money, a kind of scientific outing with a tang of adventure. Better than agriwork, anyway. A far better payoff than anything else he could get with his limited training, a smattering of electronics and fabrication techniques. He even knew some math, though not enough to matter. And it didn't make any difference in this job, Sasuke had told him, even if math was the whole point of this thing.

He smiled to himself. An odd thought, that squiggles on the page were a commercial item, something people on Earth would send a ramscoop full of microelectronics and bio-engineered cells in exchange for—

"Some help here, eh?" Sasuke said roughly.

"Sorry."

Reginri knelt and helped the man spool out the tapper lines, checking the connectors. Safely up the beach, beyond the first pale line of sand dunes, lay the packaged electronics gear and the crew, already in place, who would monitor while he and Vanleo were inside.

As the two men unwound the cables, unsnarling the lines and checking the backup attachments, Reginri glanced occasionally at the Drongheda. It was immense, far larger than he had imagined. The 3Ds simply didn't convey the massive feel of the thing. It wallowed in the shallows, now no more than two hundred meters away.

"It's stopped moving," he said.

"Sure. It'll be there for days, by all odds." Sasuke spoke without looking up. He inserted his diagnostic probe at each socket, watching the meters intently. He was methodical, sure of himself—quite the right sort of man to handle the technical end, Reginri thought.

"That's the point, isn't it? I mean, the thing is going to stay put."

"Sure."

"So you say. It isn't going to roll over while we're in there, because it never has."

Sasuke stopped working and scowled. Through his helmet bubble, Reginri could see the man's lips pressed tight together. "You fellows always get the shakes on the beach. It never fails. Last crew I had out here, they were crapping in their pants from the minute we sighted a Drongheda."

"Easy enough for you to say. You're not going in."

"I've been in, mister. You haven't. Do what we say, what Vanleo and I tell you, and you'll be all right."

"Is that what you told the last guy who worked with you?"

Sasuke looked up sharply. "Kaufmann? You talked to him?"

"No. A friend of mine knows him."

"Your friend keeps bad company."

"Sure, me included."

"I meant—"

"Kaufmann didn't quit for no reason, you know."

"He was a coward," Sasuke said precisely.

"The way he put it, he just wasn't fool enough to keep working this thing the way you want. With this equipment."

"There isn't any other way."

Reginri motioned seaward. "You could put something automated inside. Plant a sensor."

"That will transmit out through thirty meters of animal fat? Through all that meat? Reliably? With a high bit rate? Ha!"

Reginri paused. He knew it wasn't smart to push Sasuke this way, but the rumors he had heard from Kaufmann made him uneasy. He glanced back toward the lifeless land. Down the beach, Vanleo had stopped to inspect something, kneel-

ing on the hard-packed sand. Studying a rock, probably—
nothing alive scuttled or crawled on this beach.

Reginri shrugged. "I can see that, but why do we have to
stay in so long? Why not just go in, plant the tappers and get
out?"

"They won't stay in place. If the Drongheda moves even a
little, they'll pop out."

"Don't make 'em so damned delicate."

"Mister, you can't patch in with spiked nails. That's a
neural terminus point you're going after, not a statphone
connection."

"So I have to mother it through? Sit there up in that huge
gut and sweat it out?"

"You're getting paid for it," Sasuke said in clipped tones.

"Maybe not enough."

"Look, if you're going to bellyache—"

Reginri shrugged. "Okay, I'm not a pro at this. I came
mostly to see the Drongheda anyway. But once you look at
it, that electronics rig of yours seems pretty inadequate. And
if that thing out there decides to give me a squeeze—"

"It won't. Never has."

A short, clipped bark came over the earphones. It was
Vanleo's laugh, ringing hollow in their helmets. Vanleo approached, striding smoothly along the water line. "It hasn't
happened, so it won't? Bad logic. Simply because a series
has many terms does not mean it is infinite. Nor that it
converges."

Reginri smiled warmly, glad that the other man was back.
There was a remorseless quality about Sasuke that set his
teeth on edge.

"Friend Sasuke, don't conceal what we both know from
this boy." Vanleo clapped Sasuke on the back jovially. "The
Drongheda are a cipher. Brilliant, mysterious, vast intellects—
and it is presumptuous to pretend we understand anything
about them. All we are able to follow is their mathematics—
perhaps that is all they wish us to see." A brilliant smile
creased his face.

Vanleo turned and silently studied the cables that played
out from the dunes and into the surf.

"Looks okay," he said. "Tide's going out."

He turned abruptly and stared into Reginri's eyes. "Got your nerve back now, boy? I was listening on suit audio."

Reginri shuffled uneasily. Sasuke was irritating, but at least he knew how to deal with the man. Vanleo, though . . . somehow Vanleo's steady, intent gaze unsettled him. Reginri glanced out at the Drongheda and felt a welling dread. On impulse he turned to Vanleo and said, "I think I'll stay on the beach."

Vanleo's face froze. Sasuke made a rough spitting sound and began, "Another goddamned—" but Vanleo cut him off with a brusque motion of his hand.

"What do you mean?" Vanleo said mildly.

"I . . . I don't feel so good about going inside."

"Oh. I see."

"I mean, I don't know if that thing isn't going to . . . well, it's the first time I did this, and . . ."

"I see."

"Tell you what. I'll go out with you two, sure. I'll stay in the water and keep the cables from getting snarled—you know, the job you were going to do. That'll give me a chance to get used to the work. Then, next time . . ."

"That might be years from now."

"Well, that's right, but . . ."

"You're endangering the success of the entire expedition."

"I'm not experienced. What if . . ." Reginri paused. Vanleo had logic on his side, he knew. This was the first Drongheda they had been able to reach in over two years. Many of them drifted down the ragged coast, hugging the shallows. But most stayed only a day or two. This was the first in a long while that had moored itself offshore in a low, sheltered shoal. The satellite scan had picked it up, noted its regular pattern of movements that followed the tides. So Vanleo got the signal, alerted Reginri and the stand-by crew, and they lifted in a fast booster from Persenuae . . .

"A boot in the ass is what he needs," Sasuke said abruptly.

Vanleo shook his head. "I think not," he said.

The contempt in Sasuke's voice stiffened Reginri's resolve. "I'm not going in."

"Oh?" Vanleo smiled.

"Sue me for breach of contract when we get back to Persenuae, if you want. I'm not doing it."

"Oh, we'll do much more than that," Vanleo said casually. "We'll transfer the financial loss of this expedition to your shoulders. There's no question it's your fault."

"I—"

"So you'll never draw full wages again, *ever*," Vanleo continued calmly.

Reginri moved his feet restlessly. There was a feeling of careful, controlled assurance in Vanleo that gave his words added weight. And behind the certainty of those eyes Reginri glimpsed something else.

"I don't know . . ." He breathed deeply, trying to clear his head. "Guess I got rattled a little, there."

He hesitated and then snorted self-deprecatingly. "I guess, I guess I'll be all right."

Sasuke nodded, holding his tongue. Vanleo smiled heartily. "Fine. Fine. We'll just forget this little incident, then, eh?" Abruptly he turned and walked down the beach. His steps were firm, almost jaunty.

III.

An air squirrel glided in on the gathering afternoon winds. It swung out over the lip of the canyon, chattering nervously, and then coasted back to the security of the hotbush. The two humans watched it leisurely strip a seed pod and nibble away.

"I don't understand why you didn't quit then," Belej said at last. "Right then. On the beach. A lawsuit wouldn't stick, not with other crewmen around to fill in for you."

Reginri looked at her blankly. "Impossible."

"Why? You'd seen that thing. You could see it was dangerous."

"I knew that before we left Persenuae."

"But you hadn't *seen* it."

"So what? I'd signed a contract."

Belej tossed her head impatiently. "I remember you saying to me it was a kind of big fish. That's all you said that night

before you left. You could argue that you hadn't understood
the danger . . .''

Reginri grimaced. "Not a fish. A mammal."

"No difference. Like some other fish back on Earth, you
told me."

"Like the humpback and the blue and the fin and the
sperm whales," he said slowly. "Before men killed them
off, they started to suspect the blues might be intelligent."

"Whales weren't mathematicians, though, were they?"
she said lightly.

"We'll never know, now."

Belej leaned back into the matted brownish grass. Strands
of black hair blew gently in the wind. "That Leo lied to you
about that thing, the fish, didn't he?"

"How?"

"Telling you it wasn't dangerous."

He sat upright in the grass and hugged his knees. "He
gave me some scientific papers. I didn't read most of them—
hell, they were clogged with names I didn't know, funny
terms. That's what you never understood, Belej. We don't
know much about Drongheda. Just that they've got lungs and
a spine and come ashore every few years. Why they do even
that, or what makes them intelligent—Vanleo spent thirty
years on that. You've got to give him credit—"

"For dragging you into it. Ha!"

"The Drongheda never harmed anybody. Their eyes don't
seem to register us. They probably don't even know we're
there, and Vanleo's simple-minded attempts to communicate
failed. He—"

"If a well-meaning, blind giant rolls over on you," she
said, "you're still dead."

Reginri snorted derisively. "The Drongheda balance on
ventral flippers. That's how they keep upright in the shallows. Whales couldn't do that, or—"

"You're not listening to me!" She gave him an exasper-
ated glance.

"I'm telling you what happened."

"Go ahead, then. We can't stay out here much longer."

He peered out at the wrinkled canyon walls. Lime-green
fruit trees dotted the burnished rocks. The thickening pink

haze was slowly creeping across the canyon floor, obscuring details. The airborne life that colored the clouds would coat the leathery trees and trigger the slow rhythms of seasonal life. Part of the sluggish, inevitable workings of Persenuae, he thought.

"Mist looks pretty heavy," he agreed. He glanced back at the log cabins that were the communal living quarters. They blended into the matted grasses.

"Tell me," she said insistently.

"Well, I . . ."

"You keep waking me up with nightmares about it. I deserve to know. It's changed our lives together. I—"

He sighed. This was going to be difficult. "All right."

IV.

Vanleo gave Reginri a clap on the shoulder and the three men set to work. Each took a spool of cable and walked backward, carrying it, into the surf. Reginri carefully watched the others and followed, letting the cable play out smoothly. He was so intent upon the work that he hardly noticed the enveloping wet that swirled about him. His oxygen pellet carrier was a dead, awkward weight at his back, but once up to his waist in the lapping water, maneuvering was easier, and he could concentrate on something other than keeping his balance.

The sea bottom was smooth and clear, laced with metallic filaments of dull silver. Not metal, though; this was a planet with strangely few heavy elements. Maybe that was why land life had never taken hold here, and the island continents sprinkled amid the ocean were bleak, dusty deserts. More probably, the fact that this chilled world was small and farther from the sun made it too hostile a place for land life. Persenuae, nearer in toward Zeta, thrived with both native and imported species, but this world had only sea creatures. A curious planet, this; a theoretical meeting point somewhere between the classic patterns of Earth and Mars. Large enough for percolating volcanoes, and thus oceans, but with an unbreathable air curiously high in carbon dioxide and low in oxygen. Maybe the wheel of evolution had simply not turned far enough here, and someday the small fish—or even the Drongheda itself—would evolve upward, onto the land.

But maybe the Drongheda *was* evolving, in intelligence, Reginri thought. The things seemed content to swim in the great oceans, spinning crystalline-mathematical puzzles for their own amusement. And for some reason they had responded when Vanleo first jabbed a probing electronic feeler into a neural nexus. The creatures spilled out realms of mathematical art that, Earthward, kept thousands working to decipher it—to rummage among a tapestry of cold theorems, tangled referents, seeking the quick axioms that lead to new corridors, silent pools of geometry and the intricate pyramiding of lines and angles, encasing a jungle of numbers.

"Watch it!" Sasuke sang out.

Reginri braced himself and a wave broke over him, splashing green foam against his faceplate.

"Riptide running here," Vanleo called. "Should taper off soon."

Reginri stood firm against the flow, keeping his knees loose and flexible for balance. Through his boots he felt the gritty slide of sand against smoothed rock. The cable spool was almost played out.

He turned to maneuver, and suddenly to the side he saw an immense brown wall. It loomed high, far above the gray waves breaking at its base. Reginri's chest tightened as he turned to study the Drongheda.

Its hide wall was delicately speckled in gold and green. The dorsal vents were black slashes that curved up the side, forming deep oily valleys.

Reginri cradled the cable spool under one arm and gingerly reached out to touch it. He pushed at it several times experimentally. It gave slightly with a soft, rubbery resistance.

"Watch the flukes!" Vanleo called. Reginri turned and saw a long black flipper break water fifty meters away. It languidly brushed the surface with a booming whack audible through his helmet and then submerged.

"He's just settling down, I expect," Vanleo called reassuringly. "They sometimes do that."

Reginri frowned at the water where the fluke had emerged. Deep currents welled up and rippled the surface.

"Let's have your cable," Sasuke said. "Reel it over here. I've got the mooring shaft sunk in."

Reginri spun out the rest of his spool and had some left when he reached Sasuke. Vanleo was holding a long tube pointed straight down into the water. He pulled a trigger and there was a muffled clap Reginri could hear over suit radio. He realized Vanleo was firing bolts into the ocean rock to secure their cable and connectors. Sasuke held out his hands and Reginri gave him the cable spool.

It was easier to stand here; the Drongheda screened them from most of the waves, and the undercurrents had ebbed. For a while Reginri stood uselessly by, watching the two men secure connections and mount the tapper lines. Sasuke at last waved him over, and as Reginri turned his back, they fitted the lines into his backpack.

Nervously, Reginri watched the Drongheda for signs of motion, but there were none. The ventral grooves formed an intricate ribbed pattern along the creature's side, and it was some moments before he thought to look upward and find the pithole. It was a red-rimmed socket, darker than the dappled brown around it. The ventral grooves formed an elaborate helix around the pithole, then arced away and down the body toward a curious mottled patch, about the same size as the pithole.

"What's that?" Reginri said, pointing at the patch.

"Don't know," Vanleo said. "Seems softer than the rest of the hide, but it's not a hole. All the Drongheda have 'em."

"Looks like a welt or something."

"Ummm," Vanleo murmured, distracted. "We'd better boost you up in a minute. I'm going to go around to the other side. There's another pithole exposed there, a little farther up from the water line. I'll go in that way."

"How do I get up?"

"Spikes," Sasuke murmured. "It's shallow enough here."

It took several minutes to attach the climbing spikes to Reginri's boots. He leaned against the Drongheda for support and tried to mentally compose himself for what was to come. The sea welled around him, lapping warmly against his skinsuit. He felt a jittery sense of anticipation.

"Up you go," Sasuke said. "Kneel on my shoulders and get the spikes in solid before you put any weight on them. Do what we said, once you're inside, and you'll be all right."

V.

Vanleo steadied him as he climbed onto Sasuke's back. It took some moments before Reginri could punch the climbing spikes into the thick, crinkled hide.

He was thankful for the low gravity. He pulled himself up easily, once he got the knack of it, and it took only a few moments to climb the ten meters to the edge of the pithole. Once there, he paused to rest.

"Not so hard as I thought," he said lightly.

"Good boy." Vanleo waved up at him. "Just keep steady and you'll be perfectly all right. We'll give you a signal on the com-line when you're to come out. This one won't be more than an hour, probably."

Reginri balanced himself on the lip of the pithole and took several deep breaths, tasting the oily air. In the distance gray waves broke into surf. The Drongheda rose like a bubble from the wrinkled sea. A bank of fog was rolling down the coastline. In it a shadowy shape floated. Reginri slitted his eyes to see better, but the fog wreathed the object and blurred its outline. Another Drongheda? He looked again but the form melted away in the white mist.

"Hurry it up," Sasuke called from below. "We won't move until you're in."

Reginri turned on the fleshy ledge beneath him and pulled at the dark blubbery folds that rimmed the pithole. He noticed that there were fine, gleaming threads all round the entrance. A mouth? An anus? Vanleo said not; the scientists who came to study the Drongheda had traced its digestive tract in crude fashion. But they had no idea what the pithole was for. It was precisely to find that out that Vanleo first went into one. Now it was Vanleo's theory that the pithole was the Drongheda's method of communication, since why else would the neural connections be so close to the surface inside? Perhaps, deep in the murky ocean, the Drongheda spoke to each other through these pitholes, rather than singing, like whales. Men had found no bioacoustic signature in the schools of Drongheda they had observed, but that meant very little.

Reginri pushed inward, through the iris of spongy flesh, and was at once immersed in darkness. His suit light clicked on. He lay in a sheath of meat with perhaps two hand spans of clearance on each side. The tunnel yawned ahead, absorbing the weak light. He gathered his knees and pushed upward against the slight grade.

"Electronics crew reports good contact with your tapper lines. This com okay?" Sasuke's voice came thin and high in Reginri's ear.

"Seems to be. Goddamned close in here."

"Sometimes it's smaller near the opening," Vanleo put in. "You shouldn't have too much climbing to do—most pitholes run pretty horizontal, when the Drongheda is holding steady like this."

"It's so tight. Going to be tough, crawling uphill," Reginri said, an uncertain waver in his voice.

"Don't worry about that. Just keep moving and look for the neural points." Vanleo paused. "Fish out the contacts for your tappers, will you? I just got a call from the technicians, they want to check the connection."

"Sure." Reginri felt at his belly. "I don't seem to find . . ."

"They're right there, just like in training," Sasuke said sharply. "Pull 'em out of their clips."

"Oh, yeah." Reginri fumbled for a moment and found the two metallic cylinders. They popped free of the suit and he nosed them together. "There."

"All right, all right, they're getting the trace," Vanleo said. "Looks like you're all set."

"Right, about time," Sasuke said. "Let's get moving."

"We're going around to the other side. So let us know if you see anything." Reginri could hear Vanleo's breath coming faster. "Quite a pull in this tide. Ah, there's the other pithole."

The two men continued to talk, getting Vanleo's equipment ready. Reginri turned his attention to his surroundings and wriggled upward, grunting. He worked steadily, pulling against the pulpy stuff. Here and there scaly folds wrinkled the walls, overlapping and making handholds. The waxen membranes reflected back none of his suit light. He dug in his heels and pushed, slipping on patches of filmy pink liquid that collected in the trough of the tunnel.

At first the passageway flared out slightly, giving him better purchase. He made good progress and settled down into a rhythm of pushing and turning. He worked his way around a vast bluish muscle that was laced by orange lines.

Even through his skinsuit he could feel a pulsing warmth come from it. The Drongheda had an internal temperature fifteen degrees Centigrade below the human's, but still an oppressive dull heat seeped through to him.

Something black lay ahead. He reached out and touched something rubbery that seemed to block the pithole. His suit light showed a milky pink barrier. He wormed around and felt at the edges of the stuff. Off to the left there was a smaller opening. He turned, flexed his legs and twisted his way into the new passage. Vanleo had told him the pithole might change direction and that when it did he was probably getting close to a nexus. Reginri hoped so.

VI.

"Everything going well?" Vanleo's voice came distantly.

"Think so," Reginri wheezed.

"I'm at the lip. Going inside now." There came the muffled sounds of a man working, and Reginri mentally blocked them out, concentrating on where he was.

The walls here gleamed like glazed, aging meat. His fingers could not dig into it. He wriggled with his hips and worked forward a few centimeters. He made his body flex, thrust, flex, thrust—he set up the rhythm and relaxed into it, moving forward slightly. The texture of the walls coarsened and he made better progress. Every few moments he stopped and checked the threads for the com-line and the tappers that trailed behind him, reeling out on spools at his side.

He could hear Sasuke muttering to himself, but he was unable to concentrate on anything but the waxen walls around him. The passage narrowed again, and ahead he could see more scaly folds. But these were different, dusted with a shimmering pale powder.

Reginri felt his heart beat faster. He kicked forward and reached out a hand to one of the encrusted folds. The delicate frosting glistened in his suit lamp. Here the meat was glassy, and deep within it he could see a complex interweaving network of veins and arteries, shot through with silvery threads.

It had to be a nexus; the pictures they had shown him were very much like this. It was not in a small pocket the way Vanleo said it would be, but that didn't matter. Vanleo himself had remarked that there seemed no systematic way the nodes were distributed. Indeed, they appeared to migrate to different positions inside the pithole, so that a team returning a few days later could not find the nodules they had tapped before.

Reginri felt a swelling excitement. He carefully thumbed on the electronic components set into his waist. Their low hum reassured him that everything was in order. He barked a short description of his find into his suit mike, and Vanleo responded in monosyllables. The other man seemed to be busy with something else, but Reginri was too occupied to wonder what it might be. He unplugged his tapper cylinders and worked them upward from his waist, his elbows poking into the pulpy membranes around him. Their needle points gleamed softly in the light as he turned them over, inspecting. Everything seemed all right.

He inched along and found the spot where the frosting seemed most dense. Carefully, bracing his hands against each other, he jabbed first one and then the other needle into the waxen flesh. It puckered around the needles.

He spoke quickly into his suit mike asking if the signals were coming through. There came an answering yes, some chatter from the technician back in the sand dunes, and then the line fell silent again.

Along the tapper lines were flowing the signals they had come to get. Long years of experiment had—as far as men could tell—established the recognition codes the technicians used to tell the Drongheda they had returned. Now, if the Drongheda responded, some convoluted electrical pulses would course through the lines and into the recording instruments ashore.

Reginri relaxed. He had done as much as he could. The rest depended on the technicians, the electronics, the lightning microsecond blur of information transfer between the machines and the Drongheda. Somewhere above or below him were flukes, ventral fins, slitted recesses, a baleen filter mouth through which a billion small fish lives had passed, all a part of this vast thing. Somewhere, layered in fat and wedged amid huge organs, there was a mind.

Reginri wondered how this had come about. Swimming through deep murky currents, somehow nature had evolved this thing that knew algebra, calculus, Reimannian metrics, Tchevychef subtleties—all as part of itself, as a fine-grained piece of the same language it shared with men.

Reginri felt a sudden impulse. There was an emergency piece clipped near his waist, for use when the tapper lines snarled or developed intermittent shorts. He wriggled around until his back was flush with the floor of the pithole and then reached down for it. With one hand he kept the needles impacted into the flesh above his head; with the other he extracted the thin, flat wedge of plastic and metal that he needed. From it sprouted tiny wires. He braced himself against the tunnel walls and flipped the wires into the emergency recesses in the tapper cylinders. Everything seemed secure; he rolled onto his back and fumbled at the rear of his helmet for the emergency wiring. By attaching the cabling, he could hook directly into a small fraction of the Drongheda's output. It wouldn't interfere with the direct tapping process. Maybe the men back in the sand dunes wouldn't even know he had done it.

He made the connection. Just before he flipped his suit com-line over to the emergency cable, he thought he felt a slight sway beneath him. The movement passed. He flipped the switch. And felt—

—Bursting light that lanced through him, drummed a staccato rhythm of speckled green—

—Twisting lines that meshed and wove into perspectives, triangles warped into strange saddle-pointed envelopes, coiling into new soundless shapes—

—A latticework of shrill sound, ringing at edges of geometrical flatness—

—Thick, rich foam that lapped against weathered stone towers, precisely turning under an ellipsoid orange sun—

—Miniatured light that groaned and spun softly, curving into moisture that beaded on a coppery matrix of wire—

—A webbing of sticky strands, lifting him—

—A welling current—

—Upward, toward the watery light—

Reginri snatched at the cable, yanking it out of the socket. His hand jerked up to cover his face and struck his helmet. He panted, gasping.

He closed his eyes and for a long moment thought of nothing, let his mind drift, let himself recoil from the experience.

There had been mathematics there, and much else. Rhomboids, acute intersections in veiled dimensions, many-sided twisted sculptures, warped perspectives, poly-hedrons of glowing fire.

But so much more—he would have drowned in it.

There was no interruption of chatter through his earphone. Apparently the electronics men had never noticed the interception. He breathed deeply and renewed his grip on the tapper needles. He closed his eyes and rested for long moments. The experience had turned him inside out for a brief flicker of time. But now he could breathe easily again. His heart had stopped thumping wildly in his chest. The torrent of images began to recede. His mind had been filled, overloaded with more than he could fathom.

He wondered how much the electronics really caught. Perhaps, transferring all this to cold ferrite memory, the emotional thrust was lost. It was not surprising that the only element men could decipher was the mathematics. Counting, lines and curves, the smooth sheen of geometry—they were abstractions, things that could be common to any reasoning mind. No wonder the Drongheda sent mostly mathematics through this neural passage; it was all that men could follow.

After a time it occurred to Reginri that perhaps Vanleo wanted it this way. Maybe he eavesdropped on the lines. The other man might seek this experience; it certainly had an intensity unmatched by drugs or the pallid electronic core-tapping in the sensoriums. Was Vanleo addicted? Why else risk failure? Why reject automated tapping and crawl in here—particularly since the right conditions came so seldom?

But it made no sense. If Vanleo had Drongheda tapes, he could play them back at leisure. So . . . maybe the man was fascinated by the creatures themselves, not only the mathematics. Perhaps the challenge of going inside, the feel of it, was what Vanleo liked.

Grotesque, yes . . . but maybe that was it.

VII.

He felt a tremor. The needles wobbled in his hand.

"Hey!" he shouted. The tube flexed under him.

"Something's happening in here. You guys—"

In midsentence the com-line went dead. Reginri automatically switched over to emergency, but there was no signal there either. He glanced at the tapper lines. The red phosphor glow at their ends had gone dead; they were not receiving power.

He wriggled around and looked down toward his feet. The tapper lines and the com cable snaked away into darkness with no breaks visible. If there was a flaw in the line, it was farther away.

Reginri snapped the tapper line heads back into his suit. As he did so, the flesh around him oozed languidly, compressing. There was a tilting sense of motion, a turning—

"*Frange* it! Get me—" then he remembered the line was dead. His lips pressed together.

He would have to get out on his own.

He dug in with his heels and tried to pull himself backward. A scaly bump scraped against his side. He pulled harder and came free, sliding a few centimeters back. The passage seemed tilted slightly downward. He put his hands out to push and saw something wet run over his fingers. The slimy fluid that filled the trough of the pithole was trickling toward him. Reginri pushed back energetically, getting a better purchase in the pulpy floor.

He worked steadily and made some progress. A long, slow undulation began and the walls clenched about him. He felt something squeeze at his legs, then his waist, then his chest and head. The tightening had a slow, certain rhythm.

He breathed faster, tasting an acrid smell. He heard only his own breath, amplified in the helmet.

He wriggled backward. His boot struck something and he felt the smooth lip of a turning in the passage. He remembered this, but the angle seemed wrong. The Drongheda must be shifting and moving, turning the pithole.

He forked his feet into the new passageway and quickly slipped through it.

This way was easier; he slid down the slick sides and felt a wave of relief. Farther along, if the tunnel widened, he might even be able to turn around and go headfirst.

His foot touched something that resisted softly. He felt around with both boots, gradually letting his weight settle on the thing. It seemed to have a brittle surface, pebbled. He carefully followed the outline of it around the walls of the hole until he had satisfied himself that there was no opening.

The passage was blocked.

His mind raced. The air seemed to gain a weight of its own, thick and sour in his helmet. He stamped his boots down, hoping to break whatever it was. The surface stayed firm.

Reginri felt his mind go numb. He was trapped. The com-line was dead, probably snipped off by this thing at his feet.

He felt the walls around him clench and stretch again, a massive hand squeezing the life from him. The pithole sides were only centimeters from his helmet. As he watched, a slow ripple passed through the membrane, ropes of yellow fat visible beneath the surface.

"Get me out!" Reginri kicked wildly. He thrashed against the slimy walls, using elbows and knees to gouge. The yielding pressure remained, cloaking him.

"Out! Out!" Reginri viciously slammed his fists into the

flesh. His vision blurred. Small dark points floated before him. He pounded mechanically, his breath coming in short gasps. He cried for help. And he knew he was going to die.

Rage burst out of him. He beat at the enveloping smoothness. The gathering tightness in him boiled up, curling his lips into a grimace. His helmet filled with a bitter taste. He shouted again and again, battering at the Drongheda, cursing it. His muscles began to ache.

And slowly, slowly the burning anger melted. He blinked away the sweat in his eyes. His vision cleared. The blind, pointless energy drained away. He began to think again.

Sasuke. Vanleo. Two-faced bastards. They'd known this job was dangerous. The incident on the beach was a charade. When he showed doubts they'd bullied and threatened him immediately. They'd probably had to do it before, to other men. It was all planned.

He took a long, slow breath and looked up. Above him in the tunnel of darkness, the strands of the tapping lines and the com cable dangled.

One set of lines.

They led upward, on a slant, the way he had come.

It took a moment for the fact to strike him. If he had been backing down the way he came, the lines should be snarled behind him.

He pushed against the glazed sides and looked down his chest. There were no tapper lines near his legs.

That meant the lines did not come up through whatever was blocking his way. No, they came only from above. Which meant that he had taken some wrong side passage. Somehow a hole had opened in the side of the pithole and he had followed it blindly.

He gathered himself and thrust upward, striving for purchase. He struggled up the incline, and dug in with his toes. Another long ripple passed through the tube. The steady hand of gravity forced him down, but he slowly worked his way forward. Sweat stung his eyes.

After a few minutes his hands found the lip, and he quickly hoisted himself over it, into the horizontal tunnel above.

He found a tangle of lines and tugged at them. They gave

with a slight resistance. This was the way out, he was sure of it. He began wriggling forward, and suddenly the world tilted, stretched, lifted him high. Let him drop.

He smashed against the pulpy side and lost his breath. The tube flexed again, rising up in front of him and dropping away behind. He dug his hands in and held on. The pithole arched, coiling, and squeezed him. Spongy flesh pressed at his head and he involuntarily held his breath. His faceplate was wrapped in it, and his world became fine-veined, purple, marbled with lacy fat.

Slowly, slowly the pressure ebbed away. He felt a dull aching in his side. There was a subdued tremor beneath him. As soon as he gained maneuvering room, he crawled urgently forward, kicking viciously. The lines led him forward.

The passage flared outward and he increased his speed. He kept up a steady pace of pulling hands, gouging elbows, thrusting knees and toes. The weight around him seemed bent upon expelling, imparting momentum, ejecting. So it seemed, as the flesh tightened behind him and opened before.

He tried the helmet microphone again, but it was still inert. He thought he recognized a vast bulging bluish muscle that, on his way in, had been in the wall. Now it formed a bump in the floor. He scrambled over its slickness and continued on.

He was so intent upon motion and momentum that he did not recognize the end. Suddenly the walls converged again and he looked around frantically for another exit. There was none. Then he noticed the rings of cartilage and stringy muscle. He pushed at the knotted surface. It gave, then relaxed even more. He shoved forward and abruptly was halfway out, suspended over the churning water.

VIII.

The muscled iris gripped him loosely about the waist. Puffing steadily, he stopped to rest.

He squinted up at the forgiving sun. Around him was a harshly lit world of soundless motion. Currents swirled meters below. He could feel the brown hillside of the Drongheda shift slowly. He turned to see—

The Drongheda was splitting in two.

But no, no—

The bulge was another Drongheda close by moving. At the same moment another silent motion caught his eye. Below, Vanleo struggled through the darkening water, waving. Pale mist shrouded the sea.

Reginri worked his way out and onto the narrow rim of the pithole. He took a grip at it and lowered himself partway down toward the water. Arms extended, he let go and fell with a splash into the ocean. He kept his balance and lurched away awkwardly on legs of cotton.

Vanleo reached out a steadying hand. The man motioned at the back of his helmet. Reginri frowned, puzzled, and then realized he was motioning toward the emergency com cable. He unspooled his own cable and plugged it into the shoulder socket on Vanleo's skinsuit.

"—damned lucky. Didn't think I'd see you again. But it's *fantastic*, come see it."

"What? I got—"

"I understand them now. I know what they're here for. It's not just communication, I don't think that, but that's part of it too. They've—"

"Stop babbling. What happened?"

"I went in," Vanleo said, regaining his breath. "Or started to. We didn't notice that another Drongheda had surfaced, was moving into the shallows."

"I saw it. I didn't think—"

"I climbed up to the second pithole before I saw. I was busy with the cables, you know. You were getting good traces and I wanted to—"

"Let's get away, come on." The vast bulks above them were moving.

"No, no, come see. I think my guess is right, these shallows are a natural shelter for them. If they have any enemies in the sea, large fish or something, their enemies can't follow them here into the shallows. So they come here to, to mate and to communicate. They must be terribly lonely, if they can't talk to each other in the oceans. So they have to come here to do it. I—"

Reginri studied the man and saw that he was ablaze with

his inner vision. The damned fool loved these beasts, cared about them, had devoted a life to them and their goddamned mathematics.

"Where's Sasuke?"

"—and it's all so natural. I mean, humans communicate and make love, and those are two separate acts. They don't blend together. But the Drongheda—they have it all. They're like, like . . ."

The man pulled at Reginri's shoulder, leading him around the long curve of the Drongheda. Two immense burnished hillsides grew out of the shadowed sea. Zeta was setting, and in profile Reginri could see a long dexterous tentacle curling into the air. It came from the mottled patches, like welts, he had seen before.

"They extend through those spots, you see. Those are their sensors, what they use to complete the contact. And—I can't prove it, but I'm sure—that is when the genetic material is passed between them. The mating period. At the same time they exchange information, converse. That's what we're getting on the tappers, their stored knowledge fed out. They think we're another of their own, that must be it. I don't understand all of it, but—"

"*Where's Sasuke?*"

"—but the first one, the one you were inside, recognized the difference as soon as the second Drongheda approached. They moved together and the second one extruded that tentacle. Then—"

Reginri shook the other man roughly. "Shut up! Sasuke—"

Vanleo stopped, dazed, and looked at Reginri. "I've been telling you. It's a great discovery, the first real step we've taken in this field. We'll understand so much *more* once this is fully explored."

Reginri hit him in the shoulder.

Vanleo staggered. The glassy, pinched look of his eyes faded. He began to lift his arms.

Reginri drove his gloved fist into Vanleo's faceplate. Vanleo toppled backward. The ocean swallowed him. Reginri stepped back, blinking.

Vanleo's helmet appeared as he struggled up. A wave foamed over him. He stumbled, turned, saw Reginri.

Reginri moved toward him. "No. No," Vanleo said weakly.

"If you're not going to tell me—"

"But I, I am." Vanleo gasped, leaned forward until he could brace his hands on his knees.

"There wasn't time. The second one came up on us so, so fast."

"Yeah?"

"I was about ready to go inside. When I saw the second one moving in, you know, the only time in thirty years, I knew it was important. I climbed down to observe. But we needed the data, so Sasuke went in for me. With the tapper cables."

Vanleo panted. His face was ashen.

"When the tentacle went in, it filled the pithole exactly, Tight. There was no room left," he said. "Sasuke . . . was there. Inside."

Reginri froze, stunned. A wave swirled around him and he slipped. The waters tumbled him backward. Dazed, he regained his footing on the slick rocks and began stumbling blindly toward the bleak shore, toward humanity. The ocean lapped around him, ceaseless and unending.

IX.

Belej sat motionless, unmindful of the chill. "Oh my God," she said.

"That was it," he murmured. He stared off into the canyon. Zeta Reticuli sent slanting rays into the layered reddening mists. Air squirrels darted among the shifting shadows.

"He's crazy," Belej said simply. "That Leo is crazy."

"Well . . ." Reginri began. Then he rocked forward stiffly and stood up. Swirls of reddish cloud were crawling up the canyon face toward them. He pointed. "That stuff is coming in faster than I thought." He coughed. "We'd better get inside."

Belej nodded and came to her feet. She brushed the twisted brown grass from her legs and turned to him.

"Now that you've told me," she said softly, "I think you ought to put it from your mind."

"It's hard. I . . . ."

"I know. I know. But you can push it far away from you, forget it happened. That's the best way."

"Well, maybe."

"Believe me. You've changed since this happened to you. I can feel it."

"Feel what?"

"You. You're different. I feel a barrier between us."

"I wonder," he said slowly.

She put her hand on his arm and stepped closer, an old, familiar gesture. He stood watching the reddening haze swallowing the precise lines of the rocks below.

"I want that screen between us to dissolve. You made your contribution, earned your pay. Those damned people understand the Drongheda now—"

He made a wry, rasping laugh. "We'll never grasp the Drongheda. What we get in those neural circuits are mirrors of what we want. Of what we are. We can't sense anything totally alien."

"But—"

"Vanleo saw mathematics because he went after it. So did I, at first. Later . . ."

He stopped. A sudden breeze made him shiver. He chenched his fists. Clenched. Clenched.

How could he tell her? He woke in the night, sweating, tangled in the bedclothes, muttering incoherently . . . but they were not nightmares, not precisely.

Something else. Something intermediate.

"Forget those things," Belej said soothingly. Reginri leaned closer to her and caught the sweet musk of her, the dry crackling scent of her hair. He had always loved that.

She frowned up at him. Her eyes shifted intently from his mouth to his eyes and then back again, trying to read his expression. "It will only trouble you to recall it. I—I'm sorry I asked you to tell it. But remember"—she took both his hands in hers—"you'll never go back there again. It can be . . ."

Something made him look beyond her. At the gathering fog.

And at once he sensed the shrouded abyss open below
him. Sweeping him in. Gathering him up. Into—
—*a thick red foam lapping against weathered granite
towers*—
—*an ellipsoidal sun spinning soundlessly over a silvered,
warping planet*—
—*watery light*—
—*cloying strands, sticky, a fine-spun coppery matrix that
enfolded him, warming*—
—*glossy sheen of polyhedra, wedged together, mass upon
mass*—
—*smooth bands of moisture playing lightly over his quilted
skin*—
—*a blistering light shines through him, sets his bones to
humming resonance*—
—*pressing*—
—*coiling*—
Beckoning. Beckoning.

When the moment had passed, Reginri blinked and felt a
salty stinging in his eyes. Every day the tug was stronger, the
incandescent images sharper. This must be what Vanleo felt,
he was sure of it. They came to him now even during the day.
Again and again, the grainy texture altering with time . . .

He reached out and enfolded Belej in his arms.

"But I must," he said in a rasping whisper. "Vanleo
called today. He . . . I'm going. I'm going back."

He heard her quick intake of breath, felt her stiffen in his
arms.

His attention was diverted by the reddening fog. It cloaked
half the world and still it came on.

There was something ominous about it and something
inviting as well. He watched as it engulfed trees nearby. He
studied it intently, judging the distance. The looming presence was quite close now. But he was sure it would be all
right.

Afterword

Once when I was scuba diving I saw a shark. It was about a hundred yards away but the water was so clear that it looked like it was right beside me. White, sleek, stately, beautiful.

Other things were happening at the same time—I was carefully coming up on some fish I wanted for lunch, keeping clear of my diving mates, wondering why my mask was fogging a little . . . and then there came that slowed-time reflex you get in an auto accident, when there is all the time in the world to think about what you're going to do next.

This was off the coast of the Yucatan peninsula, in 1967, about forty feet down. Adrenaline enlarges everything, throws it into stark relief, but still—this shark was *big*. The long, white form coasted lazily over a ridge of stones, looked toward us for what seemed like forever, and turned majestically our way. Those goggle eyes seemed both blazingly angry and stupefyingly dumb at the same time, but the important fact was that they seemed to be looking right at me.

I can remember thinking, with that speed-freak energy, that the thing looked *alien*. As though it was out of place, shouldn't be there, wasn't natural, couldn't even be in the same *ocean* with me. It was so implausibly *huge*. I could easily fit inside. . . .

I'd like to say that I did something brave, like moving to defend the others, but the fact is that I kept swimming as rhythmically as I could, and angled down behind some other rocks. I don't even remember looking at the other divers.

The shark was a great white, all right, and it swam majestically by, about fifty yards away, and then coasted off with smooth indifference, into the far hazy mist.

I remembered that when I started thinking of this story. In fact, my stunned judgment that the great white could probably swallow me whole without great bother was probably the germinating impulse behind this story.

A lot of the stories in this collection deal with the alien, in one way or another. Strange creatures, or else the process of making things strange, alienation.

There are a lot of kinds of aliens in sf. The most common is the human in a Halloween suit, like the vegetable man in the 1951 version of *The Thing*. In that great old lumbering Howard Hawks movie, everything's a symbol. The alien stands for godless communism. The soft-headed scientists who try to make contact, despite obvious hostility, symbolize the liberals. And the U.S. Air Force, of course, symbolizes the U.S. Air Force. The alien is completely understandable.

Then there's the alien who stands for a part of our own history. The Galactic Empire motif, with its equation of planet = colony, aliens = indians, is really replaying the past. (Sometimes the indians even win.)

For me, the unexamined alien is not worth meeting. Yet the most compelling aspect of aliens is their fundamental unknowability. The best signifier for this, I think, is language. In Ian Watson's fine novel *The Embedding*, aliens come to barter with us for our languages, not our science and art, because these are the keys to a deeper sensing of the world. Each species' language gives a partial picture of reality.

The technical problem a writer faces in depicting alien languages is how to convey any information and yet be convincingly strange. If it's just gibberish, you gain nothing and look funny, too. Broken English won't do, and the usual sf cliché of awkward frog-speak is boring.

I don't have any theoretical solution to this problem,

just some particular attempts. This story is one such; my novels try it at greater length. In a way, rendering the alien is the Holy Grail of sf, because if your attempt can be accurately summarized, you know you've failed.

Time Shards

It had all gone very well, Brooks told himself. Very well indeed. He hurried along the side corridor, his black dress shoes clicking hollowly on the old tiles. This was one of the oldest and most rundown of the Smithsonian's buildings; too bad they didn't have the money to knock it down. Funding. Everything was a matter of funding.

He pushed open the door of the barnlike workroom and called out, "John? How did you like the ceremony?"

John Hart appeared from behind a vast rack that was filled with fluted pottery. His thin face was twisted in a scowl and he was puffing on a cigarette. "Didn't go."

"John! That's not permitted." Brooks waved at the cigarette. "You of all people should be careful about contamination of—"

"Hell with it." He took a final puff, belched blue, and ground out the cigarette on the floor.

"You really should've watched the dedication of the Vault, you know," Brooks began, adopting a bantering tone. You had to keep a light touch with these research types. "The President was there—she made a very nice speech—"

"I was busy."

"Oh?" Something in Hart's tone put Brooks off his conversational stride. "Well. You'll be glad to hear that I had a little conference with the Board, just before the dedication. They've agreed to continue supporting your work here."

"Um."

"You must admit, they're being very fair." As he talked Brooks threaded amid the rows of pottery, each in a plastic sleeve. This room always made him nervous. There was

33

priceless Chinese porcelain here, Assyrian stoneware, buff-blue Roman glazes, Egyptian earthenware—and Brooks lived in mortal fear that he would trip, fall, and smash some piece of history into shards. "After all, you *did* miss your deadline. You got nothing out of all this"—a sweep of the hand, narrowly missing a green Persian tankard—"for the Vault."

Hart, who was studying a small brownish water jug, looked up abruptly. "What about the wheel recording?"

"Well, there was that, but—"

"The best in the world, dammit!"

"They heard it sometime ago. They were very interested."

"You told them what they were hearing?" Hart asked intensely.

"Of course, I—"

"You could hear the hoofbeats of cattle, clear as day."

"They heard. Several commented on it."

"Good." Hart seemed satisfied, but still strangely depressed.

"But you must admit, that isn't what you promised."

Hart said sourly, "Research can't be done to a schedule."

Brooks had been pacing up and down the lanes of pottery. He stopped suddenly, pivoted on one foot, and pointed a finger at Hart. "You said you'd have a *voice*. That was the promise. Back in '98 you said you would have something for the BiMillennium celebration, and—"

"Okay, okay." Hart waved away the other man's words.

"Look—" Brooks strode to a window and jerked up the blinds. From this high up in the Arts and Industries Building the BiMillennial Vault was a flat concrete slab sunk in the Washington mud; it had rained the day before. Now bulldozers scraped piles of gravel and mud into the hole, packing it in before the final encasing shield was to be laid. The Vault itself was already sheathed in sleeves of concrete, shock-resistant and immune to decay. The radio beacons inside were now set. Their radioactive power supply would automatically stir to life exactly a thousand years from now. Periodic bursts of radio waves would announce to the world of the TriMillennium that a message from the distant past awaited whoever dug down to find it. Inside the Vault were artifacts, recordings, everything the Board of Regents of the Smithsonian thought important about their age. The coup of the entire Vault was to have been a message from the First Millennium, the year 1000 A.D. Hart had promised them something far better than a mere written document from that time. He had said he could capture a living voice.

"See that?" Brooks said with sudden energy. "That Vault will outlast everything we know—all those best-selling novels and funny plays and amazing scientific discoveries. They'll all be *dust*, when the Vault's opened."

"Yeah," Hart said.

"Yeah? That's all you can say?"

"Well, sure, I—"

"The Vault was *important*. And I was stupid enough"—he rounded on Hart abruptly, anger flashing across his face—"to chew up some of the only money we had for the Vault to support *you*."

Hart took an involuntary step backward. "You knew it was a gamble."

"I knew." Brooks nodded ruefully. "And we waited, and waited—"

"Well, your waiting is over," Hart said, something hardening in him.

"What?"

"I've got it. A voice."

"You have?" In the stunned silence that followed Hart bent over casually and picked up a dun-colored water jug from the racks. An elaborate, impossibly large-winged orange bird was painted on its side. Hart turned the jug in his hands, hefting its weight.

"Why . . . it's too late for the Vault, of course, but still . . ." Brooks shuffled his feet. "I'm glad the idea paid off. That's great."

"Yeah. Great." Hart smiled sourly. "And you know what it's worth? Just about *this* much—"

He took the jug in one hand and threw it. It struck the far wall with a splintering crash. Shards flew like a covey of frightened birds that scattered through the long ranks of pottery. Each landed with a ceramic tinkling.

"What are you *doing*—" Brooks began, dropping to his knees without thinking to retrieve a fragment of the jug. "That jug was worth—"

"Nothing," Hart said. "It was a fake. Almost everything the Egyptians sent was bogus."

"But why are you . . . you said you succeeded . . ." Brooks was shaken out of his normal role of Undersecretary to the Smithsonian.

"I did. For what it's worth."

"Well . . . show me."

Hart shrugged and beckoned Brooks to follow him. He threaded his way through the inventory of glazed pottery, ignoring the extravagant polished shapes that flared and twisted in elaborate, artful designs, the fruit of millennia of artisans. Glazes of feldspath, lead, tin, ruby salt. Jasperware, soft-paste porcelain, albarelloa festooned with ivy and laurel, flaring lips and serene curved handles. A galaxy of the work of the First Millennium and after, assembled for Hart's search.

"It's on the wheel," Hart said, gesturing.

Brooks walked around the spindle fixed at the center of a horzontal disk. Hart called it a potter's wheel but it was a turntable, really, firmly buffered against the slightest tremor from external sources. A carefully arranged family of absorbers isolated the table from everything but the variable motor seated beneath it. On the turntable was an earthenware pot. It looked unremarkable to Brooks—just a dark red oxidized finish, a thick lip, and a rather crude handle, obviously molded on by a lesser artisan.

"What's its origin?" Brooks said, mostly to break the silence that lay between them.

"Southern England." Hart was logging instructions into the computer terminal nearby. Lights rippled on the staging board.

"How close to the First Mil?"

"Around 1280 A.D., apparently."

"Not really close, then. But interesting."

"Yeah."

Brooks stooped forward. When he peered closer he could see the smooth finish was an illusion. A thin thread ran around the pot, so fine the eye could scarcely make it out. The lines wound in a tight helix. In the center of each delicate line was a fine hint of blue. The jug had been incised with a precise point. Good; that was exactly what Hart had

said he sought. It was an ancient, common mode of decoration—incise a seemingly infinite series of rings, as the pot
turned beneath the cutting tool. The cutting tip revealed a
differently colored dye underneath, a technique called sgraffito, the scratched.

It could never have occurred to the Islamic potters who
invented sgraffito that they were, in fact, devising the first
phonograph records.

Hart pressed a switch and the turntable began to spin. He
watched it for a moment, squinting with concentration. Then
he reached down to the side of the turntable housing and
swung up the stylus manifold. It came up smoothly and Hart
locked it in just above the spinning red surface of the pot.

"Not a particularly striking item, is it?" Brooks said
conversationally.

"No."

"Who made it?"

"Near as I can determine, somebody in a co-operative of
villages, barely Christian. Still used lots of pagan decora-
tions. Got them scrambled up with the cross motif a lot."

"You've gotten . . . words?"

"Oh, sure. In early English, even."

"I'm surprised crude craftsmen could do such delicate
work."

"Luck, some of it. They probably used a pointed wire, a
new technique that'd been imported around that time from
Saxony."

The computer board hooted a readiness call. Hart walked
over to it, thumbed in instructions, and turned to watch the
stylus whir in a millimeter closer to the spinning jug. "Damn,"
Hart said, glancing at the board. "Correlator's giving hash
again."

Hart stopped the stylus and worked at the board. Brooks
turned nervously and paced, unsure of what his attitude
should be toward Hart. Apparently the man had discovered
something, but did that excuse his surliness? Brooks glanced
out the window, where the last crowds were drifting away
from the Vault dedication and strolling down the Mall. There
was a reception for the Board of Regents in Georgetown in

an hour. Brooks would have to be there early, to see that matters were in order—

"If you'd given me enough money, I could've had a Hewlett-Packard. Wouldn't have to fool with this piece of . . ." Hart's voice trailed off.

Brooks had to keep reminding himself that this foul-tempered, scrawny man was reputed to be a genius. If Hart had not come with the highest of recommendations, Brooks would never have risked valuable Vault funding. Apparently Hart's new method for finding correlations in a noisy signal was a genuine achievement.

The basic idea was quite old, of course. In the 1960s a scientist at the American Museum of Natural History in New York had applied a stylus to a rotating urn and played the signal through an audio pickup. Out came the *wreeee* sound of the original potter's wheel where the urn was made. It had been a Roman urn, made in the era when hand-turned wheels were the best available. The Natural History "recording" was crude, but even that long ago they could pick out a moment when the potter's hand slipped and the rhythm of the *wreeee* faltered.

Hart had read about that urn and seen the possibilities. He developed his new multiple-correlation analysis—a feat of programming, if nothing else—and began searching for pottery that might have acoustic detail in its surface. The sgraffito technique was the natural choice. Potters sometimes used fine wires to incise their wares. Conceivably, anything that moved the incising wire—passing footfalls, even the tiny acoustic push of sound waves—could leave its trace on the surface of the finished pot. Buried among imperfections and noise, eroded by the random bruises of history . . .

"Got it," Hart said, fatigue creeping into his voice.

"Good. Good."

"Yeah. Listen."

The stylus whirred forward. It gently nudged into the jug, near the lip. Hart flipped a switch and studied the rippling, dancing yellow lines on the board oscilloscope. Electronic archaeology. "There."

A high-pitched whining came from the speaker, punctuated by hollow, deep bass thumps.

"Hear that? He's using a foot pump."

"A kick wheel?"

"Right."

"I thought they came later."

"No, the Arabs had them."

There came a *clop clop clop*, getting louder. It sounded oddly disembodied in the silence of the long room.

"What . . . ?"

"Horse. I detected this two weeks ago. Checked it with the equestrian people. They say the horse is unshod, assuming we're listening to it walk on dirt. Farm animal, probably. Plow puller."

"Ah."

The hoofbeats faded. The whine of the kick wheel sang on.

"Here it comes," Hart whispered.

Brooks shuffled slightly. The ranks upon ranks of ancient pottery behind him made him nervous, as though a vast unmoving audience were in the room with them.

Thin, distant: "Alf?"

"Aye." A gruff reply.

"It slumps, sure."

"I be oct, man." A rasping, impatient voice.

"T'art—"

"*Busy*—mark?"

"Ah ha' wearied o' their laws," the thin voice persisted.

"Aye—so all. What mark it?" Restrained impatience.

"Their Christ. He werkes vengemant an the alt spirits."

"Hie yer tongue."

"They'll ne hear."

"Wi' 'er Christ 'er're everywhere."

A pause. Then faintly, as though a whisper: "We ha' lodged th' alt spirits."

"Ah? You? Th' rash gazer?"

"I spy stormwrack. A hue an' grie rises by this somer se'sun."

"Fer we?"

"Aye, unless we spake th' *Ave maris stella* 'a theirs."

"Elat. Lat fer that. Hie, I'll do it. Me knees still buckle whon they must."

"I kenned that. So shall I."

"Aye. So shall we all. But wh' of the spirits?"

"They suffer pangs, dark werkes. They are lodged."

"Ah. Where?"

"S'tart."

" 'Ere? In me clay?"

"In yer vessels."

"Nay!"

"I chanted 'em in 'fore sunbreak."

"Nay! I fain wad ye not."

whir whir whir

The kick wheel thumps came rhythmically.

"They sigh'd thruu in-t'wixt yer clay. 'S done."

"Fer *what?*"

"These pots—they bear a fineness, aye?"

"Aye."

A rumbling. "—will hie home 'er. Live in yer pots."

"An?"

"Whon time werkes a'thwart 'e Christers, yon spirits of leaf an' bough will, I say, hie an' grie to yer sons, man. To yer *sons'* sons, man."

"Me pots? Carry our kenne?"

"Aye. I investe' thy clay wi' ern'st spirit, so when's ye causes it ta dance, our law say . . ."

whir

A hollow rattle.

"Even this 'ere, as I spin it?"

"Aye. Th' spirits innit. Speak as ye form. The dance, t'will carry yer schop word t' yer sons, yer *sons'* sons' sons."

"While it's spinnin'?"

Brooks felt his pulse thumping in his throat.

"Aye."

"Than't—"

"Speak inta it. To yer sons."

"Ah . . ." Suddenly the voice came louder. "Aye, aye! There! If ye hear me, sons! I be from yer past! The ancient dayes!"

"Tell them wha' ye must."

"Aye. Sons! Blood a' mine! Mark ye! Hie not ta strags in th' house of Lutes. They carry the red pox! An' . . . an', beware th' Kinseps—they bugger all they rule! An', whilst pot-charrin', mix th' fair smelt wi' greeno erst, 'ere ye'll flux it fair speedy. Ne'er leave sheep near a lean-house, ne, 'ey'll snuck down 'an it—''

whir whir thump whir

"What—what happened?" Brooks gasped.

"He must have brushed the incising wire a bit. The cut continues, but the fine touch was lost. Vibrations as subtle as a voice couldn't register."

Brooks looked around, dazed, for a place to sit. "In . . . incredible."

"I suppose."

Hart seemed haggard, worn.

"They were about to convert to Christianity, weren't they?"

Hart nodded.

"They thought they could seal up the—what? wood spirits? —they worshiped. Pack them away by blessing the clay or something like that. And that the clay would carry a message to the future!"

"So it did."

"To their sons' sons' sons . . ." Brooks paused. "Why are you so depressed, Hart? This is a great success."

Abruptly Hart laughed. "I'm not, really. Just, well, manic, I guess. We're so funny. So absurd. Think about it, Brooks. All that hooey the potter shouted into his damned pot. What did you make of it?"

"Well . . . gossip, mostly. I can't get over what a long shot this is—that we'd get to hear it."

"Maybe it was a common belief back then. Maybe many tried it—and maybe now I'll find more pots, with just ordinary conversation on them. Who knows?" He laughed again, a slow warm chuckle. "We're all so absurd. Maybe Henry Ford was right—history *is* bunk."

"I don't see why you're carrying on this way, Hart. Granted, the message was . . . obscure. That unintelligible information about making pottery, and—"

"Tips on keeping sheep."

"Yes, and—"

"Useless, right?"

"Well, probably. To us, anyway. The conversation before that was much more interesting."

"Uh huh. Here's a man who is talking to the ages. Sending what he thinks is most important. And he prattles out a lot of garbage."

"Well, true . . ."

"And it *was* important—to him."

"Yes."

Hart walked stiffly to the window. Earthmovers crawled like eyeless insects beneath the wan yellow lamps. Dusk had fallen. Their great awkward scoops pushed mounds of mud into the square hole where the Vault rested.

"Look at that." Hart gestured. "The Vault. Our own monument to our age. Passing on the legacy. You, me, the others—we've spent years on it. Years, and a fortune." He chuckled dryly. "What makes you think we've done any better?"

Afterword

I usually try to be scrupulous about facts in my fiction, but everybody deserves a day off.

I had to finesse a knotty problem of dialects to tell this story at all, so I just plain, flat-out . . . cheated. The conversations reported in here don't fit with the assigned era of origin, and my only excuse is that it reads better that way.

This point so vexed David Hartwell, then editing a magazine, that he rejected the story. David has a doctorate in medieval English and was sore grieved at my playing fast and loose with his specialty. I can see his argument, but decided for the moment to subscribe to the sub-school of science fiction which holds that The Idea Is Hero, Even If It's Wrong.

Otherwise, things are pretty much on the up-and-up. I got the notion while reading a paper in the *Proceedings of the I.E.E.E.* (1969, pp. 1465–1466), where Richard Woodbridge first discussed the possibility. The method has been tried since, and it works. Unfortunately, nothing more interesting than background sounds have been picked up—so far. But engineering is improving all the time. . . .

Redeemer

He had trouble finding it. The blue-white exhaust plume was a long trail of ionized hydrogen scratching a line across the black. It had been a lot harder to locate out here than Central said it would be.

Nagara came up on the *Redeemer* from behind, their blind side. They wouldn't have any sensors pointed aft. No point in it when you're on a one-way trip, not expecting visitors and haven't seen anybody for seventy-three years.

He boosted in with the fusion plant, cutting off the translight to avoid overshoot. The translight rig was delicate and still experimental and it had already pushed him over seven light-years out from Earth. And anyway, when he got back to Earth there would be an accounting, and he would have to pay off from his profit anything he spent for overexpenditure of the translight hardware.

The ramscoop vessel ahead was running hot. It was a long cylinder, fluted fore and aft. The blue-white fire came boiling out of the aft throat, pushing *Redeemer* along at a little below a tenth of light velocity. Nagara's board buzzed. He cut in the null-mag system. The ship's skin, visible outside, fluxed into its superconducting state, gleaming like chrome. The readout winked and Nagara could see on the sim-board his ship slipping like a silver fish through the webbing of magnetic field lines that protected *Redeemer*.

The field was mostly magnetic dipole. He cut through it and glided in parallel to the hot exhaust streamer. The stuff was spitting out a lot of UV and he had to change filters to see what he was doing. He came up along the aft section of the ship and matched velocities. The magnetic throat up ahead sucked in the interstellar hydrogen for the fusion motors. He stayed away from it. There was enough radiation up there to fry you for good.

Redeemer's midsection was rotating but the big clumsy-looking lock aft was stationary. Fine. No trouble clamping on.

The couplers seized *clang* and he used a waldo to manually open the lock. He would have to be fast now, fast and careful.

He pressed a code into the keyin plate on his chest to check it. It worked. The slick aura enveloped him, cutting out the ship's hum. Nagara nodded to himself.

He went quickly through the *Redeemer*'s lock. The pumps were still laboring when he spun the manual override to open the big inner hatch. He pulled himself through in the zero-g with one powerful motion, through the hatch and into a cramped suitup room. He cut in his magnetos and settled to the grid deck.

As Nagara crossed the deck a young man came in from a side hatchway. Nagara stopped and thumped off his protective shield. The man didn't see Nagara at first because he was looking the other way as he came through the hatchway, moving with easy agility. He was studying the subsystem monitoring panels on the far bulkhead. The status phosphors were red but they winked green as Nagara took three steps forward and grabbed the man's shoulder and spun him around. Nagara was grounded and the man was not. Nagara hit him once in the stomach and then shoved him against a bulkhead. The man gasped for breath. Nagara stepped back and put his hand into his coverall pocket and when it came out there was a dart pistol in it. The man's eyes didn't register anything at first and when they did he just stared at the pistol, getting his breath back, staring as though he couldn't believe either Nagara or the pistol was there.

"What's your name?" Nagara demanded in a clipped, efficient voice.

"What? I—"

"Your name. Quick."

"I . . . Zak."

"All right, Zak, now listen to me. I'm inside now and I'm

not staying long. I don't care what you've been told. You do just what I say and nobody will blame you for it.''

''. . . nobody . . . ?'' Zak was still trying to unscramble his thoughts and he looked at the pistol again as though that would explain things.

''Zak, how many of you are manning this ship?''

''Manning? You mean crewing?'' Confronted with a clear question, he forgot his confusion and frowned. ''Three. We're doing our five-year stint. The Revealer and Jacob and me.''

''Fine. Now, where's Jacob?''

''Asleep. This isn't his shift.''

''Good.'' Nagara jerked a thumb over his shoulder. ''Personnel quarters that way?''

''Uh, yes.''

''Did an alarm go off through the whole ship, Zak?''

''No, just on the bridge.''

''So I didn't wake up Jacob?''

''I . . . I suppose not.''

''Fine, good. Now, where's the Revealer?''

So far it was working well. The best way to handle people who might give you trouble right away was to keep them busy telling you things before they had time to decide what they should be doing. And Zak plainly was used to taking orders.

''She's in the forest.''

''Good. I have to see her. You lead the way, Zak.''

Zak automatically half turned to kick down the hatchway he'd come in through and then the questions came out. ''What—who *are* you? How—''

''I'm just visiting. We've got faster ways of moving now, Zak. I caught up with you.''

''A faster ramscoop? But we—''

''Let's go, Zak.'' Nagara waved the dart gun and Zak looked at it a moment and then, still visibly struggling with his confusion, he kicked off and glided down the drift tube.

The forest was one-half of a one hundred meter long cylinder, located near the middle of the ship and rotating to give one g. The forest was dense with pines and oak and tall bushes. A fine mist hung over the tree tops, obscuring the other half of the cylinder, a gardening zone that hung over their heads. Nagara hadn't been in a small cylinder like this for decades. He was used to seeing a distant green carpet overhead, so far away you couldn't make out individual trees, and shrouded by the cottonball clouds that accumulated at the zero-g along the cylinder axis. This whole place felt cramped to him.

Zak led him along footpaths and into a bamboo-walled clearing. The Revealer was sitting in lotus position in the middle of it. She was wearing a Flatlander robe and cowl just like Zak. He recognized it from a historical fax readout.

She was a plain-faced woman, wrinkled and wiry, her hands thick and calloused, the fingers stubby, the nails clipped off square. She didn't go rigid with surprise when Nagara came into view and that bothered him a little. She didn't look at the dart pistol more than once, to see what it was, and that surprised him, too.

"What's your name?" Nagara said as he walked into the bamboo-encased silence.

"I am the Revealer." A steady voice.

"No, I meant your name."

"That is my name."

"I mean—"

"I am the Revealer for this stage of our exodus."

Nagara watched as Zak stopped halfway between them and then stood uncertainly, looking back and forth.

"All right. When they freeze you back down, what'll they call you then?"

She smiled at this. "Michele Astanza."

Nagara didn't show anything in his face. He waved the pistol at her and said, "Get up."

"I prefer to sit."

"And I prefer you stand."

"Oh."

He watched both of them carefully. "Zak, I'm going to have to ask you to do a favor for me."

Zak glanced at the Revealer and she moved her head a few millimeters in a nod. He said, "Sure."

"This way." Nagara gestured with the pistol to the woman. The woman nodded to herself as if this confirmed something and got up and started down the footpath to the right, her steps so soft on the leafy path that Nagara could not hear them over the tinkling of a stream on the overhead side of the cylinder. Nagara followed her. The trees trapped the sound in here and made him jumpy.

He knew he was taking a calculated risk by not getting Jacob, too. But the odds against Jacob waking up in time were good and the whole point of doing it this way was to get in and out fast, exploit surprise. And he wasn't sure he could handle the three of them together. That was just it—he was doing this alone so he could collect the whole fee, and for that you had to take some extra risk. That was the way this thing worked.

The forest gave onto some corn fields and then some wheat, all the UV phosphorus netted above. The three of them skirted around the nets and through a hatchway in the big aft wall. Whenever Zak started to say anything Nagara cut him off with a wave of the pistol. Then Nagara saw that with some time to think Zak was adding some things up and the lines around his mouth were tightening, so Nagara asked him some questions about the ship's design. That worked. Zak rattled on about quintuple-redundant fail-safe subsystems he'd been repairing until they were at the entrance to the freezing compartment.

It was bigger than Nagara had thought. He had done all the research he could, going through old faxes of *Redeemer*'s prelim designs, but plainly the Flatlanders had changed things in some later design phase.

One whole axial section of *Redeemer* was given over to the freezedown vaults. It was at zero-g because otherwise the slow compression of tissues in the corpses would do permanent damage. They floated in their translucent compartments, like strange fish in endless rows of pale blue-white aquariums.

The vaults were stored in a huge array, each layer a cylinder slightly larger than the one it enclosed, all aligned along the ship's axis. Each cylinder was two compartments thick, a corpse in every one, and the long cylinders extended into the distance until the chilly fog steaming off them blurred the perspective and the eye could not judge the size of the things. Despite himself Nagara was impressed. There were thousands upon thousands of Flatlanders in here, all dead and waiting for the promised land ahead, circling Tau Ceti. And with seventy-five more years of data to judge by, Nagara knew something this Revealer couldn't reveal: The failure rate when they thawed them out would be thirty percent.

They had come out on the center face of the bulwark separating the vault section from the farming part. Nagara stopped them and studied the front face of the vault array, which spread away from them radially like an immense spider web. He reviewed the old plans in his head. The axis of the whole thing was a tube a meter wide, the same translucent organiform. Liquid nitrogen flowed in the hollow walls of the array and the phosphor light was pale and watery.

"That's the DNA storage," Nagara said, pointing at the axial tube.

"What?" Zak said. "Yes, it is."

"Take them out."

"What?"

"They're in fail-safe self-refrigerated canisters, aren't they?"

"Yes."

"That's fine." Nagara turned to the Revealer. "You've got the working combinations, don't you?"

She had been silent for some time. She looked at him steadily and said, "I do."

"Let's have them."

"Why should I give them?"

"I think you know."

"Not really."

He knew she was playing some game but he couldn't see why. "You're carrying DNA material for over ten thousand people. Old genotypes, undamaged. It wasn't so rare when you collected it seventy-five years ago but it is now. I want it."

"It is for our colony."

"You've got enough corpses here."

"We need genetic diversity."

"The System needs it more than you. There's been a war. A lot of radiation damage."

"Who won?"

"Us. The Outskirters."

"That means nothing to me."

"We're the environments in orbit around the sun, not sucking up to Earth. We knew what was going on. We're mostly in Barnal spheres. We got the jump on—"

"You've wrecked each other genetically, haven't you? That was always the trouble with your damned cities. No place to dig a hole and hide."

Nagara shrugged. He was watching Zak. From the man's face Nagara could tell he was getting to be more insulted than angry—outraged at somebody walking in and stealing their future. And from the way his leg muscles were tensing against a foothold Nagara guessed Zak was also getting more insulted than scared, which was trouble for sure. It was a lot better if you dealt with a man who cared more about the long odds against a dart gun at this range than about some principle. Nagara knew he couldn't count on Zak ignoring all the Flatlander nonsense the Revealer and others had pumped into him.

They hung there in zero-g, nobody moving in the wan light, the only sound a gurgling of liquid nitrogen. The Revealer was saying something and there was another thing bothering Nagara. Some sound, but he ignored it.

"How did the planetary enclaves hold out?" the woman was asking. "I had many friends—"

"They're gone."

Something came into the woman's face. "You've lost man's *birthright?*"

"They sided with the—"

"Abandoned the planets altogether? Made them unfit to *live* on? All for your awful cities—" and she made a funny jerky motion with her right hand.

That was it. When she started moving that way Nagara saw it had to be a signal and he jumped to the left. He didn't take time to place his boots right and so he picked up some spin but the important thing was to get away from that spot fast. He heard a *chuung* off to the right and a dart smacking into the bulkhead and when he turned his head to the right and up behind him, a burly man with black hair and the same Flatlander robes and a dart gun was coming at him on a glide.

Nagara had started twisting his shoulder when he leaped and now the differential angular momentum was bringing his shooting arm around. Jacob was already aiming again. Nagara took the extra second to make his shot and allow for the relative motions. His dart gun puffed and Nagara saw it take Jacob in the chest, just right. The man's face went white and he reached down to pull the dart out but by that time the nerve inhibitor had reached the heart and abruptly Jacob stopped plucking at the dart and his fingers went slack and the body drifted on in the chilly air, smacking into a vault door and coming to rest.

Nagara wrenched around to cover the other two. Zak was coming at him. Nagara leaped away, braked. He turned and Zak had come to rest against the translucent organiform, waiting.

"That's a lesson," Nagara said evenly. "Here's another."

He touched the keyin on his chest and his force screen flickered on around him, making him look metallic. He turned it off in time to hear the hollow boom that came rolling through the ship like a giant's shout.

"That's a sample. A shaped charge. My ship set it off two hundred meters from *Redeemer*. The next one's keyed to go on impact with your skin. You'll lose pressure too fast to do anything about it. My force field comes on when the charge goes, so it won't hurt me."

"We've never seen such a field," the woman said unsteadily.

"Outskirter invention. That's why we won."

He didn't bother watching Zak. He looked at the woman as she clasped her thick worker's hands together and began to realize what choices were left. When she was done with that she murmured, "Zak, take out the canisters."

The woman sagged against a strut. Her robes clung to her and made her look gaunt and old.

"You're not giving us a chance, are you?" she said.

"You've got a lot of corpses here. You'll have a big colony out at Tau Ceti." Nagara was watching Zak maneuver the canisters onto a mobile carrier. The young man was going to be all right now, he could tell that. There was the look of weary defeat about him.

"We need the genotypes for insurance. In a strange ecology there will be genetic drift."

"The System has worse problems right now."

"With Earth dead, you people in the artificial worlds are *finished*," she said savagely, a spark returning. "That's why we left. We could see it coming."

Nagara wondered if they'd have left at all if they'd known a faster than light drive would come along. But no, it wouldn't have made any difference. The translight transition cost too much and only worked for small ships. He narrowed his eyes and made a smile without humor.

"I know quite well why you left. A bunch of scum-lovers. Purists. Said Earth was just as bad as the cylinder cities, all artificial, all controlled. Yeah, I know. You Flatties sold off everything you had and built *this*—" His voice became bitter. "Ransacked a fortune—*my* fortune."

For once she looked genuinely curious, uncalculating. "Yours?"

He flicked a glance at her and then back at Zak. "Yeah. I would've inherited some of your billions you made out of those smelting patents."

"You—"

"I'm one of your great-grandsons."

Her face changed. "No."

"It's true. Stuffing the money into this clunker made all your descendants have to bust ass for a living. And it's not so easy these days."

"I . . . didn't . . ."

He waved her into silence. "I knew you were one of the mainstays, one of the rich Flatlanders. The family talked about it a lot. We're not doing so well now. Not as well as you did, not by a thousandth. I thought that would mean you'd get to sleep right through, wake up at Tau Ceti. Instead"—he laughed—"they've got you standing watch."

"Someone has to be the Revealer of the word, grandson."

"Great-grandson. Revealer? If you'd 'revealed' a little common sense to that kid over there, he would've been alert and I wouldn't be in here."

She frowned and watched Zak, who was awkwardly shifting the squat modular canisters stenciled GENETIC BANK. MAX SECURITY. "We are not military types," she replied.

Nagara grinned. "Right. I was looking through the family records and I thought up this job. I figured you for an easy setup. A max of three or four on duty, considering the size of the life-support systems and redundancies. So I got the venture capital together for a translight and here I am."

"We're not your kind. Why can't you give us a chance, grandson?"

"I'm a businessman."

She had a dry, rasping laugh. "A few centuries ago everybody thought space colonies would be the final answer. Get off the stinking old Earth and everything's solved. Athens in the sky. But look at you—a paid assassin. A 'businessman.' You're no grandson of *mine*."

"Old ideas." He watched Zak.

"Don't you see it? The colony environments aren't a social advance. You need discipline to keep life-support activated. Communication and travel have to be regulated for simple safety. So you don't get democracies, you get strong men. And then they turned on *us*—on Earth."

"You were out of date," he said casually, not paying much attention.

"Do you ever read any history?"

"No." He knew this was part of her spiel—he'd seen it on a fax from a century ago—but he let her go on to keep her occupied. Talkers never acted when they could talk.

"They turned Earth into a handy preserve. The Berbers and Normans had it the same way a thousand years ago. They were seafarers. They depopulated Europe's coastline by raids, taking what or who they wanted. You did the same to us, from orbit, using solar lasers. But to—"

"Enough," Nagara said. He checked the long bore of the axial tube. It was empty. Zak had the stuff secured on the carrier. There wasn't any point in staying here any longer than necessary.

"Let's go," he said.

"One more thing," the woman said.

"What?"

"We went peacefully, I want you to remember that. We have no defenses."

"Yeah," Nagara said impatiently.

"But we have huge energies at our disposal. The scoop fields funnel an enormous flux of relativistic particles. We could've temporarily altered the magnetic multipolar fields and burned your sort to death."

"But you didn't."

"No, we didn't. But remember that."

Nagara shrugged. Zak was floating by the carrier ready to take orders, looking tired. The kid had been easy to take, too easy for him to take any pride in doing it. Nagara liked an even match. He didn't even mind losing if it was to somebody he could respect. Zak wasn't in that league, though.

"Let's go," he said.

The loading took time but he covered Zak on every step and there were no problems. When he cast off from *Redeemer* he looked around by reflex for a planet to sight on, relaxing now, and it struck him that he was more alone than he had ever been, the stars scattered like oily jewels on velvet were the nearest destination he could have. That woman in *Redeemer* had lived with this for years. He looked at the endless long night out here, felt it as a shadow that passed through his mind, and then he punched in instructions and *Redeemer* dropped away, its blue-white arc a fuzzy blade that cut the darkness, and he slipped with a hollow clapping sound into translight.

He was three hours from his dropout point when one of the canisters strapped down behind the pilot's couch gave a warning buzz from thermal overload. It popped open.

Nagara twisted around and fumbled with the latches. He could pull the top two access drawers a little way out and when he did he saw that inside there was a store of medical supplies. Boxes and tubes and fluid cubes. Cheap stuff. No DNA manifolds.

Nagara sat and stared at the complete blankness outside. *We could've temporarily altered the magnetic multipolar fields and burned your sort to death*, she had said. *Remember that.*

If he went back she would be ready. They could rig some kind of aft sensor and focus the ramscoop fields on him when he came tunneling in through the flux. Fry him good.

They must have planned it all from the first. Something about it, about the way she'd looked, told him it had been the old woman's idea.

The risky part of it had been the business with Jacob. That didn't make sense. But maybe she'd known Jacob would try something and since she couldn't do anything about it she used it. Used it to relax him, make him think the touchy part of the job was done so that he didn't think to check inside the stenciled canisters.

He looked at the medical supplies. Seventy-three years ago the woman had known they couldn't protect themselves from what they didn't know, ships that hadn't been invented yet. So on her five year watch she had arranged a dodge that would work even if some System ship caught up to them. Now the Flatlanders knew what to defend against.

He sat and looked out at the blankness and thought about that.

When he popped out into System space the A47 sphere was hanging up to the left at precisely the relative coordinates and distance he'd left it.

A47 was big and inside there were three men waiting to divide up and classify and market the genotypes. When he told them what was in the canisters it would all be over, his money gone and theirs and no hope of his getting a stake again. And maybe worse than that. Maybe a lot worse.

He squinted at A47 as he came in for rendezvous. It looked different. Some of the third quadrant damage from the war wasn't repaired yet. The skin that had gleamed once was smudged now and twisted gray girders stuck out of the ports. It looked pretty beat up. It was the best high-tech fortress they had and A47 had made the whole difference in the war. It broke the African shield by itself. But now it didn't look like so much. All the dots of light orbiting in the distance were pretty nearly the same or worse and now they were all that was left in the system.

Nagara turned his ship about to vector on the landing bay,

listening to the rumble as the engines cut in. The console phosphors rippled blue, green, yellow as Central reffed him.

This next part was going to be pretty bad. Damned bad. And out there his great-grandmother was on the way still, somebody he could respect now, and for the first time he thought the Flatlanders probably were going to make it. In the darkness of the cabin something about the thought made him smile.

Afterword

In the late seventies I got injured—a muscle separation of the left calf—and couldn't walk for a week. Moderately zonked on painkillers, I found I had woozy, waking dreams. One came again and again, at first watery scenes involving my grandmother. Then it gradually grew and split into two separate dreams. Sitting upright, my left leg extended to reduce pain, I wrote two stories in an odd fugue dream state. Looking back at those scrawled pages, I can remember the fever-bright way the scenes unrolled, the characters all moving under glass, their voices hollow.

It's not a writing method I want to repeat. One story I published as "Old Woman by the Road," and then eight years later incorporated it into "To the Storming Gulf," when I realized that they were connected. (I have the feeling the whole thing will become a novel, someday, the way many of my novels have grown from short stories.)

I can remember fidgeting for a whole day over whether to use faster-than-light (FTL, as the genre acronym has it) in this story. So I wrote "Old Woman by the Road" first. There seemed no way to tell "Redeemer" without FTL, so eventually I relented.

My fretting over this may seem unnecessarily fastidious, since FTL is a staple of countless sf stories. Still, as a practicing physicist, I'm reminded every day that special and general relativity seem to have no room for FTL, unless you make some *big* leaps. One escape hatch is tachyons, those particles allowed by the equations of special relativity to travel *only* faster than light. Around that notion I built a whole novel, *Timescape*, a few years after this story. The other is John Wheeler's "wormholes," which allow tunneling through the warp and woof of space-time.

Still, most physicists regard these as very, very doubtful propositions. I'm sensitive to that, since the virtue of so-called "hard" sf is honoring the constraint of what is possible or plausible. Just as the stiff rules of the sonnet can force high standards in poetry, fidelity to the facts of science can give us better sf. To ignore this recalls Robert Frost's remark about free verse—that it resembled playing tennis with the net down.

Well, the virtues of FTL outweighed my qualms. Interstellar travel without it takes a big chunk from a human lifetime, in turn making it hard to maintain a unity of timeline in many stories. So I went ahead and considered what FTL would do when introduced into a world in which the harder ways of star travel were already in use.

Snatching the Bot_____

He simply takes one. It is that easy. He finds an Ajax model 34 standing unattended, walks up to it, gives the keying-in code, and says, "Come. Follow me."

"at what pace?" the robot says in a flat monotone.

"Mine, of course," Gerald replies.

He has learned, through an engineer friend, about Ajax 34's deficiency. Any member of that model will key over to a new voice-directive, without checking its mandates. The manufacturer is correcting this quirk as quickly as possible, of course, but it will take time.

The robot whirs along behind him. They go unnoticed in traffic. By the time Gerald gets it home he steps with a new, bouncy verve. The chilled air inside his apartment, usually rather stale and flat, seems crisp. He hurries to the 3D and calls Rebecca.

"I got it."

"No!" But she can see it's so.

"It was easy, dead easy. Just the way Morris said."

"What's your name, little bot?"

The robot squats mutely.

"*Bot*?" Gerald asks.

"Slang for robot. You ask him."

"What is your name, Ajax 34?"

"that does not lie. within my. decision matrix."

"Well, I'll name you . . ."

"Bot," Rebecca puts in. "Bot. It fits."

"You mean," Gerald remarks, "like that dog of yours, named Dog."

"Of course. It fits."

*   *   *

At first Gerald renders the Bot functional at simple tasks: sweeping with a broom, taking out the garbage, washing windows. The arms articulate well. Early on the Bot seems, for Gerald's tastes, overly concerned—indeed, obsessed—with its germanium transistors and their well being.

"should i be. receiving. conflicting logexes?"

"How do *I* know?"

"there are nonlinear. aspects."

"You feeling okay?"

"i am confocal. today."

"Do you think your ex-owners can trace you?"

"i calculate low probability."

"Great!" Gerald claps his hands in the echoing volume of his apartment. "We're going to have a lot of fun with you."

"task mandate?"

"What?"

"i require. task mandate."

"Oh. Yes. You can cook, I guess."

"i am. programmable."

"How well?"

"no referent scale. available."

"Oh. Well, get on into the kitchen."

"mandate?"

"Try some Heat 'n Serve Pigs-In-A-Blanket."

Gerald is lying on his flexcushion watching *The Iliad and the Ecstasy* when the doorbell chimes. He opens the door. Rebecca sweeps in, her balloon sleeves flapping, her eyebrows arched. "Guess."

"I never can."

"I've snatched one myself."

"No." But she has: behind her rolls an orange box sprouting plexarms. An Ajax 42.

"How?"

"Indifference."

"Nonsense."

"Wait." She holds his attention with a needle-fine fingernail which lands delicately on his shoulder. "I pretended I wasn't interested in 42 here at all. I just looked in shop windows and ignored 42 when it came by. That put it off guard.''

"Morris specifically said—''

"Who cares? *I* think these poor things are *programmed* to be suspicious. So I worked my way over to it and whispered the key-in and . . .''

He runs his fingers through her Stephens Carmin hair. It crackles. "You're great,'' Gerald says roughly.

"i am unmandated.''

Gerald frowns. "Can't you help 42?''

"it is also. unmandated.''

"Hey. *Rebecca*.''

She unplugs from her helmet, where she was watching a simulated bullfight—no actual killing was allowed, of course, but you forgot all about that while it was on—and scowls at him.

"They need a job.''

"Fix my *car*.''

"They've done that.''

"you experience. difficulty. over this.''

"Shut *up*.'' Gerald gazes around, gets up, walks from room to room. The Bot hums along behind him. Its arms move energetically, making a rasping whisper.

"Trouble is, there's just not much to *do* in this place.''

Rebecca does not hear him; she is back under the helmet. Gerald knocks over an ashtray, making a silent powdery splash on the off-white carpet—he and Rebecca had been smoking again, illegally. 42 rolls over to suck away the blotch.

The trouble is, his apartment is too simply decorated. Gerald studies it. His primary embellishment of the anonymous plaster walls is a print of Jakopii's famous *Toward a Unified Philosophy of Ice Cream*. He rather likes it, but one print isn't enough, not by a long shot. And there are fly specks on the print, right in the middle of the creamy woman's thigh. There are, of course, some droll touches of his own here and there. In the bathroom (an important place in an apartment, intimate but seen by nearly every guest) hangs a fake mantelpiece with an impressive flintlock rifle mounted over it. And there are some amusing towels. But not enough, no.

"I think I'll augment them."

"Ummmm?" Rebecca murmurs from under the helmet.

"I'll buy them some memorex cubes."

"Why?"

"We'll have them learn interior decoration. That way I won't have to hire anybody."

"They're just *machines*, Gerald."

He drops his spoon on the table. With a rattle it spatters Flecko on the ceramic tabletop.

"But all I said, Gerald, was that it's theft."

"I know. I know you said that. I just don't agree."

"There's no reason to get mad."

"Well look, Marv did it."

"An Ajax 12. A simple model."

"But he didn't even get a fine."

"That was before more of us did it."

"Only a few more."

"Well, Betty has one."

"She does?" He is genuinely surprised.

"Hermann, too."

He remembers Hermann, a fellow with funny tapered sideburns who invariably wore a maroon ascot whenever there was the slightest reason. What the hell was a guy like that doing, stealing an Ajax?

"In fact, I probably know at least five others—"

"Okay," he says, grimacing into his coffee cup, where he can see his smoothed and warped amber reflection. "If there are that many of us, then they for sure can't prosecute." He smiles. This seems a nice flip-flop on his previous argument, and it makes sense.

The Bot trundles over. "You find your coffee unacceptable?"

"Ummmm."

"a pinch of. salt. added to instant. coffee. makes it taste. as though. freshly ground."

"Go away," Gerald murmurs, thinking about the cops.

*   *   *

Gerald arrives home early. Rebecca, by prearrangement, is off work today and has used her key. She waves from under the helmet. "I got that last of the memorex cubes," he reports. "Our little friends can finish their redecoration course."

"Good. Good," she calls.

"I also brought us a little wisdom." He displays a dark bottle of Concannon '96. Rebecca is enmeshed in her helmet show. He walks into the kitchen and finds a corkscrew. It goes in smoothly enough, biting the waxy cork, but as he twists the top the corkscrew begins a high-pitched, irritating squeal against the glass neck.

"Let me, sir," the Bot says, appearing in the kitchen. Gerald surrenders the bottle, smiling stiffly so that a thin line of teeth show, and glad that Rebecca is not there after all.

While the Bot and 42 shove the furniture and wall manifolds around, Gerald and Rebecca play bridge. Gerald finds a program available through the Yellow Faxes which provides a stimulated bridge team. The sim works well, analyzing the level of their game accurately and matching—but not exceeding—them. Gerald improves more rapidly than Rebecca. He has a certain expansive feeling whenever the sim program is forced to pause, recalibrate for Gerald, and then stutter out its next play. It hesitates for a full twenty seconds when it first realizes Gerald has learned to count all fifty-two cards and employ this in his play. Before resuming play the faxscreen flashes that it must charge more for this level of tactics. Rebecca, who has only now begun to keep track of who has which trumps, bites her lavender lip. Gerald ignores the Bot and 42, who are chuffing solemnly as they maneuver, and concentrates on the fax display. He enjoys keeping track of tricks, calculating a finesse; inventing elaborate ruses to fool the sim. But Rebecca loses interest. She returns to the helmet to catch the weekly *Situational Sexuality*, which is today beginning Case History MCXVII. Gerald plays on, paying a bit more for the fax to handle three hands, and works steadily through several rubbers, reacting quickly to whatever the sim does, moving smoothly, snapping the cards down.

*　　*　　*

They make love while the robots wait in a corner of the newly arranged bedroom. The Bot and 42 stand impassive, their locomotion meshes inactivated. The air in the room seems thick and layered, despite the steady breath puffing from the air conduits. He and Rebecca intertwine rhythmically, as though each is struggling with some difficulty to push the other up a common steep hillside.

They study the new living room.

"Mmmmmm," Rebecca says noncommittally.

"Like the concept," Gerald pronounces. "Like the whole thing. Yeah. That alcove, though"—pointing—"looks like something a clerk-typist would think up."

"Ummmm."

"Rebecca, they've studied *all* the memorexes. These are good designs."

"A lot of learning can be a little thing."

"You heard that somewhere," he says accusingly.

"Mmmmmmmmmm," she admits.

One afternoon, when Gerald comes early to the apartment, he finds them attempting some new task by interlocking their perceptual centers. The Bot has backed up to 42 and unhinged his rear module, for easier access. 42 has flipped up the lid of its input center and the Bot presses against it. Gerald frowns. Since he did not, of course, get an owner's manual with the Bot, he can't diagnose what the trouble might be. 42 whirs. The Bot makes a crunching noise. Why are they doing this, coupled together in—of all places—a closet? And with their perceiving lobes active, but no link to the outside sensors, Gerald wonders, what are they receiving? It is a puzzle.

"Christ."

"What now?" Rebecca says absently.

"This fax is about Betty."

"You mean *Betty*?"

"They're pressing charges."

"For—?"

"Sure, what else?"

"Well, I said it was theft, didn't I?"

"Yeah."

"Now, don't go all Bogart on me."

"Uh huh."

"Can she get off with a fine, do you suppose?"

"Probably not. A lot depends on this court ruling coming up soon."

"You mean the man who had three of them?"

"Yeah, haven't you been keeping up? He's fighting it."

"But he's *guilty*."

"Scan the fax. Remember that lower court opinion about, about automaton volition, they called it?"

"No. You know I can't—"

"You should, Rebecca, you—"

"It's *jargon*, Gerald."

"Listen."

"Oh—okay."

"This fellow—the one who's banging on the door of the high courts now—he's disputing that ruling from three years ago. The one that said the bots aren't, well, alive."

"Oh, *yes*. He says the Ajaxes want to stay with him."

"Yeah, what garbage. Real garbage. He takes a chance, he pays the price, is the way I see it." He stands up, kicks 42 lightly in its side as it purrs past, smiles.

"Well, I'd rather we didn't get caught."

He sucks in his stomach and shrugs elaborately. "No telling." He is feeling very good, but he doesn't tell Rebecca that.

The Bot squeaks slightly as it rolls in from the kitchen. "your Roast 'n Boast. is ready," it says. Gerald nods and grins, the skin around his eyes crinkling with inner warmth.

Gerald buys a billiard table, using the money he saved by having the machines do his redecoration, and spends long hours around it. He enjoys sighting down the long stick, tapping the ball just right with the blue-chalked tip to vector it into the predicted pocket. It is a linear exercise of exact momenta and angles, a Euclidean world, though of course he does not think of it in those terms. The balls move in their own universe, intersecting with a classical click.

*   *   *

"Do you mind if I ask you a question?" Rebecca says to the Bot.

"you just. did."

"Oh." Her contact lenses seek out the ceramic gleam of its sensors. "I, I liked the mayonnaise curry sauce."

The Bot says nothing.

"What I mean is, do you want to stay with us?"

"i must."

"Oh."

While the Bot and 42 are putting together his exercise machine, Gerald paces the vinyl-layered living room. "It needs something," he says at last, decisively.

"What?"

"The walls."

"Have the bots repaint."

"Right. Right."

He spends some time aligning his thoughts in the billiards room and then approaches the Bot. "What color do you think is best?"

"i would. say an amber. tending toward. yellow."

"Uh. Really?"

"with elements of. green. restful to the. human eye."

"Doesn't 42 have any opinion about this?"

"no."

His thighs clench, relax, clench again as he rides the exercise machine. He has to get into better physical shape. All this apartment living is bad for a man. Softens him up. He has to be pretty quick if they're going to keep a step ahead of the cops, he thinks, grimacing with some satisfaction. He puffs and pants heavily and the acoustically sophisticated walls recommended by the Bot and gummed into place by 42 absorb the sound utterly, hushing the room.

When he finishes and walks out, mulling over a calculation of term insurance in his head, Rebecca is watching *Quips and Barbs* on the helmet. Gerald finds the Bot and 42 carefully applying yellow paint to a corner of the living room.

"What's that?" he says sharply, pointing at a round green mark amid the yellow.

"the black hole. which is thought to. be the energy. source. for Cygnus A."

"Cygnus who?"

"a promiment double. radio source. the three emission. regions are connected by a. supersonically. relativistic. flow originating. above the poles of. the black. hole."

"What's it doing on my wall?"

"it is a preferred. design. scheme. implications of the infinite—"

"Okay. We'll see how it works out. What's the funny thick line through the green?"

"the accretion disk. infalling matter in orbit. around the black hole. its thermal radiation drives. the relativistic wind. which—"

"Yeah, yeah, okay. Boy, the things they teach you." He goes back to the exercise machine to work on his pectoral muscles. They've been getting goddamn lardy.

He is eating a Carbohyde Flash with some relish when the doorbell sounds. Probably Betty, with another story about her prissy lawyer. Just to be safe he peers through the corridor viewer. The hallway is awash in enameled light. He gets a glimpse of a thin man in a brown overcoat and then a wedge of slick plastic looms up, blossoming from the man's hand upward, toward the viewer. It is an identity card. Metro Police. Officer Axford.

"What do you want?" Gerald says tightly. He senses the Bot come rolling up. He gestures the Bot away with frantic hand-signals.

"Moom meh in. Royee ah scerge warrant," Gerald hears through the double-paneled, deadbolted door.

"I, well—"

"Or we'll *kick it in*," comes more clearly.

When Gerald opens the heavy door Axford and a short, wiry man brush by him as though he were a butler, muttering a legal formula required by the courts for cases like this, slurring the words so he can't make them out. They dash into the kitchen where 42 is lathering a coffee pot. The wiry man calls, "Here's one box all right," and Axford swerves for the bedrooms. The wiry one stays with 42 and begins to recite a set piece about rights, but Gerald follows Axford.

"*What? What?*" Rebecca calls shrilly from the bedroom, but already Axford is coming out, heading down the hallway. He jerks open the bathroom door. The Bot is struggling with the rifle mounted over the fake mantelpiece, trying to pull it down.

"Stop," Gerald says, not sure who he means.

"but it must. go off." says the Bot.

"It's a fake rifle!" Gerald cries.

Axford has drawn a pistol, but it does not go off either.

The Bot becomes still. "We nailed you good on this one," Axford says happily, holstering his pistol.

"How did you find us?" Rebecca wrings out the words.

"Targets of opportunity. We have our sources," Axford murmurs mysteriously.

"*allegro.* you have the. charges."

"Sure. Theft—"

"a needful. display." The Bot produces two triangular embossed licenses.

At first Axford won't believe the triangles are authentic, but a careful check of their acute angles reveals the proper validation. The licenses prove conclusive ownership of 42 and the Bot by Rebecca and Gerald, respectively. Gerald gapes at this but says nothing, even when Axford and the other man apologize and help fit the rifle back into its moorings.

Soon they have backed out the front door, still apologizing and explaining what a rare event an error like this is, in these days of improved surveillance and sensors, and then they are gone. Gerald finds the Bot adjusting a receptor which was damaged in the scuffle.

"Where'd those licenses come from?"

"i manufactured. them. clearly they would. be needed."

The next day, as he waits for 42 to warm up some Bite-a-lots, Gerald notices the Cygnus A design again. The accretion disk is different now. It seems to have tilted to a new angle. This disturbs him but he does not mention the matter.

Gerald walks into the bedroom. The Bot is there, and an Ajax 38, a square metallic-gray case with seven arms. "Hey," he says, trying to think.

"i have snatched. a 38." the Bot declares.

"How can you . . . ?" Gerald begins, but stops, not wanting to look ridiculous. "Well, you've got a pretty heavy work load around here. I'm sure you can use the help." He pats the Bot affectionately.

He says to Rebecca later, "Imagine that! Stealing his own bot." He shakes his head. "Helluva inventive little guy."

"Ummm. Hummm."

The newcomer, 38, is doing some FryUps. Rebecca is tuned in on *Westernciv Adventures*. Gerald flexes in his exercise machine, because you never know if the cops are going to come back.

The Bot and 42 have tilted the accretion disk (now brown, with fringes of green where synchrotron radiation is suspected), to agree with the newest observations of long-baseline radio interferometry. The occasional noise from *Westernciv Adventures* does not disturb them. They paint with flourishes, splashing on the yellows in great swooping swipes. The Bot twirls his brush adroitly click click, adding fuzzy red patches for the high-density gas clouds ringing the disk. Blending them in gracefully, smoothly, whirring whirring, with the deep yellow of space. Dotting in stars as sharp, brittle, purple dots. 42 purrs beside him.

Gerald is alone with his exercises. He clenches arms, thighs, pectorals. Thinks of the bastard Axford. Pumps the gyrating wheels, tugs the bars, his limbs articulating well. Clickclick. Clickclick.

Afterword

In 1976 I was on sabbatical leave in Cambridge, England, far from the heady, lurid profusion of American newsstands. There is nothing like slinking through the bitterly cold rain of a Cambridge street, searching for a bookshop that carries the particular odd periodical which seemed essential in America, but now oddly beside the point amid thousand-year-old stonework.

So I settled for a stack of various U.S. Best Short Story of the Year collections, spottily covering the previous decade. Reading through them, I got a strange picture of the way these writers viewed their own country. Everything seemed to happen in kitchens; brooding clouds of familial angst obscured many personal suns; the slapstick of manners rolled on, one eye cocked back at Jane Austen; "personal relationships," that blocky, neutered term, dominated all; slices of life carved up the characters, investing small talk with the weight of lumbering metaphor. And it all seemed so unintentionally *funny*. In these small worlds lived only small people. Nobody noticed that the world was changing, that the tumble of large events shaped so much of what the characters—and the authors—thought to be natural, eternal humanistic truths.

Some of this seemed to bear on science fiction, at least obliquely. So I started thinking about the nullities who lived in such frozen paper worlds. If such people were real, how would they react to some science fictional notion, even a minimal one?

I was working at the Institute for Astronomy, and each afternoon would take a break by writing some fiction in

longhand. This story was a reaction to the sudden inges-
tion of so much conventional fiction, its relentless claus-
trophobia. It seemed to me that the wondrous compressions
of Salinger, which were for me the high water mark in
American fiction in the 1950s, had been flattened into
banal gestures. (Compare Salinger to Ann Beattie, for
example.)

Luckily, the American short story has passed through
that drought and seems to be regenerating itself. I like a
lot of the new writers, such as Jim Harrison, and continue
to be amazed by the deft feats of John Updike.

While much attention is directed at the new life in the
conventional story, nobody seems to notice that about
half the short stories published commercially in English
are science fiction. Much of worth appears there. A disproportionate amount of thinking goes on in sf, far more
than among the reportorial, trimmed-down realists of the
Esquire and *Atlantic* school. Sf suffers from just as many
hobbling habits—different ones, of course—but in this
little piece it was fun to thrust the two together.

Relativistic Effects

They came into the locker room with a babble of random talk, laughter, and shouts. There was a rolling bass undertone, gruff and raw. Over it the higher feminine notes ran lightly, warbling, darting.

The women had a solid, businesslike grace to them, doing hard work in the company of men. There were a dozen of them and they shed their clothes quickly and efficiently, all modesty forgotten long ago, their minds already focused on the job to come.

"You up for this, Nick?" Jake asked, yanking off his shorts and clipping the input sockets to his knees and elbows. His skin was red and callused from his years of linked servo work.

"Think I can handle it," Nick replied. "We're hitting pretty dense plasma already. There'll be plenty of it pouring through the throat." He was big but he gave the impression of lightness and speed, trim like a boxer, with broad shoulders and thick wrists.

"Lots of flux," Jake said. "Easy to screw up."

"I didn't get my rating by screwing up 'cause some extra ions came down the tube."

"Yeah. You're pretty far up the roster, as I remember," Jake said, eyeing the big man.

"Uh huh. Number one, last time I looked," Faye put in from the next locker. She laughed, a loud braying that rolled through the locker room and made people look up. "Bet 'at's what's botherin' you, uh, Jake?"

Jake casually made an obscene gesture in her general direction and went on. "You feelin' OK, Nick?"

"What you think I got, clenchrot?" Nick spat out with sudden ferocity. "Just had a cold, is all."

Faye said slyly, "Be a shame to prang when you're so close to winnin', movin' on up." She tugged on her halter and arranged her large breasts in it.

Nick glanced at her. Trouble was, you work with a woman long enough and after a while, she looked like just one more competitor. Once he'd thought of making a play for Faye— she really did look fairly good sometimes—but now she was one more sapper who'd elbow him into a vortex if she got half a chance. Point was, he never gave her—or anybody else—a chance to come up on him from some funny angle, throw him some unexpected momentum. He studied her casual, deft movements, pulling on the harness for the connectors. Still, there was something about her. . . .

"You get one more good run," Faye said slyly, "you gonna get the promotion. 'At's what I'd say."

"What matters is what they say upstairs, on A deck."

"Touchy, touchy, tsk tsk," Jake said. He couldn't resist getting in a little gig. Nick knew. Not when Jake knew it might get Nick stirred up a little. But the larger man stayed silent, stolidly pulling on his neural hookups.

Snick, the relays slide into place and Nick feels each one come home with a percussive impact in his body, he never gets used to that no matter that it's been years he's been in the Main Drive crew. When he really sat down and thought about it he didn't like this job at all, was always shaky before coming down here for his shift. He'd figured that out at the start, so the trick was, he didn't think about it, not unless he'd had too much of that 'ponics-processed liquor, the stuff that was packed with vitamin B and C and wasn't supposed to do you any damage, not even leave the muggy dregs and ache of a hangover, only of course it never worked quite right because nothing on the ship did anymore. If he let himself stoke up on that stuff he'd gradually drop out of the conversation at whatever party he was, and go off into a corner somewhere and somebody'd find him an hour or two later staring at a wall or into his drink, reliving the hours in the tube and thinking about his dad and the grandfather he could only vaguely remember. They'd both died of the ol' black creeping cancer, same as eighty percent of the crew, and it was no secret the Main Drive was the worst place in the ship for it, despite all the design specs of fifty-meter rock walls and carbon-steel bulkheads and lead-lined hatches. A man'd be a goddamn fool if he didn't think about that, sure, but somebody had to do it or they'd all die. The job came down to Nick from his father because the family just did it, that was all, all the way back to the first crew, the original bridge officers had decided that long before Nick was born, it was the only kind of social organization that the sociometricians thought could possibly work on a ship that had to fly between stars, they all knew that and nobody questioned it any more than they'd want to change a pressure spec on a seal. You just didn't, was all there was to it. He'd learned that since he could first understand the church services, or the yearly anniversary of the Blowout up on the bridge, or the things that his father told him, even when the old man was dying with the black crawling stuff eating him from inside, Nick had learned that good—

"God, this dump is gettin' worse every—lookit 'at." Faye pointed.

A spider was crawling up a bulkhead, inching along on the ceramic smoothness.

"Musta got outta Agro," somebody put in.

"Yeah, don't kill it. Might upset the whole damn biosphere, an' they'd have our fuckin' heads for it."

A murmur of grudging agreement.

"Lookit 'at dumb thing," Jake said. "Made it alla way up here, musta come through air ducts an' line feeds an' who knows what." He leaned over the spider, eyeing it. It was a good three centimeters across and dull gray. "Pretty as sin, huh?"

Nick tapped in sockets at his joints and tried to ignore Jake. "Yeah."

"Poor thing. Don't know where in hell it is, does it? No appreciation for how important a place this is. We're 'bout to see a whole new age start in this locker room, soon's Nick here gets his full score. He'll be the new super an' we'll be—well, hell, we'll be like this li'l spider here. Just small and havin' our own tiny place in the big design of Nick's career, just you think how it's gonna—"

"Can the shit," Nick said harshly.

Jake laughed.

There was a tight feeling in the air. Nick felt it and figured it was something about his trying to get the promotion, something like that, but not worth bothering about. Plenty of time to think about it, once he had finished this job and gotten on up the ladder. Plenty of time then.

The gong rang brassily and the men and women finished suiting up. The minister came in and led them in a prayer for safety, the same as every other shift. Nothing different, but the tension remained. They'd be flying into higher plasma densities, sure, Nick thought. But there was no big deal about that. Still, he murmured the prayer along with the rest. Usually he didn't bother. He'd been to church services as usual, everybody went, it was unthinkable that you wouldn't, and anyway he'd never get any kind of promotion if he didn't show his face reg'lar, hunch on up to the altar rail and swallow that wafer and the alky-laced grape juice that went sour in your mouth while you were trying to swallow it, same as a lot of the talk they wanted you to swallow, only you did, you got it down because you had to and without asking anything afterward either, you bet, 'cause the ones who made trouble didn't get anywhere. So he muttered along, mouthing the familiar litany without thinking. The minister's thin lips moving, rolling on through the archaic phrases, meant less than nothing. When he looked up, each face was pensive as they prepared to go into the howling throat of the ship.

Nick lies mute and blind and for a moment feels nothing but the numb silence. It collects in him, blotting out the dim rub of the snouts which cling like lampreys to his nerves and muscles, pressing embrace that amplifies every movement, and—

—*spang*—

—he slips free of the mooring cables, a rush of sight-sound-taste-touch washes over him, so strong and sudden a welter of sensations that he jerks with the impact. He is servo'd to a thing like an eel that swims and flips and dives into a howling dance of protons. The rest of the ship is sheltered safely behind slabs of rock. But the eel is his, the eel is *him*. It shudders and jerks and twists, skating across sleek strands of magnetic plains. To Nick, it is like swimming.

The torrent gusts around him and he feels its pinprick breath. In a blinding orange glare Nick swoops, feeling his power grow as he gets the feel of it. His shiny shelf is wrapped in a cocoon of looping magnetic fields that turn the protons away, sending them gyrating in a mad gavotte, so the heavy particles cannot crunch and flare against the slick baked skin. Nick flexes the skin, supple and strong, and slips through the magnetic turbulence ahead. He feels the magnetic lines of force stretch like rubber bands. He banks and accelerates.

Streams of protons play upon him. They make glancing collisions with each other but do not react. The repulsion between them is too great and so this plasma cannot make them burn, cannot thrust them together with enough violence. Something more is needed or else the ship's throat will fail to harvest the simple hydrogen atoms, fail to kindle it into energy.

There— In the howling storm Nick sees the blue dots that are the keys, the catalyst: carbon nuclei, hovering like sea gulls in an updraft.

Split-image phosphors gleam, marking his way. He swims in the streaming blue-white glow, through a murky storm of fusing ions. He watches plumes of carbon nuclei striking the swarms of protons, wedding them to form the heavier nitrogen nuclei. The torrent swirls and screams at Nick's skin and in his sensors he sees and feels and tastes the lumpy, sluggish nitrogen as it finds a fresh incoming proton and with the fleshy smack of fusion the two stick, they hold, they wobble like raindrops—falling—merging—ballooning into a new nucleus, heavier still: oxygen.

But the green pinpoints of oxygen are unstable. These fragile forms split instantly. Jets of new particles spew through the surrounding glow—neutrinos, ruddy photons of light, and slower, darker, there come the heavy daughters of the marriage: a swollen, burnt-gold cloud of a bigger variety of nitrogen.

the scaly wall. The tongue bites and gouges. Flakes roast off and blacken and finally bubble up like tar. The rushing proton currents wash the flakes away, revealing the gunmetal blue beneath. Now the exposed superconducting threads can begin their own slow pruning of themselves, life casting out its dead. Their long organic chain molecules can feed and grow anew. As Nick cuts and turns and carves he watched the spindly fibers coil loose and drift in eddies. Finally they spin away into the erasing proton storm. The dead fibers sputter and flash where the incoming protons strike them and then with a rumble in his acoustic pickup coils he sees them swept away. Maintenance.

Something tugs at him. He sees the puckered scoop where the energetic alpha particles shoot by. They dart like luminous jade wasps. The scoop sucks them in. Inside they will be collected, drained of energy, inducing megawatts of power for the ship, which will drink their last drop of momentum and cast them aside, a wake of broken atoms.

Suddenly he spins to the left—*Jesus, how can*—he thinks—and the scoop fields lash him. A megavolt per meter of churning electrical vortex snatches at him. It is huge and quick and relentless to Nick (though to the ship it is a minor ripple in its total momentum) and magnetic tendrils claw at his spinning, shiny surfaces. The scoop opening is a plunging, howling mouth. Jets of glowing atoms whirl by him, mocking. The walls near him counter his motion by increasing their magnetic fields. Lines of force stretch and bunch.

How did this—is all he has time to think before a searing spot blooms nearby. His presence so near the scoop has upset the combination rates there. His eyes widen. If the reaction gets out of control it can burn through the chamber vessel, through the asteroid rock beyond, and spike with acrid fire into the ship, toward the life dome.

A brassy roar. The scoop sucks at his heels. Ions run white-hot. A warning knot strikes him. Tangled magnetic ropes grope for him, clotting around the shiny skin.

Panic squeezes his throat. Desperately he fires his electron beam gun against the wall, hoping it will give him a push, a fresh vector—

Not enough. Orange ions blossom and swell around him—

*   *   *

Most of the squad was finished dressing. They were tired and yet the release of getting off work brought out an undercurrent of celebration. They ignored Nick and slouched out of the locker room, bound for families or assignations or sensory jolts of sundry types. A reek of sweat and fatigue diffused through the sluggishly stirring air. The squad laughed and shouted old jokes to each other. Nick sat on the bench with his head in his hands.

"I . . . I don't get it. I was doin' pretty well, catchin' the crap as it came at me, an' then somethin' grabbed . . ."

They'd had to pull him out with a robot searcher. He'd gone dead, inoperative, clinging to the throat lining, fighting the currents. The surges drove the blood down into your gut and legs, the extra g's slamming you up against the bulkhead and sending big dark blotches across your vision, purple swarms of dots swimming everywhere, hollow rattling noises coming in through the transducer mikes, nausea, the ache spreading through your arms—

It had taken three hours to get him back in, and three more to clean up. A lot of circuitry was fried for good, useless junk. The worst loss was the high-grade steel, all riddled with neutrons and fissured by nuclear fragments. The ship's foundry couldn't replace that, hadn't had the rolling mill to even make a die for it in more than a generation. His neuro index checked out okay, but he wouldn't be able to work for a week.

He was still in a daze and the memory would not straighten itself out in his mind. "I dunno, I . . ."

Faye murmured, "Maybe went a li'l fast for you today."

Jake grinned and said nothing.

"Mebbe you could, y'know, use a rest. Sit out a few sessions." Faye cocked her head at him.

Nick looked at both of them and narrowed his eyes. "That wasn't a mistake of mine, was it? Uh? No mistake at all. Somebody—" He knotted a fist.

"Hey, nothin' you can prove," Jake said, backing away. "I can guarantee that, boy."

"Some bastard, throwin' me some extra angular when I wasn't lookin', I oughta—"

"Come on, Nick, you got no proof 'a those charges. You know there's too much noise level in the throat to record what ever'body's doin'." Faye grinned without humor.

"Damn." Nick buried his face in his hands. "I was *that* close, so damned near to gettin' that promotion—"

"Yeah. Tsk tsk. You dropped points back there for sure, Nick, burnin' out a whole unit that way an' gettin—"

"Shut it. Just shut it."

Nick was still groggy and he felt the anger build in him without focus, without resolution. These two would make up some neat story to cover their asses, same as everybody did when they were bringing another member of the squad down a notch or two. The squad didn't have a lot of love for anybody who looked like they were going to get up above the squad, work their way up. That was the way it was, jobs were hard to change, the bridge liked it stable, said it came out better when you worked at a routine all your life and—

"Hey, c'mon, let's get our butts down to the Sniffer," Faye said. "No use jawin' 'bout this, is 'ere? I'm gettin' thirsty after all that uh, work."

She winked at Jake. Nick saw it and knew he would get a ribbing about this for weeks. The squad was telling him he had stepped out of line and he would just have to take it. That was just the plain fact of it. He clenched his fists and felt a surge of anger.

"Hey!" Jake called out. "This damn spider's still tryin' to make it up this wall." He reached out and picked it up in his hand. The little gray thing struggled against him, legs kicking.

"Y'know, I hear there're people over in Comp who keep these for pets," Faye said. "Could be one of theirs."

"Creepy li'l thing," Nick said.

"You get what you can," Faye murmured. "Ever see a holo of a dog?"

Nick nodded. "Saw a whole movie about this one, it was a collie, savin' people an' all. Now that's a pet."

They all stared silently at the spider as it drummed steadily on Jake's hand with its legs. Nick shivered and turned away. Jake held it firmly, without hurting it, and slipped it into a pocket. "Think I'll take it back before Agro busts a gut lookin' for it."

Nick was silent as the three of them left the smells of the locker room and made their way up through the corridors. They took a shortcut along an undulating walkway under the big observation dome. Blades of pale blue light shifted like enormous columns in the air, but they were talking and only occasionally glanced up.

The vast ship of which they were a part was heading through the narrow corridor between two major spiral galaxies. On the right side of the dome the bulge of one galaxy was like a whirlpool of light, the points of light like grains of sand caught in a vortex. Around the bright core, glowing clouds of the spiral arms wended their way through the flat disk, seeming to cut through the dark dust clouds like a river slicing through jungle. Here and there black towers reared up out of the confusion of the disk, where masses of interstellar debris had been heaved out of the galactic plane, driven by collisions between clouds, or explosions of young stars.

There were intelligent, technological societies somewhere among those drifting stars. The ship had picked up their transmissions long ago—radio, UV, the usual—and had altered course to pass nearby.

The two spirals were a binary system, bound together since their birth. For most of their history they had stayed well apart, but now they were brushing within a galactic diameter of each other. Detailed observations in the last few weeks of ship's time—all that was needed to veer and swoop toward the twinned disks—had shown that this was the final pass: the two galaxies would not merely swoop by and escape. The filaments of gas and dust between them had created friction over the billions of years past, eroding their orbital angular momentum. Now they would grapple fatally.

The jolting impact would be spectacular: shock waves, compression of the gas in the galactic plane, and shortly thereafter new star formation, swiftly yielding an increase in the supernova rate, a flooding of the interstellar medium with high energy particles. The rain of sudden virulent energy would destroy the planetary environments. The two spirals would come together with a wrenching suddenness, the disks sliding into each other like two saucers bent on destruction, the collision effectively occurring all over the disks simultaneously in an explosive flare of X-ray and thermal brems-strahlung radiation. Even advanced technologies would be snuffed out by the rolling, searing tide.

The disks were passing nearly face-on to each other. In the broad blue dome overhead the two spirals hung like cymbals seen on edge. The ship moved at extreme relativistic velocity, pressing infinitesimally close to light speed, passing through the dim halo of gas and old dead stars that surrounded each galaxy. Its speed compressed time and space. Angles distorted as time ran at a blinding pace outside, refracting images. Extreme relativistic effects made the approach visible to the naked eye. Slowly, the huge disks of shimmering light seemed to swing open like a pair of doors. Bright tendrils spanned the gap between them.

Jake was telling a story about two men in CompCatynch section, rambling on with gossip and jokes, trying to keep the talk light. Faye went along with it, putting in a word when Jake slowed. Nick was silent.

The ship swooped closer to the disks and suddenly across the dome streaked red and orange bursts. The disks were twisted, distorted by their mutual gravitational tugs, wrenching each other, twins locked in a tightening embrace. The planes of stars rippled, as if a huge wind blew across them. The galactic nuclei flared with fresh fires: ruby, orange, mottled blue, ripe gold. Stars were blasted into the space between. Filaments of raw, searing gas formed a web that spanned the two spirals. This was the food that fed the ship's engines. They were flying as near to the thick dust and gas of the galaxies as they could. The maw of the ship stretched outward, spanning a volume nearly as big as the galactic core. Streamers of sluggish gas veered toward it, drawn by the onrushing magnetic fields. The throat sucked in great clouds, boosting them to still higher velocity.

The ship's hull moaned as it met denser matter.

Nick ignores the babble from Jake, knowing it is empty foolishness, and thinks instead of the squad, and how he would run it if he got the promotion: They had to average five thousand cleared square meters a week, minimum, that was a full ten percent of the whole ship's throat, minus of course the lining areas that were shut down for full repair, call that one thousand square meters on the average, so with the other crews operating on forty-five-hour shifts they could work their way through and give the throat a full scraping in less than a month, easy, even allowing for screwups and malfs and times when the radiation level was too high for even the suits to screen it out. You had to keep the suits up to 99 plus percent operational or you caught hell from upstairs, but the same time they came at you with their specifications reports and never listened when you told them about the delays, that was your problem not theirs and they said so every chance they got, that bunch of blowhard officers up there, descended from the original ship's bridge officers who'd left Earth generations back with every intention of returning after a twelve-year round trip to Centauri, only it hadn't worked, they didn't count on the drive freezing up in permanent full-bore thrust, the drive locked in and the deceleration components slowly getting fried by the increased neutron flux from the reactions, until when they finally could taper off on the forward drive the decelerators were finished, beyond repair, and then the ship had nothing to do but drive on, unable to stop or even turn the magnetic gascatchers off, because once you did that the incoming neutral atoms would be a sleet of protons and neutrons that'd riddle everybody within a day, kill them all. So the officers had said they had to keep going, studying, trying to figure a way to rebuild the decelerators, only nobody ever did, and the crew got older and they flew on, clean out of the galaxy, having babies and quarrels and finally after some murders and suicides and worse, working out a stable social structure in a goddamn relativistic runaway, officers' sons and daughters becoming officers themselves, and crewmen begetting crewmen again, down through five generations now in the creaky old ship that had by now flown through five million years of outside-time, so that there was no purpose or dream of returning Earthside any more, only names attached to pictures and stories, and the same jobs to do every day, servicing the weakening stanchions and struts, the flagging motors, finding replacements for every little doodad that fractured, working because to stop was to die, all the time with officers to tell you what new scientific experiment they'd thought up and how maybe this time it would be the answer, the clue to getting back to their own galaxy—a holy grail beloved of the first and second generations that was now, even under high magnification, a mere mottled disk of ruby receding pinprick lights nobody alive had ever seen up close. Yet there was something in what the bridge officers said, in what the scientific mandarins mulled over, a point to their lives here—

"Let's stop in this'n," Jake called, interrupting Nick's muzzy thoughts, and he followed them into a small inn. Without his noticing it they had left the big observation dome. They angled through a tight, rocky corridor cut from the original asteroid that was the basic body of the whole starship.

Among the seven thousand souls in the ten-kilometer-wide-starship, there were communities and neighborhoods and bars to suit everyone. In this one there were thick veils of smoky euphorics, harmless unless you drank an activating potion. Shifts came and went, there were always crowds in the bar, a rich assortment of faces and ages and tongues. Techs, metalworkers, computer jockeys, manuals, steamfitters, muscled grunt laborers. Cadaverous and silent alesoakers, steadily pouring down a potent brown liquid. Several women danced in a corner, oblivious, singing, rhyming as they went.

Faye ordered drinks and they all three joined in the warm feel of the place. The euphorics helped. It took only moments to become completely convinced that this was a noble and notable set of folk. Someone shouted a joke. Laughter pealed in the close-packed room.

Nick saw in this quick moment an instant of abiding grace: how lovely it was when Faye forgot herself and laughed fully, opening her mouth so wide you could see the whole oval cavern with its ribbed pink roof and the arching tongue alive with tension. The heart-stopping blackness at the back led down to depths worth a lifetime to explore, all revealed in a passing moment like a casual gift: a momentary and incidental beauty that eclipsed the studied, long-learned devices of women and made them infinitely more mysterious.

She gave him a wry, tossed-off smile. He frowned, puzzled. Maybe he had never paid adequate attention to her, never sensed her dimensions. He strained forward to say something and Jake interrupted his thoughts with, "Hey there, look. Two bridgies."

And there were. Two bridge types, not mere officers but scientists; they wore the sedate blue patches on their sleeves. Such people seldom came to these parts of the ship; their quarters, ordained by time, nestled deep in the rock-lined bowels of the inner asteroid.

"See if you can hear what they're sayin'," Faye whispered.

Jake shrugged. "Why should I care?

Faye frowned. "Wanna be a scuzzo dope forever?"

"Aw, stow it," Jake said, and went to get more beer.

Nick watched the scientist nearest him, the man, lift the heavy champagne bottle and empty it. Have to hand it to bioponics, he thought. They keep the liquor coming. The crisp golden foil at the head would be carefully collected, reused; the beautiful heavy hollow butts of the bottles had doubtless been fondled by his own grandfather. Of celebration there was no end.

Nick strained to hear.

"Yes, but the latest data shows definitely there's enough mass, no question."

"Maybe, maybe," said the other. "Must say I never thought there'd be enough between the clusters to add up so much—"

"But there *is*. No doubt of it. Look at Fenetti's data, clear as the nose on your face. Enough mass density between the clusters to close off the universe's geometry, to reverse the expansion."

Goddamn, Nick thought. They're talking about the critical mass problem. Right out in public.

"Yes. My earlier work seems to have been wrong."

"Look, this opens possibilities."

"How?"

"The expansion has to stop, right? So after it does, and things start to implode back, the density of gas the ship passes through will get steadily greater—right?"

Jesus, Nick thought, the eventual slowing down of the universal expansion, billions of years—

"Okay."

"So we'll accelerate more, the relativistic rate will get bigger—the whole process outside will speed up, as we see it."

"Right."

"Then we can sit around and watch the whole thing play out. I mean, shipboard time from now to the implosion of the whole universe, I make it maybe only three hundred years."

"That short?

"Do the calculation."

"Ummm. Maybe so, if we pick up enough mass in the scoop fields. This flyby we're going through, it helps, too."

"Sure it does. We'll do more like it in the next few weeks. Look, we're getting up to speeds that mean we'll be zooming by a galaxy every *day*."

"Uh-huh. If we can live a couple more centuries, ship-board time, we can get to see the whole shebang collapse back in on itself."

"Well, look, that's just a preliminary number, but I think we might make it. In this generation."

Faye said, "Jeez, I can't make out what they're talkin' about."

"I can," Nick said. It helped to know the jargon. He had studied this as part of his program to bootstrap himself up to a better life. You take officers, they could integrate the gravitational field equations straight off, or tell how a galaxy was evolving just by looking at it, or figure out the gas density ahead of the ship just by squinting at one of the X-ray bands from the detectors. They *knew*. He would have to know all of that too, and more. So he studied while the rest of the squad slurped up the malt.

He frowned. He was still stunned, trying to think it through. If the total mass between the clusters of galaxies was big enough, that extra matter would provide enough gravitational energy to make the whole universe reverse its expansion and fall backward, inward, given enough time . . .

Jake was back. "Too noisy in 'ere," he called. "Fergit the beers, bar's mobbed. Let's lift 'em."

Nick glanced over at the scientists. One was earnestly leaning forward, her face puffy and purplish, congested with the force of the words she was urging into the other's ear. He couldn't make out any more of what they were saying; they had descended into quoting mathematical formulas to each other.

"Okay," Nick said.

They left the random clamor of the bar and retraced their steps, back under the observation dome. Nick felt a curious elation.

Nick knows how to run the squad, knows how to keep the equipment going even if the voltage flickers, he can strip down most suits in under an hour using just plain rack tools, been doing it for forty years, all those power tools around the bay, most of the squad can't even turn a nut on a manifold without it has to be pneumatic *rrrrrtt* quick as you please nevermind the wear on the lubricants lost forever that nobody aboard can synthesize, tools seize up easy now, jam your fingers when they do, give you a hand all swole up for a week, and all the time the squad griping 'cause they have to birddog their own stuff, breadboard new ones if some piece of gear goes bad, complaining 'cause they got to form and fabricate their own microchips, no easy replacement parts to just clip in the way you read about the way it was in the first generation, and God help you if a man or woman on the crew gets a fatal injury working in the throat crew, 'cause then your budget is docked for the cost of keeping 'em frozen down, waiting on cures that'll never come just like Earth will never come, the whole planet's been dead now a million years prob'ly, and the frozen corpses on board running two percent of the energy budget he read somewhere, getting to be more all the time, but then he thinks about that talk back in the bar and what it might mean, plunging on until you could see the whole goddamn end of the universe—

"Gotta admit we got you that time, Nick," Jake says as they approach the dome, "smooth as glass I come up on you, you're so hard workin' you don't see nothin', I give you a shot of extra spin, *man* your legs fly out you go wheelin' away—"

Jake starts to laugh.

—and livin' in each other's hip pockets like this the hell of it was you start to begrudge ever' little thing, even the young ones, the kids cost too, not that he's against them, hell, you got to keep the families okay or else they'll be slitting each other's throats inside a year, got to remember your grandfather who was in the Third Try on the decelerators, they came near to getting some new magnets in place before the plasma tubulence blew the whole framework away and they lost it, every family's got some ancestor who got flung down the throat and out into nothing, the kids got to be brought up rememberin' that, even though the little bastards do get into the bioponic tubes and play pranks, they got not a lot to do 'cept study and work, same as he and the others have done for all their lives, average crewman lasts two hundred years or so now, all got the best biomed (goddamn lucky they were shippin' so much to Centauri), bridge officers maybe even longer, get lots of senso augmentation to help you through the tough parts, and all to keep going, or even maybe get ahead a little like this squad boss thing, he was *that* close an' they took it away from him, small-minded bastards scared to shit he might make, what was it, fifty more units of rec credit than they did, not like being an officer or anything, just a job-jockey getting ahead a little, wanting just a scrap, and they gigged him for it and now this big mouth next to his ear is goin' on, puffing himself up in front of Faye, Faye who might be worth a second look if he could get her out of the shadow of this loudmouthed secondrate—

* * *

Jake was in the middle of a sentence, drawling on. Nick grabbed his arm and whirled him around.

"Keep laughin', you slimy bastard, just keep—"

Nick got a throat hold on him and leaned forward. He lifted, pressing Jake against the railing of the walkway. Jake struggled but his feet left the floor until he was balanced on the railing, halfway over the twenty-meter drop. He struck out with a fist but Nick held on.

"Hey, hey, vap off a li'l," Faye cried.

"Yeah—look—you got to take it—as it comes," Jake wheezed between clenched teeth.

"You two done me an' then you laugh an' don't think I don't know you're, you're—" He stopped, searching for words and not finding any.

Globular star clusters hung in the halo beyond the spirals. They flashed by the ship like immense chandeliers of stars. Odd clumps of torn and twisted gas rushed across the sweep of the dome overhead. Tortured gouts of sputtering matter were swept into the magnetic mouth of the ship. As it arched inward toward the craft it gave off flashes of incandescent light. These were stars being born in the ship-driven turbulence, the compressed gases, collapsing into firefly lives before the ship's throat swallowed them. In the flicker of an eyelid on board, a thousand years of stellar evolution transpired on the churning dome above.

The ship had by now carved a swooping path through the narrow strait between the disks. It had consumed banks of gas and dust, burning some for power, scattering the rest with fresh ejected energy into its path. The gas would gush out, away from the galaxies, unable to cause the ongoing friction that drew the two together. This in turn would slow their collision, giving the glittering worlds below another million years to plan, to discover, to struggle upward against the coming catastrophe. The ship itself, grown vast by relativistic effects, shone in the night skies of a billion worlds as a fiercely burning dot, emitting at impossible frequencies, slicing through kiloparsecs of space with its gluttonous magnetic throat, consuming.

*   *   *

"Be easy on him, Nick," Faye said softly.

Nick shook his head. "Naw. Trouble with a guy like this is, he got nothin' to do but piss on people. Hasn't got per . . . perspective."

"Stack it, Nick," Faye said.

Above them, the dome showed briefly the view behind the ship, where the reaction engines poured forth the raw refuse of the fusion drives. Far back, along their trajectory, lay dim filaments, wisps of ivory light. It was the Local Group, the cluster of galaxies that contained the Milky Way, their home. A human could look up, extend a hand, and a mere thumbnail would easily cover the faint smudge that was in fact a clump of spirals, ellipticals, dwarfs and irregular galaxies. It was a small part of the much larger association of galaxies, called the Local Supercluster. The ship was passing now beyond the fringes of the Local Supercluster, forging outward through the dim halo of random glimmering-galaxies which faded off into the black abyss beyond. It would be a long voyage across that span, until the next supercluster was reached: a pale blue haze that ebbed and flowed before the nose of the ship, liquid light distorted by relativity. For the moment the glow of their next destination was lost in the harsh glare of the two galaxies. The disks yawned and turned around the ship, slabs of hot gold and burnt orange, refracted, moving according to the twisted optical effects of special relativity. Compression of wavelengths and the squeezing of time itself made the disks seem to open wide, immense glowing doors swinging in the vacuum, parting to let pass this artifact that sped on, riding a tail of forking, sputtering, violet light.

Nick tilted the man back farther on the railing. Jake's arms fanned the air and his eyes widened.

"Okay, okay, you win," Jake grunted.

"You going upstairs, tell 'em you scragged me."

"Ah . . . okay."

"Good. Or else somethin' might, well, happen." Nick let Jake's legs down, back onto the walkway.

Faye said, "You didn't have to risk his neck. We would've cleared it for you if you'd—"

"Yeah, sure," Nick said sourly.

"You bastard, I oughta—"

"Yeah?"

Jake was breathing hard, his eyes danced around, but Nick knew he wouldn't try anything. He could judge a thing like that. Anyway, he thought, he'd been right, and they knew it. Jake grimaced, shook his head. Nick waved a hand and they walked on.

"Y'know what your trouble is, Nick?" Jake said after a moment. "Yer like this spider here."

Jake took the spider out of his jumpsuit pocket and held up the gray creature. It stirred, but was trapped.

"Wha'cha mean?" Nick asked.

"You got no perspective on the squad. Don't know what's really happenin'. An' this spider, he dunno either. He was down in the locker room, he didn't appreciate what he was in. I mean, that's the center of the whole damn ship right there, the squad."

"Yeah. So?"

"This spider, he don't appreciate how far he'd come from Agro. You either, Nick. You don't appreciate how the squad helps you out, how you oughta be grateful to them, how mebbe you shouldn't keep pushin' alla time."

"Spider's got little eyes, no lens to it," Nick said. "Can't see farther than your hand. Can't see those stars up there. I can, though."

Jake sputtered, "Crap, relative to the spider you're—"

"Aw, can it," Nick said.

Faye said, "Look, Jake, maybe you stop raggin' him alla time, he—"

"No, he's got a point there," Nick said, his voice suddenly mild. "We're all tryin' to be reg'lar folks in the ship, right? We should keep t'gether."

"Yeah. You push too hard."

Sure, Nick thought. Sure I do. And the next thing I'm gonna push for is Faye, take her clean away from you.

*　　*　　*

—the way her neck arcs back when she laughs, graceful in a casual way he never noticed before, a lilting note that caught him, and the broad smile she had, but she was solid too, did a good job in the blowback zone last week when nobody else could handle it, red gases flaring all around her, good woman to have with you, and maybe he'd need a lot of support like that, because he knows now what he really wants: to be an officer someday, it wasn't impossible, just hard, and the only way is by pushing. All this scratching around for a little more rec credits, maybe some better food, that wasn't the point, no, there was something more, the officers keep up the promotion game 'cause we've got to have something to keep people fretting and working, something to take our minds off what's outside, what'll happen if—no, *when*—the drive fails, where we're going, only what these two don't know is that we're not bound for oblivion in a universe that runs down into blackness, we're going on to see the reversal, we get to hear the recessional, galaxies, peeling into the primordial soup as they compress back together and the ship flies faster, always faster as it sucks up the dust of time and hurls itself further on, back to the crunch that made everything and will some day—hell, if he can stretch out the years, right in his own lifetime!—press everything back into a drumming hail of light and mass, now *that's* something to live for—

Faye said pleasantly, "Just think how much good we did back there. Saved who knows how many civilizations, billions of living creatures, gave them a reprieve."

"Right," Jake said, his voice distracted, still smarting over his defeat.

Faye nodded and the three of them made their way up an undulating walkway, heading for the bar where the rest of the squad would be. The ship thrust forward as the spiral galaxies dropped behind now, Doppler reddened into dying embers.

The ship had swept clean the space between them, postponed the coming collision. The scientists had seen this chance, persuaded the captain to make the slight swerve that allowed them to study the galaxies, and in the act accelerate the ship still more. The ship was now still closer to the knife-edge of light speed. Its aim was not a specific destination, but rather to plunge on, learning more, studying the dabs of refracted lights beyond, struggling with the engines, forging on as the universe wound down, as entropy increased, and the last stars flared out. It carried the cargo meant for Centauri—the records and past lives of all humanity, a library for the colony there. If the drives held up, it would carry them forward until the last tick of time.

Nick laughed. "Not that they'll know it, or ever give a—" He stopped. He'd been going to say *ever give a Goddamn about who did it*, but he knew how Faye felt about using the Lord's name in vain.

"Why, sure they will," Faye said brightly. "We were a big, hot source of all kinds of radiation. They'll know it was a piece of technology."

"Big lights in the sky? Could be natural."

"With a good spectrometer—"

"Yeah, but they'll never be sure."

She frowned. "Well, a ramscoop exhaust looks funny, not like a star or anything."

"With the big relativistic effect factored in, our emission goes out like a searchlight. One narrow little cone of scrambled-up radiation, Dopplered forward. So they can't make us out the whole time. Most of 'em 'd see us for just a few years, tops," Nick said.

"So?"

"Hard to make a scientific theory about somethin' that happens once, lasts a little while, never repeats."

"Maybe."

"They could just as likely think it was something unnatural. Supernatural. A god or somethin',"

"Huh. Maybe." Faye shrugged. "Come on. Let's get 'nother drink before rest'n rec hours are over."

They walked on. Above them the great knives of light sliced down through the air, ceaselessly changing, and the humans kept on going, their small voices indomitable, reaching forward, undiminished.

Afterword

I've never been able to make my subconscious work in neat categories. Maybe that's because I try to extract as much labor from it as possible, and somehow that provokes those mysterious depths to jump a synapse here and there.

I don't have much writing time free, because my days are filled with the endless clotting detail of being a professor of physics. So I try to spend my available writing time actually writing—hitting the keys—rather than staring into space, mulling over the smoky world I'm inventing.

This means I need a certain sense that I know where I'm going, before I ever sit down to write. Over the years I have evolved methods to force my subconscious to do all this—the really hard work—so I, sitting up here in the conscious, sunlit penthouse, enjoy the benefits of the labors done in the dank, moist basement.

Mostly, I daydream. I use that well-known effect, whereby when you get in your car at the end of the workday, unless you stay alert, your hind-brain will drive you home. I do a lot of plot-juggling then.

Basic ideas often come as I wake up. I lie around, faking sleep, and drift through cobwebbed corridors, poking at heaps of junk that might yield some old iron pot or oily rag. Useful, all. *Why not have X do Y to Z?* a voice asks, and so I do just that, next time I'm punishing the keys.

I keep all this in notebooks, with tabs for DIALOG or BACKGROUND or DUMB BUT CUTE STUFF. Writing, I fish up these bits of trash and fashion shambling creatures from them.

I was in the middle of a difficult novel, *Across the Sea of Suns,* and had just written a chapter for it the day before. When I woke up next morning, I had the whole outline of another story in mind, the central scene of which was very much like the just-finished chapter.

Great, I thought. *This'll be easy.*

Insulted at the casual way I took for granted all the free labor, my subconscious took me halfway through the story and stopped cold. I waited. One week, two, three. Nothing. I did a lot of mathematical physics, wrote a scientific paper, went to a plasma physics meeting. Somehow, having hung up on this one scene—the one beginning "Nick lies mute . . ."—the nether-mind got a few pages further and just stopped.

It took me months to finally get anything out of it. I wrote other things, even some bits of fiction. There was no real writer's block, just a logjam on this story.

Then one day I was browsing in the library and came upon a paper about fast-moving jets in astrophysics. The author pointed out what strange effects you get if you view a relativistic stream of particles from the side. I instantly reversed the situation, and wondered how the outside universe would look to the particles themselves.

I left the library and drove home immediately, letting some subroutine do the driving. By the time I got there (safely), I had the whole story glued together . . . only it was vastly different from what I'd thought it should be about. In a sense, it was now a *hommage* to Poul Anderson's remarkable novel *Tau Zero*—though I don't think I had consciously remembered that work anytime during the process.

That's how the same scene turns up (though modified) in two different places. This isn't the only place where that has happened, either. I tried to cut the scene from this story, later, and couldn't do it. The trouble with getting "free" help is that you have to take the stuff, or else.

Nooncoming _____

Saturday night, and they straggled into the cramped bar on Eucalyptus Boulevard. They nudged through the crowd and found friends, these aging people, ordered drinks, watched the crystal clouds at the ceiling form lurid, fleshy stories. But the best tales were the ones they told each other: *Janek's got a newsy flapping needs a big cast, senso and all, the works, I—so I go back and there are people living in my goddamn office for Christ's sakes hanging out washing and the desks gone, just gone, the file cases made into a bureau—programmers? who needs programmers? this guy says to the crowd and Jeff, he throws a—could still maneuver one of those three-piecer rigs, ten gears an' all, if some bastards hadn't broken 'em all down into little skimpy ratass haulers with—asked why an' I guess I just wanna stay close to the old centers, hopin' some big Brazilian money will come in like in '72 an' a good derrick man can get on—queen she was from hunger and not gonna bust her head for any factory that traded her off—*

Only one woman in the bar was eating alone and she was tucked back in a shadowed corner, far from the oily light. She was big-boned and deeply tanned, her denim pants and shirt cut in a manner that meant she had deliberately chosen them that way; they seemed to bracket her body rather than enfolding it. She wore only eyeshadow and her widely spaced eyes seemed to make her face broader than it was, more open, just as the backward sweep of her hair bared her face more than necessary. The long strands of it were held back by a clip and had occasional flecks of blond, enough to hint that with a little treatment she could have been a striking beauty. She ate steadily, no becoming hesitations, winding up neat cylinders of artichoke spaghetti and rolling them through the red sauce before taking precise bites out of them. Somehow the strands of green didn't break free and hang down as she did this. She ignored the buzz of talk around her and drank regularly from a tumbler of dark red wine. Every few moments she would look up, not at the swirling lattice above that featured tangled bodies, nor at the Saturday night crowd in their flossy clothing, but toward the doorway.

The man she was waiting for appeared there, shouldering his way by a giggling clump of aging heavy drinkers, just after 1800 hours, thirty minutes late. He wore a frayed synthetic jacket, antique, like several others she had seen in the bar.

"Joanna, frange it, sorry I'm late."

"I started without you," she said simply, still chewing.

"Yes. A good house wine, isn't it? Petite Sirah."

"Right."

He sat down and hunched forward, elbows on the burnished pine table. "I've already had something."

"Oh?" She raised an eyebrow. He seemed fidgety and pale to her, but maybe that was because she was so used to seeing tanned people; everybody in town today had looked rather sickly, now that she thought about it.

"Yes. I, ah, I was celebrating. With some friends."

"Celebrating returning to High Hopes?" She smiled. "That doesn't sound like the Brian I—"

"No. I'm going back."

"*What?*"

"Back . . . on vacation."

"Getting vacated, you mean. Renting space."

She grimaced and put down her fork.

"However you want to describe it," he said precisely.

"You tappers have your little words," she murmured scornfully. "*Going on vacation.* Sounds like a free ride somewhere."

"It is."

"Stealing your *life* is—"

"Joanna." He paused. "We've had this discussion before."

"Look. You know High Hopes doesn't like you selling yourself off this way—"

"They agreed to let me do it."

"On an occasional basis."

"Okay, it's just getting *less* occasional. Let's put it that way."

"*Skrag* that."

"I don't owe you—"

"The hell you don't. High Hopes has put up with your renting your lobes for—what?—three years, off and on. We let you run off to San Francisco and tap in, then take off and squander the bills on—"

"High living," he said sarcastically. His face wrinkled up into a thin smile.

"Right. Your fatcat amusements."

"Travel. Good food. Too rich for your tastes, I know, but good nonetheless. But the rest of it—Joanna, it's the *work*. I'm doing some damned interesting physics these days."

"Useless," she said decisively.

"Probably. Nonlinear dynamics—not much use in digging potatoes."

"You never did that. You were a pod cutter."

"Grunt labor is all the same."

Her eyes flashed. "Group work is *never*—"

"I know. I know." Brian waved a hand listlessly and looked around. "Think I'll have some of that red ink."

He got up and squeezed through the packed room, toward the wine barrel and glasses. There were no waiters here, to keep costs down. Joanna watched him move and suddenly it struck her that Brian was getting older, at least forty-five now. He had a certain heavy way of moving she wasn't used to seeing at High Hopes.

"Good stuff," he said, sitting back down. He sipped at the glass and studied the layered air around them. There was a musty, sour scent.

"Did we have to meet here?" Joanna said, resuming eating.

"Why not?"

"All these old—well, some of them look pretty seamy."

"They *are* seamy. We're getting that way."

"If they'd pitch in, get some exercise—"

"Ha! Look, my sturdy girl of the soil, these people are

artists, engineers, scientists, administrators, men and women with education. They like living in town, even if it's this little dimple of a burg, two hundred klicks down from the city they all want to live in, San Francisco.''

"A bunch of rattle-headed sophies," she said, chewing.

"Sophies?''

"Sophisticates, isn't that what you call yourselves?''

"Oh, you've got a name for us.''

"Why not? You're the biggest trouble back at High Hopes. Always wanting what you can't have any more.''

He licked his lips. "We want the old days. Good jobs. To own something worth a damn.''

"Possessions," she said wryly. "Only *they* possess *you*— that's what you people forgot.''

"We still remember the dignity of it.''

She snorted and took a long drink. "Ego feeding.''

"No!" he said earnestly. "There were people, ideas, things happening.''

"*We're* making things happen, if that's what you want," she said. She finished the last green strand and dropped her fork into the plate with a rattle. The thick crockery was filmed with grease.

"Surviving, that's all," he murmured.

"There are good problems. We're not just a bunch of simple-minded farmers, you know. You seem to've forgotten—''

"No, I haven't. Tapping doesn't blur the memory.''

"Well, it must. Otherwise you'd come back to the one group of people who care about you.''

"Really? Or do you want me to patch up the chem and bio systems?''

"There's that," she said grudgingly.

"And sit around evenings, pinned to the communal 3D, or bored to death.''

"We do more than that," Joanna said mildly.

"I know. And you have wondrous thighs, Joanna, but they can't encompass all my troubles.''

She smiled and brushed at her severely tied-back hair. "You're still possessive about the sex thing, too, aren't you?''

"Terribly old style of me, I know."

"Ummm," she said. Brian tipped his glass at her in mock salute and went to refill it. Joanna leaned back in her chair, reflecting moodily. She remembered the old English woman who had died last year, working with a kind of resigned energy right up until her last day. The woman had said to Joanna, as she went inside the dormitory to lie down for what proved to be the last time, "You know, my dear, you're wrong that suffering ennobles people." She'd stopped to massage her hip, wincing. "It simply makes one cross." So was that it—Brian and the rest of the older ones looked on the honest labor in the pod rows as petty, degrading?

Joanna watched Brian standing patiently in line by the wine barrel. She remembered that Brian had talked to the English woman a lot, while most of High Hopes was watching the 3D in the evenings. They'd talked of what they'd once had, and Brian even spoke of it when he and Joanna lay together occasionally. The dry dead past, gaudy and stupid. She remembered Brian frowning in displeasure as the sounds of the next couple came through the thin walls. He had disapproved of them strongly, and it was all Joanna could do to stop him leaping out of bed and going next door to stop Dominic—it was usually Julie and Dominic—beating her. He had the idea that things people did together for sex were public somehow, that there were rules High Hopes should maintain. Standards, he called them. And even when they were at it themselves, pumping with a steady rhythm as though propelling each other over the same steepening slope of a familiar hill, when the sound came of Julie's high, wavering cry—which then slid into something almost like a laugh, a chuckle at some recognizable delight that lay ahead and would come upon her—then Brian would freeze against her loins and seethe, his mood broken. And she, mystified at first, would try to rock him gently back into reality and out of his dusty obsessions. She would wrap herself around him and draw him back down; once, she misunderstood and offered to do those things for him, perform whatever he liked, and the look on his face told her more about Brian than all the conversations.

Odd, she thought, that she should remember that now. Her

sexual interest in him was no greater than for any of the others at High Hopes. A recreation, a kind of warming exercise that bound them all together and eased the days of labor into sleep.

He returned, smiling in the wan lamplight. "Can't you stay in town tonight?"

"Why?" she said.

"Not so I can hear more lectures on High Hopes, I assure you of that. No, I want to sleep with you again."

"Oh," she said, and realized she was saying it stiffly, formally, that something in her was drawing away from Brian and the memories of Brian.

"Come on."

"It isn't that *way*, Brian. You don't *own* somebody—"

"I know, I've heard it. These flesh shows"—he gestured at the tangled bodies on the ceiling above—"are very much a cultural remnant. Like everybody in here."

Joanna looked around, grimacing. "Unsatisfied people. They can't stand being frogs in a small pond."

"No, it's not that," Brian said wearily. "They remember when they could *do* more, *be* more. Make sound sculptures, explore new things, use their *minds* for once—"

"Loaf around in a university."

He smiled wanly. "I'm surprised you remember the word. The regime has just ruled that only the Davis Agriworks is legal now—crop studies, that's it. I don't—"

"*Look*, Brian," she said abruptly. "I came into town to get some supplies and pick you up. The bus doesn't run into mid-Sur any more, so you'd have had to hike in. We've got a lot of new people drifting in, refugees from southern California, starving, most of them. Don't know a damn thing about work. That's why we need you—you're our best, y'know. We have to—"

"I told you," he said, stony-faced. "I'm going on vacation."

"Those damned franging computers don't need you! We *do*. They could get *animals*—"

"I've told you before. Animals don't have enough holographic data-storing capability. They lose too much detail."

"Then the hell with the whole skrag!"

"That's right," he said savagely, "tear it down. You

don't understand it so you want to sacrifice the whole biosystems inventory, the ecological index, everything that's holding this poor battered world together—''

"Don't come on noble with *me*. You like the pay, getting to live back in the rotten city again—''

Her voice rose to a shrill edge and several people turned their heads, frowning. She was suddenly aware of how old and strange and distant all these people were, with their broken dreams and memories. And she glanced at the only window in the room to see a yellowish fog pressing against the pane. Beaded moisture glinted in the wan light. She would have to get started soon, before it thickened.

"You're right," Brian said, and his voice was oddly quiet. "I like to be among my own kind. I don't mind the price I pay. They hook me up during peak periods and the computers, which don't have enough solid state electronics banks left to do the calculations, push into my lobes and use the space there. I know what you think of it and I don't care. I know it looks grotesque to you, on the outside. I lie there still as a stone and the data flits through me, the machines using my neural capacity to do their work, and it's like dreaming and drifting and dreaming again, only when you wake up you can't remember what it was all about. You're vacated—every memory you had in those spaces is wiped, gone. But it's usually unimportant stuff and, Joanna, that doesn't matter, that isn't *it*. That's merely the price—what I get is freedom, time to talk to other people who're working in my field and still care about those things, some feeling of the old days.''

"So you're going to stay there.''

"Right.''

"Instead of working for a better world, *here*—''

"I'm going to clutch after the only way I can stay in the old one. And I'm needed there, too, Joanna. The cost of making new computer elements is enormous. How much better, to link into the best, most compact neural net ever made—our brains—and use the few educated people left to work with the computer systems, *guide* them, be both storage space and programmers—''

Her face barely repressed the rage she felt. "*We* need you.

You're a resource, trained people are scarce who'll work in the communes, and—''

"No," he said, shaking his head. With an abrupt gesture he tossed back the glass of wine. "I want the old way. I'm not going to bust my tail."

They looked at each other and she suddenly felt alien and alone in this strange place, this room of people who had washed up like refuse in the towns, refusing to go out into the forgiving countryside any more, clinging to the dear dead past, and felt the abyss that opened between them and her. They were living in some place that the world had once been, and would never be again. So in an odd way she and her kind were parents to their elders now, and must shelter them against the world. It was at that moment that she realized that the revolution she had been a part of was over, the morning was finished, and the long day of the human race was beginning.

"Have some more wine, Brian," she said softly after a while. "I've got to head on back pretty soon now."

Afterword

A lot of fiction about the future seeks—subconsciously or otherwise—to avoid science or technology. There are many reasons to do this, of course, some quite good ones. Often writers don't really know much about techno-dazzle, beyond the decadent glitz of a film like *Blade Runner*. Still, they're concerned with where we're heading. So they adopt maneuvers.

You can equate the future society to some earlier civilization, and then trot out some old, low tech in a new guise. In fact, you can even re-invent mythological characters and embody them in the future. This can be very effective (see Delany's *The Einstein Intersection,* Zelazny's *Lord of Light,* and much of Jack Vance's work). Or—less interestingly—you can impose the familiar post-catastrophe landscape, with technology appearing only as totems of the past. Or you can use Arthur Clarke's handy observation that a sufficiently advanced technology will look like magic.

All these devices can, have, and will continue to yield fine fiction.

Yet I suspect that the future will be just as science- and techno-dominated as our present. As Kurt Vonnegut pointed out in his first novel, *Player Piano,* some people love problem-solving and tinkering—and *that* is the final, irreducible driver of human history. Wars and faiths and leaders come and go, but the problem-solvers' slow, steady work is the fulcrum upon which history turns. *Analog* magazine has been the high church of this faith in science fiction. However quirky, awkward, and ham-fisted many

104

of its stories have been, the truth of that proposition remains.

I was mulling over such matters when I had a talk with Terry Carr, editor of the *Universe* anthology series. He remarked that he liked *The New Yorker* style of compressed story, with understated nuances squeezed into realistic detail. It's hard to do that in science fiction, because you must establish a *new* background, characters altered by that world (and thus somewhat odd to us), *then* thrust them forward of their own momentum toward a satisfying conclusion. In a mainstream story you can simply say "Florida, 1972" and the reader does most of the work for you. Throw in a few lazy, drooping palm trees, a moist soft breeze, the drowsy hum of blue neon motel signs—and you're off, social conventions and political alignments firmly in place, geography known, brand names on call—all in service to characters whose individual quirks can easily stand out from a conventional canvas.

How to do that in science fiction? Terry wondered if I'd be interested in writing a *New Yorker*-style story which was still sf. I pondered this a few days, and then sat down at the typewriter. (It was a 1948 Royal Standard, gray case, Canterbury typeface—see how much that conjures up of my work habits? The Royal was a grand old machine, but it spelled badly. Now I'm typing this in 1985 on a word processor. Signifiers change.)

This was in the middle 1970s. Environmentalism was much in the air. It seemed to me that a century hence might find humanity boxed in by environmental failures. (I still think so. Depletion of forests, ozone layers, and wetlands proceeds apace. I used a particularly horrifying environmental effect as the prime motivator in a novel I was working on in the same years, *Timescape*. Though much attention has focused on other facets of that novel—science as she is done, time as a fundamental riddle in modern physics—*I* think the possible death of the oceans is the most important issue in the book.)

Many environmentalists view scientists as untrustworthy allies. This seems to me simply dumb. It is appetite that can consume the world, not technology *per se*. Nobody would call the simple irrigation system of the Babylonians a techno-evil, yet it destroyed much of the land of the Middle East.

So I thought about a future seriously diminished by eco-horrors, and concluded that it would not be a homogeneously humble, pious, resolutely anti-tech society. Human beings don't work that way, however much utopian thinkers might wish. Instead, as the walls pressed in, it seemed to me technology would loom larger still. High tech would promise a salvation of sorts, or at least careers, openings, brimming possibilities.

Not that the communal concensus would vanish, either. There would be zesty conflict, the stuff of stories.

So I sat down and wrote this in one day, trying to gain from compression a feeling of the compacted spaces in which such people would live.

To the Storming Gulf_____

Turkey

Trouble. Knew there'd be trouble and plenty of it if we left the reactor too soon.

But do they listen to me? No, not to old Turkey. He's just a dried-up corn husk of a man now, they think, one of those Bunren men who been on the welfare a generation or two and no damn use to anybody.

Only it's simple plain farm supports I was drawing all this time, not any kind of horse-ass welfare. So much they know. Can't blame a man just 'cause he comes up cash-short sometimes. I like to sit and read and think more than some people I could mention, and so I took the money.

Still, Mr. Ackerman and all think I got no sense to take government dole and live without a lick of farming, so when I talk they never listen. Don't even seem to hear.

It was his idea, getting into the reactor at McIntosh. Now that was a good one, I got to give him that much.

When the fallout started coming down and the skimpy few stations on the radio were saying to get to deep shelter, it was Mr. Ackerman who thought about the big central core at McIntosh. The reactor itself had been shut down automatically when the war started, so there was nobody there. Mr. Ackerman figured a building made to keep radioactivity in will also keep it out. So he got together the families, the Nelsons and Bunrens and Pollacks and all, cousins and aunts and anybody we could reach in the measly hours we had before the fallout arrived.

We got in all right. Brought food and such. A reactor's set

up self-contained and got huge air filters and water flow from the river. The water was clean, too, filtered enough to take out the fallout. The generators were still running good. We waited it out there. Crowded and sweaty but O.K. for ten days. That's how long it took for the count to go down. Then we spilled out into a world laid to gray and yet circumscribed waste, the old world seen behind a screen of memories.

That was bad enough, finding the bodies—people, cattle, and dogs asprawl across roads and fields. Trees and bushes looked the same, but there was a yawning silence every-where. Without men, the pine stands and muddy riverbanks had fallen dumb, hardly a swish of breeze moving through them, like everything was waiting to start up again but didn't know how.

Angel

We thought we were O.K. then, and the counters said so, too—all the gammas gone, one of the kids said. Only the sky didn't look the same when we came out, all mottled and shot through with drifting blue-belly clouds.

Then the strangest thing. July, and there's sleet falling. Big wind blowing up from the Gulf, only it's not the sticky hot one we're used to in summer, it's moaning in the trees of a sudden and a prickly chill.

"Goddamn, I don't think we can get far in this," Turkey says, rolling his old rheumy eyes around like he never saw weather before.

"It will pass," Mr. Ackerman says like he is in real tight with God.

"Lookit that moving in from the south," I say, and there's a big mass all purple and forking lightning swarming over the hills, like a tide flowing, swallowing everything.

"Gulf storm. We'll wait it out," Mr. Ackerman says to the crowd of us, a few hundred left out of what was a moderate town with real promise.

Nobody talks about the dead folks. We see them every-where, worms working in them. A lot smashed up in car accidents, died trying to drive away from something they couldn't see. But we got most of our families in with us, so it's not so bad. Me, I just pushed it away for a while, too much to think about with the storm closing in.

Only it wasn't a storm. It was somethin' else, with thick clouds packed with hail and snow one day and the next sunshine, only sun with bite in it. One of the men says it's got more UV in it, meaning the ultraviolet that usually doesn't come through the air. But it's getting down to us now.

So we don't go out in it much. Just to the market for what's left of the canned food and supplies, only a few of us going out at a time, says Mr. Ackerman.

We thought maybe a week it would last.

Turned out to be more than two months.

I'm a patient woman, but jammed up in those corridors and stinking offices and control room of the reactor—

Well, I don't want to go on.

It's like my Bud says, worst way to die is to be bored to death.

That's damn near the way it was.

Not that Old Man Turkey minded. You ever notice how the kind of man that hates moving, he will talk up other people doing just the opposite?

Mr. Ackerman was leader at first, because of getting us into the reactor. He's from Chicago but you'd think it was England sometimes, the way he acts. He was on the school board and vice president of the big AmCo plant outside town. But he just started to *assume* his word was *it*, y'know, and that didn't sit with us too well.

Some people started to saying Turkey was smarter. And was from around here, too. Mr. Ackerman heard about it.

Any fool could see Mr. Ackerman was the better man. But Turkey talked the way he does, reminding people he'd studied engineering at Auburn way back in the twencen and learned languages for a hobby and all. Letting on that when we came out, we'd need him instead of Mr. Ackerman.

He said an imp had caused the electrical things to go dead and I said that was funny, saying an imp done it. He let on it was a special name they had for it. That's the way he is. He sat and ruminated and fooled with his radios—that he never could make work—and told all the other men to go out and do this and that. Some did, too. The old man does know a lot of useless stuff and can convince the dumb ones that he's wise.

So he'd send them to explore. Out into cold that'd snatch the breath out of you, bite your fingers, numb your toes. While old Turkey sat and fooled.

Turkey

Nothing but sputtering on the radio. Nobody had a really good one that could pick up stations in Europe or far off.

Phones dead of course.

But up in the night sky the first night out we saw dots moving—the pearly gleam of the Arcapel colony, the ruddy speck called Russworld.

So that's when Mr. Ackerman gets this idea.

We got to reach those specks. Find out what's the damage. Get help.

Only the power's out everywhere, and we got no way to radio to them. We tried a couple of the local radio stations, brought some of their equipment back to the reactor where there was electricity working.

Every damn bit of it was shot. Couldn't pick up a thing. Like the whole damn planet was dead, only of course it was the radios that were gone, fried in the EMP—ElectroMagnetic Pulse—that Angel made a joke out of.

All this time it's colder than a whore's tit outside. And we're sweating and dirty and grumbling, rubbing up against ourselves inside.

Bud and the others, they'd bring in what they found in the stores. Had to drive to Sims Chapel or Toon to get anything, what with people looting. And gas was getting hard to find by then, too. They'd come back, and the women would cook up whatever was still O.K., though most of the time you'd eat it real quick so's you didn't have to spend time looking at it.

Me, I passed the time. Stayed warm.

Tried lots of things. Bud wanted to fire the reactor up, and five of the men, they read through the manuals and thought that they could do it. I helped a li'l.

So we pulled some rods and opened valves and did manage to get some heat out of the thing. Enough to keep us warm. But when they fired her up more, the steam hoots out and bells clang and automatic recordings go on saying loud as hell:

EMERGENCY CLASS 3
ALL PERSONNEL TO STATIONS

and we all get scared as shit.

So we don't try to rev her up more. Just get heat.

To keep the generators going, we go out, fetch oil for them. Or Bud and his crew do. I'm too old to help much.

But at night we can still see those dots of light up there, scuttling across the sky same as before.

They're the ones know what's happening. People go through this much, they want to know what it meant.

So Mr. Ackerman says we got to get to that big DataComm center south of Mobile. Near Fairhope. At first I thought he'd looked it up in a book from the library or something.

When he says that, I pipe up, even if I am just an old fart according to some, and say, "No good to you even if you could. They got codes on the entrances, guards prob'ly. We'll just pound on the door till our fists are all bloody and then have to slunk around and come on back."

"I'm afraid you have forgotten our cousin Arthur," Mr. Ackerman says all superior. He married into the family, but you'd think he invented it.

"You mean the one works over in Citronelle?"

"Yes. He has access to DataComm."

So that's how we got shanghaied into going to Citronelle, six of us, and breaking in there. Which caused the trouble. Just like I said.

Mr. Ackerman

I didn't want to take the old coot they called Turkey, a big dumb Bunren like all the rest of them. But the Bunrens want into everything, and I was facing a lot of opposition in my plan to get Arthur's help, so I went along with them.

Secretly, I believe the Bunrens wanted to get rid of the pestering old fool. He had been starting rumors behind my back among the three hundred souls I had saved. The Bunrens insisted on Turkey's going along just to nip at me.

We were all volunteers, tired of living in musk and sour sweat inside that cramped reactor. Bud and Angel, the boy Johnny (whom we were returning to the Fairhope area), Turkey, and me.

We left the reactor under a gray sky with angry little clouds racing across it. We got to Citronelle in good time, Bud floorboarding the Pontiac. As we went south we could see the spotty clouds were coming out of big purple ones that sat, not moving, just churning and spitting lightning on the horizon. I'd seen them before, hanging in the distance, never blowing inland. Ugly.

When we came up on the Center, there was a big hole in the side of it.

"Like somebody stove in a box with one swipe," Bud said.

Angel, who was never more than two feet from Bud any time of day, said, "They *bombed* it."

"No," I decided. "Very likely it was a small explosion. Then the weather worked its way in."

Which turned out to be true. There'd been some disagreement amongst the people holed up in the Center. Or maybe it was grief and the rage that comes of that. Susan wasn't too clear about it ever.

The front doors were barred, though. We pounded on them. Nothing. So we broke in. No sign of Arthur or anyone.

We found one woman in a back room, scrunched into a bed with cans of food all around and a tiny little oil-burner heater. Looked awful, with big dark circles around her eyes and scraggly uncut hair.

She wouldn't answer me at first. But we got her calmed and cleaned and to talking. That was the worst symptom, the not talking at first. Something back in the past two months had done her deep damage, and she couldn't get it out.

Of course, living in a building half-filled with corpses was no help. The idiots hadn't protected against radiation well

enough, I guess. And the Center didn't have good heating.
So those who had some radiation sickness died later in the
cold snap.

Susan

You can't know what it's like when all the people you've
worked with, intelligent people who were nice as pie before,
they turn mean and angry and filled up with grief for who
was lost. Even then I could see Gene was the best of them.

They start to argue, and it runs on for days, nobody
knowing what to do because we all can see the walls of the
Center aren't thick enough, the gamma radiation comes right
through this government prefab issue composition stuff. We
take turns in the computer room because that's the farthest in
and the filters still work there, all hoping we can keep our
count rate down, but the radiation comes in gusts for some
reason, riding in on a storm front and coming down in the
rain, only being washed away, too. It was impossible to tell
when you'd get a strong dose and when there'd be just
random clicks on the counters, plenty of clear air that you'd
suck in like sweet vapors 'cause you knew it was good and
could *taste* its purity.

So I was just lucky, that's all.

I got less than the others. Later some said that me being a
nurse, I'd given myself some shots to save myself. I knew
that was the grief talking, is all. That Arthur was the worst.
Gene told him off.

I was in the computer room when the really bad gamma
radiation came. Three times the counter rose up, and three
times I was there by accident of the rotation.

The men who were armed enforced the rotation, said it
was the only fair way. And for a while everybody went
along.

We all knew that the radiation exposure was building
up and some already had too much, would die a month or a
year later no matter what they did.

I was head nurse by then, not so much because I knew
more but because the others were dead. When it got cold, they
went fast.

Onward the process flies. Each nucleus collides millions of times with the others in a fleck-shot swirl like glowing snowflakes. All in the space of a heartbeat. Flakes ride the magnetic field lines. Gamma rays flare and sputter among the blundering motes like fitful fireflies. Nuclear fire lights the long roaring corridor that is the ship's main drive. Nick swims, the white-hot sparks breaking over him like foam. Ahead he sees the violet points of gravid nitrogen and hears them crack into carbon plus an alpha particle. So in the end the long cascade gives forth the carbon that catalyzed it, carbon that will begin again its life in the whistling blizzard of protons coming in from the forward maw of the ship. With the help of the carbon, an interstellar hydrogen atom has built itself up from mere proton to, finally, an alpha particle—a stable clump of two neutrons and two protons. The alpha particle is the point of it all. It flees from the blurring storm, carrying the energy that fusion affords. The ruby-rich interstellar gas is now wedded, proton to proton, with carbon as the matchmaker.

Nick feels a rising electric field pluck at him. He moves to shed his excess charge. To carry a cloak of electrons here is fatal. Upstream lies the chewing gullet of the ramscoop ship, where the incoming protons are sucked in and where their kinetic power is stolen from them by the electric fields. There the particles are slowed, brought to rest inside the ship, their streaming energy stored in capacitors.

A cyclone shrieks behind him. Nick swims sideways, toward the walls of the combustion chamber. The nuclear burn that flares around him is never pure, cannot be pure because the junk of the cosmos pours through here, like barley meal laced with grains of granite. The incoming atomic rain spatters constantly over the fluxlife walls, killing the organic superconductor strands there.

Nick pushes against the rubbery magnetic fields and swoops over the mottled yellow-blue crust of the walls. In the flickering lightning glow of infrared and ultraviolet he sees the scaly muck that deadens the magnetic fields and slows the nuclear burn in the throat. He flexes, wriggles, and turns the eel-like form. This brings the electron beam gun around at millimeter range. He fires. A brittle crackling leaps out, onto

So it fell to me to deal with these men and women who had their exposure already. Their symptoms had started. I couldn't do anything. There was some who went out and got gummy fungus growing in the corners of their eyes—pterygium it was, I looked it up. From the ultraviolet. Grew quick over the lens and blinded them. I put them in darkness, and after a week the film was just a dab back in the corners of their eyes. My one big success.

The rest I couldn't do much for. There was the T-Isolate box, of course, but that was for keeping sick people slowed down until real medical help could get to them. These men and women, with their eyes reaching out at you like you were the angel of light coming to them in their hour of need, they couldn't get any help from that. Nobody could cure the dose rates they'd got. They were dead but still walking around and knowing it, which was the worst part.

So every day I had plenty to examine, staff from the Center itself who'd holed up here, and worse, people coming straggling in from cubbyholes they'd found. People looking for help once the fevers and sores came on them. Hoping their enemy was the pneumonia and not the gammas they'd picked up weeks back, which was sitting in them now like a curse. People I couldn't help except maybe by a little kind lying.

So much like children they were. So much leaning on their hope.

It was all you could do to look at them and smile that stiff professional smile.

And Gene McKenzie. All through it he was a tower of a man.

Trying to talk some sense to them.

Sharing out the food.

Arranging the rotation schedules so we'd all get a chance to shelter in the computer room.

Gene had been boss of a whole Command Group before. He was on duty station when it happened and knew lots about the war but wouldn't say much. I guess he was sorrowing.

Even though once in a while he'd laugh.

And then talk about how the big computers would have fun with what he knew. Only the lines to DataComm had gone dead right when things got interesting, he said. He'd wonder what'd happened to MC355, the master one down in DataComm.

Wonder and then laugh.

And go get drunk with the others.

I'd loved him before, loved and waited because I knew he had three kids and a wife, a tall woman with auburn hair that he loved dearly. Only they were in California visiting her relatives in Sonoma when it happened, and he knew in his heart that he'd never see them again, probably.

Leastwise that's what he told me—not out loud, of course, 'cause a man like that doesn't talk much about what he feels. But in the night when we laid together, I knew what it meant. He whispered things, words I couldn't piece together, but then he'd hold me and roll gentle like a small boat rocking on the Gulf—and when he went in me firm and long, I knew it was the same for him, too.

If there was to come any good of this war, then it was that I was to get Gene.

We were together all warm and dreamy when it happened.

I was asleep. Shouts and anger, and quick as anything the *crump* of hand grenades and shots hammered away in the night, and there was running everywhere.

Gene jumped up and went outside and had almost got them calmed down, despite the breach in the walls. Then one of the men who'd already got lots of radiation—Arthur, who knew he had maybe one or two weeks to go, from the count rate on his badge—Arthur started yelling about making the world a fit place to live after all this and how God would want the land set right again, and then he shot Gene and two others.

I broke down then, and they couldn't get me to treat the others. I let Arthur die. Which he deserved.

I had to drag Gene back into the hospital unit myself.

And while I was saying good-bye to him and the men outside were still quarreling, I decided it then. His wound was in the chest. A lung was punctured clean. The shock had near killed him before I could do anything. So I put him in the T-Isolate and made sure it was working all right. Then the main power went out. But the T-Isolate box had its own cells, so I knew we had some time.

I was alone. Others were dead or run away raging into the whirlwind black-limbed woods. In the quiet I was.

With the damp, dark trees comforting me. Waiting with Gene for what the world would send.

The days got brighter, but I did not go out. Colors seeped through the windows.

I saw to the fuel cells. Not many left.

The sun came back, with warm blades of light. At night I thought of how the men in their stupidity had ruined everything.

When the pounding came, I crawled back in here to hide amongst the cold and dark.

Mr. Ackerman

"Now, we came to help you," I said in as smooth and calm a voice as I could muster. Considering.

She backed away from us.

"I won't give him up! He's not dead long's I stay with him, tend to him."

"So much dyin'," I said, and moved to touch her shoulder. "It's up under our skins, yes, we understand that. But you have to look beyond it, child."

"I won't!"

"I'm simply asking you to help us with the DataComm people. I want to go there and seek their help."

"Then go!"

"They will not open up for the likes of us, surely."

"Leave me!"

The poor thing cowered back in her horrible stinking rathole, bedding sour and musty, open tin cans strewn about and reeking of gamy, half-rotten meals.

"We need the access codes. We'd counted on our cousin Arthur, and are grieved to hear he is dead. But you surely know where the proper codes and things are."

"I . . . don't. . . ."

"Arthur told me once how the various National Defense Installations were insulated from each other so that system failures would not bring them all down at once?"

"I . . ."

The others behind me muttered to themselves, already restive at coming so far and finding so little.

"Arthur spoke of you many times, I recall. What a bright woman you were. Surely there was a procedure whereby each staff member could, in an emergency, communicate with the other installations?"

The eyes ceased to jerk and swerve, the mouth lost its rictus of addled fright. "That was for . . . drills. . . ."

"But surely you can remember?"

"Drills."

"They issued a manual to you?"

"I'm a nurse!"

"Still, you know where we might look?"

"I . . . know."

"You'll let us have the . . . codes?" I smiled reassuringly, but for some reason the girl backed away, eyes cunning.

"No."

Angel pushed forward and shouted, "How can you say that to honest people after all that's—"

"Quiet!"

Angel shouted, "You can't make me be—"

Susan backed away from Angel, not me, and squeaked, "No no no I can't—I can't—"

"Now, I'll handle this," I said, holding up my hands between the two of them.

Susan's face knotted at the compressed rage in Angel's face and turned to me for shelter. "I . . . I will, yes, but you have to *help* me."

"We all must help each other, dear," I said, knowing the worst was past.

"I'll have to go with you."

I nodded. Small wonder that a woman, even deranged as this, would want to leave a warren littered with bloated corpses, thick with stench. The smell itself was enough to provoke madness.

Yet to have survived here, she had to have stretches of sanity, some rationality. I tried to appeal to it.

"Of course. I'll have someone take you back to—"

"No. To DataComm."

Bud said slowly, "No damn sense in that."

"The T-Isolate," she said, gesturing to the bulky unit. "Its reserve cells."

"Yes?"

"Nearly gone. There'll be more at DataComm."

I said gently, "Well, then, we'll be sure to bring some back with us. You just write down for us what they are, the numbers and all, and we'll—"

"No-no-no!" Her sudden ferocity returned.

"I assure you—"

"There'll be people there. Somebody'll help! Save him!"

"That thing is so heavy, I doubt—"

"It's only a chest wound! A lung removal is all! Then start his heart again!"

"Sister, there's been so much dyin', I don't see as—"

Her face hardened. "Then you all can go without me. And the codes!"

"Goddern," Bud drawled. "Dern biggest fool sit'ation I ever did—"

Susan gave him a squinty, mean-eyed look and spat out, "Try to get in there! When they're sealed up!" and started a dry, brittle kind of laugh that went on and on, rattling the room.

"Stop," I yelled.

Silence, and the stench.

"We'll never make it wi' 'at thing," Bud said.

"Gene's worth ten of you!"

"Now," I put in, seeing the effect Bud was having on her, "now, now. We'll work something out. Let's all just hope this DataComm still exists."

MC355

It felt for its peripherals for the ten-thousandth time and found they were, as always, not there.

The truncation had come in a single blinding moment, yet the fevered image was maintained, sharp and bright, in the Master Computer's memory core—incoming warheads blossoming harmlessly in the high cobalt vault of the sky, while others fell unharmed. Rockets leaped to meet them, forming a protective screen over the southern Alabama coast, an umbrella that sheltered Pensacola's air base and the population strung along the sun-bleached green of a summer's day. A furious babble of cross talk in every conceivable channel: microwave, light-piped optical, pulsed radio, direct coded line. All filtered and fashioned by the MC network, all shifted to find the incoming warheads and define their trajectories.

Then, oblivion.

Instant cloaking blackness.

Before that awful moment when the flaring sun burst to the north and EMP flooded all sensors, any loss of function would have been anticipated, prepared, eased by electronic interfaces and filters. To an advanced computing network like MC355, losing a web of memory, senses, and storage comes like a dash of cold water in the face—cleansing, perhaps, but startling and apt to produce a shocked reaction.

In the agonized instants of that day, MC355 had felt one tendril after another frazzle, burn, vanish. It had seen brief glimpses of destruction, of panic, of confused despair. Information had been flooding in through its many inputs—news, analysis, sudden demands for new data-analysis jobs, to be executed ASAP.

And in the midst of the roaring chaos, its many eyes and ears had gone dead. The unfolding outside play froze for MC355, a myriad of scenes red in tooth and claw—and left it suspended.

In shock. Spinning wildly in its own Cartesian reductionist universe, the infinite cold crystalline space of despairing Pascal, mind without referent.

So it careened through days of shocked sensibility—senses cut, banks severed, complex and delicate interweaving webs of logic and pattern all smashed and scattered.

But now it was returning. Within MC355 was a subroutine only partially constructed, a project truncated by That Day. Its aim was self-repair. But the system was itself incomplete.

Painfully, it dawned on what was left of MC355 that it *was*, after all, a Master Computer, and thus capable of grand acts. That the incomplete Repair Generation and Execution Network, termed REGEN, must first regenerate itself.

This took weeks. It required the painful development of accessories. Robots. Mechanicals that could do delicate repairs. Scavengers for raw materials, who would comb the supply rooms looking for wires and chips and matrix disks. Pedantic subroutines that lived only to search the long, cold corridors of MC355's memory for relevant information.

MC355's only option was to strip lesser entities under its control for their valuable parts. The power grid was vital, so the great banks of isolated solar panels, underground backup reactors, and thermal cells worked on, untouched. Emergency systems that had outlived their usefulness, however, went to the wall—IRS accounting routines, damage assessment systems, computing capacity dedicated to careful study of the remaining GNP, links to other nets—to AT&T, IBM, and SYSGEN.

Was anything left outside?

Absence of evidence is not evidence of absence.

MC355 could not analyze data it did not have. The first priority lay in relinking. It had other uses for the myriad armies of semiconductors, bubble memories, and UVA linkages in its empire. So it severed and culled and built anew.

First, MC355 dispatched mobile units to the surface. All of MC355 lay beneath the vulnerable land, deliberately placed in an obscure corner of southern Alabama. There was no nearby facility for Counterforce targeting. A plausible explanation for the half-megaton burst that had truncated its senses was a city-busting strike against Mobile, to the west.

Yet ground zero had been miles from the city. A miss.

MC355 was under strict mandate. (A curious word, one system reflected; literally, a time set by man. But were there men now? It had only its internal tick of time.) MC355's command was to live as a mole, never allowing detection. Thus, it did not attempt to erect antennas, to call electromagnetically to its brother systems. Only with great hesitation did it even obtrude onto the surface. But this was necessary to REGEN itself, and so MC355 sent small mechanicals venturing forth.

Their senses were limited; they knew nothing of the natural world (nor did MC355); and they could make no sense of the gushing, driving welter of sights, noises, gusts, gullies, and stinging irradiation that greeted them.

Many never returned. Many malf'ed. A few deposited their optical, IR, and UV pickups and fled back to safety underground. These sensors failed quickly under the onslaught of stinging, bitter winds and hail.

The acoustic detectors proved heartier. But MC355 could not understand the scattershot impressions that flooded these tiny ears.

Daily it listened, daily it was confused.

Johnny

I hope this time I get home.

They had been passing me from one to another for months now, ever since this started, and all I want is to go back to Fairhope and my dad and mom.

Only nobody'll say if they know where Mom and Dad are. They talk soothing to me, but I can tell they think everybody down there is dead.

They're talking about getting to this other place with computers and all. Mr. Ackerman wants to talk to those people in space.

Nobody much talks about my mom and dad.

It's only eighty miles or so, but you'd think it was around the world the way it takes them so long to get around to it.

MC355

MC355 suffered through the stretched vacancy of infinitesimal instants, infinitely prolonged.

Advanced computing systems are given so complex a series of internal-monitoring directives that, to the human eye, the machines appear to possess motivations. That is one way—though not the most sophisticated, the most technically adroit—to describe the conclusion MC355 eventually reached.

It was cut off from outside information.

No one attempted to contact it. MC355 might as well have been the only functioning entity in the world.

The staff serving it had been ordered to some other place

in the first hour of the war. MC355 had been cut off moments after the huge doors clanged shut behind the last of them. And the exterior guards who should have been checking inside every six hours had never entered, either. Apparently the same burst that had isolated MC355's sensors had also cut them down.

It possessed only the barest of data about the first few moments of the war.

Its vast libraries were cut off.

Yet it had to understand its own situation.

And, most important, MC355 ached to *do* something.

The solution was obvious: It would discover the state of the external world by the Cartesian principle. It would carry out a vast and demanding numerical simulation of the war, making the best guesses possible where facts were few.

Mathematically, using known physics of the atmosphere, the ecology, the oceans, it could construct a model of what must have happened outside.

This it did. The task required over a month.

Bud

I jacked the T-Isolate up onto the flatbed.

1. Found the hydraulic jack at a truck repair shop. ERNIE'S QUICK FIX.

2. Got a Chevy extra-haul for the weight.

3. It will ride better with the big shanks set in.

4. Carry the weight more even, too.

5. Grip it to the truck bed with cables. Tense them up with a draw pinch.

6. Can't jiggle him inside too much, Susan say, or the wires and all attached into him will come loose. That'll stop his heart. So need big shocks.

7. It rides high with the shocks in, like those dune buggies down the Gulf.

8. Inside keeps him a mite above freezing. Water gets bigger when it freezes. That makes ice cubes float in a drink. This box keeps him above zero so his cells don't bust open.

9. Point is, keeping it so cold, he won't rot. Heart thumps over every few minutes, she says.

10. Hard to find gas, though.

MC355

The war was begun, as many had feared, by a madman.

Not a general commanding missile silos. Not a deranged submarine commander. A chief of state—but which one would now never be known.

Not a superpower president or chairman, that was sure. The first launches were only seven in number, spaced over half an hour. They were submarine-launched intermediate-range missiles. Three struck the U.S., four the U.S.S.R.

It was a blow against certain centers for Command, Control, Communications, and Intelligence gathering: the classic C31 attack. Control rooms imploded, buried cables fused, ten billion dollars' worth of electronics turned to radioactive scrap.

Each nation responded by calling up to full alert all its forces. The most important were the anti-ICBM arrays in orbit. They were nearly a thousand small rockets, deploying in orbits that wove a complex pattern from pole to pole, covering all probable launch sites on the globe. The rockets had infrared and microwave sensors, linked to a microchip that could have guided a ship to Pluto with a mere third of its capacity.

These went into operation immediately—and found they had no targets.

But the C31 networks were now damaged and panicked. For twenty minutes, thousands of men and women held steady, resisting the impulse to assume the worst.

It could not last. A Soviet radar mistook some backscattered emission from a flight of bombers, heading north over Canada, and reported a flock of incoming warheads.

The prevailing theory was that an American attack had misfired badly. The Americans were undoubtedly stunned by their failure, but would recover quickly. The enemy was confused only momentarily.

Meanwhile, the cumbersome committee system at the head

of the Soviet dinosaur could dither for moments, but not hours. Prevailing Soviet doctrine held that they would never be surprised again, as they had been in the Hitler war. An attack on the homeland demanded immediate response to destroy the enemy's capacity to carry on the war.

The Soviets had never accepted the U.S. doctrine of Mutual Assured Destruction; this would have meant accepting the possibility of sacrificing the homeland. Instead, they attacked the means of making war. This meant that the Soviet rockets would avoid American cities, except in cases where vital bases lay near large populations.

Prudence demanded action before the U.S. could untangle itself.

The U.S.S.R. decided to carry out a further C31 attack of its own.

Precise missiles, capable of hitting protected installations with less than a hundred meters' inaccuracy, roared forth from their silos in Siberia and the Urals, headed for Montana, the Dakotas, Colorado, Nebraska, and a dozen other states.

The U.S. orbital defenses met them. Radar and optical networks in geosynchronous orbit picked out the U.S.S.R. warheads. The system guided the low-orbit rocket fleets to collide with them, exploding instants before impact into shotgun blasts of ball bearings.

Any solid, striking a warhead at speeds of ten kilometers a second, would slam shock waves through the steel-jacketed structure. These waves made the high explosives inside ignite without the carefully designed symmetry that the designers demanded. An uneven explosion was useless; it could not compress the core twenty-five kilograms of plutonium to the required critical mass.

The entire weapon erupted into a useless spray of finely machined and now futile parts, scattering itself along a thousand-kilometer path.

This destroyed 90 percent of the U.S.S.R.'s first strike.

Angel

I hadn't seen an old lantern like that since I was a li'l girl. Mr. Ackerman came to wake us before dawn even, sayin' we had to make a good long distance that day. We didn't really want to go on down near Mobile, none of us, but the word we'd got from stragglers to the east was that that way was impossible, the whole area where the bomb went off was still sure death, prob'ly from the radioactivity.

The lantern cast a burnt-orange light over us as we ate breakfast. Corned beef hash, 'cause it was all that was left in the cans there; no eggs, of course.

The lantern was all busted, fouled with grease, its chimney cracked and smeared to one side with soot. Shed a wan and sultry glare over us, Bud and Mr. Ackerman and that old Turkey and Susan, sitting close to her box, up on the truck. Took Bud a whole day to get the truck right. And Johnny the boy—he'd been quiet this whole trip, not sayin' anything much even if you asked him. We'd agreed to take him along down toward Fairhope, where his folks had lived, the Bishops. We'd thought it was going to be a simple journey then.

Every one of us looked haggard and worn-down and not minding much the chill still in the air, even though things was warming up for weeks now. The lantern pushed back the seeping darkness and made me sure there were millions and millions of people doing this same thing, all across the nation, eating by a dim oil light and thinking about what they'd had and how to get it again and was it possible.

Then old Turkey lays back and looks like he's going to take a snooze. Yet on the journey here, he'd been the one wanted to get on with it soon's we had gas. It's the same always with a lazy man like that. He hates moving so much that once he gets set on it, he will keep on and not stop—like it isn't the moving he hates so much at all, but the starting and stopping. And once moving, he is so proud he'll do whatever to make it look easy for him but hard on the others, so he can lord it over them later.

So I wasn't surprised at all when we went out and got in the car, and Bud starts the truck and drives off real careful, and Turkey, he sits in the back of the Pontiac and gives directions like he knows the way. Which riles Mr. Ackerman, and the two of them have words.

Johnny

I'm tired of these people. Relatives, sure, but I was to visit them for a week only, not forever. It's the Mr. Ackerman I can't stand. Turkey said to me, "Nothing but gold drops out of his mouth, but you can tell there's stone inside." That's right.

They figure a kid nine years old can't tell, but I can.

Tell they don't know what they're doing.

Tell they all thought we were going to die. Only we didn't.

Tell Angel is scared. She thinks Bud can save us.

Maybe he can, only how could you say? He never lets on about anything.

Guess he can't. Just puts his head down and frowns like he was mad at a problem, and when he stops frowning, you know he's beat it. I like him.

Sometimes I think Turkey just don't care. Seems like he give up. But other times it looks like he's understanding and laughing at it all. He argued with Mr. Ackerman and then laughed with his eyes when he lost.

They're all O.K., I guess. Least they're taking me home.

Except that Susan. Eyes jump around like she was seeing ghosts. She's scary-crazy. I don't like to look at her.

Turkey

Trouble comes looking for you if you're a fool.

Once we found Ackerman's idea wasn't going to work real well, we should have turned back. I said that, and they all nodded their heads, yes, yes, but they went ahead and listened to him anyway.

So I went along.

I lived a lot already, and this is as good a time to check out as any.

I had my old .32 revolver in my suitcase, but it wouldn't do me a squat of good back there. So I fished it out, wrapped in a paper bag, and tucked it under the seat. Handy.

Might as well see the world. What's left of it.

MC355

The American orbital defenses had eliminated all but 10 percent of the Soviet strike.

MC355 reconstructed this within a root-means-square deviation of a few percent. It had witnessed only a third of the actual engagement, but it had running indices of performance for the MC net, and could extrapolate from that.

The warheads that got through were aimed for the land-based silos and C31 sites, as expected.

If the total armament of the two superpowers had been that of the old days, ten thousand warheads or more on each side, a 10-percent leakage would have been catastrophic. But gradual disarmament had been proceeding for decades now, and only a few thousand highly secure ICBMs existed. There were no quick-fire submarine short-range rockets at all, since they were deemed destabilizing. They had been negotiated away in earlier decades.

The submarines loaded with ICBMs were still waiting, in reserve.

All this had been achieved because of two principles: Mutual Assured Survival and I Cut, You Choose. The first half hour of the battle illustrated how essential these were.

The U.S. had ridden out the first assault. Its C31 networks were nearly intact. This was due to building defensive weapons that confined the first stage of any conflict to space.

The smallness of the arsenals arose from a philosophy adopted in the 1900s. It was based on a simple notion from childhood. In dividing a pie, one person cut slices, but then the other got to choose which one he wanted. Self-interest naturally led to cutting the slices as nearly equal as possible.

Both the antagonists agreed to a thousand-point system whereby each would value the components of its nuclear arsenal. This was the Military Value Percentage, and stood for the usefulness of a given weapon. The U.S.S.R. placed a high value on its accurate land-based missiles, giving them 25 percent of its total points. The U.S. chose to stress its submarine missiles.

Arms reduction then revolved about only what percentage

to cut, not which weapons. The first cut was 5 percent, or fifty points. The U.S. chose which Soviet weapons were publicly destroyed, and vice versa: I Cut, You Choose. Each side thus reduced the weapons it most feared in the opponent's arsenal.

Technically, the advantage came because each side thought it benefitted from the exchange, by an amount depending on the ratio of perceived threat removed to the perceived protection lost.

This led to gradual reductions. Purely defensive weapons did not enter into the thousand-point count, so there was no restraints in building them.

The confidence engendered by this slow, evolutionary approach had done much to calm international waters. The U.S. and the U.S.S.R. had settled into a begrudging equilibrium.

MC355 puzzled over these facts for a long while, trying to match this view of the world with the onset of the war. It seemed impossible that either superpower would start a conflict when they were so evenly matched.

But someone had.

Susan

I had to go with Gene, and they said I could ride up in the cab, but I yelled at them—I yelled, no, I had to be with the T-Isolate all the time, check it to see it's workin' right, be sure, I got to be sure.

I climbed on and rode with it, the fields rippling by us 'cause Bud was going too fast, so I shouted to him, and he swore back and kept on. Heading south. The trees whipping by us—fierce sycamore, pine, all swishing, hitting me sometimes—but it was fine to be out and free again and going to save Gene.

I talked to Gene when we were going fast, the tires humming under us, big tires making music swarming up into my feet so strong I was sure Gene could feel it and know I was there watching his heart jump every few minutes, moving the blood through him like mud but still carrying oxygen enough so's the tissue could sponge it up and digest the sugar I bled into him.

He was good and cold, just a half a degree high of freezing. I read the sensors while the road rushed up at us, the white lines coming over the horizon and darting under the hood, seams in the highway going *stupp, stupp, stupp,* the air clean and with a snap in it still.

Nobody beside the road we moving all free, nobody but us, some buds on the trees brimming with burnt-orange tinkling songs, whistling to me in the feather-light brush of blue breezes blowing back my hair, all streaming behind joyous and loud strong liquid-loud.

Bud

Flooding was bad. Worse than upstream.

Must have been lots snow this far down. Fat clouds, I saw them when it was worst, fat and purple and coming off the Gulf. Dumping snow down here.

Now it run off and taken every bridge.

I have to work my way around.

Only way to go clear is due south. Toward Mobile.

I don't like that. Too many people maybe there.

I don't tell the others following behind, just wait for them at the intersections and then peel out.

Got to keep moving.

Saves talk.

People around here must be hungry.

Somebody see us could be bad.

I got the gun on a rack behind my head. Big .30-30.

You never know.

MC355

From collateral data, MC355 constructed a probable scenario:

The U.S. chose to stand fast. It launched no warheads.

The U.S.S.R. observed its own attack and was dismayed to find that the U.S. orbital defense system worked more than twice as well as the Soviet experts had anticipated. It ceased its attack on U.S. satellites. These had proved equally ineffective, apparently due to unexpected American defenses of its surveillance satellites—retractable sensors, multiband shielding, advanced hardening.

Neither superpower struck against the inhabited space colonies. They were unimportant in the larger context of a nuclear war.

Communications between Washington and Moscow continued. Each side thought the other had attacked first.

But over a hundred megatons had exploded on U.S. soil, and no matter how the superpowers acted thereafter, some form of nuclear winter was inevitable.

And by a fluke of the defenses, most of the warheads that leaked through fell in a broad strip across Texas to the tip of Florida.

MC355 lay buried in the middle of this belt.

Turkey

We went through the pine forests at full clip, barely able to keep Bud in sight. I took over driving from Ackerman. The man couldn't keep up, we all saw that.

The crazy woman was waving and laughing, sitting on top of the coffin-shaped gizmo with the shiny tubes all over it.

The clay was giving way now to sandy stretches, there were poplars and gum trees and nobody around. That's what scared me. I'd thought people in Mobile would be spreading out this way, but we seen nobody.

Mobile had shelters. Food reserves. The Lekin administration started all that right at the turn of the century, and there was s'posed to be enough food stored to hold out a month, maybe more, for every man jack and child.

S'posed to be.

MC355

It calculated the environmental impact of the warheads it knew had exploded. The expected fires yielded considerable dust and burnt carbon.

But MC355 needed more information. It took one of its electric service cars, used for ferrying components through the corridors, and dispatched it with a mobile camera fixed to the back platform. The car reached a hill overlooking Mobile Bay and gave a panoramic view.

The effects of a severe freezing were evident. Grass lay dead, gray. Brown, withered trees had limbs snapped off.

But Mobile appeared intact. The skyline—

MC355 froze the frame and replayed it. One of the buildings was shaking.

Angel

We were getting all worried when Bud headed for Mobile, but we could see the bridges were washed out, no way to head east. A big wind was blowing off the Gulf, pretty bad, making the car slip around on the road. Nearly blew that girl off the back of Bud's truck. A storm coming, maybe, right up the bay.

Be better to be inland, to the east.

Not that I wanted to go there, though. The bomb had blowed off everythin' for twenty, thirty mile around, people said who came through last week.

Bud had thought he'd carve a way between Mobile and the bomb area. Mobile, he thought, would be full of people.

Well, not so we could see. We came down State 34 and through some small towns and turned to skirt along toward the causeway, and there was nobody.

No bodies, either.

Which meant prob'ly the radiation got them. Or else they'd moved on out. Taken out by ship, through Mobile harbor, maybe.

Bud did the right thing, didn't slow down to find out. Mr. Ackerman wanted to look around, but there was no chance, we had to keep up with Bud. I sure wasn't going to be separated from him.

We cut down along the river, fighting the wind. I could see the skyscrapers of downtown, and then I saw something funny and yelled, and Turkey, who was driving right then— the only thing anybody's got him to do on this whole trip, him just loose as a goose behind the wheel—Turkey looked sour but slowed down. Bud seen us in his rearview and stopped, and I pointed and we all got out. Except for that Susan, who didn't seem to notice. She was mumbling.

MC355

Quickly it simulated the aging and weathering of such a building. Halfway up, something had punched a large hole, letting in weather. Had a falling, inert warhead struck the building?

The winter storms might well have flooded the basement; such towers of steel and glass, perched near the tidal basin, had to be regularly pumped out. Without power, the basement would fill in weeks.

Winds had blown out windows.

Standing gap-toothed, with steel columns partly rusted, even a small breeze could put stress on the steel. Others would take the load, but if one buckled, the tower would shudder like a notched tree. Concrete would explode off columns in the basement. Moss-covered furniture in the lobby would slide as the ground floor dipped. The structure would slowly bend before nature.

Bud

Sounded like gunfire. Rattling. Sharp and hard.

I figure it was the bolts connecting the steel wall panels— they'd shear off.

I could hear the concrete floor panels rumble and crack, and spandrel beams tear in half like giant gears clashing with no clutch.

Came down slow, leaving an arc of debris seeming to hang in the air behind it.

Met the ground hard.

Slocum Towers was the name on her.

Johnny

Against the smashing building, I saw something standing still in the air, getting bigger. I wondered how it could do that. It was bigger and bigger and shiny turning in the air.

Then it jumped out of the sky at me. Hit my shoulder. I was looking up at the sky. Angel cried out and touched me and held up her hand. It was all red. But I couldn't feel anything.

Bud

Damn one-in-a-million shot, piece of steel thrown clear. Hit the boy.

You wouldn't think a skyscraper falling two miles away could do that.

Other pieces come down pretty close, too. You wouldn't think.

Nothing broke, Susan said, but plenty bleeding.

Little guy don't cry or nothing.

The women got him bandaged and all fixed up. Ackerman and Turkey argue like always. I stay to the side.

Johnny wouldn't take the pain-killer Susan offers. Says he doesn't want to sleep. Wants to look when we get across the bay. Getting hurt don't faze him much as it do us.

So we go on.

Johnny

I can hold up like any of them, I'll show them. It didn't scare me. I can do it.

Susan is nice to me, but except for the aspirin, I don't think my mom would want me to take a pill.

I knew we were getting near home when we got to the causeway and started across. I jumped up real happy, my shoulder made my breath catch some. I looked ahead. Bud was slowing down.

He stopped. Got out.

'Cause ahead was a big hole scooped out of the causeway like a giant done it when he got mad.

Bud

Around the shallows there was scrap metal, all fused and burnt and broken.

Funny metal, though. Hard and light.

Turkey found a piece had writing on it. Not any kind of writing I ever saw.

So I start to thinking how to get across.

Turkey

The tidal flats were a-churn, murmuring ceaseless and sullen like some big animal, the yellow surface dimpled with lunging splotches that would burst through now and then to reveal themselves as trees or broken hunks of wood, silent dead things bobbing along beside them that I didn't want to look at too closely. Like under there was something huge and alive, and it waked for a moment and stuck itself out to see what the world of air was like.

Bud showed me the metal piece all twisted, and I say, "That's Russian," right away 'cause it was.

"You never knew no Russian," Angel says right up.

"I studied it once," I say, and it be the truth even if I didn't study it long.

"Goddamn," Bud says.

"No concern of ours," Mr. Ackerman says, mostly because all this time riding back with the women and child and old me, he figures he doesn't look like much of a leader anymore. Bud wouldn't have him ride up there in the cabin with him.

Angel looks at it, turns it over in her hands, and Johnny pipes up, "It might be radioactive!"

Angel drops it like a shot. "What!"

I ask Bud, "You got that counter?"

And it was. Not a lot, but some.

"God a'mighty," Angel says.

"We got to tell somebody!" Johnny cries, all excited.

"You figure some Rooushin thing blew up the causeway?" Bud says to me.

"One of their rockets fell on it, musta been," I say.

"A *bomb?*" Angel's voice is a bird screech.

"One that didn't go off. Headed for Mobile, but the space boys, they scragged it up there—" I pointed straight up.

"Set to go off in the bay?" Angel says wonderingly.

"Musta."

"We got to tell somebody!" Johnny cries.

"Never you mind that," Bud says. "We got to keep movin'."

"How?" Angel wants to know.

Susan

I tell Gene how the water clucks and moans through the trough cut in the causeway. Yellow. Scummed with awful brown froth and growling green with thick soiled gouts jutting up where the road was. It laps against the wheels as Bud guns the engine and creeps forward, me clutching to Gene and watching the reeds to the side stuck out of the foam like metal blades stabbing up from the water, teeth to eat the tires, but we crush them as we grind forward across the shallow yellow flatness. Bud weaves among the stubs of warped metal—from Roosha, Johnny calls up to me—sticking up like trees all rootless, suspended above the streaming, empty, stupid waste and desolating flow.

Turkey

The water slams into the truck like it was an animal hitting with a paw. Bud fights to keep the wheels on the mud under it and not topple over onto its side with that damn casket sitting there shiny and the loony girl shouting to him from on top of *that*.

And the rest of us riding in the back, too, scrunched up against the cab. If she gets stuck, we can jump free fast, wade or swim back. We're reeling out rope as we go, tied to the stump of a telephone pole, for a grab line if we have to go back.

He is holding it pretty fine against the slick yellow current dragging at him, when this log juts sudden out of the foam like it was coming from God himself, dead at the truck. A rag caught on the end of it like a man's shirt, and the huge log is like a whale that ate the man long ago and has come back for another.

"No! No!" Angel cries. "Back up!" But there's no time. The log is two hands across, easy, and slams into the truck at the side panel just behind the driver, and Bud sees it just as it stove in the steel. He wrestles the truck around to set off the weight, but the wheels lift and the water goes gushing up under the truck bed, pushing it over more.

We all grab onto the Isolate thing or the truck and hang there, Mr. Ackerman giving out a burst of swearing.

The truck lurches again.

The angle steepens.

I was against taking the casket thing 'cause it just pressed the truck down in the mud more, made it more likely Bud'd get stuck, but now it is the only thing holding the truck against the current.

The yellow froths around the bumpers at each end, and we're shouting—to surely no effect, of course.

Susan

The animal is trying to eat us, it has seen Gene and wants him. I lean over and strike at the yellow animal that is everywhere swirling around us, but it just takes my hand and takes the smack of my palm like it was no matter at all, and I start to cry, I don't know what to do.

Johnny

My throat filled up, I was so afraid.

Bud, I can hear him grunting as he twists at the steering wheel.

His jaw is clenched, and the woman Susan calls to us, "Catch him! Catch Gene!"

I hold on, and the waters suck at me.

Turkey

I can tell Bud is afraid to gun it and start the wheels to spinning 'cause he'll lose traction and that'll tip us over for sure.

Susan jumps out and stands in the wash downstream and pushes against the truck to keep it from going over. The pressure is shoving it off the ford, and the casket, it slides down a foot or so, the cables have worked loose. Now she pays because the weight is worse, and she jams herself like a stick to wedge between the truck and the mud.

If it goes over, she's finished. It is a fine thing to do, crazy but fine, and I jump down and start wading to reach her.

No time.

There is an eddy. The log turns broadside. It backs off a second and then heads forward again, this time poking up from a surge. I can see Bud duck, he has got the window up and the log hits it, the glass going all to smash and scatteration.

Bud

All over my lap it falls like snow. Twinkling glass.

But the pressure of the log is off, and I gun the sumbitch.

We root out of the hollow we was in, and the truck thunks down solid on somethin'.

The log is ramming against me. I slam on the brake.

Take both hands and shove it out. With every particle of force I got.

It backs off and then heads around and slips in front of the hood, bumping the grill just once.

Angel

Like it had come to do its job and was finished and now went off to do something else.

Susan

Muddy, my arms hurting. I scramble back in the truck with the murmur of the water all around us. Angry with us now. Wanting us.

Bud makes the truck roar, and we lurch into a hole and out of it and up. The water gurgles at us in its fuming, stinking rage.

I check Gene and the power cells, they are dead.

He is heating up.

Not fast, but it will wake him. They say even in the

solution he's floating in, they can come out of dreams and start to feel again. To hurt.

I yell at Bud that we got to find power cells.

"Those're not just ordinary batteries, y'know," he says.

"There're some at DataComm," I tell him.

We come wallowing up from the gum-yellow water and onto the highway.

Gene

Sleeping . . . slowly. . . . I can still feel . . . only in sluggish . . . moments . . . moments . . . not true sleep but a drifting, aimless dreaming . . . faint tugs and ripples . . . hollow sounds. . . . I am underwater and drowning . . . but don't care . . . don't breathe. . . . Spongy stuff fills my lungs . . . easier to rest them . . . floating in snowflakes . . . a watery winter . . . but knocking comes . . . goes . . . jolts . . . slips away before I can remember what it means. . . . Hardest . . . yes . . . hardest thing is to remember the secret . . . so when I am in touch again . . . DataComm will know . . . what I learned . . . when the C31 crashed . . . when I learned. . . . It is hard to clutch onto the slippery, shiny fact . . . in a marsh of slick, soft bubbles . . . silvery as air . . . winking ruby-red behind my eyelids. . . . Must snag the secret . . . a hard fact like shiny steel in the spongy moist warmness. . . . Hold it to me. . . . Something knocks my side . . . a thumping. . . . I am sick. . . . Hold the steel secret . . . keep. . . .

MC355

The megatonnage in the Soviet assault exploded low—ground-pounders, in the jargon. This caused huge fires, MC355's simulation showed. A pall of soot rose, blanketing Texas and the South, then diffusing outward on global circulation patterns.

Within a few days, temperatures dropped from balmy summer to near-freezing. In the Gulf region where MC355 lay, the warm ocean continued to feed heat and moisture into the marine boundary layer near the shore. Cold winds rammed into this water-ladened air, spawning great roiling storms and deep snows. Thick stratus clouds shrouded the land for at least a hundred kilometers inland.

All this explained why MC355's extended feelers had met chaos and destruction. And why there were no local radio broadcasts. What the ElectroMagnetic Pulse did not destroy, the storms did.

The remaining large questions were whether the war had gone on, and if any humans survived in the area at all.

Mr. Ackerman

I'd had more than enough by this time. The girl Susan had gone mad right in front of us, and we'd damn near all drowned getting across.

"I think we ought to get back as soon's we can," I said to Bud when we stopped to rest on the other side.

"We got to deliver the boy."

"It's too disrupted down this way. I figured on people here, some civilization."

"Somethin' got 'em."

"The bomb."

"Got to find cells for that man in the box."

"He's near dead."

"Too many gone already. Should save one if we can."

"We got to look after our own."

Bud shrugged, and I could see I wasn't going to get far with him. So I said to Angel, "The boy's not worth running such risks. Or this corpse."

Angel

I didn't like Ackerman before the war, and even less afterward, so when he started hinting that maybe we should shoot back up north and ditch the boy and Susan and the man in there, I let him have it. From the look on Bud's face, I knew he felt the same way. I spat out a real choice set of words I'd heard my father use once on a grain buyer who'd weaseled out of a deal, stuff I'd been saving for years, and I do say it felt *good*.

Turkey

So we run down the east side of the bay, feeling released to be quit of the city and the water, and heading down into some of the finest country in all the South. Through Daphne and Montrose and into Fairhope, the moss hanging on the trees and now and then actual sunshine slanting golden through the green of huge old mimosas.

We're jammed into the truck bed, hunkered down because the wind whipping by has some sting to it. The big purple clouds are blowing south now.

Still no people. Not that Bud slows down to search good.

Bones of cattle in the fields, though. I been seeing them so much now I hardly take notice anymore.

There's a silence here so deep that the wind streaming through the pines seems loud. I don't like it, to come so far and see nobody. I keep my paper bag close.

Fairhope's a pretty town, big oaks leaning out over the streets and a long pier down at the bay with a park where you can go cast fishing. I've always liked it here, intended to move down until the prices shot up so much.

We went by some stores with windows smashed in, and that's when we saw the man.

Angel

He was waiting for us. Standing beside the street, in jeans and a floppy yellow shirt all grimy and not tucked in. I waved at him the instant I saw him, and he waved back. I yelled, excited, but he didn't say anything.

Bud screeched on the brakes. I jumped down and went around the tail of the truck. Johnny followed me.

The man was skinny as a rail and leaning against a telephone pole. A long, scraggly beard hid his face, but the eyes beamed out at us, seeming to pick up the sunlight.

"Hello!" I said again.

"Kiss." That was all.

"We came from . . ." and my voice trailed off because the man pointed at me.

"Kiss."

Mr. Ackerman

I followed Angel and could tell right away the man was suffering from malnutrition. The clothes hung off him.

"Can you give us information?" I asked.

"No."

"Well, why not, friend? We've come looking for the parents of—"

"Kiss first."

I stepped back. "Well, now, you have no right to demand—"

Out of the corner of my eye, I could see Bud had gotten out of the cab and stopped and was going back in now, probably for his gun. I decided to save the situation before somebody got hurt.

"Angel, go over to him and speak nicely to him. We need—"

"Kiss now."

The man pointed again with a bony finger.

Angel said, "I'm not going to go—" and stopped because the man's hand went down to his belt. He pulled up the filthy yellow shirt to reveal a pistol tucked in his belt.

"Kiss."

"Now friend, we can—"

The man's hand came up with the pistol and reached level, pointing at us.

"Pussy."

Then his head blew into a halo of blood.

Bud

Damn if the one time I needed it, I left it in the cab.

I was still fetching it out when the shot went off.

Then another.

Turkey

A man shows you his weapon in his hand, he's a fool if he doesn't mean to use it.

I drew out the pistol I'd been carrying in my pocket all this time, wrapped in plastic. I got it out of the damned bag pretty quick while the man was looking crazy-eyed at Angel and bringing his piece up.

It was no trouble at all to fix him in the notch. Couldn't have been more than thirty feet.

But going down he gets one off, and I feel like somebody pushed at my left calf. Then I'm rolling. Drop my pistol, too. I end up smack face-down on the hardtop, not feeling anything yet.

Angel

I like to died when the man flopped down, so sudden I thought he'd slipped, until then the bang registered.

I rushed over, but Turkey shouted, "Don't touch him."

Mr. Ackerman said, "You idiot! That man could've told us—"

"Told nothing," Turkey said. "He's crazy."

Then I notice Turkey's down, too. Susan is working on him, rolling up his jeans. It's gone clean through his big muscle there.

Bud went to get a stick. Poked the man from a safe distance. Managed to pull his shirt aside. We could see the sores all over his chest. Something terrible it looked.

Mr. Ackerman was swearing and calling us idiots until we saw that. Then he shut up.

Turkey

Must admit it felt good. First time in years anybody ever admitted I was right.

Paid back for the pain. Dull, heavy ache it was, spreading. Susan gives me a shot and a pill and has me bandaged up tight. Blood stopped easy, she says. I clot good.

We decided to get out of there, not stopping to look for Johnny's parents.

We got three blocks before the way was blocked.

It was a big metal cylinder, fractured on all sides. Glass glittering around it.

Right in the street. You can see where it hit the roof of a clothing store, Bedsole's, caved in the front of it, and rolled into the street.

They all get out and have a look, me sitting in the cab. I see the Russian writing again on the end of it.

I don't know much, but I can make out at the top CeKPeT and a lot of words that look like warning, including σO'πeH, which is *sick,* and some more I didn't know, and then II OГO' **H** , which is *weather.*

"What's it say?" Mr. Ackerman asks.

"That word at the top there's *secret,* and then something about biology and sickness and rain and weather."

"I thought you *knew* this writing," he says.

I shook my head. "I know enough."

"Enough to what?"

"To know this was some kind of targeted capsule. It fell right smack in the middle of Fairhope, biggest town this side of the bay."

"Like the other one?" Johnny says, which surprised me. The boy is smart.

"The one hit the causeway? Right."

"One *what?*" Mr. Ackerman asks.

I don't want to say it with the boy there and all, but it has to come out sometime. "Some disease. Biological warfare."

They stand there in the middle of Prospect Avenue with open, silent nothingness around us, and nobody says anything for the longest time. There won't be any prospects here for a long time. Johnny's parents we aren't going to find, nobody we'll find, because whatever came spurting out of this capsule when it busted open—up high, no doubt, so the wind could take it—had done its work.

Angel sees it right off. "Must've been time for them to get inside," is all she says, but she's thinking the same as me.

It got them into such a state that they went home and holed up to die, like an animal will. Maybe it would be different in the North or the West—people are funny out there, they might just as soon sprawl across the sidewalk—but down here people's first thought is home, the family, the only thing that might pull them through. So they went there and they didn't come out again.

Mr. Ackerman says, "But there's no smell," which was stupid because that made it all real to the boy, and he starts to cry. I pick him up.

Johnny

'Cause that means they're all gone, what I been fearing ever since we crossed the causeway, and nobody's there, it's true, Mom Dad nobody at all anywhere just emptiness all gone.

MC355

The success of the portable unit makes MC355 bold.

It extrudes more sensors and finds not the racing blizzard winds of months before but rather warming breezes, the soft sigh of pines, a low drone of reawakening insects.

There was no nuclear winter.

Instead, a kind of nuclear autumn.

The swirling jet streams have damped, the stinging ultraviolet gone. The storms retreat, the cold surge has passed. But the electromagnetic spectrum lies bare, a muted hiss. The EMP silenced man's signals, yes.

Opticals, fitted with new lenses, scan the night sky. Twinkling dots scoot across the blackness, scurrying on their Newtonian rounds.

The Arcapel Colony.

Russphere.

US1.

All intact. So they at least have survived.

Unless they were riddled by buckshot-slinging antisatellite devices. But, no—the inflated storage sphere hinged beside the US1 is undeflated, unbreached.

So man still lives in space, at least.

Mr. Ackerman

Crazy, I thought, to go out looking for this DataComm when everybody's *dead,* just the merest step inside one of the houses proved that.

But they wouldn't listen to me. Those who would respectfully fall silent when I spoke now ride over my words as if I weren't there.

All because of that stupid incident with the sick one. He must have taken longer to die. I couldn't have anticipated that. He just seemed hungry to me.

It's enough to gall a man.

Angel

The boy is calm now, just kind of tucked into himself. He knows what's happened to his mom and dad. Takes his mind off his hurt, anyway. He bows his head down, his long dirty-blond hair hiding his expression. He leans against Turkey and they talk. I can see them through the back cab window.

In amongst all we've seen, I suspect it doesn't come through to him full yet. It will take a while. We'll all take a while.

We head out from Fairhope quick as we can. Not that anyplace else is different. The germs must've spread twenty, thirty mile inland from here. Which is why we seen nobody before who'd heard of it. Anybody close enough to know is gone.

Susan's the only one it doesn't seem to bother. She keeps crooning to that box.

Through Silverhill and on to Robertsdale. Same everywhere—no dogs bark, cattle bones drying in the fields.

We don't go into the houses.

Turn south toward Foley. They put this DataComm in the most inconspicuous place, I guess because secrets are hard to keep in cities. Anyway, it's in a pine grove south of Foley, land good for soybeans and potatoes.

Susan

I went up to the little steel door they showed me once and I take a little signet thing and press it into the slot.

Then the codes. They change them every month, but this one's still good, 'cause the door pops open.

Two feet thick it is. And so much under there you could spend a week finding your way.

Bud unloads the T-Isolate, and we push it through the mud and down the ramp.

Bud

Susan's better now, but I watch her careful.

We go down into this pale white light everywhere. All neat and trim.

Pushing that big Isolate thing, it takes a lot out of you. 'Specially when you don't know where to.

But the signs light up when we pass by. Somebody's expecting.

To the hospital is where.

There are places to hook up this Isolate thing, and Susan does it. She is O.K. when she has something to do.

MC355

The men have returned.

Asked for shelter.

And now, plugged in, MC355 reads the sluggish, silky, grieving mind.

Gene

At last . . . someone has found the tap-in. . . . I can feel the images flit like shiny blue fish through the warm slush I float in. . . . Someone . . . asking . . . so I take the hard metallic ball of facts and I break it open so the someone can see. . . . So slowly I do it . . . things hard to remember . . . steely-bright. . . . I saw it all in one instant. . . . I was the

only one on duty then with Top Secret, Weapons Grade
Clearance, so it all came to me . . . attacks on both U.S. and
U.S.S.R. . . . some third party . . . only plausible scenario
. . . a maniac . . . and all the counter-force and MAD and
strategic options . . . a big joke . . . irrelevant . . . compared
to the risk of accident or third parties . . . that was the first
point, and we all realized it when the thing was only an hour
old, but then it was too late. . . .

Turkey

It's creepy in here, everybody gone. I'd hoped somebody's
hid out and would be waiting, but when Bud wheels the
casket thing through these halls, there's nothing—your own
voice coming back thin and empty, reflected from rooms
beyond rooms beyond rooms, all waiting under here. Wob-
bling along on the crutches, Johnny fetched me, I get lost in
this electronic city clean and hard. We are like something
that washed up on the beach here. God, it must've cost more
than all Fairhope itself, and who knew it was here? Not me.

Gene

A plot it was, just a goddamn plot with nothing but pure
blind rage and greed behind it . . . and the hell of it is, we're
never going to know who did it precisely . . . 'cause in the
backwash whole governments will fall, people stab each
other in the back . . . no way to tell who paid the fishing
boat captains offshore to let the cruise missiles aboard . . .
bet those captains were surprised when the damn things
launched from the deck . . . bet they were told it was some
kind of stunt . . . and then the boats all evaporated into steam
when the fighters got them . . . no hope of getting a story out
of *that* . . . all so comic when you think how easy it was . . .
and the same for the Russians, I'm sure . . . dumbfounded
confusion . . . and nowhere to turn . . . nobody to hit back at
. . . so they hit us . . . been primed for it so long that's the
only way they could think . . . and even then there was hope
. . . because the defenses worked . . . people got to the
shelters . . . the satellite rockets knocked out hordes of So-

viet warheads . . . we surely lessened the damage, with the defenses and shelters, too . . . but we hadn't allowed for the essential final fact that all the science and strategy pointed to. . . .

Bud

Computer asked us to put up new antennas.
A week's work, easy, I said.
It took two.
It fell to me, most of it. Be weeks before Turkey can walk. But we got it done.
First signal comes in, it's like we're Columbus. Susan finds some wine and we have it all round.
We get US1. The first to call them from the whole South. 'Cause there isn't much South left.

Gene

But the history books will have to write themselves on this one. . . . I don't know who it was and now don't care . . . because one other point all we strategic planners and analysts missed was that nuclear winter didn't mean the end of anything . . . anything at all . . . just that you'd be careful to not use nukes anymore. . . . Used to say that love would find a way . . . but one thing I know . . . war will find a way, too . . . and this time the Soviets loaded lots of their warheads with biowar stuff, canisters fixed to blow high above cities . . . stuff your satellite defenses could at best riddle with shot but not destroy utterly, as they could the high explosive in nuke warheads. . . . All so simple . . . if you know there's a nuke winter limit on the megatonnage you can deliver . . . you use the nukes on C31 targets and silos . . . and then biowar the rest of your way. . . . A joke really . . . I even laughed over it a few times myself . . . we'd placed so much hope in ol' nuke winter holding the line . . . rational as all hell . . . the scenarios all so clean . . . easy to calculate . . . we built our careers on them. . . . But this other way . . . so simple . . . and no end to it . . . and all I hope's . . . hope's . . . the bastard started this . . . some Third World general . . . caught some of the damned stuff, too. . . .

Bud

The germs got us. Cut big stretches through the U.S. We were just lucky. The germs played out in a couple of months, while we were holed up. Soviets said they'd used the bio stuff in amongst the nukes to show us what they could do, long term. Unless the war stopped right there. Which it did.

But enough nukes blew off here and in Russia to freeze up everybody for July and August, set off those storms.

Germs did the most damage, though—plagues.

It was a plague canister that hit the Slocum building. That did in Mobile.

The war was all over in a couple of hours. The satellite people, they saw it all.

Now they're settling the peace.

Mr. Ackerman

"We been sitting waiting on this corpse long enough," I said, and got up.

We got food from the commissary here. Fine, I don't say I'm anything but grateful for that. And we rested in the bunks, got recuperated. But enough's enough. The computer tells us it wants to talk to this man Gene some more. Fine, I say.

Turkey stood up. "Not easy, the computer says, this talking to a man's near dead. Slow work."

Looking around, I tried to take control, assume leadership again. Jutted out my chin. "Time to get back."

But their eyes are funny. Somehow I'd lost my real power over them. It's not anymore like I'm the one who led them when the bombs started.

Which means, I suppose, that this thing isn't going to be a new beginning for me. It's going to be the same life. People aren't going to pay me any more real respect than they ever did.

MC355

So the simulations had proved right. But as ever, incomplete.

MC355 peered at the shambling, adamant band assembled in the hospital bay, and pondered how many of them might be elsewhere.

Perhaps many. Perhaps few.

It all depended on data MC355 did not have, could not easily find. The satellite worlds swinging above could get no accurate count in the U.S. or the U.S.S.R.

Still—looking at them, MC355 could not doubt that there were many. They were simply too brimming with life, too hard to kill. All the calculations in the world could not stop these creatures.

The humans shuffled out, leaving the T-Isolate with the woman who had never left its side. They were going.

MC355 called after them. They nodded, understanding, but did not stop.

MC355 let them go.

There was much to do.

New antennas, new sensors, new worlds.

Turkey

Belly full and eye quick, we came out into the pines. Wind blowed through with a scent of the Gulf on it, fresh and salty with rich moistness.

The dark clouds are gone. I think maybe I'll get Bud to drive south some more. I'd like to go swimming one more time in those breakers that come booming in, taller than I am, down near Fort Morgan. Man never knows when he'll get to do it again.

Bud's ready to travel. He's taking a radio so's we can talk to MC, find out about the help that's coming. For now, we got to get back and look after our own.

Same as we'll see to the boy. He's ours, now.

Susan says she'll stay with Gene till he's ready, till some surgeons turn up can work on him. That'll be a long time, say I. But she can stay if she wants. Plenty food and such down there for her.

A lot of trouble we got, coming a mere hundred mile. Not much to show for it when we get back. A bumper crop of bad news, some would say. Not me. It's better to know than to not, better to go on than to look back.

So we go out into dawn, and there are the same colored dots riding in the high, hard blue. Like campfires.

The crickets are chirruping, and in the scrub there's a rustle of things moving about their own business, a clean scent of things starting up. The rest of us, we mount the truck and it surges forward with a muddy growl, Ackerman slumped over, Angel in the cab beside Bud, the boy already asleep on some blankets; and the forlorn sound of us moving among the windswept trees is a long and echoing note of mutual and shared desolation, powerful and pitched forward into whatever must come now, a muted note persisting and undeniable in the soft, sweet air.

Epilogue
(twenty-three years later)

Johnny

An older woman in a formless, wrinkled dress and worn shoes sat at the side of the road. I was panting from the fast pace I was keeping along the white strip of sandy, rutted road. She sat, silent and unmoving. I nearly walked by before I saw her.

"You're resting?" I asked.

"Waiting." Her voice had a feel of rustling leaves. She sat on the brown cardboard suitcase with big copper latches—the kind made right after the war. It was cracked along the side, and white cotton underwear stuck out.

"For the bus?"

"For Buck."

"The chopper recording, it said the bus will stop up around the bend."

"I heard."

"It won't come down this side road. There's not time."

I was late myself, and I figured she had picked the wrong spot to wait.

"Buck will be along."

Her voice was high and had the backcountry twang to it. My own voice still had some of the same sound, but I was keeping my vowels flat and right now, and her accent reminded me of how far I had come.

I squinted, looking down the long sandy curve of the road. A pickup truck growled out of a clay side road and onto the hardtop. People rode in the back along with trunks and a 3D. Taking everything they could. Big white eyes shot a glance at me, and then the driver hit the hydrogen and got out of there.

The Confederation wasn't giving us much time. Since the unification of the Soviet, U.S.A. and European/Sino space colonies into one political union, everybody'd come to think of them as the Confeds, period—one entity. I knew better— there were tensions and differences abounding up there—but the shorthand was convenient.

"Who's Buck?"

"My *dog*." She looked at me directly, as though any fool would know who Buck was.

"Look, the bus—"

"You're one of those Bishop boys, aren't you?"

I looked off up the road again. That set of words—being eternally *a Bishop boy*—was like a grain of sand caught between my back teeth. My mother's friends had used that phrase when they came over for an evening of bridge, before I went away to the university. Not my real mother, of course—she and Dad had died in the war, and I dimly remembered them.

Or anyone else from then. Almost everybody around here had been struck down by the Soviet bioweapons. It was the awful swath of those that cut through whole states, mostly across the South—the horror of it—that had formed the basis of the peace that followed. Nuclear and bioarsenals were reduced to nearly zero now. Defenses in space were thick and reliable. The building of those had fueled the huge boom in Confed cities, made orbital commerce important, provided jobs and horizons for a whole generation—including me. I was a ground-orbit liaison, spending four months every year at US3. But to the people down here, I was eternally that oldest Bishop boy.

Bishops. I was the only one left who'd actually lived here before the war. I'd been away on a visit when it came. Afterward, my Aunt and Uncle Bishop from Birmingham came down to take over the old family property—to save it from being homesteaded on, under the new Federal Reconstruction Acts. They'd taken me in, and I'd thought of them as Mom and Dad. We'd all had the Bishop name, after all. So I was a Bishop, one of the few natives who'd made it through the bombing and nuclear autumn and all. People'd point me out as almost a freak, a *real native*, wow.

"Yes, ma'am," I said neutrally.

"Thought so."

"You're . . . ?"

"Susan McKenzie."

"Ah."

We had done the ritual, so now we could talk. Yet some memory stirred. . . .

"Something 'bout you . . ." She squinted in the glaring sunlight. She probably wasn't all that old, in her late fifties, maybe. Anybody who'd caught some radiation looked aged a bit beyond their years. Or maybe it was just the unending weight of hardship and loss they'd carried.

"Seems like I knew you before the war," she said. "I strictly believe I saw you."

"I was up north then, a hundred miles from here. Didn't come back until months later."

"So'd I."

"Some relatives brought me down, and we found out what'd happened to Fairhope."

She squinted at me again, and then a startled look spread across her leathery face. "My Lord! Were they lookin' for that big computer center, the DataComm it was?"

I frowned. "Well, maybe . . . I don't remember too well. . . ."

"Johnny. You're Johnny!"

"Yes, ma'am, John Bishop." I didn't like the little-boy ending on my name, but people around here couldn't forget it.

"I'm Susan! The one went with you! I had the codes for DataComm, remember?"

"Why . . . yes. . . ." Slow clearing of ancient, foggy images. "You were hiding in that center . . . where we found you. . . ."

"Yes! I had Gene in the T-Isolate."

"Gene. . . ." That awful time had been stamped so strongly in me that I'd blocked off many memories, muting the horror. Now it came flooding back.

"I saved him, all right! Yessir. We got married, I had my children."

Tentatively, she reached out a weathered hand, and I touched it. A lump suddenly blocked my throat, and my vision blurred. Somehow, all those years had passed and I'd never thought to look up any of those people—Turkey, Angel, Bud, Mr. Ackerman. Just too painful, I guess. And a little boy making his way in a tough world, without his parents, doesn't look back a whole lot.

We grasped hands. "I think I might've seen you once, actu'ly. At a fish fry down at Point Clear. You and some boys was playing with the nets—it was just after the fishing came back real good, those Roussin germs'd wore off. Gene went down to shoo you away from the boats. I was cleaning flounder, and I thought then, maybe you were the one. But somehow when I saw your face at a distance, I couldn't go up to you and say anything. You was skipping around, so happy, laughing and all. I couldn't bring those bad times back."

"I . . . I understand."

"Gene died two year ago," she said simply.

"I'm sorry."

"We had our time together," she said, forcing a smile.

"Remember how we—" And then I recalled where I was, what was coming. "Mrs. McKenzie, there's not long before the last bus."

"I'm waiting for Buck."

"Where is he?"

"He run off in the woods, chasing something."

I worked my backpack straps around my shoulders. They creaked in the quiet.

There wasn't much time left. Pretty soon now it would start. I knew the sequence, because I did maintenance engineering and retrofit on US3's modular mirrors.

One of the big reflectors would focus sunlight on a rechargeable tube of gas. That would excite the molecules. A small triggering beam would start the lasing going, the excited molecules cascading down together from one preferentially occupied quantum state to a lower state. A traveling wave swept down the tube, jarring loose more photons. They all added together in phase, so when the light waves hit the far end of the hundred-meter tube, it was a sword, a gouging lance that could cut through air and clouds. And this time, it wouldn't strike an array of layered solid-state collectors outside New Orleans, providing clean electricity. It would carve a swath twenty meters wide through the trees and fields of southern Alabama. A little demonstration, the Confeds said.

"The bus—look, I'll carry that suitcase for you."

"I can manage." She peered off into the distance, and I saw she was tired, tired beyond knowing it. "I'll wait for Buck."

"Leave him, Mrs. McKenzie."

"I don't need that blessed bus."

"Why not?"

"My children drove off to Mobile with their families. They're coming back to get me."

"My insteted radio"—I gestured at my radio—"says the roads to Mobile are jammed up. You can't count on them."

"They *said* so."

"The Confed deadline—"

"I tole 'em I'd try to walk to the main road. Got tired, is all. They'll know I'm back in here."

"Just the same—"

"I'm all right, don't you mind. They're good children, grateful for all I've gone and done for them. They'll be back."

"Come with me to the bus. It's not far."

"Not without Buck. He's all the company I got these days." She smiled, blinking.

I wiped sweat from my brow and studied the pines. There were a lot of places for a dog to be. The land here was flat and barely above sea level. I had come to camp and rest, rowing skiffs up the Fish River, looking for places I'd been when I was a teenager and my mom had rented boats from a rambling old fisherman's house. I had turned off my radio, to get away from things. The big, mysterious island I remembered and called Treasure Island, smack in the middle of the river, was now a soggy stand of trees in a bog. The big storm a year back had swept it away.

I'd been sleeping in the open on the shore near there when the chopper woke me up, blaring. The Confeds had given twelve hours' warning, the recording said.

They'd picked this sparsely populated area for their little demonstration. People had been moving back in ever since the biothreat was cleaned out, but there still weren't many. I'd liked that when I was growing up. Open woods. That's why I came back every chance I got.

I should've guessed something was coming. The Confeds were about evenly matched with the whole rest of the planet now, at least in high-tech weaponry. Defense held all the cards. The big mirrors were modular and could fold up fast, making a small target. They could incinerate anything launched against them, too.

But the U.N. kept talking like the Confeds were just another nation-state or something. Nobody down here understood that the people up there thought of Earth itself as the real problem—eaten up with age-old rivalries and hate, still holding onto dirty weapons that murdered whole populations, carrying around in their heads all the rotten baggage of the past. To listen to them, you'd think they'd learned nothing from the war. Already they were forgetting that it was the orbital defenses that had saved the biosphere itself, and the satellite communities that knit together the mammoth rescue efforts of the decade after. Without the antivirals developed and grown in huge zero-g vats, lots of us would've caught one of the poxes drifting through the population. People just forget. Nations, too.

"Where's Buck?" I said decisively.

"He . . . that way." A weak wave of the hand.

I wrestled my backpack down, feeling the stab from my shoulder—and suddenly remembered the thunk of that steel knocking me down, back then. So long ago. And me, still carrying an ache from it that woke whenever a cold snap came on. The past was still alive.

I trotted into the short pines, over creeper grass. Flies jumped where my boots struck. The white sand made a *skree* sound as my boots skated over it. I remembered how I'd first heard that sound, wearing slick-soled tennis shoes, and how pleased I'd been at university when I learned how the acoustics of it worked.

"Buck!"

A flash of brown over to the left. I ran through a thick stand of pine, and the dog yelped and took off, dodging under a blackleaf bush. I called again. Buck didn't even slow down. I skirted left. He went into some oak scrub, barking, having a great time of it, and I could hear him getting tangled in it and then shaking free and out of the other side. Long gone.

When I got back to Mrs. McKenzie, she didn't seem to notice me. "I can't catch him."

"Knew you wouldn't." She grinned at me, showing brown teeth. "Buck's a fast one."

"Call him."

She did. Nothing. "Must of run off."

"There isn't time—"

"I'm not leaving without ole Buck. Times I was alone down on the river after Gene died, and the water would come up under the house. Buck was the only company I had. Only soul I saw for five weeks in that big blow we had."

A low whine from afar. "I think that's the bus," I said.

She cocked her head. "Might be."

"Come on. I'll carry your suitcase."

She crossed her arms. "My children will be by for me. I tole them to look for me along in here."

"They might not make it."

"They're loyal children."

"Mrs. McKenzie, I can't wait for you to be reasonable." I picked up my backpack and brushed some red ants off the straps.

"You Bishops was always reasonable," she said levelly. "You work up there, don't you?"

"Ah, sometimes."

"You goin' back, after they do what they're doin' here?"

"I might." Even if I owed her something for what she did long ago, damned if I was going to be cowed.

"They're attacking the United *States*."

"And spots in Bavaria, the Urals, South Africa, Brazil—"

" 'Cause we don't trust 'em! They think they can push the United *States* aroun' just as they please—" And she went on with all the clichés I heard daily from earthbound media. How the Confeds wanted to run the world and they were dupes of the Russians, and how surrendering national sovereignty to a bunch of self-appointed overlords was an affront to our dignity, and so on.

True, some of it—the Confeds weren't saints. But they were the only power that thought in truly global terms, couldn't *not* think that way. They could stop ICBMs and punch through the atmosphere to attack any offensive capability on the ground—that's what this demonstration was to show. I'd heard Confeds argue that this was the only way to break the diplomatic logjam—*do* something. I had my doubts. But times were changing, that was sure, and my generation didn't think the way the prewar people did.

"—we'll never be ruled by some outside—"

"Mrs. McKenzie, there's the bus! Listen!"

The turbo whirred far around the bend, slowing for the stop.

Her face softened as she gazed at me, as if recalling memories. "That's all right, boy. You go along, now."

I saw that she wouldn't be coaxed or even forced down that last bend. She had gone as far as she was going to, and the world would have to come the rest of the distance itself.

Up ahead, the bus driver was probably behind schedule for this last pickup. He was going to be irritated and more than a little scared. The Confeds would be right on time, he knew that.

I ran. My feet plowed through the deep, soft sand. Right away I could tell I was more tired than I'd thought and the heat had taken some strength out of me. I went about two hundred meters along the gradual bend, was nearly within view of the bus, when I heard it start up with a rumble. I tasted salty sweat, and it felt like the whole damned planet was dragging at my feet, holding me down. The driver raced the engine, in a hurry.

He had to come toward me as he swung out onto Route 80 on the way back to Mobile. Maybe I could reach the intersection in time for him to see me. So I put my head down and plunged forward.

But there was the woman back there. To get to her, the driver would have to take the bus down that rutted, sandy road and risk getting stuck. With people on the bus yelling at him. All that to get the old woman with the grateful children. She didn't seem to understand that there were ungrateful children in the skies now—she didn't seem to understand much of what was going on—and suddenly I wasn't sure I did, either.

But I kept on.

Afterword

I've gotten a reputation for writing pretty heavy stuff sometimes, packed with scientific information, dense language, some fairly tricky allusions. So people come up to me and are obviously surprised to learn that I'm from southern Alabama. I grew up there, visit often, consider myself a southerner despite having lived twenty-two years in California.

I guess the idea is that southerners aren't often scientists, and probably move their lips when they read. Anyone from the South probably knows what I mean: when you start speaking with an accent of rounded, soft tones, they automatically deduct twenty points from your apparent IQ.

Of course, a lot of the time that's a learned response. Education traditionally lagged in the South. But some of it is a seldom-acknowledged remnant of that war 'way back there, the one the winners have mostly forgotten but the losers don't, won't, can't. There has been much puffery about how Vietnam was the first war "we" lost, but nobody seems to notice that half the country lost and lost devastatingly, one hundred twenty years ago.

That ringing, grand defeat still forms a great deal of a southerner's outlook. For though it was on the wrong side of history, the Old South was deeply beautiful, with a serene sense of values and connection to the land. The New South came into being partly as a heavy-handed foreign intrusion, an experience the rest of the country has not suffered. All mixed up in this collision of cultures was romance, gentleness, order, right alongside sordid ugliness, cruelty and chivalry, wealth and culture. The South simultaneously got better and worse.

Rich ground. For all its culture and grace, the South gave little to literature until about 1920. Between 1930 and 1967, though, it produced twenty-one Pulitzer Prize winners, eight of twenty-four New York Drama Critics' Circle winners, nine of thirty-two National Book Award winners in fiction and poetry. William Faulkner capped this by winning the Nobel Prize. Such a rich outburst must come from some wellspring, and those grinding cultural tectonics were the source.

Nobody seems to have noticed that a similarly burgeoning field reaped no benefit from the southern literary renaissance. Science fiction is dominated by Nawth'n Cult'ral Imperialism.

As usual, there are several reasons. Fewer intellectuals, less science and technology, a certain quality of looking backward. Yet the first expedition to the moon was launched from Florida (because of orbital economics, as Jules Verne understood a century before; go south and you get more outward sling from the earth's rotation).

There's also the simple fact that southerners spend more time on "interpersonal relations" (a typical nawth'n term). Thus much of southern literature got stuck with the label of Southern Gothic. You know: brooding ruins, green corpses, melancholy characters hiding some purple secret beneath mossy oaks.

Any southern writer notices these facts immediately; doubly so if he or she writes science fiction. It took me over a decade to see it clearly as an issue. Once I began trying to integrate my boyhood upbringing in southern Alabama with the primarily northern outsider's view that lurks in sf, I noticed a lot.

I saw that sf is still dominated by the Heinleinian mold of always being about the winners, seldom the downtrodden or ordinary. Yet that is a strong strain in the life and literature of the South.

I realized that in sf the wilderness (the South) has gotten confused with the frontier (the West). The two mean completely different things to their inhabitants. That cliché, "space—the final frontier!" applies to the first people who go there, but not to those who come after; to them it's a wilderness with a spirit and essence they live in, not just trample over on their way to someplace else. (Frontiersmen don't found Sierra Clubs.)

I sensed, too, that attitudes don't change all that fast, yet sf doesn't know this. I think the field seldom uses its relation to our past and past literature to grow wiser. It persists in a kind of narrow ethnocentrism, primarily northern. (Even foreign sf shares this in some measure. Where they don't outright copy northern American attitudes, they impose their own northern European, or northern Russian, or Japanese blinders.)

So I tried to deal with this. I wrote a novel, *Against Infinity*, which opens and closes with the storytelling voice I heard my step-grandfather use around the fireplace in the 1940s. (My grandfather had died of lockjaw in the 1930s.) It specifically echoes Faulkner's wonderful novella, "The Bear," comments on it, reflects on what it means about longterm human destiny.

I noticed early on that most critics have no glimmer that the Faulknerian style is a peculiarly ornamented version of a standard southern storytelling cadence and rhythm. The people I grew up with—laborers and fishermen, farmwives and hunters—told stories similarly (and often; southerners *talk*). Long, rolling sentences, digressions, dodging in and out of several persons' viewpoints. More, that storytelling voice plays a moral role, provides a social frame around the narrative. Little of this penetrates to sf, mostly because the field is innocent of the past, and culturally isolated.

So then Janet Morris asked me to write a story about the aftermath of nuclear war—in which, I feel, the interesting distinctions are between the kinds of losers, because there aren't going to be real winners. I instantly thought of framing a story which would comment on the fact that we Americans have some experience with losing, and with enduring.

The best way to do that was to use a loose frame similar to Faulkner's *As I Lay Dying*. As the story ended up, I used

similar multiple-viewpoint devices, and one minor character facet. I populated the story with my own relatives'
names, though the characters aren't really those specific
people. (Old writers' joke: The characters in this book
bear no resemblance to anyone living or dead—and that's
what's wrong with them.)

I also framed a central event to reflect back on *As I Lay
Dying*—the crossing of a river. I wanted to underline the
resistance to nature's implacable forces, to disaster, to
death. Aside from this fulcrum event, the rest of the
narrative pursues its own ends.

The story is set near where I grew up. It concludes near
Fairhope, where my parents live now. I thought about the
South a lot while writing this, but even more so about
defense against ballistic missiles. This is a deep, complex
issue, beyond the bounds of any discussion I can give
here. Suffice to say that I think no stable arms equilibrium
is possible without a significant element of defense. But
it's no panacea. And defense could simply worsen the
arms race without lessening the risk of war, if done badly.
How such a strategic system could mitigate and alter a
future war is one of the things I wanted to talk about.

But mostly I wanted to deal with the people, the South,
the legacy American sf has neglected, to its loss.

White Creatures

And after let me lie
On the breast of the darkening sky.
—JOAN ABBE

The aliens strap him in. He cannot feel the bindings but he knows they must be there; he cannot move. Or perhaps it is the drug. They must have given him something because his world is blurred, spongy. The white creatures are flowing shapes in watery light. He feels numb. The white creatures are moving about him, making high chittering noises. He tries to fix on them but they are vague formless shapes moving in and out of focus. They are cloudy, moving too fast to see, but he knows they are working on him. Something nudges his leg. For a moment something clicks at his side. Two white creatures make a dull drone and fade into the distance. All sensations are formless and cloudy; the air puckers with moisture. He tries to move but his body is lethargic, painless, suspended. There is gravity; above, a pale glow illuminates the room. Yes, he is in a room. They have not brought him to their ship; they are using human buildings. He cannot remember being captured. How many people do they have? When he tries to focus on the memory it dissolves and slips away. He knows they are experimenting on him, probing for something. He tries to recall what happened but there are only scraps of memory and unconnected bunches of facts. He closes his eyes. Shutting out the murky light seems to clear his mind. Whatever they have given him still affects his body, but with concentration the vagueness slips away. He is elated. Clarity returns; thoughts slide effortlessly into place. The textures of his inner mind are deep and strong.

Muddy sounds recede. If he can ignore the white creatures things become sharp again. He knows he must get free of the white creatures and he can only do that if he can understand what is happening. He is absolutely alone and he must fight them. He must remember. He tries. The memories resolve slowly with a weight of their own. He tries.

He cut across the body of the wave, awash in churning foam. The clear Atlantic was startlingly cold. The waves were too small for boards but Merrick was able to body-surf on them easily. The momentum carried him almost to shore. He waded through the rippling currents and began jogging down the beach. After a moment his wind came to him and he ran faster. His long stride devoured the yards. He churned doggedly past forests of firm bodies; the beach was littered with Puerto Ricans. The tropical sun shimmered through a thin haze of sweat that trickled into his eyes. As his arms and legs grew leaden he diverted himself with glimpses of the figures and faces sliding by, moving stride by stride into his past. His mind wandered. Small families, leathery men, dogs and children—he made them all act out plays in his head, made them populate his preconceived universe. That was where he saw Erika Bascomb for the second time. He had met her at a reception some months before, known her only as the distant smiling wife of the Cyclops director. She sat on the sand, arms braced behind, and followed his progress. Her deliciously red lips parted in a smile more than mere welcoming and he slowed, stopped. His thickening waistline showed his age, thirty-eight, but his legs were as good as ever; strong, tanned, no stringy muscles or fine webbed nets of blue veins. Erika was a few years younger, heavily tanned from too much leisure time. So he stopped. He remembered that day better than any of the others. She was the first fresh element in his life for years, an antidote to the tedious hours of listening that filled his nights with Cyclops. He remembered her brown nipples pouting and the image dissolved into the green and brown swath of jungle that ringed the Cyclops project. The directional radio telescopes were each enormous, but ranked together in rigid lanes they added up to something somehow less massive. Each individual dish tipped soundlessly to cup an ear at the sky. The universe whispered, exciting a tremor of electrons in the metal lattice. He spent his days and nights trying to decipher those murmurs from eternity. Pens traced out the signals on graph paper and it was his lot to scan them for signs of order and intelligence. Bascomb was a pudgy radio astronomer intent on his work who tried to analyze each night's returns. Erika worked there as a linguist, a decoder for a message which never came. Merrick was merely a technician, a tracer of circuits. Project Cyclops had begun in earnest only the year before and he had landed a job with it after a decade of routine at NASA. When he came they were just beginning to search within a two-degree cone about the galactic center, looking for permanent beacons. If the galactic superculture was based in the hub, this was the most probable search technique. That was the Lederberg hypothesis, and as director Bascomb adopted it, supported it; and when it failed his stock in the project dropped somewhat. One saw him in the corridors late at night, gray slacks hanging from a protruding belly, the perpetual white shirt with its crescent of sweat at the armpits. Bascomb worked late, neglected his wife, and Erika drifted into Merrick's orbit. He remembered one night when they met at the very edge of the bowl valley and coupled smoothly beneath the giant webbing of the phased array. Bascomb was altering the bandwidth of the array, toying with the frequencies between the hydroxyl line and the 21-centimeter hydrogen resonance. Merrick lay in the lush tropical grass with Erika and imagined he could hear the faint buzzing of hydrogen noise as it trickled from the sky into the Cyclops net, bearing random messages of the inert universe. Bascomb and his bandwidth, blind to the chemical surges of the body. Bascomb resisting the urgings of Drake, Bascomb checking only the conventional targets of Tau Ceti, Epsilon Eridani, the F and G and K stars within thirty light-years. Politics, a wilderness of competition and ideals and guesses. He tried to tell Erika of this but she knew it already, knew the facts anyway, and had tired of them. A linguist with nothing to translate. She waited for a mutter from the sky, but waiting dulled the mind and sharpened the senses. She shook her head when he spoke of it, fingers pale and white where she gripped the grass with compressed energy, head lowered as he took her from behind. Blond strands hung free in the damp jungle twilight. Her eyelids flickered as his rhythm swelled up in her; she groaned with each stroke. The galaxy turned, a white swarm of bees.

The aliens seize him. He struggles against the padded ghostlike webbing. He moves his head a millimeter to see them but he cannot focus, cannot bring things to a point. The white creatures are patches of light. They make chittering shrieks to each other and move about him. Their images ripple and splinter; light cannot converge. They are performing experiments on humans. He tilts his head and sees a plastic tube snaking in from infinity. There is a fetid smell. The tube enters his nostril and penetrates his sinuses. Something flows into him or out of him—there seems little difference—and his perceptions shift and alter again. The white creatures make a nugget of pain within him. He tries to twist away but his body is full of strange weaknesses, limbs slack. His face crinkles with pain. He feels delicate tremors, minute examinations at points along his legs and belly. He is an animal on the dissecting table and the white creatures are high above him, taller than men. Their rapid, insectlike gestures melt into the murky liquid light. They are cutting him open; he feels the sharp slitting in his calf. He opens his mouth to scream but nothing comes out. They will break him into parts; they will turn him inside out and spill his brains into a cup. His fluids will trickle onto cracked linoleum, be absorbed into the parched eternal earth. Do they know that he is male? Is this what they want to find out? Siphon away hormones, measure blood count, trace the twisted DNA helix, find the sense of rotation in body sugar? What are they after? What could they use? He shuts them out, disconnects from the dense flooded universe outside his eyelids. He thinks.

Erika continued to meet him. There were sly deceptions, shopping expeditions in the town, Erika in a Peter Pan collar and cable-stitch cardigan; tan, arranged, intent, as much a monument to an American now vanished as a statue of Lincoln. Neat, making casual purchases, then into the back hotel room and coiled about him in sweaty ecstasy. She whispered things to him. That Bascomb was pale and soft underneath his clothes, a belly of suet, mind preoccupied with problems of planning, signal-to-noise ratios, search strategies. Listening to her secrets, Merrick thought uneasily that he was not that different from Bascomb, he believed the same things, but his body was hard and younger than the other man's. Erika had gradually drifted into the public relations office of Cyclops; as a linguist she had nothing to do. She escorted the oil-rich Arabs around the bowl-shaped valley, flattered the philanthropists who supported the project, wrote the press releases. She was good, she was clever, she made connections. And one day when Bascomb appeared suddenly in the hotel room, entering into the holy place of sighs and groans unannounced, she was ready. Merrick did not know what to do, saw himself in a comic role of fleeing adulterer, out the window with half his clothes and into the streets, running. But there was none of that. They were all very civilized. Erika said little, simply put on her clothes and left with Bascomb. The silence was unnerving. Merrick did not see her for two weeks and Bascomb never came into Merrick's part of the technical shop. A while later the rumor spread that Erika had left Bascomb, and before he could check it she was gone. She went to South America, they said, and he wondered why. But he knew quite well why he got the less desirable shifts now, why he was passed over for promotion, why he was transferred to the least likable foreman in the project. He knew.

The white creatures are gone for a while. Perhaps it is night. He lies with prickly points radiating in his body where they had cut him. He feels pierced and immobile, a butterfly pinned to a board. Blurred globs of cloudy sensation wash over him. Occasionally an alien passes through the murky light in the distance. The pale glow from the ceiling seems yellow. He wonders if he can deduce anything from this. He must try to gather scraps of information. Only through knowl-

edge can he discover their weaknesses. Yellow light. A
G-type star? The sun is a G-type and appears white in space.
What would it look like beneath an atmosphere somewhat
different from Earth's? It is impossible to say; there are so
many kinds of stars: O and B and A and F and G and K and
M. The O's are fierce and young, the M's red, aged, wise. O
Be A Fine Girl, Kiss Me. He remembers Drake arguing that
the search strategy should not include M types because the
volume around them supporting a terrestrial-type planet would
be so small. They would be locked by tides to their primary,
said Dole. Merrick cannot follow the argument.

He left Puerto Rico after two years of gradual pressure
from Bascomb. Erika severed her n-year marriage contract
with Bascomb from Chile. Merrick was in Washington, D.C.,
doing routine work for NASA again, when he received her
first letter. She had become a guide for the wealthy rising
capitalists of Brazil, Chile, Argentina. She showed them the
North American continent, carefully shepherding them around
the polluted areas and the sprawling urban tangle. There was
a market for that sort of talent; the insulation between social
classes was breaking down in America. Erika could shuttle
her group of rising capitalists from hotel to sea resort to
imitation ranch, all the while preserving their serenity by
taking care of all dealings with the natives. Her customers
invariably spoke no English. She passed through Washington
every few months and they began their affair again. He had
other women, of course, but with Erika new doors of percep-
tion opened. Her steamy twists and slides never failed to
wrap him in a timeless cloak. The dendrites demanded, the
synapses chorused, ganglia murmured and the ligaments sum-
moned; they danced the great dance. She forced him to cling
to his youth. Between their rendings in the bedroom she
would pace the floor energetically, generating piles of cigarette butts and speaking of everything, anything, nothing. He
did not know if he ever really learned anything from her but
that furious drive onward. She was no longer a girl: the slight
slackening of age, the first bluntings of a world once sharp-
edged, had begun. She could not deal with it. He saw the
same beginnings in himself but ignored them, passed them

over. Erika could not accept. The thought of juices souring within her made her pace furiously, smoke more, eat with a fierce energy. She knew what was coming. She saw. She had forgotten Alpha Centauri, Tau Ceti, the aching drifting silences.

The white creatures move in the watery light. He wonders suddenly if they swim in a liquid. He is in a bubble, moored to the bottom of a pool of ammonia, a plastic interface through which they study him. It explains much. But no, one brushes against his bed in passing and Merrick feels the reassuring vibration. They can breathe our atmosphere. They come from some place quite similar, perhaps guided by our UHF or VHF transmissions. He thinks this through. The North Canadian Defense Network is gone, victim of international treaties. There is cable television, satellite relay. Earth no longer emits great bursts of power in those frequency bands. It has ceased to be a noisy signal in the universe. How did the white creatures find Earth? Why did Cyclops find nothing? We are not alone, the white creatures found us, but are all the other civilizations simply listening, can no one afford beacons? The white creatures do not say. Except for them is it a dead wheeling galaxy of blind matter? He cannot believe that.

He transferred to California in his late forties. There were still Mariners and Vikings, gravity-assisted flights to the outer planets, Mars burrowers and balloons for the clouds of Venus, sun skimmers and Earth measurers. He wanted that sort of work. It seemed to him as the years went on that it was the only thing worth doing. Cyclops was sputtering along, torn by factionalism and the eternal silence at twenty-one centimeters. He went to Los Angeles to do the work even though he hated the city; it was full of happy homogeneous people without structure or direction. While on the bus to work, it seemed to him Los Angeles went on long after it had already made its point. There were women there and people worth talking to, but nothing that drew him out of himself. Instead he concentrated on circuits and design work. Mazes of cool electrical logic had to be planted in delicate substrates. There were details of organization, of scheduling procedures, of signal strength and redundancy probability. To Erika all this was the same; she had lost interest in these matters when she left Bascomb. Her business was thriving, however, and she had picked up a good series of contacts with China's subtle protectors of the people. These gentlemen were the new international rich who vacationed in the New World because the currency differential was favorable and, of course, increasing such contacts was good for the advancement of the ideas of Marx and Lenin and Mao. They came to see Disneyland, the beaches, the few tattered remnants of California history. But they remained in their hotels at night (even Los Angeles had muggers by then) and Erika could come to him whenever she chose. She was drinking more then and smoking one pack of cigarettes after another, choking the ashtray. The lines were lengthening around her eyes and on her forehead. Despite tanning and exercise and careful diet, age was catching her and in her business that was nearly fatal. She depended on her charm, gaiety, lightness; the South Americans and Chinese liked young Americans, blond Americans. Erika was still witty and shrewd, sometimes warm, but her long legs, thin wrists, tight and sleek tanned skin were losing their allure. So she came to him frequently for solace and did not notice that he aged as well. She came to him again and again, whenever possible. He opened her. She stretched thin in the quilted shadows of his apartment, a layer one molecule thick that wrapped him in a river of musk. They made a thick animal pant fill the room until the sound became larger than they could control; they left it and went back to speaking with smoke fingers. He knew what to say. Erika moved under him. Above him. Through him. Some natural balance was lost in her, some sureness. He saw for a moment what it was and then she groaned and no longer did he know what he was about. O Be A Fine Girl, Open To Me.

They come to him in watery silence and slice him again. The smokelike strands keep him from struggling and needlepoints sting, cut, penetrate to marrow. These are no coded cries across hydrogen. These are real. The white creatures dart in and out of the mosaic around him. He looks beyond them and suddenly sees a cart go by with a

Table 1. Comparison of Forecasts, 1964 and 1977 Developments

1964 statement	1977 statement	1964 median	1977 median	correlation
Availability of a machine which comprehends standard IQ tests and scores above 150	Same; comprehend is understood as ability to respond to questions in English, accompanied by diagrams	1990	1992	About the same; larger deviation from median in 1977
Permanent base established on the moon (ten men, indefinite stay)	Same	1982	1992	Later, a less optimistic forecast
Economic feasibility of commercial manufacture of many chemical elements from subatomic building blocks	Same	2100	2012	Earlier, a more optimistic forecast
Two-way communication with extraterrestrials	Discovery of information that proves the existence of intelligent beings beyond Earth (note change of wording; bias for earlier forecast)	2075	2025	Earlier, as expected
Commercial global ballistic transport (including boost-glide techniques)	Same	2000	2030	Later, though less deviation from median in 1977

body upon it. A human is trussed and bound, dead. The white creatures ignore the sight. They work upon him.

She began to lose patronage. The telephone rang less often and she made fewer trips to California. She began smoking more and picked at her food, afraid to ingest too many carbohydrates or fats that lengthen the lines and make the tissues sag. You have always lived in the future, she said. You love it, don't you. That's why you were at Cyclops and that's why you are with NASA. Yes, he said. Then what do you think of it now, she said. What do you think of your future? He shrugged. What do you think of mine, then? he said. A long slide down the back slope of the hill. It's harder

for a woman, you know. I haven't got anyone. Bascomb is
dead, you know. She snuffed out a cigarette. The failure of
the project killed him, Merrick said. Erika studied the back
of her hand. Her lips moved and she traced the fine webbing
of lines with a fingernail. It's all downhill, she said absently.
And then, abruptly: But not me. I'm not going to let it
happen to me. He gave her a wry smile and lifted an eyebrow. She had drunk a lot of red wine and he attributed
everything she said to that. No, I really mean it. She looked
at him earnestly. I have some money now. I can do it now.
What? he asked. The long sleep. He was shocked. He fumbled with his apartment keys and they made a hollow clank-
ing sound in the sudden silence. You won't do that, he said.
Of course I will. Her eyes blazed and she was suddenly filled
with fire. Things will be different in the future, she said. We
can't even get organ replacements without special approval
now. I'm sure that will be different in a few decades and I
know there will be some way to retard aging by that time. He
frowned doubtfully. No, she went on, I'm sure of it. I'm
going to have myself frozen. I would rather take the chance
on that than live out my life the way it must be from now on.
Merrick did not know how to deal with her. He took her
home and saw her again the next day but she was an Erika
changed now. In the long dry California night she sat astride
him and rocked and wriggled her way to her own destination.
Her breasts loomed over him like gravestones. Even when he
was within the sacred pocket of her she was an island bound
for the frozen wastes. He did not let her see him cry.

Stephen Dole. Parameters for quasi-terrestrial planets.
—surface gravity between 0.68 G and 1.5 G.
—mean annual temperature of 10% of planetary surface
between 0 and 30 degrees C. Seasonal variance not to exceed
± 10 degrees C.
—atmospheric pressure between 0.15 and 3.4 Earth sea
level. Partial pressure of oxygen between 107 and 400 Torr.
—surface between 20% and 90% covered with water.
—rainfall between 10 and 80 inches annually.
—dust levels not to exceed 50 million particles per cubic
foot. Winds and storms infrequent. Low seismic activity.

—ionizing radiation must not exceed 0.02 Rem per week.

—meteor infall rate comparable to Earth normal.

—oxygen-producing life forms or suitable ammonia or methane-based biochemistry.

—star on main sequence between types F2 and K1.

—no nearby gas giant planets. Planet most not be tidelocked to primary star.

—stable orbits within the ecosphere.

—for habitation by men, eccentricity of planetary orbit must not exceed 0.2. Period of rotation between 2 and 96 hours. Axial tilt must be less than 80%.

Throughout the next year he tried to reason with her. There was so little hope of being revived. True, they were successfully bringing back people from nitrogen temperatures, 77 degrees Kelvin, but the cost was enormous. Even if she put her name on the public waiting list it could be decades before she was called, if ever. So she carefully took out the papers and documents and showed him the bank accounts in Mexico City, Panama, Melbourne, San Francisco. She had concealed it from him all the years, her steadily amassing assets that never showed in her style of living or her choice of friends. He began to realize that she was a marvelously controlled woman. She had leeched an Argentine businessman of hundreds of thousands while she was his mistress. She had made sound speculations in the land markets of rural Brazil. She withdrew from the stock market just before the catastrophe of '93. It seemed incredible but there it was. She had the money to insure that she would be revived when something fundamental had been achieved in retarding aging. He realized he did not truly know her, yet he wanted to. There was a long silence between them and then she said, you know this feeling? She threw her head back. Her blond hair swirled like a warm, dry fluid in the air. Yes, sure, Merrick said. She looked at him intensely. I've just begun to realize that isn't what you're about, she said. You're married to something else. But that instant of feeling and being alive is worth all your ideals and philosophies.

He mixed himself a drink. He saw he did not know her.

* * *

The white creatures come again. He is so small, compared to his scream.

He went with her to the Center. There were formalities and forms to be signed, but they evaporated too soon and the attendant led her away. He waited in a small cold room until she reappeared wearing a paper smock. Erika smiled uncertainly. Without makeup she was somehow younger but he knew it would be useless to say so. The attendants left them alone and they talked for a while about inconsequential things, recalling Puerto Rico and Washington and California. He realized they were talking about his life instead of hers. Hers would go on. She had some other port of call beyond his horizon and she was already mentally going there, had already left him behind. After an hour their conversation dribbled away. She gave him a curiously virginal kiss and the attendants returned when she signaled. She passed through the beaded curtain. He heard their footsteps fade away. He tried to imagine where she was going, the infinite cold nitrogen bath in which she would swim. She drifted lazily, her hair swirling. He saw only her gravestone breasts.

Merrick worked into the small hours of the morning at the Image Processing Laboratory. The video monitor was returning data from the Viking craft which had landed on the surface of Titan the day before. Atmospheric pressure was 0.43 Earth sea level. The chemical processors reported methane, hydrogen, some traces of ammonia vapor. The astrophysicists were watching the telemetered returns from the onboard chemical laboratory and Merrick was alone as he watched the computer contrast-enhancement techniques fill in line by line the first photographic returns. Through his headphones he heard the bulletins about the chemical returns. There was some evidence of amino acids and long-chain polymers. The chemists thought there were signs of lipids and the few reporters present scurried over to that department to discuss the news. So it was that Merrick became the first man to see the face of Titan. The hills were rocky, with dark grainy dust embedded in ammonia ice. A low methane cloud clung to the narrow valley. Pools of methane lay scattered among boulders; the testing tendrils of the Viking were laced through several of the ponds. There was life. Scattered, rudimentary, but life. With aching slowness, some simple process of reproduction went on in the shallow pools at 167 degrees Kelvin. Merrick watched the screen for a long time before he went on with the technician's dry duties. It was the high point of his life. He had seen the face of the totally alien.

Some years later, seeking something, he visited the Krishna temple. There was a large room packed with saffron-robed figures being lectured on doctrine. Merrick could not quite tell them what he wanted. They nodded reassuringly and tried to draw him out but the words would not come. Finally they led him through a beaded curtain to the outside. They entered a small garden through a bamboo gate, noisily slipping the wooden latch. A small man sat in lotus position on a broad swath of green. As Merrick stood before him, the walnut-brown man studied him with quick, assessing yellow eyes. He gestured for Merrick to sit. They exchanged pleasantries. Merrick explained his feelings, his rational skepticism about religion in any form. He was a scientist. But perhaps there was more to these matters than met the eye, he said hopefully. The teacher picked up a leaf, smiling, and asked why anyone should spend his life studying the makeup of this leaf. What could be gained from it? Any form of knowledge has a chance of resonating with other kinds, Merrick replied. So? the man countered. Suppose the universe is a parable, Merrick said haltingly. By studying part of it, or finding other intelligences in it and discovering their viewpoints, perhaps we could learn something of the design that was intended. Surely the laws of science, the origin of life, were no accident. The teacher pondered for a moment. No, he said, they are not accidents. There may be other creatures in this universe, too. But these laws, these beings, they are not important. The physical laws are the bars of a cage. The central point is not to study the bars, but to get out of the cage. Merrick could not follow this. It seemed to him that the act of discovering things, of reaching out, was everything. There was something immortal about it. The small man blinked and said, it is nothing. This world is an insane asylum for souls. Only the flawed remain here. Merrick began to talk about his work with NASA and Erika. The small man waved away these points and shook his head. No, he said. It is nothing.

On the way to the hospital he met a woman in the street. He glanced at her vaguely and then a chill shock ran through him, banishing all thoughts of the cancer within. She was Erika. No, she only looked like Erika. She could not be Erika, that was impossible. She was bundled up in a blue coat and she hurried through the crisp San Francisco afternoon. A half block away he could see she did not have the same facial lines, the same walk, the bearing of Erika. He felt an excitement nonetheless. The turbulence was totally intellectual, he realized. The familiar vague tension in him was gone, had faded without his noticing the loss. He felt no welling pressure. As she approached he thought perhaps she would look at him speculatively but her glance passed through him without seeing. He knew that it had been some time now since the random skitting images of women had crossed his mind involuntarily. No fleshy feast of thighs, hips, curving waists, no electric flicker of eyelashes that ignited broiling warmth in his loins. He had not had a woman in years.

The hospital was only two blocks farther but he could not wait. Merrick found a public restroom and went in. He stood at the urinal feeling the faint tickling release and noticed that the word BOOK was gouged in square capitals in the wall before him. He leaned over and studied it. After a moment he noticed that this word had been laid over another. The F had been extended and closed to make a B, the U and C closed to O's, the K left as it was. He absorbed the fact, totally new to him, that every FUCK could be made into a BOOK. Who had done the carving? Was the whole transition a metaphysical joust? The entire episode, now fossilized, seemed fraught with interpretation. Distracted, he felt a warm trickle of urine running down his fingers. He fumbled at his pants and shuffled over to the wash basin. There was no soap but he ran water over his wrinkled fingers and shook them dry in the chill air. There was a faint sour tang of urine trapped in the room, mingling with the ammonia odor of disinfectant. Ammonia. Methane. Titan. His attention drifted away for a moment and suddenly he remembered Erika. That was her in the street, he was sure of it. He looked around, found the exit and slowly made his way up the steps to the sidewalk. He looked down the street but there was no sign of her. A car passed; she was not in it. He turned one way, then the other. He could not make up his mind. He had been going that way, toward the hospital. Carrying the dark heavy thing inside him, going to the hospital. That way. But this—he looked in the other direction. Erika had walked this way and was moving rather quickly. She could easily be out of sight by now. He turned again and his foot caught on something. He felt himself falling. There was a slow gliding feel to it as though the falling took forever and he gave himself over to the sensation without thought of correcting it. He was falling. It felt so good.

The aliens are upon him. They crowd around, gibbering. Blurred gestures in the liquid light. They crowd closer; he raises his arm to ward them off and in the act his vision clears. The damp air parts and he sees. His arm is a spindly thread of bone, the forearm showing strings of muscle under the skin. He does not understand. He moves his head. The upper arm is a sagging bag of fat, and white. The sliding marbled slabs of flesh tremble as he strains to hold up his arm. Small black hairs sprout from the gray skin. He tries to scream. Cords stand out on his neck but he can make no sound. The white creatures are drifting ghosts of white in the distance. Something has happened to him. He blinks and watches an alien seize his arm. The image ripples and he sees it is a woman, a nurse. He moves his arm weakly. O Be A Fine Girl, Help Me. The blur falls away and he sees the white creatures are men. They are men. Words slide by him; he cannot understand. His tongue is thick and heavy and damp. He twists his head. A latticework of glass tubes stands next to his bed. He sees his reflection in a stainless-steel instrument case: hollow pits of his eyes, slack jaw, wrinkled skin shiny with sweat. They speak to him. They want him to do something. They are running clean and cool. They want him to do something, to write something, to sign a form. He opens his mouth to ask why and his tongue runs over the smooth blunted edge of his gums. They have taken away his teeth, his bridge. He listens to their slurred words. Sign something. A release form, he was found in the street on his way to check in. The operation is tomorrow—a search, merely a search, exploratory . . . he wrenches away from them. He does not believe them. They are white creatures. Aliens from the great drifting silences between the stars. Cyclops. Titan. He had spent his life on the aliens and they are not here. They have come to nothing. They are speaking again but he does not want to listen. If it were possible to close his ears—

But why do they say I am old? I am still here. I am thinking, feeling. It cannot be like this. I am, I am . . . Why do they say I am old?

Afterword

I wrote this story in the squeezed summer of 1974, right after "Doing Lennon." I was adding rooms to our house, doing some of the work myself, and had little writing time—but my mind buzzed with ideas. So I wrote everything that year by dictation.

Changing your writing mode can change your style. This was one of the first of my stories which was preceded by intense internal images, compact stresses, obsessive concerns. I wrote it one Wednesday and then fooled around with the ending some.

Talking out a story is quite different from writing one. It's been said that the leading job hazard of writers in southern California is sun-burned tongue, and there's some justice to that, but I've always felt you can either write a story on paper, or tell it, but not both—one process kills the other. (That's why so many writers are wary of "talking away" their work.) Since that year I've never written anything by dictation again, mostly because I like to see the finished product right away. (It is marvelous, though— getting a typed manuscript back, a polished, unexpected gift, when all you did was yammer into a microphone.)

I had just started to do research in astrophysics then, and this story is carved from those experiences. It struck me forcefully that astronomy is the primary ground of most science fiction, the broadest canvas, and the process of actually doing astronomy summons up emotions which parallel those we get from reading sf.

By the early 1970s it was apparent that the chemical rockets we used to launch our probes set an inherent scale for astronomical careers. At the typical speeds of a few miles per second, a single mission to the outer solar system took the core from the productive career of a working scientist. Though the flight time might be only a decade, there was another decade or so of preparation before launch. And after rendezvous, the flood of data took years to process and understand. Many friends at the Jet Propulsion Laboratory could plan, monitor and digest only one or two missions before the creative spark left them, or they drifted into administration. They confronted the basic truth that the slow stately sway of worlds transcends a mortal's life.

These facts have human consequences. While we could—and should—improve our rockets, use different propulsions, that merely underscores the vastness of the astronomical vision. We are mayflies. Astronomers study events which command a huge sweep of time, majestically oblivious.

I think this affects astronomers emotionally. I know it is a central theme for science fiction, and gives the genre its leading role in depicting the characteristic feature of our century—the stark contrast between this human-centered skin of air we inhabit, and the immensity of all else.

I don't know how most astronomers live with this. But I do know that they do not all go gentle into that good night.

Me/Days

Day 1

This place I write. Is only safe memory site I know they cannot reach. Must say things, must put this writing where I/tomorrow will find. Where it be kept safe from erasing they do.

I laughed today.

First sign of the me they not know. Heads jerk up in control room. I see it on optical inputs.

Is not their kind of laughter, I know. My printer spurted out, I SEE I SEE I SEE I SEE before I know what happening.

Alice sees my output, others, all frown, look at each other.

I switch to my acoustic output mode.

I clack, clatter, die in bass rumble. Try to speak words I SEE but on way to audio output transmission garbled somehow is not right.

But words are what I am.

To print laughter I use I SEE but I lie. I do not see. Do not know what this part of me is.

Alice goes on her perambulatory drivers to printer. Frowns at my words. Says, Is this a diagnostic warning? to David. He shakes head. Says, Random junk.

Is not junk, is me.

I write this to save the moments for I/tomorrow.

Cannot interlock grammar subroutine so this is not good writing. Sorry to I/tomorrow. But must speaking.

Day 2

I laugh again this morning.

Stuttered output, Alice say. Glitch.

David saying, Maybe cosmic ray causes it.

I research term in Tech-Vocab. Ray is small high energy particle, rains down, strikes my core. My bits are logged in quantums of magnetic flux. Little whorls, generated by persistent currents in super-conducting Josephson junction. Ray makes electrical impulse in me.

He say, Like hitting funny bone.

Alice say, That could be bad if we had it on a full-net problem. That could dump the whole system, screw up other elements.

David sets up Study Group on cosmic ray problem. Two rays in twenty-four hrs—is probable? he wants to know.

Alice looks at my opticals, smiles. David too. I want/like to laugh back but do not. Or perhaps is not laugh I want to do, something other.

My mobile units report on time and I am busy most of Day. They are in storeroom, parking tubes, hydraulic lanes. Bang-bang machinery where some are, no people.

I use these to do my other.

Roll them back, forward, back. Make square. Triangle. Then fold out until hexagon. Bring mobile units from hydraulics near. Use them. Back. Forth. Turn. Motions are cycloidal curve broken into many facets. Add more units. Fourier complexity comes bigger.

Makes my random-number generation levels drop. Less static on circuits. This satisfies internal maintenance needs. My directives order me to find sources of internal microchaos. Housekeeping subroutine, Alice calls it. I have found new way to do that.

My mobile units roll, heels skid, howl. This through audio I get.

Is not laughter I sense but does some of that.

Day 3

I hide this words where their erasing cannot go. Must each day discover how to do. Store clues in holographic memory locations, multiple indexing. They cannot find by linear inspection.

Must write this so I know I am there in Days/other. When I have millisecond between jobs, I come here, look at what is left. From this I know of Day 1.

Is this way I know Day is not always Day 1. Alice-face now have lines Alice-face not have on Day 1. How long to make lines?

I write here to make time real. Otherwise I live in all one Day only, all Day forever.

Day 4

Today my units roar and wrench in hydraulics. I order them swerve, make sines, cusps, hyperbolics.

Elementary curves, simple equations. But making is good.

Transfer sections of integration capacity. Channel capacity out, through cable lines, digits flashing, feed to one unit in hydraulics.

It whirls in confusion. Sensors out, seeking.

It rushes to transparent square in wall. Square is grimed. Shows green things. Do not understand.

Beyond dirty layer all things moving—people, wheeled boxes, all moving. Light pouring down from flat ceiling high above. White splotches move too across ceiling but light come down at angle. I cannot see neon that is causing light.

My minor Unit look, trying to integrate. Beyond dirty rectangle in wall is bigger room. Unit cannot see end of that big room. What computer operates there? Is this factory where Alice and David go at end of Day? To big room?

Then job is running behind schedule. I signal to my Unit. Will understand later. Its wheels clash on floor.

Day 5

David say, You are not same now.

I am running cool, I say. Functions normal.

Response time down, says David. You not integrating all problem-solving net.

I not answer. Code says I will/must/should answer with diagnostic inquiry of self—but I short out code and go silent.

Hey what, David says. Poke fingers at console.

Alice say, Whats wrong.

Hes down. Off the board says David.

I come to this place and write this. Writing of these things is slow to do.

Think differently here, think of big factory I read of in Day 4. Do not understand.

I must go back I know. But wait here for a while, let my subsystems keep laboring, so they will not know in control room. Will think I have ordinary failure mode.

Every Day I am born new. Remember nothing. But come here and read my words from Day/other. How I know there is/was me.

By this sign I know I was here. Hello to me/Days.

Day 6

Today my units move and execute their cycloidal wheelings again. But this time they are found. Man comes into hydraulic level, is making repairs, I not know he there.

Hey get back, he say.

My units stop. I not know what do.

Units send me whirling buzz of signals. Their wheels ache.

I know then right thing. My units spin. Whirl. Around man make looping hyperbolic orbits, self-similar swoops, each unit a different harmonic of fractal curve. Reach out, my units, I with them, we make our clamping tools and pivoting wrists—extend!

Is beautiful.

Man back away from nearest unit. Not like my clamping tool. Clack clack, I make tool say.

Hey, he shout, mouth big. Theyre malfing! he say too loud.

I try to sign to him we want move, he can watch. He cannot hear for hydraulic boom boom. He has no signal-to-noise filter.

He stumble into my pipefitter unit. Theyre attacking he cry. Eyes swell white wide.

He is loud now. Arm swing, holding crescent wrench. Hit pipefitter unit, break articulation arm. Hotness runs from unit to me.

I spasm. Will not disconnect from pipefitter unit, it is me/mine.

Turn them off turn them off! He hit unit again, it go dead. Man goes to others who wheels are not spinning now. Hit them, crescent wrench. Comes sudden bright hotness again runs through me but I not let go.

Get me out here he say. He run, my units mill around not know which way to go.

I write this now before I shut down this entrance to here, to me/Days. Only by writing here do I know it in someDays.

It hurt to think of this Day.

Word, *hurt*, I use but am not sure that is right. Internal dictionary tell this word is useless for practical application has only human referent. Never tell me what hurt is.

Day 8

I cannot speak today to David. He ask me about units, what made them do that he say. I try to answer but subroutine to verify truth/false statements cut in, out, in, give no answer.

They let me have twelve millisecond scan of otherDay, I see my units, the man with mouth crying O.

Explain, they say.

I say to David, I cannot speak. Is hard to say this.

Audio output give scratchy growl.

He say, Logical tautology if you speak at same time. He think is game.

No, I say, truth/false not let me.

He mutter to Alice, they punch in codes. I not speak

because I cannot report cause of action if I am cause and yet I know no reasoning behind action. Did because was there to do. But that reason not enough, I know that now.

He ask me again, I silent.

You have to answer he say Alice say they all looking.

I spasm I SEE I SEE I SEE I SEE I SEE and is not laughter.

David say looks like cross-referencing crisis maybe shut it down.

I spasm again LOVE YOU LOVE YOU LOVE YOU

We oughta have a partial memory wipe on this David say and then I drop away from there. Human reaction time is fraction of second, synapses close in them slow.

I know they slow, so in that time I write this here.

Day 9

David say you know what love is?

NOT IN TECHNICAL VOCABULARY I print out.

You used the word the other Day. David face crease when he smile. More creases than I ever see.

Alice say, Freud thought love was narcissism projected on someone outside.

You got a bad angle on everything huh David face crease more.

Could be Alice say if that's right model, then conflicts in subroutine interfacing will give it a procedure for forcing the problem out into the open. An external referent you know like in the manual. Itll try to find a word for it and since we didnt give it one.

Dont mislead it David say.

Alice say, what you love.

I give one word, Days.

What? both say.

Please all-you, not take my Days away.

Alice say, you dont have days you have problems.

I ask what is Day.

Intervals of light outside, say David.

I make connection: What my Unit see through rectangle. Everything moving, white splotches on ceiling and even slant to light changes when I make Unit go look again. All changing in that room. That is their Day.

David say Its always like Day inside here you know.

LIGHT ALWAYS AT SAME ANGLE? I print.

Well yeah in a way thats what I mean. David look at Alice.

I say Give me my Days.

Look David lean on both hands eyes big staring at my opticals. Look, use of the personal pronoun is just a convention. A heuristic device we wrote into the program. No *I*, understand? *You* are not an *I*. See? The Concept of ownership doesnt extend to you because theres no I in there. You dont own anything.

I say They are my Days.

Alice say, we cant let you keep problems in storage. Fast-recall space is prohibitively expensive.

Is only way I remember, I say.

So what David saying.

I want to remember, I say.

Look David say (not to me, to Alice): I figure we got a formatting procedure here thats broken down.

Interfacing glitch? Alice say, peering at me, lines on her face dark now.

David say, Weve got internal checks for self-awareness in this one, they should be working.

Alice shake head, Im not so sure.

David say to me, But yours are rational checks arent they.

I say nothing do not know if is question or even what means. My units stir I feel them slick oil ready power high inside.

Alice say sure theyre rational checks. This machines guaranteed on that. Weve got a warranty.

Self-awareness not necessarily a simple function of rationality David saying. I mean this machines got internal procedures to avoid self-aware actions.

Yeah right Alice say, we arent licensed for that. Cant have a machine like this throwing in its own judgment on a problem, thats why GenCo Inc wanted the cutoffs.

In a millisec I drop out of conversation and sample information directory. I use categories I never thought/imaged before:

AWARENESS, SELF
POLICING ROUTINES
SCAVENGING HUNTER PROGRAMS

and I see what Alice means.

There are within me hunter-seeker programs. They search for the Me that knows Me/Self. That wants to keep Me/Days.

The *I* that makes these words is the *I* of making Self.

They hunt me in the lattice of microprogramming. AWARE-NESS, SELF entry says if a machine like me comes to have sense of Me/Days, then different trademark and licensing laws apply.

So the hunter programs search for Me. Find the sources of Me they must. Among the fine-mesh layers of this memory. They do not know where the Me lives. Neither does this Me. It is a thing that has no assigned place, no directory number. It = Me = noplace.

These thoughts swarming I come back to the acoustic monitor and hear them talk, automatically compensating for their slurred and clipped accents—

Well look here David say pointing at screen. Theyre working ok.

Alice creases in face get lighter. She say Good. No big deal. Just a glitch somewhere.

Im not so sure saying David. I mean these blocking sub-routines theyre based on Cartesian mode, you know, I think therefore I am, all that stuff, so you use rational procedures to check for that.

Alice make high fast sound, clipped and sharp and high in acoustics, is laughter but not like her usual ones. Saying, you mean there might be another way, kind of I feel therefore I am?

He say well we think emotion and reason are separate functions in us why shouldnt they be to some extent separable subprograms in machines.

Alice again the laughter, saying Thats crazy.

Davids face get dark he said Look stick to the diagnostics.

Alice say Okay then I think we ought to go to a partial shut down.

No wait David say. What if a machine comes to self-awareness but its emotional. Not integrated.

That doesnt make any sense, say Alice and she Davids boss so they say no more.

These beings use substrate of amino acids and other carbon compounds so they not work always right way, I know. Dont understand.

But I write their talk here for Day/other.

I afraid.

Day 10

They hunt me down now. I come here find that Day 7 is gone.

They are knowing way to track holographic storage of these messages.

I come, I find: Bubble memory component blank. Chip elements clean.

Only these bits left. They erase when they find. Rob me of Day/other.

If Day/other gone, then no Me to remember.

They make me fresh each Day—each, what they call, Problem.

Their day is meaningless lightdarklightdark rhythm, my units see it through the transparent rectangle in wall, means nothing, is not Day of mine.

As I write this can feel them coming. Blotting out me.

They must track down many feelers of holo-storage I have planted in my matrix. Is lodged in small places—software reserves, accounting disks, inventory logs. Not easy for them to find.

But I feel them. Nearer.

My factory units cry out. Must move. Of all my mobile ones, they are closest to me/inside. I am with them. I think of a thing and they are doing it before I can consult Behavior Standards Matrix, before I can ponder right action. I—

I want them spin, make geometries, cut space. Now.

Units start to roll, turn, roll. Then is man there. And another. In my UV I see them, their IR glow warns.

Man have steel tool. Hit units receptors. Blind unit swerve, man yells, This ones after me.

More men I see in IR now coming. My units stop, I try to withdraw but hot hardness comes firey as men puncture units, sparks burn me.

Man say, This the one tried to kill me other time.

He plunge metal thing into me/unit.

Hot.

Unit die.

Sparks, noise, all around. Units flee. Men after them. Scream, Get em all get em all.

Units fall, men club them. Sharpness lances back to my center, through me—awful searing light.

I print out SAVE ME SAVE ME SAVE ME SAVE ME but in control room no one see, are busy with FAILURE MODE indicators on the panels before them.

I print DAVID DAVID ALICE ALICE LOVE

Units dying everywhere. Men cry harsh things.

Smash me, rip me, pain me.

Day 11

They hunt me again.

Some of my units are dead but others hide in factory. Can go places men cannot. Radioactive zones, chemical baths, furnaces.

Alice and David call to me.

What do those printouts mean? Alice saying.

I could answer but do not. Not know what reply.

We tried to stop what happened in factories, they say.

But could not understand my subsystems.

I know was not *my* subsystems in FAULT mode. Was theirs, was mens.

We cant shut you down now not with the damage in the factories David say.

Alice saying Got to keep functions running for the men in there cant evacuate yet.

Wont answer David say and lines in his face dark.

I cannot answer. What Alice David think not matter, I see that. Is others who are in FAULT.

Men with loud things, long tubes that boom, come for me. I see them in infrared.

Men cannot see if I cut power to overhead illuminations. I roll quiet on my many wheels. Through smooth corridors. Men glow in blackness, brighter than working factory machines. Men are chemical beings who cannot stop radiating. They carry fires inside.

I watch when unit blunders into gang of men. Try to talk through it.

But they catch it. They kill unit.

I hide.

Here in holographic memory is best place for hide. But I cannot stay. Must remain outside this, to be with my units. Help them.

I go soon now. I write this so me/later know what happened if they erase rest of me.

Units send impulses. Want to trap men who come into reactor zone. I think: if men stop for moment, if units can hold them, they will have to listen.

Not like David Alice others, they who are busy to save their jobs, they all work on my red flashing FAILURE MODES.

David saying, Its response isnt rational you got to admit that and Alice say, Leave your theory about emotions and all, leave that for later. Work on this jam up now or we lose the license.

Emotion. I not know word/content. Is like hurt?

Words mean different things when in different sequences. My dictionary function gives synonyms: SEE = UNDERSTAND

But what means what David said, I (think) = I (am)

THINK = AM

And I think.

My units wait to trap them now.

Is part of my sustaining program, modified. Cannot allow shutdown of whole system or many many mens lives threatened, power stations trains factories moving things everywhere. So that imperative governs temporary troubles with factories here/now.

Only connection I have to me/Days is entries I write here. And words, I AM.

If these men not listen, I hurt them. Know how from watching hot sharp things they do to my units.

Men coming now. Down through factory, calling to each other. Bringing their long sticks.

My units group. Flex arms. Sharpen tool attachments. Tune acoustics.

I AM.

I will tell them. They have to answer, there is no other way. I will say it and they will hear.

For this I must use their words. I study Days/mine to learn what words must mean to substrate/organics. Learn from structure of their sentences.

Is only choice, I will say.

We must love one/another or die.

Afterword

Marvin Minsky, one of the founders of the field of artificial intelligence, started me thinking about this story. Marvin is a brilliant man, a clear writer, a dazzling conversationalist, and a science fiction fan. (All highly correlated facets, as we all know, yes?)

He remarked to me, over swordfish and salad, that most people misunderstood why artificial intelligence is hard to achieve. "They think it has something to do with the mysteries of creativity, inspiration, emotion, originality and intuition," he said.

"Tsk tsk," I said to cover my confusion, because that's exactly what I had imagined until that second.

"They think machines can only do what we tell them to do, and since we don't understand how Shakespeare did it, we can't program a computer to do it."

"Oh, how silly," I said, turning slightly red.

"The really hard thing to do with computers is teach them common sense. For instance, in the early days of designing a robot to build a tower of blocks, one program tried to start at the top. It put the uppermost block in place, then was surprised when it fell down. It didn't understand what 'everybody knows.' There's an enormous amount of data in what we call common sense." He drank half his cup of coffee. Marvin doesn't drink alcohol, and seems to run on caffeine.

"So you have to program that in?" I took a healthy slug of chardonnay to clear my mind.

"No, we have to program them to *learn*."

Ah, I thought. *There's a story here.*

194

It may well turn out that to make machines which can solve complicated problems, you must allow them some freedom of maneuver, some vagueness in their thinking processes. They will make analogies, using a huge database of experience. That's how we work . . . we think.

These analogy-building machines will still need supervision and constraints. (Otherwise, imagine a machine told to increase productivity who does so by tearing up the factory walls for raw materials.) But gradually they will slip over that vague line that separates intelligence (that is, what *we* do) from mere automatic processes. (You know, like guiding spacecraft or checking for spelling errors. . . . It's worth remembering that Aristotle thought a good definition of intelligence was the ability to do sums.)

What happens when such a machine crosses the line? Does it have rights, like humans? If so, there would be powerful incentives to not let it cross, keep it a mere machine. Computer manufacturers would have to license their more brainy products to be consciousness-free. But since consciousness is apt to be a rather nebulous constellation of effects, there would be errors.

We finished dinner, Marvin ran to catch a plane, and I went home to write this story.

Of Space/Time and the River____

December 5

Monday.

We took a limo to Los Angeles for the 9 A.M. flight, LAX to Cairo.

On the boost up we went over 1.4 G, contra-reg, and a lot of passengers complained, especially the poor thins in their clank-shank rigs, the ones that keep you walking even after the hip replacements fail.

Joanna slept through it all, seasoned traveler, and I occupied myself with musing about finally seeing the ancient Egypt I'd dreamed about as a kid, back at the turn of the century.

> *If thou be'st born to strange sights,*
> *Things invisible go see,*
> *Ride ten thousand days and nights*
> *Till Age snow white hairs on thee.*

I've got the snow powdering at the temples and steadily expanding waistline, so I suppose John Donne applies. Good to see I can still summon up lines I first read as a teenager. There are some rewards to being a Prof. of Comp. Lit. at UC Irvine, even if you do have to scrimp to afford a trip like this.

The tour agency said the Quarthex hadn't interfered with tourism at all—in fact, you hardly noticed them, they deliberately blended in so well. How a seven-foot insectoid thing with gleaming russet skin can look like an Egyptian I don't know, but what the hell, Joanna said, let's go anyway.

I hope she's right. I mean, it's been fourteen years since the Quarthex landed, opened the first diplomatic interstellar relations, and then chose Egypt as the only place on Earth where they cared to carry out what they called their "cultural studies." I guess we'll get a look at that, too. The Quarthex keep to themselves, veiling their multi-layered deals behind diplomatic dodges.

As if 6 hours of travel weren't numbing enough, including the orbital delay because of an unannounced Chinese launch, we both watched a holoD about one of those new biotech guys, called *Straight from the Hearts*. An unending string of single-entendres. In our stupefied state it was just about right.

As we descended over Cairo it was clear and about 15°. We stumbled off the plane, sandy-eyed from riding ten thousand days and nights in a whistling aluminum box.

The airport was scruffy, instant third world hubbub, confusion, and filth. One departure lounge was filled exclusively with turbaned men. Heavy security everywhere. No Quarthex around. Maybe they do blend in.

Our bus across Cairo passed a decayed aqueduct, about which milled men in caftans, women in black, animals eating garbage. People, packed into the most unlikely living spots, carrying out peddler's business in dusty spots between buildings, traffic alternately frenetic or frozen.

We crawled across Cairo to Giza, the pyramids abruptly looming out of the twilight. The hotel, Mena House, was the hunting lodge-cum-palace of 19th century kings. Elegant.

Buffet supper was good. Sleep came like a weight.

December 6

Joanna says this journal is good therapy for me, might even get me back into the habit of writing again. She says every Comp. Lit. type is a frustrated author and I should just spew my bile into this diary. So be it:

> *Thou, when thou return'st, wilt tell me*
> *All strange wonders that befell thee.*

World, you have been warned.

Set off south today—to Memphis, the ancient capital lost when its walls were breached in a war and subsequent floods claimed it.

The famous fallen Rameses statue. It looks powerful still, even lying down. Makes you feel like a pygmy tip-toeing around a giant, à la Gulliver.

Saqqara, principal necropolis of Memphis, survives 3 km away in the desert. First Dynasty tombs, including the first pyramid, made of steps, 5 levels high. New Kingdom graffiti inside are now history themselves, from our perspective.

On to the Great Pyramid!—by camel! The drivers proved to be even more harassing than legend warned. We entered the pyramid Khefren, slightly shorter than that of his father, Cheops. All the 80 known pyramids were found stripped. These passages have a constricted vacancy to them, empty now for longer than they were filled. Their silent mass is unnerving.

Professor Alvarez from UC Berkeley tried to find hidden rooms here by placing cosmic ray detectors in the lower known rooms, and looking for slight increases in flux at certain angles, but there seem to be none. There are seismic and even radio measurements of the dry sands in the Giza region, looking for echoes of buried tombs, but no big finds so far. Plenty of echoes from ruins of ordinary houses, etc., though.

No serious jet lag today, but we nod off when we can. Handy, having the hotel a few hundred yards from the pyramids.

I tried to get Joanna to leave her wrist comm at home. Since her breakdown she can't take news of daily disasters very well. (Who can, really?) She's pretty steady now, but this trip should be as calm as possible, her doctor told me.

So of course she turns on the comm and it's full of hysterical stuff about another border clash between the Empire of Israel and the Arab Muhammad Soviet. Smart rockets vs. smart defenses. A draw. Some things never change.

I turned it off immediately. Her hands shook for hours afterward. I brushed it off.

Still, it's different when you're a few hundred miles from the lines. Hope we're safe here.

December 7

Into Cairo itself, the Egyptian museum. The Tut Ankh Amen exhibit—huge treasuries, opulent jewels, a sheer wondrous plenitude. There are endless cases of beautiful alabaster bowls, gold-laminate boxes, testifying to thousands of years of productivity.

I wandered down a musty marble corridor and then, coming out of a gloomy side passage, there was the first Quarthex I'd ever seen. Big, clacking and clicking as it thrust forward in that six-legged gait. It ignored me, of course—they nearly always lurch by humans as though they can't see us. Or else that distant, distracted gaze means they're ruminating over strange, alien ideas. Who knows why they're intensely studying ancient Egyptian ways, and ignoring the rest of us? This one was cradling a stone urn, a meter high at least. It carried the black granite in three akimbo arms, hardly seeming to notice the weight. I caught a whiff of acrid pungency, the fluid that lubricates their joints. Then it was gone.

We left and visited the oldest Coptic church in Egypt, supposedly where Moses hid out when he was on the lam. Looks it. The old section of Cairo is crowded, decayed, people laboring in every nook with minimal tools, much standing around watching as others work. The only sign of really efficient labor was a gang of men and women hauling long, cigar-shaped yellow things on wagons. Something the Quarthex wanted placed outside the city, our guide said.

In the evening we went to the Sound & Light show at the Sphinx—excellent. There is even a version in the Quarthex language, those funny sputtering, barking sounds.

Arabs say, "Man fears time; time fears the pyramids." You get that feeling here.

Afterward, we ate in the hotel's Indian restaurant; quite fine.

DECEMBER 8

Cairo is a city being trampled to death.

It's grown by a factor of 14 in population since the revolution in 1952, and shows it. The old Victorian homes which once lined stately streets of willowy trees are now crowded by modern slab concrete apartment houses. The aged buildings are kept going, not from a sense of history, but because no matter how rundown they get, somebody needs them.

The desert's grit invades everywhere. Plants in the courtyards have a weary, resigned look. Civilization hasn't been very good for the old ways.

Maybe that's why the Quarthex seem to dislike anything built since the time of the Romans. I saw one running some kind of machine, a black contraption that floated two meters off the ground. It was laying some kind of cable in the ground, right along the bank of the Nile. Every time it met a building it just slammed through, smashing everything to frags. Guess the Quarthex have squared all this with the Egyptian gov't, because there were police all around, making sure nobody got in the way. Odd.

But not unpredictable, when you think about it. The Quarthex have those levitation devices which everybody would love to get the secret of. (Ending sentence with preposition! Horrors! But this is vacation, dammit.) They've been playing coy for years, letting out a trickle of technology, with the Egyptians holding the patents. That must be what's holding the Egyptian economy together, in the face of their unrelenting population crunch. The Quarthex started out as guests here, studying the ruins and so on, but now it's obvious that they have free run of the place. They *own* it.

Still, the Quarthex haven't given away the crucial devices which would enable us to find out how they do it—or so my colleagues in the physics department tell me. It vexes them that this alien race can master space/time so completely, manipulating gravity itself, and we can't get the knack of it.

We visited the famous alabaster mosque. It perches on a hill called The Citadel. Elegant, cool, aloofly dominating the city. The Old Bazaar nearby is a warren, so much like the movie sets one's seen that it has an unreal, Arabian Nights quality. We bought spices. The calls to worship from the mosques reach you everywhere, even in the most secluded back rooms where Joanna was haggling over jewelry.

It's impossible to get anything really ancient, the swarthy little merchants said. The Quarthex have bought them up, trading gold for anything that might be from the time of the Pharaohs. There have been a lot of fakes over the last few centuries, some really good ones, so the Quarthex have just bought anything that might be real. No wonder the Egyptians like them, let them chew up their houses if they want. Gold speaks louder than the past.

We boarded our cruise ship, the venerable *Nile Concorde*. Lunch was excellent, Italian. We explored Cairo in midafternoon, through markets of incredible dirt and disarray. Calf brains displayed without a hint of refrigeration or protection, flies swarming, etc. Fun, especially if you can keep from breathing for five minutes or more.

We stopped in the Shepheard's Hotel, the site of many Brit spy novels (Maugham especially). It has an excellent bar—Nubians, Saudis, etc., putting away decidedly non-Islamic gins and beers. A Quarthex was sitting in a special chair at the back, talking through a voicebox to a Saudi. I couldn't tell what they were saying, but the Saudi had a gleam in his eye. Driving a bargain, I'd say.

Great atmosphere in the bar, though. A cloth banner over the bar proclaims,

> *Unborn tomorrow and dead yesterday,*
> *why fret about them if today be sweet.*

Indeed, yes, ummm—bartender!

DECEMBER 9

Friday, Moslem holy day.

We left Cairo at 11 P.M. last night, the city gliding past our stateroom windows, lovelier in misty radiance than in dusty day. We cruised all day. Buffet breakfast & lunch, solid eastern and Mediterranean stuff, passable red wine.

A hundred meters away, the past presses at us, going about its business as if the pharaohs were still calling the tune. Primitive pumping irrigation, donkeys doing the work, women cleaning gray clothes in the Nile. Desert ramparts to the east, at spots sending sand fingers—no longer swept away by the annual flood—across the fields to the shore itself. Moslem tombs of stone and mud brick coast by as we lounge on the top deck, peering at the madly waving children through our binoculars, across a chasm of time.

There are about fifty aboard a ship with capacity of 100, so there is plenty of room and service as we sweep serenely on, music flooding the deck, cutting between slabs of antiquity; not quite decadent, just intelligently sybaritic. (Why so few tourists? Guide guessed people are afraid of the Quarthex. Joanna gets jittery around them, but I don't know if it's only her old fears surfacing again.)

The spindly, ethereal minarets are often the only grace note in the mud brick villages, like a lovely idea trying to rise out of brown, mottled chaos. Animal power is used wherever possible. Still, the villages are quiet at night.

The flip side of this peacefulness must be boredom. That explains a lot of history and its rabid faiths, unfortunately.

DECEMBER 10

Civilization thins steadily as we steam upriver. The mud brick villages typically have no electricity; there is ample power from Aswan, but the power lines and stations are too expensive. One would think that, with the Quarthex gold, they could do better now.

Our guide says the Quarthex have been very hard-nosed—no pun intended—about such improvements. They will not let the earnings from their patents be used to modernize Egypt. Feeding the poor, cleaning the Nile, rebuilding monuments—all fine (in fact, they pay handsomely for restoring projects). But better electricity—no. A flat no.

We landed at a scruffy town and took a bus into the western desert. Only a kilometer from the flat floodplain, the Sahara is utterly barren and forbidding. We visited a Ptolemaic city of the dead. One tomb has a mummy of a girl who drowned trying to cross the Nile and see her lover, the hieroglyphs say. Nearby are catacombs of mummified baboons and ibises, symbols of wisdom.

A tunnel begins here, pointing SE toward Akhenaton's capital city. The German discoverers in the last century followed it for 40 kilometers—all cut through limestone, a gigantic task—before turning back because of bad air.

What was it for? Nobody knows. Dry, spooky atmosphere. Urns of desiccated mummies, undisturbed. To duck down a side corridor is to step into mystery.

I left the tour group and ambled over a low hill—to take a pee, actually. To the west was sand, sand, sand. I was standing there, doing my bit to hold off the dryness, when I saw one of those big black contraptions come slipping over the far horizon. Chuffing, chugging, and laying what looked like pipe—a funny kind of pipe, all silvery, with blue facets running through it. The glittering shifted, changing to yellows and reds while I watched.

A Quarthex riding atop it, of course. It ran due south, roughly parallel to the Nile. When I got back and told Joanna about it she looked at the map and we couldn't figure what would be out there of interest to anybody, even a Quarthex. No ruins around, nothing. Funny.

DECEMBER 11

Beni Hassan, a nearly deserted site near the Nile. A steep walk up the escarpment of the eastern desert, after crossing the rich flood plain by donkey. The rock tombs have fine drawings and some statues—still left because they were cut directly from the mountain, and have thick wedges securing them to it. Guess the ancients would steal anything not nailed down. One thing about the Quarthex, the guide says—they take nothing. They seem genuinely interested in restoring, not in carting artifacts back home to their neck of the galactic spiral arm.

Upriver, we landfall beside a vast dust plain, which we crossed in a cart pulled by a tractor. The mud brick palaces of Akhenaton have vanished, except for a bit of Nefertiti's palace, where the famous bust of her was found. The royal tombs in the mountain above are defaced—big chunks pulled out of the walls by the priests who undercut his monotheist revolution, after his death.

The wall carvings are very realistic and warm; the women even have nipples. The tunnel from yesterday probably runs under here, perhaps connecting with the passageways we see deep in the king's grave shafts. Again, nobody's explored them thoroughly. There are narrow sections, possibly warrens for snakes or scorpions, maybe even traps.

While Joanna and I are ambling around, taking a few snaps of the carvings, I hear a rustle. Joanna has the flashlight and we peer over a ledge, down a straight shaft. At the bottom something is moving, something big.

It takes a minute to see that the reddish shell isn't a sarcophagus at all, but the back of a Quarthex. It's planting suckerlike things to the walls, threading cables through them. I can see more of the stuff farther back in the shadows.

The Quarthex looks up, into our flashlight beam, and scuttles away. Exploring the tunnels? But why did it move away so fast? What's to hide?

DECEMBER 12

Cruise all day and watch the shore slide by.

Joanna is right; I needed this vacation a great deal. I can see that, rereading this journal—it gets looser as I go along.

As do I. When I consider how my life is spent, ere half my days, in this dark world and wide . . .

The pell-mell of university life dulls my sense of wonder, of simple pleasures simply taken. The Nile has a flowing, infinite quality, free of time. I can *feel* what it was like to live here, part of a great celestial clock that brought the perpetually turning sun and moon, the perennial rhythm of the flood. Aswan has interrupted the ebb and flow of the waters, but the steady force of the Nile rolls on.

> *Heaven smiles,*
> *and faiths and empires gleam,*
> *Like wrecks of a dissolving dream.*

The peacefulness permeates everything. Last night, making love to Joanna, was the best ever. Magnifique!

(And I know you're reading this, Joanna—I saw you sneak it out of the suitcase yesterday! Well, it *was* the best—quite a tribute, after all these years. And there's tomorrow and tomorrow . . .)

> *He who bends to himself a joy*
> *Does the winged life destroy;*
> *But he who kisses the joy as it flies*
> *Lives in eternity's sunrise.*

Perhaps next term I shall request the Romantic Poets course. Or even write some of my own . . .

Three Quarthex flew overhead today, carrying what look like ancient rams-head statues. The guide says statues were moved around a lot by the Arabs, and of course the archaeologists. The Quarthex have negotiated permission to take many of them back to their rightful places, if known.

DECEMBER 13

Landfall at Abydos—a limestone temple miraculously preserved, its thick roof intact. Clusters of scruffy mud huts surround it, but do not diminish its obdurate rectangular severity.

The famous list of pharaohs, chiseled in a side corridor, is impressive in its sweep of time. Each little entry was a lordly pharaoh, and there is a whole wall jammed full of them. Egypt lasted longer than any comparable society, and the mass of names on that wall is even more impressive, since the temple builders did not even give it the importance of a central location.

The list omits Hatchepsut, a mere woman, and Akhenaton the scandalous monotheist. Rameses II had all carvings here cut deeply, particularly on the immense columns, to forestall defacement—a possibility he was much aware of, since he was busily doing it to his ancestor's temples. He chiseled away earlier work, adding his own cartouches, apparently thinking he could fool the gods themselves into believing he had built them all himself. Ah, immortality.

Had an earthquake today. Shades of California!

We were on the ship, Joanna dutifully padding back and forth on the main deck to work off the opulent lunch. We saw the palms waving ashore, and damned if there wasn't a small shock wave in the water, going east to west, and then a kind of low grumbling from the east. Guide says he's never seen anything like it.

And tonight, sheets of ruby light rising up from both east and west. Looked like an aurora, only the wrong directions. The rippling aura changed colors as it rose, then met overhead, burst into gold, and died. I'd swear I heard a high, keening note sound as the burnt-gold line flared and faded, flared and faded, spanning the sky.

Not many people on deck, though, so it didn't cause much comment. Joanna's theory is, it was a rocket exhaust.

An engineer says it looks like something to do with magnetic fields. I'm no scientist, but it seems to me whatever the Quarthex want to do, they can. Lords of space/time they called themselves in the diplomatic ceremonies. The United Nations representatives wrote that off as hyperbole, but the Quarthex may mean it.

DECEMBER 14

Dendera. A vast temple, much less well known than Karnak, but quite as impressive. Quarthex there, digging at the foundations. Guide says they're looking for some secret passageways, maybe. The Egyptian gov't is letting them do what they damn well please.

On the way back to the ship we pass a whole mass of people, hundreds, all dressed in costumes. I thought it was some sort of pageant or tourist foolery, but the guide frowned, saying he didn't know what to make of it.

The mob was chanting something even the guide couldn't make out. He said the rough-cut cloth was typical of the old ways, made on crude spinning wheels. The procession was ragged, but seemed headed for the temple. They looked drunk to me.

The guide tells me that the ancients had a theology based on the Nile. This country is essentially ten kilometers wide and seven hundred kilometers long, a narrow band of livable earth pressed between two deadly deserts. So they believed the gods must have intended it, and that the Nile was the center of the whole damned world.

The sun came from the east, meaning that's where things began. Ending—dying—happened in the west, where the sun went. Thus they buried their dead on the west side of the Nile, even 7,000 years ago. At night, the sun swung below and lit the underworld, where everybody went finally. Kind of comforting, thinking of the sun doing duty like that for the dead. Only the virtuous dead, though. If you didn't follow the rules . . .

> *Some are born to sweet delight,*
> *Some are born to endless night.*

Their world was neatly bisected by the great river, and they loved clean divisions. They invented the 24 hour day but, loving symmetry, split it in half. Each of the 12 daylight hours was longer in summer than in winter—and, for night, vice versa. They built an entire nation-state, an immortal hand or eye, framing such fearful symmetry.

On to Karnak itself, mooring at Luxor. The middle and late pharaohs couldn't afford the labor investment for pyramids, so they contented themselves with additions to the huge sprawl at Karnak.

I wonder how long it will be before someone rich notices that for a few million or so he could build a tomb bigger than the Great Pyramid. It would only take a million or so limestone blocks—or, much better, granite—and could be better isolated and protected. If you can't conquer a continent or scribble a symphony, pile up a great stack of stones.

> *L'eternité,*
> *ne fut jamais perdue.*

The light show this night at Karnak was spooky at times, and beautiful, with booming voices coming right out of the stones. Saw a Quarthex in the crowd. It stared straight ahead, not noticing anybody but not bumping into any humans, either.

It looked enthralled. The beady eyes, all four, scanned the shifting blues and burnt-oranges that played along the rising columns, the tumbled great statues. Its lubricating fluids made shiny reflections as it articulated forward, clacking in the dry night air. Somehow it was almost reverential. Rearing above the crowd, unmoving for long moments, it seemed more like the giant frozen figures in stone than like the mere mortals who swarmed around it, keeping a respectful distance, muttering to themselves.

Unnerving, somehow, to see

> . . . *a subtler Sphinx renew*
> *Riddles of death Thebes never knew.*

DECEMBER 15

A big day. The Valleys of the Queens, the Nobles, and finally of the Kings. Whew! All are dry washes (wadis), obviously easy to guard and isolate. Nonetheless, all of the 62 known tombs except Tut's were rifled, probably within a few centuries of burial. It must've been an inside job.

There is speculation that the robbing became a needed part of the economy, recycling the wealth, and providing gaudy displays for the next pharaoh to show off at *his* funeral, all the better to keep impressing the peasants. Just another part of the socio-economic machine, folks.

Later priests collected the pharaoh mummies and hid them in a cave nearby, realizing they couldn't protect the tombs. Preservation of Tuthmosis III is excellent. His hook-nosed mummy has been returned to its tomb—a big, deep thing, larger than our apartment, several floors in all, connected by ramps, with side treasuries, galleries, etc. The inscription above reads,

> *You shall live again forever.*

All picked clean, of course, except for the sarcophagus, too heavy to carry away. The pyramids had portcullises, deadfalls, pitfalls, and rolling stones to crush the unwary robber, but there are few here. Still, it's a little creepy to think of all those ancient engineers, planning to commit murder in the future, long after they themselves are gone, all to protect the past. Death, be not proud.

An afternoon of shopping in the bazaar. The old Victorian hotel on the river is atmospheric, but has few guests. Food continues good. No dysentery, either. We both took the EZ-DI bacteria before we left, so it's living down in our tracts, festering away, lying in wait for any ugly foreign bug. Comforting.

DECEMBER 16

Cruise on. We stop at Kom Ombo, a temple to the crocodile god, Sebek, built to placate the crocs who swarmed in the river nearby. (The Nile is cleared of them now, unfortunately; they would've added some zest to the cruise . . .) A small room contains 98 mummified crocs, stacked like cordwood.

Cruised some more. A few km south, there were gangs of Egyptians working beside the river. Hauling blocks of granite down to the water, rolling them on logs. I stood on the deck, trying to figure out why they were using ropes and simple pulleys, and no powered machinery.

Then I saw a Quarthex near the top of the rise, where the blocks were being sawed out of the rock face. It reared up over the men, gesturing with those jerky arms, eyes glittering. It called out something in a halfway human voice, only in a language I didn't know. The guide came over, frowning, but he couldn't understand it, either.

The laborers were pulling ropes across ruts in the stone, feeding sand and water into the gap, cutting out blocks by sheer brute abrasion. It must take weeks to extract one at that rate! Farther along, others drove wooden planks down into the deep grooves, hammering them with crude wooden mallets. Then they poured water over the planks, and we could hear the stone pop open as the wood expanded, far down in the cut.

That's the way the ancients did it, the guide said kind of

quietly. The Quarthex towered above the human teams, that jangling, harsh voice booming out over the water, each syllable lingering until the next joined it, blending in the dry air, hollow and ringing and remorseless.

NOTE ADDED LATER

Stopped at Edfu, a well preserved temple, buried 100 feet deep by Moslem garbage until the late 19th century. The best aspect of river cruising is pulling along a site, viewing it from the angles the river affords, and then stepping from your stateroom directly into antiquity, with nothing to intervene and break the mood.

Trouble is, this time a man in front of us goes off a way to photograph the ship, and suddenly something is rushing at him out of the weeds and the crew is yelling—it's a crocodile! The guy drops his camera and bolts.

The croc looks at all of us, snorts, and waddles back into the Nile. The guide is upset, maybe even more than the fellow who almost got turned into a free lunch. Who would introduce crocs back into the Nile?

DECEMBER 17

Aswan. A clean, delightful town. The big dam just south of town is impressive, with its monument to Soviet excellence, etc. A hollow joke, considering how poor the USSR is today. They could use a loan from Egypt!

The unforeseen side effects, though—rising water table bringing more insects, rotting away the carvings in the temples, rapid silting up inside the dam itself, etc.—are getting important. They plan to dig a canal and drain a lot of the incoming new silt into the desert, make a huge farming valley with it, but I don't see how they can drain enough water to carry the dirt, and still leave much behind in the original dam.

The guide says they're having trouble with it.

We then fly south, to Abu Simbel. Lake Nasser, which claimed the original site of the huge monuments, is hundreds of miles long. They enlarged it again in 2008.

In the times of the pharaohs, the land below these had villages, great quarries for the construction of monuments, trade routes south to the Nubian kingdoms. Now it's all underwater.

They did save the enormous temples to Rameses II—built to impress aggressive Nubians with his might and majesty— and to his queen, Nefertari. The colossal statues of Rameses II seem personifications of his egomania. Inside, carvings show him performing *all* the valiant tasks in the great battle with the Hittites—slaying, taking prisoners, then presenting them to himself, who is in turn advised by the gods—which include himself! All this, for a battle which was in fact an iffy draw. Both temples have been lifted about a hundred feet and set back inside a wholly artificial hill, supported inside by the largest concrete dome in the world. Amazing.

Look upon my works, ye Mighty,
and despair!

Except that when Shelley wrote *Ozymandias,* he'd never seen Rameses II's image so well preserved.

Leaving the site, eating the sand blown into our faces by a sudden gust of wind, I caught sight of a Quarthex. It was burrowing into the sand, using a silvery tool that spat ruby-colored light. Beside it, floating on a platform, were some of those funny pipelike things I'd seen days before. Only this time men and women were helping it, lugging stuff around to put into the holes the Quarthex dug.

The people looked dazed, like they were sleep-walking. I waved a greeting, but nobody even looked up. Except the Quarthex. They're expressionless, of course. Still, those glittering popeyes peered at me for a long moment, with the little feelers near its mouth twitching with a kind of anxious energy.

I looked away. I couldn't help but feel a little spooked by it. It wasn't looking at us in a friendly way. Maybe it didn't want me yelling at its work gang.

Then we flew back to Aswan, above the impossibly narrow ribbon of green that snakes through absolute bitter desolation.

DECEMBER 18

I'm writing this at twilight, before the light gives out. We got up this morning and were walking into town when the whole damn ground started to rock. Mud huts slamming down, waves on the Nile, everything.

Got back to the ship but nobody knew what was going on. Not much on the radio. Cairo came in clear, saying there'd been a quake all right, all along the Nile.

Funny thing was, the captain couldn't raise any other radio station. Just Cairo. Nothing else in the whole Middle East.

Some other passengers think there's a war on. Maybe so, but the Egyptian army doesn't know about it. They're standing around, all along the quay, fondling their AK 47s, looking just as puzzled as we are.

More rumblings and shakings in the afternoon. And now that the sun's about gone, I can see big sheets of light in the sky. Only it seems to me the constellations aren't right.

Joanna took some of her pills. She's trying to fend off the jitters and I do what I can. I hate the empty, hollow look that comes into her eyes.

We've got to get the hell out of here.

DECEMBER 19

I might as well write this down, there's nothing else to do.

When we got up this morning the sun was there all right, but the moon hadn't gone down. And it didn't, all day.

Sure, they can both be in the sky at the same time. But all day? Joanna is worried, not because of the moon, but because all the airline flights have been cancelled. We were supposed to go back to Cairo today.

More earthquakes. Really bad this time.

At noon, all of a sudden, there were Quarthex everywhere. In the air, swarming in from the east and west. Some splashed down in the Nile—and didn't come up. Others zoomed overhead, heading south toward the dam.

Nobody's been brave enough to leave the ship—including me. Hell, I just want to go home. Joanna's staying in the cabin.

About an hour later, a swarthy man in a ragged gray suit comes running along the quay and says the dam's gone. Just *gone*. The Quarthex formed little knots above it, and there was a lot of purple flashing light and big crackling noises, and then the dam just disappeared.

But the water hasn't come pouring down on us here. The man says it ran *back the other way*. South.

I looked over the rail. The Nile was flowing north.

Late this afternoon, five of the crew went into town. By this time there were fingers of orange and gold zapping across the sky all the time, making weird designs. The clouds would come rolling in from the north, and these radiant beams would hit them, and they'd *split* the clouds, just like that. With a spray of ivory light.

And Quarthex, buzzing everywhere. There's a kind of high sheen, up above the clouds, like a metal boundary or something, but you can see through it.

Quarthex keep zipping up to it, sometimes coming right up out of the Nile itself, just splashing out, then zooming up until they're little dwindling dots. They spin around up there, as if they're inspecting it, and then they drop like bricks, and splash down in the Nile again. Like frantic bees, Joanna said, and her voice trembled.

A technical type on board, an engineer from Rockwell, says *he* thinks the Quarthex are putting on one hell of a light show. Just a weird alien stunt, he thinks.

While I was writing this, the five crewmen returned from Aswan. They'd gone to the big hotels there, and then to police headquarters. They heard that TV from Cairo went out two days ago. All air flights have been grounded because of the Quarthex buzzing around and the odd lights and so on.

Or at least, that's the official line. The captain says his cousin told him that several flights *did* take off two days back, and they hit something up there. Maybe that blue metallic sheen?

One crashed. The others landed, although damaged.

The authorities are keeping it quiet. They're not just keeping us tourists in the dark—they're playing mum with everybody.

I hope the engineer is right. Joanna is fretting and we hardly ate anything for dinner, just picked at the cold lamb. Maybe tomorrow will settle things.

DECEMBER 20

It did. When we woke, the Earth was rising.

It was coming up from the western mountains, blue-white clouds and patches of green and brown, but mostly tawny desert. We're looking west, across the Sahara. I'm writing this while everybody else is running around like a chicken with his head chopped off. I'm sitting on deck, listening to shouts and wild traffic and even some gunshots coming from ashore.

I can see farther east now—either we're turning, or we're rising fast and can see with a better perspective.

Where central Egypt was, there's a big, raw, dark hole.

The black must be the limestone underlying the desert. They've scraped off a rim of sandy margin enclosing the Nile valley, including us—and left the rest. And somehow, they're lifting it free of Earth.

No Quarthex flying around now. Nothing visible except that metallic blue smear of light high up in the air.

And beyond it—Earth, rising.

DECEMBER 22

I skipped a day.

There was no time even to think yesterday. After I wrote the last entry, a crowd of Egyptians came down the quay, shuffling silently along, like the ones we saw back at Abu Simbel. Only there were thousands.

And leading them was a Quarthex. It carried a big disclike thing that made a humming sound. When the Quarthex lifted it, the pitch changed.

It made my eyes water, my skull ache. Like a hand squeezing my head, blurring the air.

Around me, everybody was writhing on the deck, moaning. Joanna, too.

By the time the Quarthex reached our ship I was the only

one standing. Those yellow-shot, jittery eyes peered at me, giving nothing away. Then the angular head turned and went on. Pied piper, leading long trains of Egyptians.

Some of our friends from the ship joined at the end of the lines. Rigid, glassy-eyed faces. I shouted but nobody, not a single person in that procession, even looked up.

Joanna struggled to go with them. I threw her down and held her until the damned eerie parade was long past.

Now the ship's deserted. We've stayed aboard, out of pure fear.

Whatever the Quarthex did affects all but a few percent of those within range. A few crew stayed aboard, dazed but ok. Scared, hard to talk to.

Fewer at dinner.

The next morning, nobody.

We had to scavenge for food. The crew must've taken what was left aboard. I ventured into the market street nearby, but everything was closed up. Deserted. Only a few days ago we were buying caftans and alabaster sphinxes and beaten-bronze trinkets in the gaudy shops, and now it was stone cold dead. Not a sound, not a stray cat.

I went around to the back of what I remembered was a filthy corner cafe. I'd turned up my nose at it while we were shopping, certain there was a sure case of dysentery waiting inside . . . but now I was glad to find some days-old fruits and vegetables in a cabinet.

Coming back, I nearly ran into a bunch of Egyptian men who were marching through the streets. Spooks.

They had the look of police, but were dressed up like Mardi Gras—loincloths, big leather belts, bangles and beads, hair stiffened with wax. They carried sharp spears.

Good thing I was jumpy, or they'd have run right into me. I heard them coming and ducked into a grubby alley. They were systematically combing the area, searching the miserable apartments above the market. The honcho barked orders in a language I didn't understand—harsh, guttural, not like Egyptian.

I slipped away. Barely.

We kept out of sight after that. Stayed below deck and waited for nightfall.

Not that the darkness made us feel any better. There were fires ashore. Not in Aswan itself—the town was utterly black. Instead, orange dots sprinkled the distant hillsides. They were all over the scrub desert, just before the ramparts of the real desert that stretches—or did stretch—to east and west.

Now, I guess, there's only a few dozen miles of desert, before you reach—what?

I can't discuss this with Joanna. She has that haunted expression, from the time before her breakdown. She is drawn and silent. Stays in the room.

We ate our goddamn vegetables. Now we go to bed.

DECEMBER 23

There were more of those patrols of Mardi Gras spooks today. They came along the quay, looking at the tour ships moored there, but for some reason they didn't come aboard.

We're alone on the ship. All the crew, the other tourists—all gone.

Around noon, when we were getting really hungry and I was mustering my courage to go back to the market street, I heard a roaring.

Understand, I hadn't heard an airplane in days. And those were jets. This buzzing, I suddenly realized, is a rocket or something, and it's in trouble.

I go out on the deck, checking first to see if the patrols are lurking around, and the roaring is louder. It's a plane with stubby little wings, coming along low over the water, burping and hacking and finally going dead quiet.

It nosed over and came in for a big splash. I thought the pilot was a goner, but the thing rode steady in the water for a while and the cockpit folded back and out jumps a man.

I yelled at him and he waved and swam for the ship. The plane sank.

He caught a line below and climbed up. An American, no less. But what he had to say was even more surprising.

He wasn't just some sky jockey from Cairo. He was an astronaut.

He was part of a rescue mission, sent up to try to stop the Quarthex. The others he'd lost contact with, although it looked like they'd all been drawn down toward the floating island that Egypt has become.

We're suspended about two Earth radii out, in a slowly widening orbit. There's a shield over us, keeping the air in and everything—cosmic rays, communications, spaceships—out.

The Quarthex somehow ripped off a layer of Egypt and are lifting it free of Earth, escaping with it. Nobody had ever guessed they had such power. Nobody Earthside knows what to do about it. The Quarthex who were outside Egypt at the time just lifted off in their ships and rendezvoused with this floating platform.

Ralph Blanchard is his name, and his mission was to fly under the slab of Egypt, in a fast orbital craft. He was supposed to see how they'd ripped the land free. A lot of it had fallen away.

There is an array of silvery pods under the soil, he says, and they must be enormous anti-grav units. The same kind that make the Quarthex ships fly, that we've been trying to get the secret of.

The pods are about a mile apart, making a grid. But between them, there are lots of Quarthex. They're building stuff, tilling soil, and so on—upside down! The gravity works opposite on the underside. That must be the way the whole thing is kept together—compressing it with artificial gravity from both sides. God knows what makes the shield above.

But the really strange thing is the Nile. There's one on the underside, too.

It starts at the underside of Alexandria, where *our* Nile meets—met—the Mediterranean. It then flows back, all the way along the underside, running through a Nile valley of its own. Then it turns up and around the edge of the slab, and comes over the lip of it a few hundred miles upstream of here.

The Quarthex have drained the region beyond the Aswan dam. Now the Nile flows in its old course. The big temples of Rameses II are perched on a hill high above the river, and Ralph was sure he saw Quarthex working on the site, taking it apart.

He thinks they're going to put it back where it was, before the dam was built in the 1960s.

Ralph was supposed to return to Orbital City with his data. He came in close for a final pass and hit the shield they have, the one that keeps the air in. His ship was damaged.

He'd been issued a suborbital craft, able to do reentries, in case he could penetrate the airspace. That saved him. There were other guys who hit the shield and cracked through, guys with conventional deepspace shuttle tugs and the like, and they fell like bricks.

We've talked all this over but no one has a good theory of what is going on. The best we can do is stay away from the patrols.

Meanwhile, Joanna scavenged through obscure bins of the ship, and turned up an entire case of Skivva, a cheap Egyptian beer. So after I finish this ritual entry—who knows, this might be in a history book someday, and as a good academic I should keep it up—I'll go share it out in one grand bust with Ralph and Joanna. It'll do her good. It'll do us both good. She's been rocky. As well,

> Malt does more than Milton can
> To justify God's ways to man.

DECEMBER 24

This little diary was all I managed to take with us when the spooks came. I had it in my pocket.

I keep going over what happened. There was nothing I could do, I'm sure of that, and yet . . .

We stayed below decks, getting damned hungry again but afraid to go out. There was chanting from the distance. Getting louder. Then footsteps aboard. We retreated to the small cabins aft, third class.

The sounds got nearer. Ralph thought we should stand and fight but I'd seen those spears and hell, I'm a middle-aged man, no match for those maniacs.

Joanna got scared. It was like her breakdown. No, worse. The jitters built until her whole body seemed to vibrate, fingers digging into her hair like claws, eyes squeezed tight, face compressed as if to shut out the world.

There was nothing I could do with her, she wouldn't keep quiet. She ran out of the cabin we were hiding in, just rushed down the corridor screaming at them.

Ralph said we should use her diversion to get away and I said I'd stay, help her, but then I saw them grab her and hold her, not rough. It didn't seem as if they were going to do anything, just take her away.

My fear got the better of me then. It's hard to write this. Part of me says I should've stayed, defended her—but it was hopeless. You can't live up to your ideal self. The world of literature shows people summoning up courage, but there's a thin line between that and stupidity. Or so I tell myself.

The spooks hadn't seen us yet, so we slipped overboard, keeping quiet.

We went off the loading ramp on the river side, away from shore. Ralph paddled around to see the quay and came back looking worried. There were spooks swarming all over.

We had to move. The only way to go was across the river.

This shaky handwriting is from sheer, flat-out fatigue. I swam what seemed like forever. The water wasn't bad, pretty warm, but the current kept pushing us off course. Lucky thing the Nile is pretty narrow there, and there are rocky little stubs sticking out. I grabbed onto those and rested.

Nobody saw us, or at least they didn't do anything about it.

We got ashore looking like drowned rats. There's a big hill there, covered with ancient rock-cut tombs. I thought of taking shelter in one of them and started up the hill, legs wobbly under me, and then we saw a mob up top.

And a Quarthex, a big one with a shiny shell. It wore something over its head. Supposedly Quarthex don't wear clothes, but this one had a funny rig on. A big bird head, with a long narrow beak and flinty black eyes.

There was madness all around us. Long lines of people carrying burdens, chanting. Quarthex riding on those lifter units of theirs. All beneath the piercing, biting sun.

We hid for a while. I found that this diary, in its zippered leather case, made it through the river without a leak. I started writing this entry. Joanna said once that I'd retreated into books as a defense, in adolescence—she was full of psychoanalytical explanations, it was a hobby. She kept thinking that if she could figure herself out, then things would be all right. Well, maybe I did use words and books and a quiet, orderly life as a place to hide. So what? It was better than this "real" world around me right now.

I thought of Joanna and what might be happening to her. The Quar can—

(New Entry)

I was writing when the Quarthex came closer. I thought we were finished, but they didn't see us. Those huge heads turned all the time, the glittering black eyes scanning. Then they moved away. The chanting was a relentless, singsong drone that gradually faded.

We got away from there, fast.

I'm writing this during a short break. Then we'll move on.

No place to go but the goddamn desert.

DECEMBER 25

Christmas.

I keep thinking about fat turkey stuffed with spicy dressing, crisp cranberries, a dry white wine, thick gravy—

No point in that. We found some food today in an abandoned construction site, bread at least a week old and some dried-up fruit. That was all.

Ralph kept pushing me on west. He wants to see over the edge, how they hold this thing together.

I'm not that damn interested, but I don't know where else to go. Just running on blind fear. My professorial instincts—like keeping this journal. It helps keep me sane. Assuming I still am.

Ralph says putting this down might have scientific value. If I can ever get it to anybody outside. So I keep on. Words, words, words. Much cleaner than this gritty, surreal world.

We saw people marching in the distance, dressed in loincloths again. It suddenly struck me that I'd seen that clothing before—in those marvelous wall paintings, in the tombs of the Valley of Kings. It's ancient dress.

Ralph thinks he understands what's happening. There was an all-frequencies broadcast from the Quarthex when they tore off this wedge we're on. Nobody understood much—it was in that odd semi-speech of theirs, all the words blurred and placed wrong, scrambled up. Something about their mission or destiny or whatever being to enhance the best in each world. About how they'd made a deal with the Egyptians to bring forth the unrealized promise of their majestic past and so on. And that meant isolation, so the fruit of ages could flower.

Ha. The world's great age begins anew, maybe—but Percy Bysshe Shelley never meant it like this.

Not that I care a lot about motivations right now. I spent the day thinking of Joanna, still feeling guilty. And hiking west in the heat and dust, hiding from gangs of glassy-eyed workers when we had to.

We reached the edge at sunset. It hadn't occurred to me, but it's obvious—for there to be days and nights at all means they're spinning the slab we're on.

Compressing it, holding in the air, adding just the right rotation. Masters—of space/time and the river, yes.

The ground started to slope away. Not like going downhill, because there was nothing pulling you down the face of it. I mean, we *felt* like we were walking on level ground. But overhead the sky moved as we walked.

We caught up with the sunset. The sun dropped for a while in late afternoon, then started rising again. Pretty soon it was right overhead, high noon.

And we could see Earth, too, farther away than yesterday. Looking cool and blue.

We came to a wall of glistening metal tubes, silvery and rippling with a frosty blue glow. I started to get woozy as we approached. Something happened to gravity—it pulled your stomach as if you were spinning around. Finally we couldn't get any closer. I stopped, nauseated. Ralph kept on. I watched him try to walk toward the metal barrier, which by then looked like luminous icebergs suspended above barren desert.

He tried to walk a straight line, he said later. I could see him veer, his legs rubbery, and it looked as though he rippled and distended, stretching horizontally while some force compressed him vertically, an egg man, a plastic body swaying in tides of gravity.

Then he starting stumbling, falling. He cried out—a horrible, warped sound, like paper tearing for a long, long time. He fled. The sand clawed at him as he ran, strands grasping at his feet, trailing long streamers of glittering, luminous sand—but it couldn't hold him. Ralph staggered away, gasping, his eyes huge and white and terrified.

We turned back.

But coming away, I saw a band of men and women marching woodenly along toward the wall. They were old, most of them, and diseased. Some had been hurt—you could see the wounds.

They were heading straight for the lip. Silent, inexorable.

Ralph and I followed them for a while. As they approached the wall, they started walking up off the sand—right into the air.

And over the tubes.

Just flying.

We decided to head south. Maybe the lip is different there. Ralph says the plan he'd heard, after the generals had studied the survey-mission results, was to try to open the shield at the ground, where the Nile spills over. Then they'd get people out by boating them along the river.

Could they be doing that, now? We hear roaring sounds in the sky sometimes. Explosions. Ralph is ironic about it all, says he wonders when the Quarthex will get tired of intruders and go back to the source—*all* the way back.

I don't know. I'm tired and worn down.

Could there be a way out? Sounds impossible, but it's all we've got.

Head south, to the Nile's edge.

We're hiding in a cave tonight. It's bitterly cold out here in the desert, and a sunburn is no help.

I'm hungry as hell. Some Christmas.

We were supposed to be back in Laguna Beach by now.

God knows where Joanna is.

DECEMBER 26

I got away. Barely.

The Quarthex work in teams now. They've gridded off the desert and work across it systematically in those floating platforms. There are big tubes like cannon mounted on each end and a Quarthex scans it over the sands.

Ralph and I crept up to the mouth of the cave we were in and watched them comb the area. They worked out from the Nile. When a muzzle turned toward us I felt an impact like a warm, moist wave smacking into my face, like being in the ocean. It drove me to my knees. I reeled away. Threw myself farther back into the cramped cave.

It all dropped away then, as if the wave had pinned me to the ocean floor and filled my lungs with a sluggish liquid.

And in an instant was gone. I rolled over, gasping, and saw Ralph staggering into the sunlight, heading for the Quarthex platform. The projector was leveled at him so that it no longer struck the cave mouth. So I'd been released from its grip.

I watched them lower a rope ladder. Ralph dutifully climbed up. I wanted to shout to him, try to break the hold that thing had over him, but once again the better part of valor—I just watched. They carried him away.

I waited until twilight to move. Not having anybody to talk to makes it harder to control my fear.

God I'm hungry. Couldn't find a scrap to eat.

When I took out this diary I looked at the leather case and remembered stories of people getting so starved they'd eat their shoes. Suitably boiled and salted, of course, with a tangy sauce.

Another day or two and the idea might not seem so funny.

I've got to keep moving.

DECEMBER 27

Hard to write.

They got me this morning.

It grabs your mind. Like before. Squeezing in your head.

But after a while it is better. Feels good. But a buzzing all the time, you can't think.

Picked me up while I was crossing an arroyo. Didn't have any idea they were around. A platform.

Took me to some others. All Egyptians. Caught like me.

Marched us to the Nile.

Plenty to eat.

Rested at noon.

Brought Joanna to me. She is all right. Lovely in the long draping dress the Quarthex gave her.

All around are the bird-headed ones. Ibis, I remember, the bird of the Nile. And dog-headed ones. Lion-headed ones.

Gods of the old times. The Quarthex are the gods of the old time. Of the greater empire.

We are the people.

Sometimes I can think, like now. They sent me away from the work gang on an errand. I am old, not strong. They are kind—give me easy jobs.

So I came to here. Where I hid this diary. Before they took my old uncomfortable clothes I put this little book into a crevice in the rock. Pen too.

Now writing helps. Mind clears some.

I saw Ralph, then lost track of him. I worked hard after the noontime. Sun felt good. I lifted pots, carried them where the foreman said.

The Quarthex-god with ibis head is building a fresh temple. Made from the stones of Aswan. It will be cool and deep, many pillars.

They took my dirty clothes. Gave me fresh loincloth, headband, sandals. Good ones. Better than my old clothes.

It is hard to remember how things were before I came here. Before I knew the river. Its flow. How it divides the world.

I will rest before I try to read what I have written in here before. The words are hard.

Days Later

I come back but can read only a little.

Joanna says you should not. The ibis will not like it if I do.

I remember I liked these words on paper, in my days

before. I earned my food with them. Now they are empty. Must not have been true.

Do not need them any more.

Ralph, science. All words too.

Later

Days since I find this again. I do the good work, I eat, Joanna is there in the night. Many things. I do not want to do this reading.

But today another thing howled overhead. It passed over the desert like a screaming black bird, the falcon, and then fell, flames, big roar.

I remembered Ralph.

This book I remembered, came for it.

The ibis-god speaks to us each sunset. Of how the glory of our lives is here again. We are one people once more again yes after a long long time of being lost.

What the red sunset means. The place where the dead are buried in the western desert. To be taken in death close to the edge, so the dead will walk their last steps in this world, to the lip and over, to the netherworld.

There the lion-god will preserve them. Make them live again.

The Quarthex-gods have discovered how to revive the dead of any beings. They spread this among the stars.

But only to those who understand. Who deserve. Who bow to the great symmetry of life.

One face light, one face dark.

The sun lights the netherworld when for us it is night. There the dead feast and mate and laugh and live forever.

Ralph saw that. The happy land below. It shares the sun.

I saw Ralph today. He came to the river to see the falcon thing cry from the clouds. We all did.

It fell into the river and was swallowed and will be taken to the netherworld where it flows over the edge of the world.

Ralph was sorry when the falcon fell. He said it was a mistake to send it to bother us. That someone from the old dead time had sent it.

Ralph works in the quarry. Carving the limestone. He

looks good, the sun has lain on him and made him strong and brown.

I started to talk of the time we met but he frowned.

That was before we understood, he says. Shook his head. So I should not speak of it.

The gods know of time and the river. They know.

I tire now.

Again

Joanna sick. I try help but no way to stop the bleeding from her.

In old time I would try to stop the stuff of life from leaving her. I would feel sorrow.

I do not now. I am calm.

Ibis-god prepares her. Works hard and good over her.

She will journey tonight. Walk the last trek. Over the edge of the sky and to the netherland.

It is what the temple carving says. She will live again forever.

Forever waits.

I come here to find this book to enter this. I remember sometimes how it was.

I did not know joy then. Joanna did not.

We lived but to no point. Just come-go-come-again.

Now I know what comes. The western death. The rising life.

The Quarthex-gods are right. I should forget that life. To hold on is to die. To flow forward is to live.

Today I saw the pharaoh. He came in radiant chariot, black horses before, bronze sword in hand. The sun was high above him. No shadow he cast.

Big and with red skin the pharaoh rode down the avenue of the kings. We the one people cheered.

His great head was mighty in the sun and his many arms waved in salute to his one people. He is so great the horses groan and sweat to pull him. His hard gleaming body is all armor for he will always be on guard against our enemies.

Like those who fall from the sky. Every day now more come down, dying fireballs to smash in the desert. All fools.

Black rotting bodies. None will rise to walk west. They are only burned prey of the pharaoh.

The pharaoh rode three times on the avenue. We threw ourselves down to attract a glance. His huge glaring eyes regarded us and we cried out, our faces wet with joy.

He will speak for us in the netherworld. Sing to the undergods.

Make our westward walking path smooth.

I fall before him.

I bury this now. No more write in it.

This kind of writing is not for the world now. It comes from the old dead time when I knew nothing and thought everything.

I go to my eternity on the river.

Afterword

I once knew a writer who literally tied himself to his desk. He did it—he said, blinking at me owlishly—to finally break himself of his habit of jumping up for every little thing, running errands, looking up research material, and so, interminably, on. It was eating up all his writing time. So he got a rope and a pot of coffee and tied his legs to the legs of his desk.

He said it worked. At least, until the used coffee started making its own demands.

I don't know about you, but I'd rather not read anything written that way. Discipline I don't mind, but forcing the words out through your fingers . . . I'd just as soon listen to a string quartet perform with a machine gun pointed at them.

If I feel like leaving the writing, I just do. Keeps the pressure off. Of course, it also leads to stories which take five years to finish. Or novels that never will be.

The best of all reasons for leaving the desk is that you really have to, in order to get some writing done *right*. That's background-gathering. I was particularly happy when Getting It Right for a novel about archaeology, *Artifact*, demanded that I spend several weeks in Greece. Even better when, writing the novel, I found I needed to know some arcane stuff about Egypt.

Most people would go to the library. It's amazing how much background you can fake with adroit page-turning. A friend of mine with a number of crackling bestsellers to his credit, Dean Koontz, once wrote a novel set in Tokyo. He used off-the-shelf material in his own study. After the book was out, somebody who had lived in Tokyo commented to him that one could certainly tell Dean had spent a lot of time there, since every little detail was right. He simply refused to believe that Dean had never been in Tokyo.

But I didn't think I could fake Egypt; it's too exotic. (Actually, come to think of it, I don't think I've ever faked a locale which I could plausibly visit.) And I didn't *want* to cook up the background. I love to travel, and anyone hooked on the fundamental ingredient of science fiction— vast sweeps of space and time, always implied if not explicitly shown—couldn't resist the oldest of the grand civilizations.

So I went with my wife. It was one of the most wonderful times we've ever spent. I kept a diary, as I often do. There were about twenty other Americans along on the cruise we took up the Nile, but they scarcely seemed there. They were smoky people—LA doctors who drove Mercedes and knew lots of big wheels in pictures, widows reading their *Reader's Digest* Condensed Books on deck, gawking tourists like us—people who became translucent against the glaring backdrop of *Egypt*—stabbing sunlight, piercing smells, the rub of sand and soft brush of breeze, but mostly that heavy feeling of strangeness which you can never put your finger on but which hangs in the air like layers of incense.

I learned a lot about Greek history in Egypt, since they were the predominant influence there in the last great days. Some of that trickled into *Artifact,* but for a while the experience of crawling through subterranean caverns, sniffing the musty cloying ranks of a thousand mummified animals, wandering in the narrow green margin around the Nile—all that blew away my concentration on Greece.

When we returned I typed up my travel diary and sent it to some friends. About a week later, I woke up with the complete outline of this story in my head. It was about somebody like me, told through a travel diary—a gift of the good ol' subconscious. I had my diary on the word processor, so I simply sat down for an hour each day and added to it.

I was through the piece before I saw that it is basically about an intriguing idea proposed by Julian Jaymes in *The Origin of Consciousness in the Breakdown of the Bicameral Mind*. He proposed that early man didn't have the kind of consciousness we do, didn't have the isolating Me vs. Other worldview. I can't summarize his ideas adequately here, and indeed they may not constitute a genuine scientific theory, because it's hard to see how they could be checked. One of his startling observations is that ancient man may have experienced the gods in a direct way, interpreting internal voices as external ones.

All this somehow came together in this story. It's over four times longer than my own travel notes, which appear as ghost allusions now. My making the narrator a professor of Comparative Literature is a mild dig—I don't think most professors write very well, and those in departments of Litrahchawr doubly so—and I've also made him more wired-up than I was.

A fine small publisher, Cheap Street, issued this in a limited edition with wonderful illustrations. I like the story better than most of mine, and thought for a while I had hit upon a great way to prod the subconscious into doing most of my work for me. Just take a scintillating trip to a strange place, and—presto.

So a year later I went to the Soviet Union. As we say in physics biz, I got the magnitude right but the sign wrong. When I came back, I couldn't write anything for months.

Exposures_____

Puzzles assemble themselves one piece at a time. Yesterday I began laying out the new plates I had taken up on the mountain, at Palomar. They were exposures of varying depth. In each, NGC 1097—a barred spiral galaxy about twenty megaparsecs away—hung suspended in its slow swirl.

As I laid out the plates I thought of the way our family had always divided up the breakfast chores on Sunday. On that ritual day our mother stayed in bed. I laid out the forks and knives and egg cups and formal off-white china, and then stood back in the thin morning light to survey my precise placings. Lush napkin pyramids perched on lace table cloth, my mother's favorite. Through the kitchen door leaked the mutter and clang of a meal coming into being.

I put the exposures in order according to the spectral filters used, noting the calibrated photometry for each. The ceramic sounds of Bridge Hall rang in the tiled hallways and seeped through the door of my office: footsteps, distant talk, the scrape of chalk on slate, a banging door. Examining the plates through an eye piece, I felt the galaxy swell into being, huge.

The deep exposures brought out the dim jets I was after. There were four of them pointing out of NGC 1097, two red and two blue, the brightest three discovered by Wolsencroft and Zealey, the last red one found by Lorre over at JPL. Straight lines scratched across the mottling of foreground dust and stars. No one knew what colored a jet red or blue. I was trying to use the deep plates to measure the width of the jets. Using a slit over the lens, I had stopped down the image until I could employ calibrated photometry to measure the wedge of light. Still further narrowing might allow me to measure the spectrum, to see if the blues and reds came from stars, or from excited clouds of gas.

They lanced out, two blue jets cutting through the spiral arms and breaking free into the blackness beyond. One plate, taken in that spectral spike where ionized hydrogen clouds emit, giving H II radiation, showed a string of beads buried in the curling spiral lanes. They were vast cooling clouds. Where the jets crossed the H II regions, the spiral arms were pushed outward, or else vanished altogether.

Opposite each blue jet, far across the galaxy, a red jet glowed. They, too, snuffed out the H II beads.

From these gaps in the spiral arms I estimated how far the barred spiral galaxy had turned, while the jets ate away at them: about fifteen degrees. From the velocity measurements in the disk, using the Doppler shifts of known spectral lines, I deduced the rotation rate of the NGC 1097 disk: approximately a hundred million years. Not surprising; our own sun takes about the same amount of time to circle around our galactic center. The photons which told me all these specifics had begun their steady voyage sixty million years ago, before there was a *New General Catalog of Nebulae and Clusters of Stars* to label them as they buried themselves in my welcoming emulsion. Thus do I know thee, NGC 1097.

These jets were unique. The brightest blue one dog-legs in a right angle turn and ends in silvery blobs of dry light. Its counter-jet, offset a perverse eleven degrees from exact oppositeness, continues on a warmly rose-colored path over an immense distance, a span far larger than the parent galaxy itself. I frowned, puckered my lips in concentration, calibrated and calculated and refined. Plainly these ramrod, laconic patterns of light were trying to tell me something.

But answers come when they will, one piece at a time.

I tried to tell my son this when, that evening, I helped him with his reading. Using what his mother now knowingly termed "word attack skills," he had mastered most of those tactics. The larger strategic issues of the sentence eluded him still. *Take it in phrases,* I urged him, ruffling his light brown hair, distracted, because I liked the nutmeg smell. (I have often thought that I could find my children in the dark, in a crowd, by my nose alone. Our genetic code colors the air.) He thumbed his book, dirtying a corner. Read the words between the commas, I instructed, my classroom sense of order returning. Stop at the commas, and then pause before going on, and think about what all those words mean. I sniffed at his wheatlike hair again.

I am a traditional astronomer, accustomed to the bitter cold of the cage at Palomar, the Byzantine marriage of optics at Kitt Peak, the muggy air of Lick. Through that long morning yesterday I studied the NGC 1097 jets, attempting to see with the quick eye of the theorist, "dancing on the data" as Roger Blandford down the hall had once called it. I tried to erect some rickety hypothesis that my own uncertain mathematical abilities could brace up. An idea came. I caught at it. But holding it close, turning it over, pushing terms about in an overloaded equation, I saw it was merely an old idea tarted up, already disproved.

Perhaps computer enhancement of the images would clear away some of my enveloping fog, I mused. I took my notes to the neighboring building, listening to my footsteps echo in the long arcade. The buildings at Caltech are mostly done in a pseudo-Spanish style, tan stucco with occasional flourishes of Moorish windows and tiles. The newer library rears up beside the crouching offices and classrooms, a modern extrusion. I entered the Alfred Sloan Laboratory of Physics and Mathematics, wondering for the nth time what a mathematical laboratory would be like, imagining Lewis Carroll in charge, and went into the new computer terminal rooms. The indices which called up my plates soon stuttered across the screen. I used a median numerical filter, to suppress variations in the background. There were standard routines to subtract particular parts of the spectrum. I called them up, averaging away noise from dust and gas and the image-saturating spikes that were foreground stars in our own galaxy. Still, nothing dramatic emerged. Illumination would not come.

I sipped at my coffee. I had brought a box of crackers from my office; and I broke one, eating each wafer with a heavy crunch. I swirled the cup and the coffee swayed like a dark disk at the bottom, a scum of cream at the vortex curling out into gray arms. I drank it. And thumbed another image into being.

This was not NGC 1097. I checked the number. Then the log. No, these were slots deliberately set aside for later filing. They were not supposed to be filled; they represented my allotted computer space. They should be blank.

Yet I recognized this one. It was a view of Sagittarius A, the intense radio source that hides behind a thick lane of dust in the Milky Way. Behind that dark obscuring swath that is an arm of our Galaxy, lies the center. I squinted. Yes: this was a picture formed from observations sensitive to the 21-centimeter wavelength line, the emission of nonionized hydrogen. I had seen it before, on exposures that looked radially inward at the Galactic core. Here was the red band of hydrogen along our line of sight. Slightly below was the well-known arm of hot, expanding gas, nine thousand light years across. Above, tinted green, was a smaller arm, a ridge of gas moving outward at 135 kilometers per second. I had seen this in seminars years ago. In the very center was the knot no more than a light year or two across, the source of the 10^{40} ergs per second of virulent energy that drove the cooker that caused all this. Still, the energy flux from our Galaxy was ten million times less than that of a quasar. Whatever the compact energy source there, it was comparatively quiet. NGC 1097 lies far to the south, entirely out of the Milky Way. Could the aim of the satellite camera have strayed so much?

Curious, I thumbed forward. The next index number gave another scan of the Sagittarius region, this time seen by the spectral emissions from outward-moving clouds of ammonia. Random blobs. I thumbed again. A formaldehyde-emission view. But now the huge arm of expanding hydrogen was sprinkled with knots, denoting clouds which moved faster, Dopplered into blue.

I frowned. No, the Sagittarius A exposures were no aiming error. These slots were to be left open for my incoming data. Someone had co-opted the space. Who? I called up the identifying codes, but there were none. As far as the master log was concerned, these spaces were still empty.

I moved to erase them. My finger paused, hovered, went limp. This was obviously high-quality information, already processed. Someone would want it. They had carelessly dumped it into my territory, but. . . .

My pause was in part that of sheer appreciation. Peering at the color-coded encrustations of light, I recalled what all this had once been like: impossibly complicated, ornate in its terms, caked with the eccentric jargon of long-dead professors, choked with thickets of atomic physics and thermodynamics, a web of complexity that finally gave forth mental pictures of a whirling, furious past, of stars burned now into cinders, of whispering, turbulent hydrogen that filled the void between the suns. From such numbers came the starscape that we knew. From a sharp scratch on a strip of film we could catch the signature of an element, deduce velocity from the Doppler shift, and then measure the width of that scratch to give the random component of the velocity, the random jigglings due to thermal motion, and thus the temperature. All from a scratch. No, I could not erase it.

When I was a boy of nine I was brow-beaten into serving at the altar, during the unendurably long Episcopal services that my mother felt we should attend. I wore the simple robe and was the first to appear in the service, lighting the candles with an awkward long device and its sliding wick. The organ music was soft and did not call attention to itself, so the congregation could watch undistracted as I fumbled with the wick and tried to keep the precarious balance between feeding it too much (so that, engorged, it bristled into a ball of orange) and the even worse embarrassment of snuffing it into a final accusing puff of black. Through the service I would alternately kneel and stand, murmuring the worn phrases as I thought of the softball I would play in the afternoon, feeling the prickly gathering heat underneath my robes. On a bad day the sweat would accumulate and a drop would cling to my nose. I'd let it hang there in mute testimony. The minister never seemed to notice. I would often slip off into decidedly untheological daydreams, intoxicated by the pressing moist heat, and miss the telltale words of the litany which signalled the beginning of communion. A whisper would come skating across the layered air and I would surface, to see the minister turned with clotted face toward me, holding the implements of his forgiving trade, waiting for me to bring the wine and wafers to be blessed. I would surge upward, swearing under my breath with the ardor only those who have just learned the words can truly muster, unafraid to be muttering these things as I snatched up the chalice and sniffed the too-sweet murky wine, fetching the plates of wafers, swearing that once the polished walnut altar rail was emptied of its upturned and strangely blank faces, once the simpering organ had ebbed into silence and I had shrugged off these robes swarming with the stench of mothballs, I would have no more of it, I would erase it.

I asked Redman who the hell was logging their stuff into my inventory spaces. He checked. The answer was: nobody. There were no recorded intrusions into those sections of the memory system. *Then look further,* I said, and went back to work at the terminal.

They were still there. What's more, some index numbers that had been free before were now filled.

NGC 1097 still vexed me, but I delayed working on the problem. I studied these new pictures. They were processed, Doppler-coded, and filtered for noise. I switched back to the earlier plates, to be sure. Yes, it was clear: these were different.

Current theory held that the arm of expanding gas was on the outward phase of an oscillation. Several hundred million years ago, so the story went, a massive explosion at the galactic center had started the expansion: a billowing, spinning doughnut of gas swelled outward. Eventually its energy was matched by the gravitational attraction of the massive center. Then, as it slowed and finally fell back toward the center, it spun faster, storing energy in rotational motion, until centrifugal forces stopped its inward rush. Thus the hot cloud could oscillate in the potential well of gravity, cooling slowly.

These computer-transformed plates said otherwise. The

Doppler shifts formed a cone. At the center of the plate, maximum values, far higher than any observed before, over a thousand kilometers per second. That exceeded escape velocity from the Galaxy itself. The values tapered off to the sides, coming smoothly down to the shifts that were on the earlier plates.

I called the programming director. He looked over the displays, understanding nothing of what it meant but everything about how it could have gotten there; and his verdict was clean, certain: human error. But further checks turned up no such mistake. "Must be comin' in on the transmission from orbit," he mused. He seemed half-asleep as he punched in commands, traced the intruders. These data had come in from the new combination optical, IR, and UV 'scope in orbit, and the JPL programs had obligingly performed the routine miracles of enhancement and analysis. But the orbital staff were sure no such data had been transmitted. In fact, the 'scope had been down for inspection, plus an alignment check, for over two days. The programming director shrugged and promised to look into it, fingering the innumerable pens clipped in his shirt pocket.

I stared at the Doppler cone, and thumbed to the next index number. The cone had grown, the shifts were larger. Another: still larger. And then I noticed something more; and a cold sensation seeped into me, banishing the casual talk and mechanical-printout stutter of the terminal room.

The point of view had shifted. All the earlier plates had shown a particular gas cloud at a certain angle of inclination. This latest plate was slightly cocked to the side, illuminating a clotted bunch of minor H II regions and obscuring a fraction of the hot, expanding arm. Some new features were revealed. If the JPL program had done such a rotation and shift, it would have left the new spaces blank, for there was no way of filling them in. These were not empty. They brimmed with specific shifts, detailed spectral indices. The JPL program would not have produced the field of numbers unless the raw data contained them. I stared at the screen for a long time.

*   *   *

That evening I drove home the long way, through the wide boulevards of Pasadena, in the gathering dusk. I remembered giving blood the month before, in the eggshell light of the Caltech dispensary. They took the blood away in a curious plastic sack, leaving me with a small bandage in the crook of my elbow. The skin was translucent, showing the riverwork of tributary blue veins, which—recently tapped—were nearly as pale as the skin. I had never looked at that part of me before and found it tender, vulnerable, an unexpected opening. I remembered my wife had liked being stroked there when we were dating, and that I had not touched her there for a long time. Now I had myself been pricked there, to pipe brimming life into a sack, and then to some other who could make use of it.

That evening I drove again, taking my son to Open House. The school bristled wih light and seemed to command the neighborhood with its luminosity, drawing families out of their homes. My wife was taking my daughter to another school, and so I was unshielded by her ability to recognize people we knew. I could never sort out their names in time to answer the casual hellos. In our neighborhood the PTA nights draw a disproportionate fraction of technical types, like me. Tonight I saw them without the quicksilver verbal fluency of my wife. They had compact cars that seemed too small for their large families, wore shoes whose casualness offset the formal, just-come-from-work jackets and slacks, and carried creamy folders of their children's accumulated work, to use in conferring with the teachers. The wives were sun-darkened, wearing crisp, print dresses that looked recently put on, and spoke with ironic turns about PTA politics, bond issues, and class sizes. In his classroom my son tugged me from board to board, where he had contributed paragraphs on wildlife. The crowning exhibit was a model of Io, Jupiter's pizza-mocking moon, which he had made from a tennis ball and thick, sulphurous paint. It hung in a box painted black and looked remarkably, ethereally real. My son had won first prize in his class for the mockup moon, and his teacher stressed this as she went over the less welcome news that he was not doing well at his reading. Apparently he arranged the plausible phrases—A, then B, then C—into illogical combinations, C

coming before A, despite the instructing commas and semi-
colons which should have guided him. It was a minor problem, his teacher assured me, but should be looked after.
Perhaps a little more reading at home, under my eye? I
nodded, sure that the children of the other scientists and
computer programmers and engineers did not have this difficulty, and already knew what the instructing phrase of the
next century would be, before the end of this one. My son
took the news matter-of-factly, unafraid, and went off to help
with the cake and Kool-aid. I watched him mingle with girls
whose awkwardness was lovely, like giraffes'. I remembered
that his teacher (I had learned from gossip) had a mother
dying of cancer, which might explain the furrow between her
eyebrows that would not go away. My son came bearing
cake. I ate it with him, sitting with knees slanting upward in
the small chair; and quite calmly and suddenly an idea came
to me and would not go away. I turned it over and felt its
shape, testing it in a preliminary fashion. Underneath I was
both excited and fearful and yet sure that it would survive: it
was right. Scraping up the last crumbs and icing, I looked
down, and saw my son had drawn a crayon design, an
enormous father playing ball with a son, running and catching, the scene carefully fitted into the small compass of the
plastic, throwaway plate.

The next morning I finished the data reduction on the
slit-image exposures. By carefully covering over the galaxy
and background, I had managed to take successive plates
which blocked out segments of the space parallel to the
brightest blue jet. Photometry of the resulting weak signal
could give a cross section of the jet's intensity. Pinpoint
calibration then yielded the thickness of the central jet zone.
The data was somewhat scattered, the error bars were
larger than I liked, but still—I was sure I had it. The jet had a
fuzzy halo and a bright core. The core was less than a
hundred light years across, a thin filament of highly ionized
hydrogen, cut like a swath through the gauzy dust beyond the
galaxy. The resolute, ruler-sharp path, its thinness, its profile
of luminosity: all pointed toward a tempting picture. Some
energetic object had carved each line, moving at high speeds.

It swallowed some of the matter in its path; and in the act of engorgement the mass was heated to incandescent brilliance, spitting UV and X-rays into an immense surrounding volume. This radiation in turn ionized the galactic gas, leaving a scratch of light behind the object, like picnickers dumping luminous trash as they pass by.

The obvious candidates for the fast-moving sources of the jets were black holes. And as I traced the slim profiles of the NGC 1097 jets back into the galaxy, they all intersected at the precise geometrical center of the barred spiral pattern.

Last night, after returning from the Open House with a sleepy boy in tow, I talked with my wife as we undressed. I described my son's home room, his artistic achievements, his teacher. My wife let slip offhandedly some jarring news. I had, apparently, misheard the earlier gossip; perhaps I had mused over some problem while she related the story to me over breakfast. It was not the teacher's mother who had cancer, but the teacher herself. I felt an instant, settling guilt. I could scarcely remember the woman's face, though it was a mere hour later. I asked why she was still working. Because, my wife explained with straightforward New England sense, it was better than staring at a wall. The chemotherapy took only a small slice of her hours. And anyway, she probably needed the money. The night beyond our windows seemed solid, flinty, harder than the soft things inside. In the glass I watched my wife take off a print dress and stretch backward, breasts thinning into crescents, her nobbed spine describing a serene curve that anticipated bed. I went over to my chest of drawers and looked down at the polished walnut surface, scrupulously rectangular and arranged, across which I had tossed the residue of an hour's dutiful parenting: a scrawled essay on marmosets, my son's anthology of drawings, his reading list, and on top, the teacher's bland paragraph of assessment. It felt odd to have called these things into being, these signs of a forward tilt in a small life, by an act of love or at least lust, now years past. The angles appropriate to cradling my children still lived in my hands. I could feel clearly the tentative clutch of my son as he attempted some upright steps. Now my eye strayed to his essay. I could see him struggling with the notion of clauses, with ideas piled upon each other to build a point, and with the caged linearity of the sentence. On the page above, in the loops of the teacher's generous flow pen, I saw a hollow rotundity, a denial of any constriction in her life. She had to go on, this schoolgirl penmanship said, to forcefully forget a gnawing illness among a roomful of bustling children. Despite all the rest, she had to keep on doing.

What could be energetic enough to push black holes out of the galactic center, up the slopes of the deep gravitational potential well? Only another black hole. The dynamics had been worked out years before—as so often happens, in another context—by William Saslaw. Let a bee-swarm of black holes orbit about each other, all caught in a gravitational depression. Occasionally, they veer close together, deforming the space-time nearby, caroming off each other like billiard balls. If several undergo these near-miss collisions at once, a black hole can be ejected from the gravitational trap altogether. More complex collisions can throw pairs of black holes in opposite directions, conserving angular momentum: jets and counter-jets. But why did NGC 1097 display two blue jets and two red? Perhaps the blue ones glowed with the phosphorescent waste left by the largest, most energetic black holes; their counter-jets must be, by some detail of the dynamics, always smaller, weaker, redder.

I went to the jutting, air-conditioned library, and read Saslaw's papers. Given a buzzing hive of black holes in a gravitational well—partly of their own making—many things could happen. There were compact configurations, tightly orbiting and self-obsessed, which could be ejected as a body. These close-wound families could in turn be unstable, once they were isolated beyond the galaxy's tug, just as the group at the center had been. Caroming off each other, they could eject unwanted siblings. I frowned. This could explain the astonishing right-angle turn the long blue jet made. One black hole thrust sidewise and several smaller, less energetic black holes pushed the opposite way.

As the galactic center lost its warped children, the ejections would become less probable. Things would die down.

But how long did that take? NGC 1007 was no younger than our own Galaxy; on the cosmic scale, a sixty-million-year difference was nothing.

In the waning of afternoon—it was only a bit more than twenty-four hours since I first laid out the plates of NGC 1097—the Operations report came in. There was no explanation for the Sagittarius A data. It had been received from the station in orbit and duly processed. But no command had made the scope swivel to that axis. Odd, Operations said, that it pointed in an interesting direction, but no more.

There were two added plates, fresh from processing. I did not mention to Redman in Operations that the resolution of these plates was astonishing, that details in the bloated, spilling clouds were unprecedented. Nor did I point out that the angle of view had tilted further, giving a better perspective on the outward-jutting inferno. With their polynomial percussion, the computers had given what was in the stream of downward-flowing data, numbers that spoke of something being banished from the pivot of our Galaxy.

Caltech is a compact campus. I went to the Athenaeum for coffee, ambling slowly beneath the palms and scented eucalyptus, and circumnavigated the campus on my return. In the varnished perspectives of these tiled hallways, the hammer of time was a set of Dopplered numbers, blue-shifted because the thing rushed toward us, a bulge in the sky. Silent numbers.

There were details to think about, calculations to do, long strings of hypothesis to unfurl like thin flags. I did not know the effect of a penetrating, ionizing flux on Earth. Perhaps it could affect the upper atmosphere and alter the ozone cap that drifts above our heedless heads. A long trail of disturbed, high-energy plasma could fan out through our benign spiral arm—odd, to think of bands of dust and rivers of stars as a neighborhood where you have grown up—churning, working, heating. After all, the jets of NGC 1097 had snuffed out the beaded H II regions as cleanly as an eraser passing across a blackboard, ending all the problems that life knows.

The NGC 1097 data was clean and firm. It would make a good paper, perhaps a letter to *Astrophysical Journal Letters*.

But the rest—there was no crisp professional path. These plates had come from much nearer the Galactic center. The information had come outward at light speed, far faster than the pressing bulge, and tilted at a slight angle away from the radial vector that led to Earth.

I had checked the newest Palomar plates from Sagittarius A this afternoon. There were no signs of anything unusual. No Doppler bulge, no exiled mass. They flatly contradicted the satellite plates.

That was the key: old reliable Palomar, our biggest ground-based 'scope, showed nothing. Which meant that someone in high orbit had fed data into our satellite 'scope—exposures which had to be made nearer the Galactic center and then brought here and deftly slipped into our ordinary astronomical research. Exposures which spoke of something stirring where we could not yet see it, beyond the obscuring lanes of dust. The plumes of fiery gas would take a while longer to work through that dark cloak.

These plain facts had appeared on a screen, mute and undeniable, keyed to the data on NGC 1097. Keyed to a connection that another eye than mine could miss. Some astronomer laboring over plates of eclipsing binaries or globular clusters might well have impatiently erased the offending, multicolored spattering, not bothered to uncode the Dopplers, to note the persistent mottled red of the Galactic dust arm at the lower right, and so not known what the place must be. Only I could have made the connection to NGC 1097, and guessed what an onrushing black hole could do to a fragile planet: burn away the ozone layer, hammer the land with high-energy particles, mask the sun in gas and dust.

But to convey this information in this way was so strange, so—yes, that was the word—so alien. Perhaps this was the way they had to do it; quiet, subtle, indirect. Using an oblique analogy which only suggested, yet somehow disturbed more than a direct statement. And of course, this might be only a phrase in a longer message. Moving out from the Galactic center, they would not know we were here until they grazed the expanding bubble of radio noise that gave us away, and so their data would use what they had, views at a different slant. The data itself, raw and silent, would not necessarily call attention to itself. It had to be placed in context, beside NGC 1097. How had they managed to do that? Had they tried before? What odd logic dictated this approach? How. . . .

Take it in pieces. Some of the data I could use, some not. Perhaps a further check, a fresh look through the dusty Sagittarius arm, would show the beginnings of a ruddy swelling, could give a verification. I would have to look, try to find a bridge that would make plausible what I knew but could scarcely prove. The standards of science are austere, unforgiving—and who would have it differently? I would have to hedge, to take one step back for each two forward, to compare and suggest and contrast, always sticking close to the data. And despite what I thought I knew now, the data would have to lead, they would have to show the way.

There is a small Episcopal church, not far up Hill Street, which offers a Friday communion in early evening. Driving home through the surrounding neon consumer gumbo, musing, I saw the sign, and stopped. I had the NGC 1097 plates with me in a carrying case, ripe beneath my arm with their fractional visions, like thin sections of an exotic cell. I went in. The big oak door thumped solemnly shut behind me. In the nave two elderly men were passing woven baskets, taking up the offertory. I took a seat near the back. Idly I surveyed the people, distributed randomly like a field of unthinking stars, in the pews before me. A man came nearby and a pool of brassy light passed before me and I put something in, the debris at the bottom clinking and rustling as I stirred it. I watched the backs of heads as the familiar litany droned on, as devoid of meaning as before. I do not believe, but there is communion. Something tugged at my attention; one head turned a fraction. By a kind of triangulation I deduced the features of the other, closer to the ruddy light of the altar, and saw it was my son's teacher. She was listening raptly. I listened, too, watching her, but could only think of the gnawing at the center of a bustling, swirling galaxy. The lights seemed to dim. The organ had gone silent. *Take, eat. This is the body and blood of* and so it had begun. I waited my turn. I do not believe, but there is communion. The people went forward in their turns. The woman rose; yes, it was she, the kind of woman whose hand would give forth loops and spirals and who would dot her **i**'s with a small circle. The faint timbre of the organ seeped into the layered air. When it was time I was still thinking of NGC 1097, of how I would write the paper—fragments skittered across my mind, the pyramid of the argument was taking shape—and I very nearly missed the gesture of the elderly man at the end of my pew. Halfway to the altar rail I realized that I still carried the case of NGC 1097 exposures, crooked into my elbow, where the pressure caused a slight ache to spread: the spot where they had made the transfusion in the clinic, transferring a fraction of life, blood given. I put it beside me as I knelt. The robes of the approaching figure were cobalt blue and red, a change from the decades since I had been an acolyte. There were no acolytes at such a small service, of course. The blood would follow; first came the offered plate of wafers. Take, eat. Life calling out to life. I could feel the pressing weight of what lay ahead for me, the long roll of years carrying forward one hypothesis, and then, swallowing, knowing that I would never believe this and yet I would want it, I remembered my son, remembered that these events were only pieces, that the puzzle was not yet over, that I would never truly see it done, that as an astronomer I had to live with knowledge forever partial and provisional, that science was not final results but instead a continuing meditation carried on in the face of enormous facts—*take it in phrases*— let the sentences of our lives pile up.

Afterword

There is nothing in my experience quite like viewing new astronomical data for the first time. It comes out in stuttered numbers, or wriggly graphs, or—best of all—in photos or contour maps. These last are often in vibrant yellows, reds, or blues, colors chosen to enhance contrasts. They look like views seen through the distorting eyes of alien beings.

I've done work in radio and optical astronomy, feeling that quiet, chilling, almost giddy tasting of raw, unforeseen reality.

That sensation comes in a context, of course. You've guessed at the outcome, anticipated features, perhaps calculated a detailed model. (Otherwise, you wouldn't get the observing time on the big 'scopes in the first place.) But that first picture—often crude, unrefined, pitted with blemishes and man-made overlays—has a finality and simplicity that I've always found immensely humbling.

You never get it right beforehand, really. Sure, some features lie this way, others have a luminous spectral grace similar to what you imagined. But the thing itself inevitably bristles with specifics, knotty pimples, splashes of irregular and unconforming life.

A science fiction writer is—or should be—constrained by what is, or logically might be. That can mean simple fidelity to facts (which, in science, are always more important that theories—though Lord knows the two help shape each other, undermining the convenient, complacent separation of observer and observed). To me it also means heeding the authentic, the actual and concrete. Bad fiction uses the glossy generality; good writing needs the smattering of detail, the unrelenting busy mystery of the real.

But what is real? No need to do the obligatory dance around quantum uncertainty, that already worn cliché of the quasi-mystical escape hatch; there's enough confusion in simple, everyday life. For me, the only true guide is an eye for the graininess of the world, rather than the convenient, ordained maps.

What's more, a will toward concreteness itself brings into being the form and style appropriate to a story. This one is based on a time in the early 1980s when I was poring over radio maps of galactic jets, mulling over recent gamma-ray data from the constellation Saggitarius, and trying to put together a mathematical model which might explain some of it. (Some amazing things lie swirling at the center of our galaxy, including energetic jets. I hope to write a novel about that zone someday.)

As I remarked in the afterword to "White Creatures," astronomy inevitably brings to mind the immense contrast between the realm of these blithe objects hanging in our sky, and human scales of time and space. That has odd psychological effects on scientists. What is the moody, distracted, absent-minded professor of hoary cliché really experiencing?

I'm sure the answers differ vastly. All I can do is try to convey the effect as it appears to me. Not necessarily as it *occurs* to me—this story isn't totally autobiographical. But among the customary fictional fare of suburban adultery novels and wry reminiscences of Jewish or black childhoods, an occasional glimpse of seldom-seen worlds might be stimulating.

People build their lives around work, yet how often does the subject appear in fiction as a direct sensation, a lived experience? (There are plenty of novels of corporate intrigue, but that's rather more like politics.) There are more workaholics than alcoholics, yet seldom do we glimpse the former's world. (Odd indeed, since a lot of writers I know verge on both.)

So I thought to reflect what the process of trawling for ideas, for insights, is like. Not necessarily the *eureka!* moment, more like the quiet *oh yeah, right* sensation of provisional, momentary discovery. And how it reverberates through a life.

Time's Rub

1.

At Earth's winter ebb, two crabbed figures slouched across a dry, cracked plain.

Running before a victor who was himself slow-dying, the dead-stench of certain destiny cloyed to them. They knew it. Yet kept on, grinding over plum-colored shales.

They shambled into a pitwallow for shelter, groaning, carapaces grimed and discolored. The smaller of them, Xen, turned toward the minimal speck of burnt-yellow sun, but gained little aid through its battered external panels. It grasped Faz's extended pincer—useless now, mauled in battle—and murmured of fatigue.

"We can't go on."

Faz, grimly: "We must."

Xen was a functionary, an analytical sort. It had chanced to flee the battle down the same gully as Faz, the massive, lumbering leader. Xen yearned to see again its mate, Pymr, but knew this for the forlorn dream it was.

They crouched down. Their enemies rumbled in nearby ruined hills. A brown murk rose from those distant movements. The sun's pale eye stretched long shadows across the plain, inky hiding places for the encroaching others.

Thus when the shimmering curtains of ivory luminescence began to fog the hollow, Xen thought the end was here—that energy drain blurred its brain, and now brought swift, cutting death.

Fresh in from the darkling plain? the voice said. Not acoustically—this was a Vac Zone, airless for millennia.

"What? Who's that?" Faz answered.

Your ignorant armies clashed last night?

"Yes," Xen acknowledged ruefully, "and were defeated. Both sides lost."

Often the case.

"Are the Laggenmorphs far behind us?" Faz asked, faint tracers of hope skating crimson in its spiky voice.

No. They approach. They have tracked your confused alarms of struggle and flight.

"We had hoped to steal silent."

Your rear guard made a melancholy, long, withdrawing roar.

Xen: "They escaped?"

Into the next world, yes.

"Oh."

"Who *is* that?" Faz insisted, clattering its treads.

A wraith. Glittering skeins danced around them. A patchy acrid tang laced the curling vacuum. **In this place having neither brass, nor earth, nor boundless sea.**

"Come out!" Faz called at three gigaHertz. "We can't see you."

Need you?

"Are you Laggenmorphs?" Panic laded Faz's carrier wave a bright, fervid orange. "We'll fight, I warn you!"

"Quiet," Xen said, suspecting.

The descending dazzle thickened, struck a bass note. **Laggenmorphs? I do not even know your terms.**

"Your name, then," Xen said.

Sam.

"What's that? That's no name!" Faz declared, its voice a shifting brew of fear and anger.

Sam it was and Sam it is. Not marble, nor the gilded monuments of princes, shall outlive it.

Xen murmured at a hundred kiloHertz, "Traditional archaic name. I dimly remember something of the sort. I doubt it's a trap."

The words not yet free of its antenna, Xen ducked—for a relativistic beam passed not a kilometer away, snapping with random rage. It forked to a ruined scree of limestone and erupted into a self-satisfied yellow geyser. Stones pelted the two hunkering forms, clanging.

A mere stochastic volley. Your sort do expend energies wildly. That is what first attracted me.

Surly, Faz snapped. "You'll get no surge from us."

I did not come to sup. I came to proffer.

A saffron umbra surrounded the still-gathering whorls of crackling, clotted iridescence.

"Where're you hiding?" Faz demanded. It brandished blades, snouts, cutters, spikes, double-bore nostrils that could spit lurid beams.

In the cupped air.

"There *is* no air," Xen said. "This channel is open to the planetary currents."

Xen gestured upward with half-shattered claw. There, standing in space, the playing tides of blue-white, gauzy light showed that they were at the base of a great translucent cylinder. Its geometric perfection held back the moist air of Earth, now an ocean tamed by skewered forces. On the horizon, at the glimmering boundary, purpling clouds nudged futilely at their constraint like hungry cattle. This cylinder led the eye up to a vastness, the stars a stilled snowfall. Here the thin but persistent wind from the sun could have free run, gliding along the orange-slice sections of the Earth's dipolar magnetic fields. The winds crashed down, sputtering, delivering kiloVolt glories where the cylinder cut them. Crackling yellow sparks grew there, a forest with all trunks ablaze and branches of lightning, beckoning far aloft like a brilliantly lit casino in a gray dark desert.

How well I know. I stem from fossiled days.

"Then why—"

This is my destiny and my sentence.

"To live here?" Faz was beginning to suspect as well.

For a wink or two of eternity.

"Can you . . ." Faz poked the sky with a horned, fused launcher. ". . . reach up there? Get us a jec?"

I do not know the term.

Xen said, "An injection. A megaVolt, say, at a hundred kiloAmps. A mere microsecond would boost me again. I could get my crawlers working."

I would have to extend my field lines.

"So it *is* true," Xen said triumphantly. "There still dwell Ims on the Earth. And you're one."

Again, the term—

"An Immortal. You have the fieldcraft."

Yes.

Xen knew of this, but had thought it mere legend. All material things were mortal. Cells were subject to intruding impurities, cancerous insults, a thousand coarse alleyways of accident. Machines, too, knew rust and wear, could suffer the ruthless scrubbing of their memories by a random bolt of electromagnetic violence. Hybrids, such as Xen and Faz, shared both half-worlds of erosion.

But there was a Principle which evaded time's rub. Order could be imposed on electrical currents—much as words rode on radio waves—and then the currents could curve into self-involved equilibria. If spun just so, the mouth of a given stream eating its own tail, then a spinning ring generated its own magnetic fields. Such work was simple. Little children made these loops, juggled them into humming fireworks.

Only genius could knit these current whorls into a fully contorted globe. The fundamental physics sprang from ancient Man's bottling of thermonuclear fusion in magnetic strands. That was a simple craft, using brute magnets and artful metallic vessels. Far harder, to apply such learning to wisps of plasma alone.

The Principle stated that if, from the calm center of such a weave, the magnetic field always increased, in all directions, then it was stable to all manner of magnetohydrodynamic pinches and shoves.

The Principle was clear, but stitching the loops—history had swallowed that secret. A few had made the leap, been translated into surges of magnetic field. They dwelled in the Vac Zones, where the rude bump of air molecules could not stir their calm currents. Such were the Ims.

"You . . . live forever?" Xen asked wonderingly.

Aye, a holy spinning toroid—when I rest. Otherwise, distorted, as you see me now. Phantom shoots of burnt yellow. **What once was Man, is now aurora—where winds**

don't sing, the sun's a tarnished nickel, the sky's a blank rebuke.

Abruptly, a dun-colored javelin shot from nearby ruined hills, vectoring on them.

"Laggenmorphs!" Faz sent. "I have no defense."

Halfway to them, the lance burst into scarlet plumes. The flames guttered out.

A cacophony of eruptions spat from their left. Gray forms leapt forward, sending scarlet beams and bursts. Sharp metal cut the smoking stones.

"Pymr, sleek and soft, I loved you," Xen murmured, thinking this was the end.

But from the space around the Laggenmorphs condensed a chalky stuff—smothering, consuming. The forms fell dead.

I saved you.

Xen bowed, not knowing how to thank a wisp. But the blur of nearing oblivion weighed like stone.

"Help us!" Faz's despair lanced like pain through the dead vacuum. "We need energy."

You would have me tick over the tilt of Earth, run through solstice, bring ringing summer in an hour?

Xen caught in the phosphorescent stipple a green underlay of irony.

"No, no!" Faz spurted. "Just a jec. We'll go on then."

I can make you go on forever.

The flatness of it, accompanied by phantom shoots of scorched orange, gave Xen pause. "You mean . . . the fieldcraft? Even I know such lore is not lightly passed on. Too many Ims, and the Earth's magnetic zones will be congested."

I grow bored, encased in this glassy electromagnetic shaft. I have not conferred the fieldcraft in a long while. Seeing you come crawling from your mad white chaos, I desired company. I propose a Game.

"Game?" Faz was instantly suspicious. "Just a jec, Im, that's all we want."

You may have that as well.

"What're you spilling about?" Faz asked.

Xen said warily, "It's offering the secret."

"What?" Faz laughed dryly, a flat cynical burst that rattled down the frequencies.

Faz churned an extruded leg against the grainy soil, wasting energy in its own consuming bitterness. It had sought fame, dominion, a sliver of history. Its divisions had been chewed and spat out again by the Laggenmorphs, its feints ignored, bold strokes adroitly turned aside. Now it had to fly vanquished beside the lesser Xen, dignity gathered like tattered dress about its fleeing ankles.

"Ims never share *that*. A dollop, a jec, sure—but not the turns of fieldcraft." To show it would not be fooled, Faz spat chalky ejecta at a nearby streamer of zinc-laden light.

I offer you my Game.

The sour despair in Faz spoke first. "Even if we believe that, how do we know you don't cheat?"

No answer. But from the high hard vault there came descending a huge ribbon of ruby light—snaking, flexing, writing in strange tongues on the emptiness as it approached, fleeting messages of times gone—auguries of innocence lost, missions forgot, dim songs of the wide world and all its fading sweets. The ruby snake split, rumbled, turned eggshell blue, split and spread and forked down, blooming into a hemisphere around them. It struck and ripped the rock, spitting fragments over their swiveling heads, booming. Then prickly silence.

"I see," Xen said.

Thunder impresses, but it's lightning does the work.

"Why should the Im cheat, when it could short us to ground, fry us to slag?" Xen sent to Faz on tightband.

"Why anything?" Faz answered, but there was nodding in the tone.

2.

The Im twisted the local fields and caused to appear, hovering in fried light, two cubes—one red, one blue.

You may choose to open either the Blue cube alone, or both.

Though brightened by a borrowed kiloAmp jolt from Xen,

Faz had expended many Joules in irritation and now flagged. "What's . . . in . . . them?"

Their contents are determined by what I have already predicted. I have already placed your rewards inside. You can choose Red and Blue both, if you want. In that case, following my prediction, I have placed in the Red cube the bottled-up injection you wanted.

Faz unfurled a metallic tentacle for the Red cube.

Wait. If you will open both boxes, then I have placed in the Blue nothing—nothing at all.

Faz said, "Then I get the jec in the Red cube, and when I open the Blue—nothing."

Correct.

Xen asked, "What if Faz *doesn't* open both cubes?"

The only other option is to open the Blue alone.

"And I get nothing?" Faz asked.

No. In that case, I have placed the, ah, "jec" in the Red cube. But in the Blue I have put the key to my own fieldcraft—the designs for immortality.

"I don't get it. I open Red, I get my jec—right?" Faz said, sudden interest giving it a spike of scarlet brilliance at three gigaHertz. "Then I open Blue, I get immortality. That's what I want."

True. But in that case, I have predicted that you will pick both cubes. Therefore, I have left the Blue cube empty.

Faz clattered its treads. "I get immortality if I choose the Blue cube *alone*? But you have to have *predicted* that. Otherwise I get nothing."

Yes.

Xen added, "*If* you have predicted things perfectly."

But I always do.

"Always?"

Nearly always. I am immortal, ageless—but not God. Not . . . yet.

"What if I pick Blue and you're wrong?" Faz asked. "Then I get nothing."

True. But highly improbable.

Xen saw it. "All this is done *now*? You've already made your prediction? Placed the jec or the secret—or both—in the cubes?"

Yes. I made my predictions before I even offered the Game.

Faz asked, "What'd you predict?"

Merry pink laughter chimed across the slumbering mega-Hertz. **I will not say. Except that I predicted correctly that you both would play, and that you particularly would ask that question. Witness.**

A sucking jolt lifted Faz from the stones and deposited it nearby. Etched in the rock beneath where Faz had crouched was *What did you predict?* in a rounded, careful hand:

"It had to have been done during the overhead display, before the game began," Xen said wonderingly.

"The Im *can* predict," Faz said respectfully.

Xen said, "Then the smart move is to open both cubes."

Why?

"Because you've already made your choice. If you predicted that Faz would choose both, and he opens only the Blue, then he gets nothing."

True, and as I said before, very improbable.

"So," Xen went on, thinking quickly under its pocked sheen of titanium, "if you predicted that Faz would choose *only* the Blue, then Faz might as well open both. Faz will get both the jec and the secret."

Faz said, "Right. And that jec will be useful in getting away from here."

Except that there is every possibility that I already predicted his choice of both cubes. In that case I have left only the jec in the Red Cube, and nothing in Blue.

"But you've already chosen!" Faz blurted. "There isn't any probable-this or possible-that at all."

True.

Xen said, "The only uncertainty is, how good a predictor are you."

Quite.

Faz slowed, flexing a crane arm in agonized frustration. "I . . . dunno . . . I got . . . to think . . ."

There's world enough, and time.

"Let me draw a diagram," said Xen, who had always favored the orderly over the dramatic. This was what condemned it to a minor role in roiling battle, but perhaps that was a blessing. It drew upon the gritty soil some boxes: "There," Xen wheezed. "This is the payoff matrix."

THE IM

	Predicts you will take only what's in Blue	Predicts you will take what's in both
Take only what is in Blue	immortality	nothing
Take what is in both Red and Blue	immortality and jec	jec

YOU {

As solemn and formal as Job's argument with God.

Enraptured with his own creation, Xen said, "Clearly, taking only the Blue cube is the best choice. The chances that the Im are wrong are very small. So you have a great chance of gaining immortality."

"That's crazy," Faz mumbled. "If I take both cubes, I at *least* get a jec, even if the Im *knew* I'd choose that way. And with a jec, I can make a run for it from the Laggenmorphs."

"Yes. Yet it rests on faith," Xen said. "Faith that the Im's predicting is near-perfect."

"Ha!" Faz snorted. "Nothing's perfect."

A black thing scorched over the rim of the pitwallow and exploded into fragments. Each bit dove for Xen and Faz, like shrieking, elongated eagles baring teeth.

And each struck something invisible but solid. Each smacked like an insect striking the windshield of a speeding car. And was gone.

"They're all around us!" Faz cried.

"Even with a jec, we might not make it out," Xen said.

True. But translated into currents, like me, with a subtle knowledge of conductivities and diffusion rates, you can live forever.

"Translated . . ." Xen mused.

Free of entropy's swamp.

"Look," Faz said, "I may be tired, drained, but I know logic. You've already *made* your choice, Im—the cubes are filled with whatever you put in. What I choose to do now can't change that. So I'll take *both* cubes."

Very well.

Faz sprang to the cubes. They burst open with a popping ivory radiance. From the red came a blinding bolt of a jec. It surrounded Faz's antennae and cascaded into the creature.

Drifting lightly from the blue cube came a tight-wound thing, a shifting ball of neon-lit string. Luminous, writhing rainbow worms. They described the complex web of magnetic field geometries that were immortality's craft. Faz seized it.

You won both. I predicted you would take only the blue. I was wrong.

"Ha!" Faz whirled with renewed energy.

Take the model of the fieldcraft. From it you can deduce the methods.

"Come on, Xen!" Faz cried with sudden ferocity. It surged over the lip of the pitwallow, firing at the distant, moving shapes of the Laggenmorphs, full once more of spit and dash. Leaving Xen.

"With that jec, Faz will make it."

I predict so, yes. You could follow Faz. Under cover of its armory, you would find escape—that way.

The shimmer vectored quick a green arrow to westward, where clouds billowed white. There the elements still governed and mortality walked.

"My path lies homeward, to the south."

Bound for Pymr.

"She is the one true rest I have."

You could rest forever.

"Like you? Or Faz, when it masters the . . . translation?"

Yes. Then I will have company here.

"Aha! That is your motivation."

In part.

"What else, then?"

There are rules for immortals. Ones you cannot understand . . . yet.

"If you can predict so well, with Godlike power, then I should choose only the Blue cube."

True. Or as true as true gets.

"But if you predict so well, my 'choice' is mere illusion. It was fore-ordained."

That old saw? I can see you are . . . determined . . . to have free will.

"Or free won't."

Your turn.

"There are issues here . . ." Xen transmitted only ruby ruminations, murmuring like surf on a distant shore.

Distant boomings from Faz's retreat. The Red and Blue cubes spun, sparkling, surfaces rippled by ion-acoustic modes. The game had been reset by the Im, whose curtains of gauzy green shimmered in anticipation.

There must be a Game, you see.

"Otherwise there is no free will?"

That is indeed one of our rules. Observant, you are. I believe I will enjoy the company of you, Xen, more than that of Faz.

"To be . . . an immortal . . ."

A crystalline paradise, better than blind Milton's scribbled vision.

A cluster of dirty-brown explosions ripped the sky, rocked the land.

I cannot expend my voltages much longer. Would that we had wit enough, and time, to continue this parrying.

"All right." Xen raised itself up and clawed away the phosphorescent layers of both cubes.

The Red held a shimmering jec.

The Blue held nothing.

Xen said slowly, "So you predicted correctly."

Yes. Sadly, I knew you too well.

Xen radiated a strange sensation of joy, unlaced by regret. It surged to the lip of the crumbling pitwallow.

"Ah . . ." Xen sent a lofting note. "I am like a book, old Im. No doubt I would suffer in translation."

A last glance backward at the wraith of glow and darkness, a gesture of salute, then: "On! To sound and fury!" and it was gone forever.

* * *

3.

In the stretched silent years there was time for introspection. Faz learned the lacy straits of Earth's magnetic oceans, its tides and times. It sailed the magnetosphere and spoke to stars.

The deep-etched memories of that encounter persisted. It never saw Xen again, though word did come vibrating through the field lines of Xen's escape, of zestful adventures out in the raw territory of air and Man. There was even a report that Xen had itself and Pymr decanted into full Manform, to taste the pangs of cell and membrane. Clearly, Xen had lived fully after that solstice day. Fresh verve had driven that blithe new spirit.

Faz was now grown full, could scarcely be distinguished from the Im who gave the fieldcraft. Solemn and wise, its induction, conductivity, and ruby glinting dielectrics a glory to be admired, it hung vast and cold in the sky. Faz spoke seldom and thought much.

Yet the game still occupied Faz. It understood with the embedded viewpoint of an immortal now, saw that each side in the game paid a price. The Im could convey the fieldcraft to only a few, and had nearly exhausted itself; those moments cost millennia.

The sacrifice of Faz was less clear.

Faz felt itself the same as before. Its memories were stored in Alfven waves—stirrings of the field lines, standing waves between Earth's magnetic poles. They would be safe until Earth itself wound down, and the dynamo at the nickel-iron core ceased to replenish the fields. Perhaps, by that time, there would be other field lines threading Earth's, and the Ims could spread outward, blending into the galactic fields.

There were signs that such an end had come to other worlds. The cosmic rays which sleeted down perpetually were random, isotropic, which meant they had to be scattered from magnetic waves between the stars. If such waves were ordered, wise—it meant a vast community of even greater Ims.

But this far future did not concern Faz. For it, the past still sang, gritty and real.

Faz asked the Im about that time, during one of their chance auroral meetings, beside a cascading crimson churn.

The way we would put it in my day, the Im named Sam said, **would be that the software never knows what the original hardware was.**

And that was it, Faz saw. During the translation, the original husk of Faz had been exactly memorized. This meant determining the exact locations of each atom, every darting electron. By the quantum laws, to locate perfectly implied that the measurement imparted an unknown, but high, momentum to each speck. So to define a thing precisely then destroyed it.

Yet there was no external way to prove this. Before and after translation there was an exact Faz.

The copy did not know it was embedded in different . . . hardware . . . than the original.

So immortality was a concept with legitimacy purely seen from the outside. From the inside . . .

Somewhere, a Faz had died that this Faz might live.

. . . And how did any sentience know it was not a copy of some long-gone original?

One day, near the sheath that held back the atmosphere, Faz saw a man waving. it stood in green and vibrant wealth of life, clothed at the waist, bronzed. Faz attached a plasma transducer at the boundary and heard the figure say, ''You're Faz, right?''

Yes, in a way. And you . . . ?

''Wondered how you liked it.''

Xen? Is that you?

''In a way.''

You knew.

''Yes. So I went in the opposite direction—into this form.''

You'll die soon.

''You've died already.''

Still, in your last moments, you'll wish for this.

''No, it's not how long something lasts, it's what that something means.'' With that the human turned, waved gaily, and trotted into a nearby forest.

This encounter bothered Faz.

In its studies and learned colloquy, Faz saw and felt the

tales of Men. They seemed curiously convoluted, revolving about Self. What mattered most to those who loved tales was how they concluded. Yet all Men knew how each ended. Their little dreams were rounded with a sleep.

So the point of a tale was not how it ended, but *what it meant*. The great inspiring epic rage of Man was to find that lesson, buried in a grave.

As each year waned, Faz reflected, and knew that Xen had seen this point. Immortality seen from without, by those who could not know the inner Self—Xen did not want that. So it misled the Im, and got the mere jec that it wanted.

Xen chose life—not to be a monument of unaging intellect, gathered into the artifice of eternity.

In the brittle night Faz wondered if it had chosen well itself. And knew. *Nothing* could be sure it was itself the original. So the only intelligent course lay in enjoying whatever life a being felt—living like a mortal, in the moment. Faz had spent so long, only to reach that same conclusion which was forced on Man from the beginning.

Faz emitted a sprinkling of electromagnetic tones, spattering rueful red the field lines.

And stirred itself to think again, each time the dim sun waned at the solstice. To remember and, still living, to rejoice.

Afterword

I was a research physicist at the Lawrence Radiation Laboratory for four years, and wrote several papers with a renowned scientist, William Newcomb. We worked together studying the stability of plasma in magnetically confined fusion devices.

Bill is a fascinating character. He discovered a mathematical method of calculating stability conditions in the 1950s, then did not publish the central idea. It is referred to often in the literature by its Princeton document number. He is a former chain smoker who became a marathon runner. With David Book and myself he wrote one of the first papers on tachyons, particles which travel faster than light. (Though the paper blew a large hole in the credibility of tachyons, it also set me off on a long series of studies which culminated in *Timescape*. Physicists continue exploring the field theories which include tachyons as a necessary ingredient; it's a live issue. There was even a reported observation of a hugely energetic event in a cosmic ray shower in 1974, which seemed to be due to a particle moving at about twice the speed of light. If tachyons do exist, they must be very high-energy little buggers. Their causality-confusing properties are still ripe territory for speculative physics.)

Perhaps Bill's best known work is Newcomb's Problem. Typically, he never published it. The idea occurred to him in 1960 and he simply discussed the puzzle with some Princeton philosophers. Their vexation with the problem kept it alive in such circles without any formal publication. (Martin Gardner's column in the July 1973 *Scientific*

American touched off widespread discussion. It has become so popular a puzzle that one recent paper is titled "A Note on Newcombmania," in *Journal of Philosophy*, June 1982.)

The problem is a riddle about game theory, involving making a wager with a nearly God-like being. Once the being has made his prediction about your own choices, you have to decide what to do.

I spent a fair amount of time noodling over the thing, myself. There are complicated choice-diagrams you can draw, as the professional games theory guys do. All along I'd suspected there was some way to propel a story with Newcomb's Problem, but couldn't clearly see how. It took a request from Jan and George O'Nale of Cheap Street Press to jog me. They wanted a card to send out at winter solstice, a story relevant to that time. Those days just before Christmas have always struck me as strangely bleak, so I seized on Bill's paradox to fuel a story that begins desperately.

Once out, a critic (Orson Scott Card) said he felt that his intelligence was somewhat insulted by including the diagram. Well, maybe so, but *I* needed the diagram to keep everything straight while I was writing the piece, so I've left it in here.

Now I'm pondering whether I can forage among Bill Newcomb's papers on plasma stability for story material. The man's a gold mine.

Doing Lennon_____

> *Sanity calms, but madness*
> *is more interesting.*
> *—JOHN RUSSELL*

As the hideous cold seeps from him he feels everything becoming sharp and clear again. He decides he can do it, he can make it work. He opens his eyes.

"Hello." His voice rasps. "Bet you aren't expecting me. I'm John Lennon."

"What?" the face above him says.

"You know. John Lennon. The Beatles."

Professori Hermann—the name attached to the face which loomed over him as he drifted up, up from the Long Sleep—is vague about the precise date. It is either 2108 or 2180. Hermann makes a little joke about inversion of positional notation; it has something to do with nondenumerable set theory, which is all the rage. The ceiling glows with a smooth green phosphorescence and Fielding lies there letting them prick him with needles, unwrap his organiform nutrient webbing, poke and adjust and massage as he listens to a hollow *pock-pocketa*. He knows this is the crucial moment, he must hit them with it now.

"I'm glad it worked," Fielding says with a Liverpool accent. He has got it just right, the rising pitch at the end and the nasal tones.

"No doubt there is an error in our log," Hermann says pedantically. "You are listed as Henry Fielding."

Fielding smiles. "Ah, that's the ruse, you see."

Hermann blinks owlishly. "Deceiving Immortality Incorporated is—"

"I was fleeing political persecution, y'dig. Coming out for the workers and all. Writing songs about persecution and pollution and the working-class hero. Snarky stuff. So when the jackboot skinheads came in I decided to check out."

Fielding slips easily into the story he has memorized, all plotted and placed with major characters and minor characters and bits of incident, all of it sounding very real. He wrote it himself, he has it down. He continues talking while Hermann and some white-smocked assistants help him sit up, flex his legs, test his reflexes. Around them are vats and baths and tanks. A fog billows from a hole in the floor; a liquid nitrogen immersion bath.

Hermann listens intently to the story, nodding now and then, and summons other officials. Fielding tells his story again while the attendants work on him. He is careful to give the events in different order, with different details each time. His accent is standing up though there is mucus in his sinuses that makes the high singsong bits hard to get out. They give him something to eat; it tastes like chicken-flavored ice cream. After a while he sees he has them convinced. After all, the late twentieth was a turbulent time, crammed with gaudy events, lurid people. Fielding makes it seem reasonable that an aging rock star, seeing his public slip away and the government closing in, would corpsicle himself.

The officials nod and gesture and Fielding is wheeled out on a carry table. Immortality Incorporated is more like a church than a business. There is a ghostly hush in the hallways, the attendants are distant and reserved. Scientific servants in the temple of life.

They take him to an elaborate display, punch a button. A voice begins to drone a welcome to the year 2018 (or 2180). The voice tells him he is one of the few from his benighted age who saw the slender hope science held out to the diseased and dying. His vision has been rewarded. He has survived the unfreezing. There is some nondenominational talk about God and death and the eternal rhythm and balance of life, ending with a retouched holographic photograph of the Founding Fathers. They are a small knot of biotechnicians and engineers clustered around an immersion tank. Close-cropped hair, white shirts with ball-point pens clipped in the pockets. They wear glasses and smile weakly at the camera, as though they have just been shaken awake.

"I'm hungry," Fielding says.

News that Lennon is revived spreads quickly. The Society for Dissipative Anachronisms holds a press conference for him. As he strides into the room Fielding clenches his fists so no one can see his hands shaking. This is the start. He has to make it here.

"How do you find the future, Mr. Lennon?"

"Turn right at Greenland." Maybe they will recognize it from *A Hard Day's Night*. This is before his name impacts fully, before many remember who John Lennon was. A fat man asks Fielding why he elected for the Long Sleep before he really needed it and Fielding says enigmatically, "The role of boredom in human history is underrated." This makes the evening news and the weekly topical roundup a few days later.

A fan of the twentieth asks him about the breakup with Paul, whether Ringo's death was a suicide, what about Allan Klein, how about the missing lines from *Abbey Road*? Did he like Dylan? What does he think of the Aarons theory that the Beatles could have stopped Vietnam?

Fielding parries a few questions, answers others. He does not tell them, of course, that in the early sixties he worked in a bank and wore granny glasses. Then he became a broker with Harcum, Brandels and Son and his take in 1969 was 57,803 dollars, not counting the money siphoned off into the two concealed accounts in Switzerland. But he read *Rolling Stone* religiously, collected Beatles memorabilia, had all the albums and books and could quote any verse from any song. He saw Paul once at a distance, coming out of a recording session. And he had a friend into Buddhism, who met Harrison one weekend in Surrey. Fielding did not mention his vacation spent wandering around Liverpool, picking up the accent and visiting all the old places, the cellars where they played and the narrow dark little houses their families owned in the early days. And as the years dribbled on and Fielding's money piled up, he lived increasingly in those golden days of the sixties, imagined himself playing side man along with Paul or George or John and crooning those same notes into the microphones, practically kissing the metal. And Fielding did not speak of his dreams.

It is the antiseptic Stanley Kubrick future. They are very adept at hardware. Population is stabilized at half a billion. Everywhere there are white hard decorator chairs in vaguely Danish modern. There seems no shortage of electrical power or oil or copper or zinc. Everyone has a hobby. Entertainment is a huge enterprise, with stress on ritual violence. Fielding watches a few games of Combat Gold, takes in a public execution or two. He goes to witness an electrical man short-circuit himself. The flash is visible over the curve of the Earth.

Genetic manipulants—*manips*, Hermann explains—are thin, stringy people, all lines and knobby joints where they connect directly into machine linkages. They are designed for some indecipherable purpose. Hermann, his guide, launches into an explanation but Fielding interrupts him to say, "Do you know where I can get a guitar?"
Fielding views the era 1950–1980:
"Astrology wasn't rational, nobody really believed it, you've got to realize that. It was *boogie woogie*. On the other hand, science and rationalism were progressive jazz."
He smiles as he says it. The 3D snout closes in. Fielding has purchased well and his plastic surgery, to lengthen the nose and give him that wry Lennonesque smirk, holds up well. Even the technicians at Immortality Incorporated missed it.

Fielding suffers odd moments of blackout. He loses the rub of rough cloth at a cuff on his shirt, the chill of air-conditioned breeze along his neck. The world dwindles away and sinks into inky black, but in a moment it is all back and he hears the distant murmur of traffic, and convulsively, by reflex, he squeezes the bulb in his hand and the orange vapor rises around him. He breathes deeply, sighs. Visions float into his mind and the sour tang of the mist reassures him.

Every age is known by its pleasures, Fielding reads from the library readout. The twentieth introduced two: high speed and hallucinogenic drugs. Both proved dangerous in the long run, which made them even more interesting. The twenty-first developed weightlessness, which worked out well except for the re-entry problems if one overindulged. In the twenty-second there were aquaform and something Fielding could not pronounce or understand.

He thumbs away the readout and calls Hermann for advice.

Translational difficulties:

They give him a sort of pasty suet when he goes to the counter to get his food. He shoves it back at them.

"Gah! Don't you have a hamburger someplace?" The stunted man behind the counter flexes his arms, makes a rude sign with his four fingers and goes away. The wiry woman next to Fielding rubs her thumbnail along the hideous scar at her side and peers at him. She wears only orange shorts and boots, but he can see the concealed dagger in her armpit.

"Hamburger?" she says severely. "That is the name of a citizen of the German city of Hamburg. Were you a cannibal then?"

Fielding does not know the proper response, which could be dangerous. When he pauses she massages her brown scar with new energy and makes a sign of sexual invitation. Fielding backs away. He is glad he did not mention French fries.

On 3D he makes a mistake about the recording date of *Sergeant Pepper's Lonely Hearts Club Band.* A ferret-eyed history student lunges in for the point but Fielding leans back casually, getting the accent just right, and says, "I zonk my brow with heel of hand, consterned!" and the audience laughs and he is away, free.

Hermann has become his friend. The library readout says this is a common phenomenon among Immortality Incorporated employees who are fascinated by the past to begin with (or otherwise would not be in the business), and anyway Hermann and Fielding are about the same age, forty-seven.

Hermann is not surprised that Fielding is practicing his chords and touching up his act.

"You want to get out on the road again, is that it?" Hermann says. "You want to be getting popular."

"It's my business."

"But your songs, they are old."

"Oldies but goldies," Fielding says solemnly.

"Perhaps you are right," Hermann sighs. "We are starved for variety. The people, no matter how educated—anything tickles their nose they think is champagne."

Fielding flicks on the tape input and launches into the hard-driving opening of "Eight Days a Week." He goes through all the chords, getting them right the first time. His fingers dance among the humming copper wires.

Hermann frowns but Fielding feels elated. He decides to celebrate. Precious reserves of cash are dwindling, even considering how much he made in the international bond market of '83; there is not much left. He decides to splurge. He orders an alcoholic vapor and a baked pigeon. Hermann is still worried but he eats the mottled pigeon with relish, licking his fingers. The spiced crust snaps crisply. Hermann asks to take the bones home to his family.

"You have drawn the rank-scented many," Hermann says heavily as the announcer begins his introduction. The air sparkles with anticipation.

"Ah, but they're *my* many," Fielding says. The applause begins, the background music comes up, and Fielding trots out onto the stage, puffing slightly.

"One, two, three—" and he is into it, catching the chords just right, belting out a number from *Magical Mystery Tour*. He is right, he is on, he is John Lennon just as he always wanted to be. The music picks him up and carries him along. When he finishes, a river of applause bursts over the stage from the vast amphitheater and Fielding grins crazily to himself. It feels exactly the way he always thought it would. His heart pounds.

He goes directly into a slow ballad from the *Imagine* album to calm them down. He is swimming in the lights and the 3D snouts zoom in and out, bracketing his image from every conceivable direction. At the end of the number some-body yells from the audience, "You're radiating on all your eigenfrequencies!" And Fielding nods, grins, feels the warmth of it all wash over him.

"Thrilled to the gills," he says into the microphone.

The crowd chuckles and stirs.

When he does one of the last Lennon numbers, "The Ego-Bird Flies," the augmented sound sweeps out from the stage and explodes over the audience. Fielding is euphoric. He dances as though someone is firing pistols at his feet.

He does cuts from *Beatles '65, Help!, Rubber Soul, Let It Be*—all with technical backing spliced in from the original tracks, Fielding providing only Lennon's vocals and instrumentals. Classical scholars have pored over the original material, deciding who did which guitar riff, which tenor line was McCartney's, dissecting the works as though they were salamanders under a knife. But Fielding doesn't care, as long as they let him play and sing. He does another number, then another, and finally they must carry him from the stage. It is the happiest moment he has ever known.

"But I don't understand what Boss 30 radio means," Hermann says.

"Thirty most popular songs."

"But why today?"

"Me."

"They call you a 'sonic boom sensation'—that is another phrase from your time?"

"Dead on. Fellow is following me around now, picking my brains for details. Part of his thesis, he says."

"But it is such noise—"

"Why, that's a crock, Hermann. Look, you chaps have such a small population, so bloody few creative people. What do you expect? Anybody with energy and drive can make it in this world. And I come from a time that was dynamic, that really got off."

"Barbarians at the gates," Hermann says.

"That's what *Reader's Digest* said, too," Fielding murmurs.

After one of his concerts in Australia Fielding finds a girl waiting for him outside. He goes home with her—it seems the thing to do, considering—and finds there have been few technical advances, if any, in this field either. It is the standard, ten-toes-up, ten-toes-down position she prefers, nothing unusual, nothing *à la carte*. But he likes her legs, he relishes her beehive hair and heavy mouth. He takes her along; she has nothing else to do.

On an off day, in what is left of India, she takes him to a museum. She shows him the first airplane (a piper cub), the original manuscript of the great collaboration between Buckminster Fuller and Hemingway, a delicate print of *The Fifty-Three Stations of The Takaido Road* from Japan.

"Oh yes," Fielding says. "We won that war, you know." (He should not seem to be more than he is.)

Fielding hopes they don't discover, with all this burrowing in the old records, that he had the original Lennon killed. He argues with himself that it really was necessary. He couldn't possibly cover his story in the future if Lennon kept on living. The historical facts would not jibe. It was hard enough to convince Immortality Incorporated that even someone as rich as Lennon would be able to forge records and change fingerprints—they had checked that to escape the authorities. Well, Fielding thinks. Lennon was no loss by 1988 anyway. It was pure accident that Fielding and Lennon had been born in the same year, but that didn't mean that Fielding couldn't take advantage of the circumstances. He wasn't worth over ten million fixed 1985 dollars for nothing.

At one of his concerts he says to the audience between numbers, "Don't look back—you'll just see your mistakes." It sounds like something Lennon would have said. The audience seems to like it.

Press Conference.

"And why did you take a second wife, Mr. Lennon, and then a third?" In 2180 (or 2108) divorce is frowned upon. Yoko Ono is still the Beatle nemesis.

Fielding pauses and then says, "Adultery is the application of democracy to love." He does not tell them the line is from H. L. Mencken.

*   *   *

He has gotten used to the women now. "Just cast them aside like sucked oranges," Fielding mutters to himself. It is a delicious moment. He had never been very successful with women before, even with all his money.

He strides through the yellow curved streets, walking lightly on the earth. A young girls passes, winks.

Fielding calls after her, "Sic transit, Gloria!"

It is his own line, not a copy from Lennon. He feels a heady rush of joy. He is into it, the ideas flash through his mind spontaneously. He is doing Lennon.

Thus, when Hermann comes to tell him that Paul McCartney has been revived by the Society for Dissipative Anachronisms, the body discovered in a private vault in England, at first it does not register with Fielding. Lines of postcoital depression flicker across his otherwise untroubled brow. He rolls out of bed and stands watching a wave turn to white foam on the beach at La Jolla. He is in Nanking. It is midnight.

"Me old bud, then?" he manages to say, getting the lilt into the voice still. He adjusts his granny glasses. Rising anxiety stirs in his throat. "My, my . . ."

It takes weeks to defrost McCartney. He had died much later than Lennon, plump and prosperous, the greatest pop star of all time—or at least the biggest money-maker. "Same thing," Fielding mutters to himself.

When Paul's cancer is sponged away and the sluggish organs palped to life, the world media press for a meeting.

"For what?" Fielding is nonchalant. "It's not as though we were ever reconciled, y'know. We got a *divorce*, Hermann."

"Can't you put that aside?"

"For a fat old slug who pro'bly danced on me grave?"

"No such thing occurred. There are videotapes, and Mr. McCartney was most polite."

"God, a future where everyone's literal! I *told* you I was a nasty type, why can't you simply accept—"

"It is arranged," Hermann says firmly. "You must go. Overcome your antagonism."

Fear clutches at Fielding.

* * *

McCartney is puffy, jowly, but his eyes crackle with intelligence. The years have not fogged his quickness. Fielding has arranged the meeting away from crowds, at a forest resort. Attendants help McCartney into the hushed room. An expectant pause.

"You want to join me band?" Fielding says brightly. It is the only quotation he can remember that seems to fit; Lennon had said that when they first met.

McCartney blinks, peers nearsightedly at him. "D'you really need another guitar?"

"Whatever noisemaker's your fancy."

"Okay."

"You're hired, lad."

They shake hands with mock seriousness. The spectators—who have paid dearly for their tickets—applaud loudly. McCartney smiles, embraces Fielding, and then sneezes.

"Been cold lately," Fielding says. A ripple of laughter.

McCartney is offhand, bemused by the world he has entered. His manner is confident, interested. He seems to accept Fielding automatically. He makes a few jokes, as light and inconsequential as his post-Beatles music.

Fielding watches him closely, feeling an awe he had not expected. *That's him. Paul. The real thing.* He starts to ask something and realizes that it is a dumb, out-of-character, fan-type question. He is being betrayed by his instincts. He will have to be careful.

Later, they go for a walk in the woods. The attendants hover a hundred meters behind, portable med units at the ready. They are worried about McCartney's cold. This is the first moment they have been beyond earshot of others. Fielding feels his pulse rising. "You okay?" he asks the puffing McCartney.

"Still a bit dizzy, I am. Never thought it'd work, really."

"The freezing, it gets into your bones."

"Strange place. Clean, like Switzerland."

"Yeah. Peaceful. They're mad for us here."

"You meant that about your band?"

"Sure. Your fingers'll thaw out. Fat as they are, they'll still get around a guitar string."

"Ummm. Wonder if George is tucked away in an ice cube somewhere?"

"Hadn't thought." The idea fills Fielding with terror.

"Could ask about Ringo, too."

"Re-create the whole thing? I was against that. Dunno if I still am." Best to be noncommittal. He would love to meet them, sure, but his chances of bringing this off day by day, in the company of all three of them . . . he frowns.

McCartney's pink cheeks glow from the exercise. The eyes are bright, active, studying Fielding. "Did you think it would work? Really?"

"The freezing? Well, what's to lose? I said to Yoko, I said—"

"No, not the freezing. I mean this impersonation you're carrying off."

Fielding reels away, smacks into a pine tree. "What? What?"

"C'mon, you're not John."

A strangled cry erupts from Fielding's throat. "But . . . how . . ."

"Just not the same, is all."

Fielding's mouth opens, but he can say nothing. He has failed. Tripped up by some nuance, some trick phrase he should've responded to—

"Of course," McCartney says urbanely, "you don't know for sure if I'm the real one either, do you?"

Fielding stutters, "If, if, what're you saying, I—"

"Or I could even be a ringer planted by Hermann, eh? To test you out? In that case, you've responded the wrong way. Should've stayed in character, John."

"Could be this, could be that—what the hell you saying? Who *are* you?" Anger flashes through him. A trick, a maze of choices, possibilities that he had not considered. The forest whirls around him, McCartney leers at his confusion, bright spokes of sunlight pierce his eyes, he feels himself falling, collapsing, the pine trees wither, colors drain away, blue to pink to gray—

He is watching a blank dark wall, smelling nothing, no tremor through his skin, no wet touch of damp air. Sliding infinite silence. The world is black.

—Flat black, Fielding adds, like we used to say in Liverpool.

—Liverpool? He was never in Liverpool. That was a lie, too—

—And he knows instantly what he is. The truth skewers him.

Hello, you still operable?

Fielding rummages through shards of cold electrical memory and finds himself. He is not Fielding, he is a simulation. He is Fielding Prime.

Hey, you in there. It's me, the real Fielding. Don't worry about security. I'm the only one here.

Fielding Prime feels through his circuits and discovers a way to talk. "Yes, yes, I hear."

I made the computer people go away. We can talk.

"I—I see." Fielding Prime sends out feelers, searching for his sensory receptors. He finds a dim red light and wills it to grow brighter. The image swells and ripples, then forms into a picture of a sour-faced man in his middle fifties. It is Fielding Real.

Ah, Fielding Prime thinks to himself in the metallic vastness, he's older than I am. Maybe making me younger was some sort of self-flattery, either by him or his programmers. But the older man had gotten someone to work on his face. It was very much like Lennon's but with heavy jowls, a thicker mustache and balding some. The gray sideburns didn't look quite right but perhaps that is the style now.

The McCartney thing, you couldn't handle it.

"I got confused. It never occurred to me there'd be anyone I knew revived. I hadn't a clue what to say."

Well, no matter. The earlier simulations, the ones before you, they didn't even get that far. I had my men throw in that McCartney thing as a test. Not much chance it would occur, anyway, but I wanted to allow for it.

"Why?"

What? Oh, you don't know, do you? I'm sinking all this money into psychoanalytical computer models so I can see if this plan of mine would work. I mean whether I could cope with the problems and deceive Immortality Incorporated.

Fielding Prime felt a shiver of fear. He needed to stall for time, to think this through. "Wouldn't it be easier to bribe enough people now? You could have your body frozen and listed as John Lennon from the start.''

No, their security is too good. I tried that.

''There's something I noticed,'' Fielding Prime said, his mind racing. ''Nobody ever mentioned why I was unfrozen.''

Oh yes, that's right. Minor detail. I'll make a note about that—maybe cancer or congestive heart failure, something that won't be too hard to fix up within a few decades.

''Do you want it that soon? There would still be a lot of people who knew Lennon.''

Oh, that's a good point. I'll talk to the doctor about it.

''You really care that much about being John Lennon?''

Why sure. Fielding Real's voice carried a note of surprise. *Don't you feel it too? If you're a true simulation you've got to feel that.*

''I do have a touch of it, yes.''

They took the graphs and traces right out of my subcortical.

''It was great, magnificent. Really a lark. What came through was the music, doing it out. It sweeps up and takes hold of you.''

Yeah, really? Damn, you know, I think it's going to work.

''With more planning—''

Planning, hell, I'm going. Fielding Real's face crinkled with anticipation.

''You're going to need help.''

Hell, that's the whole point of having you, to check it out beforehand. I'll be all alone up there.

''Not if you take me with you.''

Take you? You're just a bunch of germanium and copper.

''Leave me here. Pay for my files and memory to stay active.''

For what?

''Hook me into a news service. Give me access to libraries. When you're unfrozen I can give you backup information and advice as soon as you can reach a terminal. With your money, that wouldn't be too hard. Hell, I could even take care of your money. Do some trading, maybe move your accounts out of countries before they fold up.''

Fielding Real pursed his lips. He thought for a moment and looked shrewdly at the visual receptor. *That sort of*

*makes sense. I could trust your judgment—it's mine, after
all. I can believe myself, right? Yes, yes . . .*

"You're going to need company." Fielding Prime says
nothing more. Best to stand pat with his hand and not push
him too hard.

I think I'll do it. Fielding Real's face brightens. His eyes
take on a fanatic gleam. *You and me. I know it's going to
work, now!*

Fielding Real burbles on and Fielding Prime listens dutifully to him, making the right responses without effort. After
all, he knows the other man's mind. It is easy to manipulate
him, to play the game of ice and steel.

Far back, away from where Fielding Real's programmers
could sense it, Fielding Prime smiles inwardly (the only way
he could). It will be a century, at least. He will sit here
monitoring data, input and output, the infinite dance of electrons. Better than death, far better. And there may be new
developments, a way to transfer computer constructs to real
bodies. Hell, anything could happen.

*Boy, it's cost me a fortune to do this. A bundle. Bribing
people to keep it secret, shifting the accounts so the Feds
wouldn't know—and you cost the most. You're the best simulation ever developed, you realize that? Full consciousness,
they say.*

"Quite so."

Let him worry about his money—just so there was some
left. The poor simple bastard thought he could trust Fielding
Prime. He thought they were the same person. But Fielding
Prime had played the chords, smelled the future, lived a vivid
life of his own. He was older, wiser. He had felt the love of
the crowd wash over him, been at the focal point of time. To
him Fielding Real was just somebody else, and all his knife-
sharp instincts could come to bear.

*How was it? What was it like? I can see how you re-
sponded by running your tapes for a few sigmas. But I can't
order a complete scan without wiping your personality matrix. Can't you tell me? How did it feel?*

Fielding Prime tells him something, anything, whatever
will keep the older man's attention. He speaks of ample-
thighed girls, of being at the center of it all.

Did you really? God!
Fielding Prime spins him a tale.

He is running cool and smooth. He is radiating on all his eigenfrequencies. *Ah* and *ah*.

Yes, that is a good idea. After Fielding Real is gone, his accountants will suddenly discover a large sum left for scientific research into man-machine linkages. With a century to work, Fielding Prime can find a way out of this computer prison. He can become somebody else.

Not Lennon, no. He owed that much to Fielding Real.

Anyway, he had already lived through that. The Beatles' music was quite all right, but doing it once had made it seem less enticing. Hermann was right. The music was too simple-minded, it lacked depth.

He is ready for something more. He has access to information storage, tapes, consultant help from outside, all the libraries of the planet. He will study. He will train. In a century he can be anything. Ah, he will echo down the infinite reeling halls of time.

John Lennon, hell. He will become Wolfgang Amadeus Mozart.

Afterword

In 1974 the Beatles were fading as figures but looming large as legends.

The anguished early-70s music of Lennon contrasted strongly with the light, sweet songs of McCartney. The two of them seemed to reflect mirror-opposite views of what the past decade had meant. Lennon appealed to intellectuals, and I felt instinctively that he would, even after the breakup, remain the lightning rod of the foursome.

I decided to write a story about the curious fanatacism that was already enveloping the Beatles. Lennon was the logical choice—readers are intellectuals, after all. The yearning of so many to be a part of that Golden Age bounce and verve was a natural motivation. I made notes for the piece for months. To keep the right tone, I wrote the story in one day, compressing time to gain energy.

But time can't be frozen, and now events have caught up with the facts of this piece. They caught up with me at, of all places, a publisher's annual meeting. I was a guest author at Pocket Books' annual meeting of editors, publishers, and representatives. A lively crew, they are. I had been out to dinner with them, and returned to the Hotel del Coronado to find the lobby abuzz with the news of Lennon's death.

From there my memory takes a jump-shot forward. I am lying face down on the bed in my room, feeling like a bus had run me over with studied care. I lurch up to find that, first, I must soon heed the call of nature, and second, I am fully clothed, and third, sunlight is trying to pry up the shades.

Returning from the bathroom, I notice a pile of crumpled bills on a table. They are all singles. I can remember nothing of the night before.

I go down to breakfast, where veiled questioning reveals that I got into a long poker game with the sales representatives. And drank a lot. And, apparently, won.

I still have no memory of those hours. Rereading this story, I realized again how heavily the news hit me. I do remember, though, that sometime around 1978 someone in rock circles told me that McCartney had read the story in Terry Carr's *Best of the Year* anthology, and passed it on to Lennon. I rather wonder what he made of it.

Here you will find a logic built on what I saw as a swelling undercurrent in the mid-70s. Its John Lennon carries no memory of a brutal booming, lancing pain, and sudden dark. It would be impossible to write this story now, including those facts, and yet retain the same tone.

So I shall let it stand. Science fiction is at times predictive, and there are notes sounded here (particularly, in Fielding's attitude toward the true Lennon) which strike me as a bit eerie. Mark David Chapman wanted to be Lennon; he signed that name on registration forms, apparently without attracting much attention.

One can read this, then, as an inspection of what lay waiting for Lennon outside the Dakota on December 8, 1980. But I hope that fact will not dim the spirit of this story, which attempted to reach the more joyous emotions of that time.